**Praise for *New York Times* bestselling author
Stella Cameron**

Stella Cameron's novels "keep readers
thoroughly entertained."
—*Publishers Weekly*

"Stella Cameron's 7 Mayfair books
are always fun to read and her latest
may be her most entertaining to date."
—*The Midwest Book Review* on 7B

**Praise for two-time RITA® Award winner
Fay Robinson**

"Fay Robinson's novels stir the heart and
make you remember how it feels to fall in love."
—Stef Ann Holm, MIRA Books author

"Ms. Robinson's marvelous cast of characters,
emotional highs and lows, and strong storyline
will touch readers' hearts!"
—*Romantic Times* on *A Man Like Mac*

STELLA CAMERON

is a national bestselling author of historical romances and mainstream women's fiction. Readers love her character-driven stories of heartfelt emotion and everlasting romantic sentiment. Stella draws from people in her own life to create these memorable characters. She and her husband make their home in Washington State.

FAY ROBINSON

writes for Harlequin Superromance. *A Man Like Mac* won the RITA® Award in 2001 from the Romance Writers of America for Best First Book, and her second title, *Coming Home to You,* won a Maggie award from Georgia Romance Writers as an unpublished manuscript and the RITA® Award in 2002 for Best Long Contemporary Romance. Fay believes in love at first sight, in happily-ever-after endings and in hearts destined to be together. She lives in Alabama within one hundred miles of the place where her paternal ancestors settled in the early 1800s. Fay spends her spare time canning vegetables from her husband's garden and researching her family history.

STELLA CAMERON
FAY ROBINSON

COURAGE MY LOVE

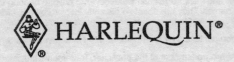

HARLEQUIN®

TORONTO • NEW YORK • LONDON
AMSTERDAM • PARIS • SYDNEY • HAMBURG
STOCKHOLM • ATHENS • TOKYO • MILAN • MADRID
PRAGUE • WARSAW • BUDAPEST • AUCKLAND

ISBN 0-373-83543-4

COURAGE MY LOVE

Copyright © 2003 by Harlequin Books S.A.

The publisher acknowledges the copyright holders of the individual works as follows:

RISKS
Copyright © 1990 by Stella Cameron

A MAN LIKE MAC
Copyright © 2000 by Carmel Thomaston

This edition published by arrangement with Harlequin Books S.A.

® and TM are trademarks of the publisher. Trademarks indicated with ® are registered in the United States Patent and Trademark Office, the Canadian Trade Marks Office and in other countries.

Visit us at www.eHarlequin.com

Printed in U.S.A.

CONTENTS

RISKS
Stella Cameron

For Ferd—
I wish I could tell him why

CHAPTER ONE

"I'm telling you, Mrs. Andrews, he was totally cool. Tall and blond, with green eyes, and—"

"Bliss, look at me, and listen." Jennie leaned on her sole employee's desk and waited for the girl's almost-black eyes to regain focus. "I'm not interested in who ogles you through the window. Where did you file Gucci?"

"My parents are kind of old-world. They say I should marry a nice Japanese boy. I tell them I'm not interested in marrying anyone for ages yet, not till I'm at least twenty."

"Which gives you a whole two years. Very sensible." Jennie couldn't help enjoying Bliss Matsui, an ebullient eighteen-year-old who had managed to talk her way into a job as Jennie's "assistant," Bliss's self-coined title for her office-girl duties.

"But if I was into older Caucasian men..."

"Bliss. Gucci?"

"Oh, of course. Under C."

Jennie bowed her head. "C?"

"Yeah. I decided to put some pizzazz into the filing system. You know, make it different. I call it organization by association." Bliss hooked her straight black hair behind her ear and speared a pencil on top. "For instance, that man would have been filed under, um, H maybe. For hunk."

Jennie refused to be distracted. Renting this tiny studio could turn out to be the best investment she ever made. On the main floor of Cincinnati's Terminal Building, the Fourth Avenue location was perfect, central to the kind of successful people who were potential clients for Executive Images. The space was also expensive enough to stretch Jennie's budget, which meant there weren't enough hours in a day to allow for getting sidetracked.

"Could we get back to my Gucci file?"

"Oh...yeah." A brilliant smile showed Bliss's small and perfect teeth. "Under C for Charo."

"Charo," Jennie repeated slowly. In one hour—or fifty-eight minutes now—she was expected at the office of a museum curator. He'd already let her know he was seeking her services reluctantly at the suggestion of a colleague. Keeping him waiting wouldn't improve her chances of convincing him how badly he needed to be made over by Jennie Andrews. "Why Charo...? Oh. Oh, Bliss, that's ridiculous. Do you mean because of the way she says, cucci, cucci...?"

"You've got it!" The girl leaned back in her chair, still grinning. "I saw her on an old Johnny Carson show. That's what I mean by association."

Jennie marched to a file cabinet and pulled open the top drawer. "And now, you get this," she said, locating and extracting the folder in question. "Most of my associations are twenty years older than yours, and I expect to find what I want, when I want it—and quickly. Save your creativity for your design classes."

"Now you're angry. And it's only eighteen years."

"I'm not—" Jennie looked over her shoulder at Bliss. "How do you know how old I am?"

"He did."

She closed the drawer slowly. *"He?"* These coded conversations might wear down the most patient woman, and Jennie was anything but patient.

"You know. *Him.* He asked if you were the Jennie Andrews who was about thirty-six with two teenage boys. So I said Steven's seventeen and Bobby's fifteen, and he said that would be right."

"What are you talking about, Bliss?" Jennie felt suddenly nervous. "Some man you don't know asked questions about me, and you told him my personal business?"

The smile slipped from Bliss's exotic face. "He was the

one who came in here. The good-looking one I told you about.''

"In? I thought you were talking about someone who looked at you through the window.'' She glanced out into the mall, where lunch-hour crowds bustled to and fro past the offices and shops that lined the concourse of the domed building.

"He opened the door," Bliss said, sounding anxious. "I didn't think there was anything wrong, because he knows you."

Jennie picked up her briefcase and stuffed folders and catalogs inside. "I don't know anyone who looks like your description of this man."

"But he knows how you look. Long, dark, wavy hair, brown eyes, slim and about five-five. And pretty, he said."

"Five-six," Jennie said, and drew in a sharp breath. "If I had time, I'd feel sick. This guy's probably some kook who hangs around this place looking for vulnerable women. Steven and Bobby have both been here with me, so he could have seen them. You've got to learn some self-defense techniques—like suspicion."

"But—"

"*Don't* talk to any more strange men and don't give out information about me. You didn't tell him my address, did you?"

The girl studied her hands.

"Bliss?"

"He, er, he asked if you lived in Eden Park, and I said yes."

Jennie groaned. "I'm not going to sleep at night, waiting for some crazed sex fiend to break into the house." She paused in the act of opening her organizer. "You didn't let him know… You didn't say there isn't a Mr. Andrews?"

Bliss pulled the pencil from behind her ear and pointed it triumphantly at Jennie. "That proves he already knew you. I almost forgot. It was the last thing he said. It was kind of like he didn't quite believe you were you. He said, 'Mark Andrews's widow?' And I said yes." She jutted her lower lip and sent up a relieved breath that lifted her straight bangs.

"This makes absolutely no sense. I can't think who this man is." And there was no more time. "We'll continue this fascinating discussion when I get back from persuading Mr. Gertson to give up his baggy corduroys. That should be by about three. In the meantime, concentrate on confirming my appointments for tomorrow and don't talk to strangers unless they're customers. I'm expecting a call from Francine at Saks. Tell her I intend to bring Mr. Cronin from Proctor and Gamble by in the morning and I'd like her to arrange for the shoes I picked out to be available with everything else." Under her breath she murmured, *"Just in case he doesn't cancel again and I can finally persuade him to make some decisions."*

Pulling on her raincoat as she went, Jennie hurried from the studio to mingle with the throng. The fall of many feet on marble floors sent up a vibrating clatter that rose past a second-floor balcony, visible through curved arches, to vaulted blue ceilings decorated with gold filigree. Executive Images by Jennie Andrews had been in residence here only two weeks, since April 1—April Fools' Day, as Steven had been quick to point out, and didn't she think that was an omen?

She smiled as she pushed through heavy glass doors into a blustery wet day. Her oldest son tried her patience daily, but she chose to believe that Steven would eventually outgrow his mouthy, rebellious stage. And what she'd done was anything but foolish—she was sure of that. Deciding to invest in professional premises rather than continuing to operate from her kitchen table would make all the difference to her success.

Mr. Gertson was even more of a challenge than most of her primarily male clientele. Usually she made a visit to the customer's office and his home environment. After going through the existing wardrobe to see what could be salvaged, she shopped alone to pick out items for consideration, then took the client with her to try on what she recommended and to make final selections.

This would not do for Mr. Gertson. For her "outrageous" fee, he expected her to transport everything to him. Jennie had an uncomfortable conviction that by later this afternoon, she'd be taking most of her suggested purchases back, but she couldn't afford to pass up any potential business until she was established.

She turned the corner from Fourth onto Walnut, walking along the side of the Terminal Building toward her car. Visible above the roofs of low-lying warehouses ahead, the dome of Riverfront Stadium wore a mantle of gray cloud. Jennie wrapped her flapping coat more tightly about her legs to keep spatterings of rain off her skirt...and jarred to a halt.

Tall, blond, green eyed?

Muscle around her ribs tightened.

It couldn't be. The last she'd heard, he was on an extended lecture tour raising funds for the drug research foundation he worked for. The corners of her mouth trembled involuntarily. No, it couldn't be him. She walked on more slowly. The last time they'd met, his closing comment had been that she'd hear from him again. That had been over a year ago—closer to eighteen months. Since then, he hadn't contacted her. And she'd put a new lifetime between them and had forgotten their exchange of that day...almost.

Jennie reached her silver Mercedes sedan, unlocked the passenger door and put her briefcase and purse on the seat. The back of the car was loaded with items intended to streamline Mr. Gertson.

Once behind the wheel, she slipped the key into the ignition but didn't immediately start the engine. She was fooling herself. That old conversation wasn't forgotten at all. It was as clear as if it was taking place now. With the passing months, reason had convinced her she'd been lashing out in the heat of grief, mindlessly blaming one of the best friends she and Mark had ever had because he was convenient. Only it was more than that. Mark had sewed the seeds before he died, and she'd been too distraught to recognize his accusations as the probable result of frustration over his illness.

She turned the key. If Peter Kynaston had come to her again, as he'd said he would, she'd have apologized. But he'd stayed away, and Jennie had assumed he didn't want to hear from her again.

Who could blame him? Her parting words had been: "Stay away. We both know you killed my husband."

WRANGLING WITH CRUSTY old members of the foundation always wore him out. Half of them didn't know HIV from DNA, but they had the power to approve or squash every move undertaken in his lab.

"Loosen up, Peter." Liz Meadows, his assistant and frequently his main link to sanity on these occasions, followed him down the stairs from the foundation's conference rooms.

Peter emerged onto the main floor of the Terminal Building and waited for her to catch up. As usual, dark pins were working loose from the knot of almost-white hair at her nape, and wiry wisps sprang free to give her a harried look.

"What d'they know?" he said when Liz stood beside him. "Not a blamed thing. They just have to keep reminding us they hold the old purse strings."

She laughed. "Have I ever told you that anger makes you sound more Aussie than ever?"

"Once or twice," he said, attempting a scowl. Liz could always defuse his too-ready temper. "Trouble is that while I was more or less out of their clutches for so long, I managed to forget what it was like to be here permanently. Now I'm back for good, the thought of facing them again and again makes me crazy."

"Look—" she took his arm and steered him closer to the windows of a hair salon and out of the path of the rushing crowd "—they gave you everything you wanted, didn't they?"

"This time. But you'll notice we're going to have to go through one of these inquisitions every two weeks."

"Just to keep them abreast of things, Peter, nothing more. You'll always get the okay—you know that."

"And I'm being unreasonable. I know. But I've got work to do, lots of it. Things are finally moving, and I don't want to waste valuable time coming here to explain our findings. Even they should understand that drug research can be slow."

Liz hitched the strap of her brown leather purse over her

shoulder, straightened the bottoms of her beige twinset about the hips of a sensible tan pleated skirt and planted her flat brown brogues more firmly. "You've got to remember that the heat's on in this business. We're dealing with the biggies. AIDS is going to keep on being hot news, and chemotherapy touches most people's lives one way or another. Those guys up there are under pressure from whoever they answer to *and* to the press. Everyone wants to know what people like us are coming up with."

"And I'll tell them." He sounded as irritable as he felt. "But I can't give them answers I don't have."

"They don't expect you to," Liz said gently. "It's just that you're so arrogant you can't bear to answer to anyone. Am I right?"

He opened his mouth to remind her that he was the boss around here, but changed his mind. There was too much potential truth in what she said for comfort, although he wouldn't have used the word "arrogant" to describe himself. "I'm not answering that," he said after meeting her eyes for several uncomfortable seconds. "You go on back. There's something I want—" Glancing past Liz, he forgot the rest of what he'd intended to say. There was absolutely no mistake—not that he'd thought there could be. Jennie Andrews, weighed down by an oversize briefcase, a purse and a stack of papers clamped under her arm, walked rapidly toward him. Not really toward him, but in his direction.

Liz turned around, and he heard her pleased "Oh!" before she hurried to head Jennie off.

Peter stayed where he was. A vast and unfamiliar wave of nostalgia rushed over him. She looked just the same—not just the same as when he'd last seen her, but the way she'd been in the years after they'd met, when they'd become friends…before Mark died. After that, she'd been different in every way.

Part of him wanted to turn around and leave by the back entrance to the building. A stronger part kept him rooted to the spot, watching, waiting for her reaction when she saw him.

Liz must think he was close on her heels, equally enthusiastic at the sight of their old boss's wife. He might be glad to see Jennie—but he was also apprehensive. But Liz didn't know what had passed between him and Jennie after Mark's death. Only the two of them had stood in her kitchen after the funeral, a place that had become as familiar to him as any place ever had, while she said she never wanted to see him again.

He was too far away to hear what they said, but he saw Jennie smile, and nod and manage to return Liz's hug with one arm. Jennie looked just as he remembered—from before Mark's death, when they all did so many things together. Her hair was even longer, perhaps, past her shoulders, but the way light caught the mass of bouncy dark waves was the same, and her wide smile, the sparkle in her tawny eyes... She wore a belted navy raincoat with the collar turned up and a bright red scarf at her neck. His chest expanded. Relief. Jennie looked her old self again, and regardless of how she felt about him, he was so glad for her.

Liz said something and turned towards him. "Peter! It's Jennie." Liz had been well aware of the tension between Mark and Peter at the lab, but she didn't know what had passed between him and Jennie later.

He looked, not at Liz, but at Jennie. The smile had gone, and the brightness in her eyes as they met his. Juggling, she shifted the papers to hold them in front of her chest like a shield. She appeared...shocked. He should have followed his first instinct and ducked out. Now it was too late.

"Come here," Liz called to him. "Come and see who I've found."

There was no choice. He strode forward and stopped a few feet from Jennie. He'd automatically raised his arms to hug her. Quickly he stuck his hand in the pockets of his jeans and pasted on a smile that stretched his face. "Hello, Jennie. Long time no see." God, that sounded inane.

She nodded, juggled some more and extended a hand. "How are you, Peter? I thought...I knew you... How long have you been back in town?" Her long slender fingers were cool in his, and the brief squeeze was that of an impersonal stranger. But did he imagine a slight trembling as she withdrew her hand?

"They decided to bring me home about two months ago." He did think of Cincinnati as home now. The last ties to Sydney had broken irrevocably months ago. Nodding up at the balcony, he said, "The foundation has meeting rooms here now, so they'll be dragging us over regularly."

"Well," Liz said, a little too brightly. "Sounds as if you two have a lot of catching up to do."

Peter gritted his teeth and avoided looking at Jennie.

"I'd better go," Liz continued. "Good to see you, Jennie. Don't be such a stranger. I haven't felt we should, well, intrude. You understand. But you look ready for anything now, and Fred and I won't take no for an answer, so expect to come for dinner." Liz turned her enthusiastic face to Peter and frowned. His discomfort must be very obvious. "See you at the lab," she said, and he noticed the unfamiliar heightening of her color. Later she was going to ask questions he'd rather not field.

He studied the scuffed toes of his boots, unable to think of a thing to say to this woman who used to make him feel so comfortable.

"So you're back for good."

"Yeah. Jennie, I meant to—"

"Did Ellie come back with you?" The words tumbled out and let him know she was as uneasy as he was.

"Ellie and I called it quits months ago. We should have done it long before." Ellie had been his fiancé, but they'd learned that long-distance courtships were generally doomed to failure. Not that distance was all that had pushed them apart.

"I'm sorry," Jennie said.

"Don't be. We're both better for the break." He hunched his shoulders inside his jean jacket. "So, what does Jennie Andrews do—Executives Images, I mean?"

She shrugged, and he saw her throat move convulsively. "You wouldn't be interested."

"Yes, I would," he blurted out, meaning what he said but

regretting the display of enthusiasm that was likely to make her retreat…again. Another instant, and he'd be throwing himself at her feet and begging her for friendship again. She'd never know how much he'd missed the niche her family had made for him…or how he'd grieved alone for Mark's loss. But she wouldn't believe that. Their final encounter and the harsh words she'd heaped on him proved that.

"It must have been you who talked to Bliss," she said. Her knuckles, folded around the papers, were white. "The girl in my studio."

He stared at her blankly, then remembered. "Oh, yeah. Cute kid. I think I made her nervous. She didn't string two words together."

Jennie laughed, and the effect was delightful. Her full soft mouth parted to show very white teeth, and her brown eyes glittered. "One of the things I always liked about you was the fact that you never seemed to know the stunning effect you have on women. She said you were, er, totally cool, a hunk." Her voice slowed and she turned pink.

Peter was aware of a warm, satisfied feeling. "So there were things you liked about me, Jen," he said quietly, satisfaction giving way to sadness for what they'd lost.

She took a step in the direction of her studio. "You know there were." Reaching up awkwardly to push back her hair, she regarded him somberly.

"Well, I'm sure you have better things to do than stand around talking to me." And he didn't want to bring up old hurts.

He almost saw her making up her mind to say something. "Give my love…give my best to the boys." He drew in a sharp breath and added impulsively, "I miss all of you. Goodbye, Jen."

"Peter!"

He'd only taken two strides when her urgent voice stopped him. "Yes." If he looked her directly in the eye, she'd see just how affected he was.

"Nothing."

"No. Okay, take care of yourself."

"Do you ever have any spare time?"

His heart seemed to twist. "Of course." Now he did look at her and he could have sworn tears hovered in her eyes. "Why?"

She hunched her shoulders. "I've had a lot of time to think."

"So have I."

Jennie backed away. "There are things I should say to you, Peter."

"Me, too." His heart hammered now.

"You don't have to, but if you feel like it, stop by the house. Bobby still asks about you."

"When are you all home?" Mentally he included Steven, although he couldn't visualize the boy's face without seeing accusation in his dark eyes, eyes so much like his father's.

"Any evening," Jennie said. "But really, only come if you don't have anything better to do. We aren't very exciting, but the coffee's still good."

Not exciting? He'd sought out the Andrewses, not for excitement but for the warm family feeling that hovered in every inch of their home. It couldn't be the same without Mark, but there still had to be so much more there than in his own house, empty except for one hostile Siamese cat who'd come with the property.

Peter took a step toward Jennie, but she retreated some more. "Forget I said that," she said. "Don't feel obligated. I know how busy you are."

He bowed his head before aiming a grin and a salute in her direction. "In my whole life, girl, I never did anything out of a sense of obligation." For a moment he considered what he'd said. "Well, almost never. I'll call first, but I'll be over for that coffee."

CHAPTER TWO

Okay, Jennie thought, this was one time when Steven would see just how tough she could get. "Watch my mouth, Steven. No. End of discussion."

"Great, Mom. But I'm going to the movies with Gigi, and that's the way it is. Or are you gonna try to lock me in my room without supper?"

Why did he have to stage another rebellion when she was tired and wanted nothing more than a long hot bath? This tall, striking, seventeen-year-old son who'd inherited his father's dark good looks, had been the nicest guy...until a year or so ago, when he'd started turning into a mouthy monster.

"I need to borrow some money against my allowance. I told Gigi we'd grab a hamburger first."

A teeny red light in Jennie's brain grew rapidly bigger and brighter. "Is that a fact, Steven Andrews? You need to borrow money so you can take a girl out to eat and to the movies on a school night. I've told you I don't want you to go. Sounds like we're getting a demonstration of final authority around here. No, I'm not going to lock you in your room. Yes, I've said you can't go. And no, you can't borrow money. Does that spell out all the angles?"

"Fine." He shrugged and tugged forward a hank of gelled black hair. "I'll borrow it from Gigi. Keep up the tough stuff, Mom, and I'll stop telling you where I'm going. I was just being polite. See ya."

"Can I come, Steve?" Bobby, two years his brother's junior, had been silent throughout what had become an almost nightly session of wrangling. "I'll get lost in the movie house."

Jennie turned on the younger boy. "That's it, Bobby. Get upstairs. And you, Steven, go in the den and do your homework. You can call Gigi and make arrangements to go out this weekend if you like. But this rude behavior has to stop. Since your father—"

"Yeah, I know." He rolled his eyes. "Since Dad died I've deteriorated into a nothing. Change the tape, will ya?"

She felt a foreign urge to strike and was immediately overwhelmed with self-disgust. She wasn't the only single parent struggling with an angry teenager. In time his mind would catch up with the growth of his body. He had to be over six feet and he was muscular—a man in appearance, but an angry, misplaced boy inside. But she wasn't about to give up on him, no matter how much he tested her; she loved him too much and he had too much potential.

Frustration slithered through her veins. She pulled out a chair and sat at the big kitchen table. Mark's death had changed so much more than the obvious. She could cope with having discovered that he hadn't left them as well provided for as she'd expected—and with the subtle transformation that took place in so many of their old friends' attitudes toward her—but nothing had prepared her for the job of trying to be both mother and father to a confused teenager who still hadn't accepted the loss of his father.

Bobby hadn't left the room. "I thought I told you to go upstairs, young man." She couldn't bring herself to sound angry. Bobby was always the one who tried to smooth things over between her and Steven, and she felt guilty that he considered maintaining peace was his family role.

"Gee, Mom. I was only kidding about the movies." Keeping one eye on her to monitor her reaction, he took a Coke from the fridge and popped the tab.

Jennie couldn't help smiling. Bobby, a slim, smaller but rapidly growing version of Steven, was a charming manipulator. He evidently sighted the chink he'd made in her armor and slid companionably into a chair beside her.

Steven muttered something that sounded like "creep," and

Jennie sighed. "Steven, why don't you go and call Gigi about tomorrow?"

He hovered near the back door, fingering yellow flowered drapes looped back over a square-paned window. His eyes moved from the rain that still slanted down outside to the toes of his worn sneakers. "Look. It's time we talked some of this stuff through, but I don't have time now 'cause Gigi'll wonder where I am."

Jennie recognized the smoothing-over tactics he used before any fresh offensive. "Why don't we go ahead and discuss your 'stuff,' Steven? I've got plenty of time. But I've already said you aren't going anywhere tonight."

"You don't understand," he shouted, his face turning red. "It's getting tough to explain why I'm the only kid my age living in Eden Park who doesn't get to do what he wants. And I always have less money than anyone else."

"Steven, don't shout at me." She glanced at Bobby, wishing he weren't witnessing this and probably taking notes for future use. "You know we have to be a little careful with the budget these days. And that doesn't mean I think you're underprivileged. You have plenty, more than most of the world."

He looked at the ceiling. "Don't give me that starving-millions routine. Just because I do without, it doesn't mean some kid in Ethiopia's going to get the difference, does it?"

"I've had a busy day," Jennie said. "And I've got work to do this evening. We're not going to discuss this anymore." She got a sudden, vivid picture of Peter Kynaston smiling at her this afternoon. Talking to someone who'd been a part of her life as it used to be, in less complicated days, would feel so good.

"There's something else we have to talk about." Steven crossed his arms and leaned against the door. "The Honda's falling apart."

"Oh, really?" Losing her temper would accomplish nothing. What he meant was that most of his friends had new cars, not hand-me-downs. "That's the breaks, Steven," she said evenly. "That car was good enough for me and now it'll have to be good enough for you until you can buy something else of your own. That's the way it's going to be.''

"Probably more than I'm gonna get," Bobby put in, and immediately grinned. "Just joking, Mom."

She spared him a frown. "This discussion is closed."

"You're all right," Steven said to her, undaunted. "You've got Dad's Mercedes. And you'd have had another new car by now if he hadn't—"

Jennie stared at him, not even slightly mollified by the faint flush that spread over his cheekbones.

"I'm sorry," he said quietly. "I shouldn't have said that."

She didn't comment.

"Would it be okay if I just went out for a little while? Gigi and I need to talk. I won't be long, honest."

"I don't think—"

"Ple-e-e-ase, Mom. Look, I didn't have a great day at school and I came home in a bad mood. I shouldn't have taken it out on you, okay?"

Jennie stared at him and saw, with a disturbing sense of déjà vu, his father standing there. Steven could have been Mark apologizing for being short with her and promising that when the breakthrough at the lab came, he wouldn't be so uptight.

"Just for an hour, Mom?" Steven wheedled now.

"Okay." She made herself smile at him. Their happiness and success as a family was the fuel that drove whatever ambition she had, including the business venture. And thinking about the business reminded her she'd made up her mind that the time had come to discuss a major plan she had in mind that would affect them all. "Steven, when you get back, I'd like to talk to you about something I'm mulling over."

He wasn't listening. "I could use a few bucks," he said, leafing through his wallet. "Gigi'll be disappointed about the movies, but we could still eat."

Steven already got a perfectly adequate allowance. "You'll have to make do," she told him, and when he opened his mouth to argue, she added, "unless you'd rather not go at all."

For a few moments he scowled at her, and she felt the first real apprehension over what his reaction would be when she told him she was considering selling this large and much too expensive house in order to plow more money into Executive Images.

"I think you'd better forget—" Before she could finish, he left, rattling the glass in its wooden frame.

"Steve can be a butt," Bobby said conspiratorially, his dark brows drawn together. She didn't have the heart to complain about his language.

"Did you get that biology paper back?" Jennie gave her whole attention to Bobby. Too often he got what little time she had left after fielding Steven's constant demands.

Bobby's response was cut off by a gust of cold air and Steven, who whipped back into the kitchen and stood with his back to the door. His face was red once more, his brown eyes bright.

"What is it?" Jennie got up.

"Him," Steven said. "After the last time, I didn't think he'd come back, but he has. He just turned into the driveway. Don't answer the door."

She wound her wedding ring around and around while she thought. There was no need to ask who *he* was. Peter must have come.

"Geez. You should see *his* car," Steven continued. "New. Black Lotus Esprit. I've only seen 'em in magazines. I bet they cost a bundle."

"I wouldn't know. But he can afford it. He's a very successful man." The roof of her mouth turned dry, and she ran her tongue back. "I should have talked to you about this a long time ago. There isn't time now. But please remember we aren't rude to people, Steven. We have no reason to be."

"Not even—"

"*Don't* say it. Don't even suggest it. All that's past, and I've come to believe we made some hasty judgments because we weren't thinking clearly. We never did have any real proof that he had anything to do with what happened."

"Yeah, I do," Steven said with a stubborn lift of his

pointed chin. "My dad told me the way it was. I believed him then and I do now. Why wouldn't I? Stress makes Parkinson's get worse faster. Dad was stressed out by that guy, and because he was already weak he had the heart attack."

"There's no real evidence that that's what caused—"

"Dad to die before he had to? Yeah, there is. Who's getting all the glory—and the bucks—from Dad's work?"

"Oh, Steven, don't." Regret, sadness and so much more crowded in, not for herself or even for Mark, anymore, but for their son.

The front doorbell rang. Jennie dithered, weighing her options. Not answering the door was out. She didn't play games. And anyway, whether it had been a good idea or not, she had invited Peter to come over. Managing a smile at Steven, she ran a hand over her hair. It seemed important for Peter to see that she was coping well. "Why don't you stay and visit with Peter, too. I saw him this afternoon and invited him to come over sometime. He was such good friends with you boys, and we shouldn't—"

"I'm leaving." Wearing the mutinous frown that was becoming all too standard, Steven went outside again.

"Is it really Peter?" Bobby asked, his eyes wide. When she nodded, he said, "I didn't think he'd ever come by again."

"Peter's been traveling all over the world," she told Bobby. She couldn't remember feeling as anxious as she did in this moment.

The doorbell rang again, and Jennie walked into the hall. "Coming," she said as levelly as she could.

Through the wide, parquet-tiled foyer she went, past the foot of the soaring stairs with glistening oak banisters. The shadow beyond the glass insert in one of the double doors loomed tall and broad.

Jennie opened the door and looked at Peter Kynaston.

"Hi." He leaned against the jamb and smiled, but the slight narrowing of green eyes suggested he wasn't smiling with anything but his wide mouth. Peter was gauging her mood, assessing what might be in store for him here.

"Hi." She inclined her head and waited.

He brought expressive brows together, forming a deep crease between. How old was he now, thirty-two? He looked it, and the maturity suited him. Thirty-two, successful and striking with curly sun-streaked brown hair and those impossible-to-ignore green eyes…an almost stereotypical Australian outdoors type. The mythical Ellie, the woman he'd been engaged to in Sydney, had given up quite a catch.

He bowed his head and placed the heel of one booted foot on the threshold. "I got home from the lab and went out to work on the greenhouse I'm building. The rain kept running down my neck. Then I remembered the coffee you promised me. It sounded too good to pass up, so here I am." He smiled, but she felt his wariness, saw the speculation in his gaze. There was so much between them that needed to be said if they were to try to mend bridges—maybe too much. "It's been a long time, Jennie. Over a year and a half."

"That long?" She managed to sound surprised, although she could have told him the day and the month.

"Hmm." His gaze returned to her face. "You're looking good…great. I thought that when I saw you this afternoon."

For a thirty-six-year-old widow? "Thanks."

"How're things going, Jennie?"

She'd always found his accent fascinating. "Fine."

"Managing all right with everything around here?"

"I've become a fix-it whiz," she said, feeling a flash of pride. There weren't too many things she couldn't do.

Peter glanced at the broad sweep of lawn rising to terraced beds in front of the Tudor-style house. "Growing season's about on us, but Steven's got a strong back and Bobby's up to it, too, so I don't suppose you have to worry there."

"True." And there she was a liar. Steven moaned with every shove of the mower. *No one else's kids had to do this stuff.* Steven couldn't, or wouldn't, understand the need for any change, and although Bobby helped willingly enough, she was determined that he shouldn't do more than his share.

"Hi, there, Jennie!"

She peered past Peter and saw Carl Ramstet, her next-door

neighbor, swathed in yellow oilskins and clipping dead branches from shrubs. Carl wasn't a man who could be idle. "Don't work too hard," she called, trying for an airy tone. "Tell Lou I'll be over for that drink she promised me." Lou had promised just that, and it should be enough to make sure Peter didn't stay too long. Earlier she'd felt so certain she was ready to clear away any misunderstandings. Now she wasn't sure.

"I brought this for you," Peter said, picking up a pot she hadn't noticed. "Do you like orchids?"

Looking at his hopeful face, she felt overwhelming empathy. Peter's ambition, his undeniable brilliance and absorption in his work weren't enough to completely obliterate his conscience. Jennie saw now that although, as she'd come to realize, he would never have wittingly set out to undermine Mark, still there might be moments when he wondered if he had contributed to his benefactor's death, which had come so much earlier than expected. Peter, as Mark's assistant—his protégé—had been heir apparent to the star research role, and Mark had come to believe that Peter was impatient with his understudy status. Impatience was one thing; deliberate efforts to bring about another man's downfall was something quite different. Peter Kynaston couldn't have planned what happened.

"Jennie?"

"Oh." She'd been staring at him blankly. She couldn't leave him on the front step any longer, not with Carl watching the whole scene. "I love orchids. Come in out of the wet. The coffee's hot."

Without taking the plant, she turned away and headed for the kitchen, letting him close the door and follow her. The solid thud of his boots brought flashes of other times when he hadn't felt he needed to ring the bell before coming in. Jennie could visualize his loose-limbed stride, and the way he looked, without having to see him. An oversize navy-blue windbreaker, denim shirt and jeans were a uniform for Peter. These and the cowboy boots that had caused so much amusement at first, particularly at the lab, where his white coat looked like an incongruous nod to convention.

"How's the new hobby coming?"

Jennie set her teeth and kept walking. "You mean my business?"

In the kitchen she was surprised to find that Bobby had disappeared. She often forgot that his jaunty front tended to be a cover for shyness. She poured a mug of coffee, faced Peter and stood with one hand splayed on the table that was covered with catalogs and client files.

Peter hooked back his coat and anchored his thumbs in his pockets. "Looks like you're getting into some serious stuff. With the little shop and everything. Well, I suppose it fills up some time. I thought you were happy with the salesgirl job at that department store." He didn't add what he'd voiced at the time she'd taken the job, that he couldn't understand why she'd decided to leave her home and children. And she hadn't told him that even if she hadn't needed to augment her income, with Mark gone there were too many empty hours, too much time to think and remember.

"I liked the store," she said stiffly, setting the mug down near Peter. "But after six months I realized I was really good at helping people fit their wardrobes to their life-styles." And he didn't know, didn't have any idea, that "filling time" had nothing to do with her determination to move her financial footing from adequate to comfortable—and to be totally independent. "I decided to turn the talent into a real career and I'm starting to make some headway."

"Good," Peter said vaguely. He set the green pot with its heavy spray of creamy orchids beside the sink. "Mist it about twice a week and make sure it doesn't get direct sun." He bent his big shoulders over what Jennie knew was only one of the dozens of varieties he raised. "Needs watering twice a week, but the bark has to completely dry out in between." Watching his strong hands, gentle with the flowers that were his passion, touched a chord in her.

"Who looked after your plants while you were away?" She

wanted to ask why, in the two months since he'd returned, he hadn't tried to contact her. But she knew she had no right.

"Boarded them out," Peter remarked. "Costs almost as much as boarding a dog, I'd say." He laughed and reached for the coffee.

"It was funny seeing you today," she said. Her throat seemed to close. "I felt as if there hadn't been any time since we last met—only it's been so long. Strange."

He drank deeply and sniffed appreciatively. "Yeah, strange. How are the boys? I saw Steven driving out, but he didn't see me."

Didn't choose to see him, Jennie thought. She couldn't face any silences. "The boys are good, very good."

"Great." He turned and leaned against the sink, his boots crossed at the ankles. "How does all that work?" He indicated her papers.

"It wouldn't interest you." And, if she could make herself face the truth, she'd say that she wouldn't expect a renowned scientist who set his own style in all things to relate to what she did.

Peter went to the table, turned a chair backward and sat astride the seat, putting his coffee aside while he leafed through a jewelry catalog. He rested his chin atop his forearm on the chair back and concentrated. "Do you make your contacts by phone, or what?"

"Actually I've got a coat with safety pins all over the lining."

He glanced at her blankly, then frowned. "What for?"

She almost laughed. There had always been areas of naïveté in Peter—maybe because of the cultural difference—that amused her.

"Oh, Peter, you know how it's done. I pin fake Gucci watches inside my coat and wait around Greyhound Bus stations for incoming passengers. Or outside men's rooms. That's a good spot. It's called very direct sales."

His smile spread very slowly, driving deep dimples into the grooves beneath his cheekbones. He slapped his muscular, jean-clad thighs. "You always did enjoy making fun of me. Come on, Jennie-o, explain. I am interested."

The temptation to let down and enjoy him, to put aside the past, was overwhelmingly tempting. Why not. "I shop for executives and anybody else who's too busy to shop or who thinks it's a status symbol to have someone do the job for them.

"I analyze the client's business and private life-styles and assemble appropriate wardrobes designed to maximize their best physical assets. Of course, playing to the need for an aura of power is very important, and since I've spent a lot of time around successful people, I have a feel for what's needed."

"I guess you work mostly for women."

She hid a smile. "Actually most of my clients are men. Men are used to asking women's advice about such things as clothes—or even how their offices or apartments should be furnished. A lot of women still feel perfect taste is something they should be born with and they aren't prepared to admit they could use help from someone like me."

Peter's brow raised. "Men, huh? I suppose I understand what you mean. How do you find your customers?"

"I made a lot of contacts while I was still working at the store. From there, it's been through advertising and word of mouth. More word of mouth than anything. It's really working, Peter." There was a warm rush of satisfaction at the thought. For the first time in her life, she was responsible for her own fate and she liked it.

"You sound pretty involved," Peter said. "I'd have thought you had enough to do with the boys at the age they are. You and Mark were always so adamant about kids needing a parent available at all times."

Getting irritated would be pointless. "I'm here when I'm needed. The boys are pretty independent now."

Before she could react, Peter took her cold hands in his warm ones and stared up at her. His eyes were gentle, thoughtful, but they always had been. "It's probably a good idea," he said quietly. "Being alone isn't much fun, and they'll be gone before you know it. Seems funny to see Steven driving his own car already."

"They're growing up." If she wasn't careful, she'd start confiding in Peter out of habit, telling him how concerned she was about Steven. Apart from Lou and Carl Ramstet, there was no one anymore. All the old crowd had melted away since she'd ceased to fit their mold. Jennie realized her own expression could betray her mood. She smiled and removed her hands. "You've been alone awhile, Peter. It's too bad things didn't work out between you and Ellie."

Now what was in his eyes? Speculation? She could still feel the firm warmth of his fingers on hers. How long had it been since a man held her hand?

Peter stirred and stood up. "The final break was months ago now, and I know it was the right decision. We didn't want the same things. How about you? Any new love interests in your life?"

The question hit like a blow. "Mark's only been dead... No, there's no one." Her knees shook. She'd never been asked the question before, and it seemed unconscionable that Peter should be the one to do so now.

"Mark's been dead almost two years. That's a long time," he said, but his voice was mild, detached even. "Particularly since he was ill for several years."

The bluntness, the clinical approach, unnerved her. "I'm not—"

"Mom, I just talked to Derek." Bobby scuffed into the kitchen, his eyes on Peter. "He says the registration for the bike trip has to be in by tomorrow."

"Hi, Bob," Peter said.

Bobby hunched his shoulders and gave a lopsided smile. "Hi, Peter. How's Killer?"

Jennie looked away. Bobby and Peter's Siamese cat had been firm friends.

"Ornery," Peter said. "But she's only bitten me twice today. You'll have to come over and see if you can improve her disposition."

"I'd like that," Bobby said, but not without a wary check

of Jennie's reaction. "Can I take the registration over to Derek's, Mom?"

"We didn't make a definite decision on this," Jennie said, inwardly cursing Bobby's rotten timing. She didn't want to discuss potential problems in front of Peter.

"All the guys are going," Bobby said tentatively. Jennie knew how much he wanted to go. "We've gotta get my bike in for new tires, too."

"Could we discuss this later?" she said, her chest getting tighter with every breath, her face hotter. An adult was supposed to accompany each child, and even if she had time to go, she knew every other boy's father would be along and she'd feel awkward.

Bobby sighed, then smiled. "It's okay—I don't really want to go anyway."

She wiped her palms on the loose weave of her beige woolen skirt. "We don't have to make a final decision now."

"What's wrong with your tires?" Peter said. "Are they really shot or just needing a patch, maybe?"

Bobby shrugged. "Dunno. They won't stay pumped up."

"Tell you what, sport. How about I fix 'em for you? I'm a bike whiz. I bet you didn't know that."

"You don't have time, Peter." Jennie turned to Bobby. "I'll work something out. Don't worry." She had no idea what, or how she'd fit it in. The trip was on Sunday, and she'd be working until Saturday afternoon.

"This is man's stuff," Peter said, grinning, deliberately not looking at her. "Leave it to me, huh?"

"Okay," Bobby said, and Jennie heard how badly he wanted to feel good about this. "What about the registration?"

"Give it to me," she said, more shortly than she intended. After signing the form, she handed it to him. "Run it over, then get to your homework. We'll talk some more later."

Jennie sat in a chair as far as possible from Peter, trying to come up with some nonchalant comment about teenage boys and feeling unaccountably shaky.

"It isn't easy, is it?" he said, destroying any inspiration

she might have had. "Bringing up kids alone, I mean. I'd be glad to help if you'd let me. Boys need a man around, and I could try to fill the gap a bit."

"You don't know about kids, Peter. You never had any." Pride made her want to hide how she'd struggled with a longing for them to be good friends again. "But thanks for the offer."

Peter appeared lost in thought. The slow drip of the faucet that needed repair sounded deafening to Jennie.

"You do have enough money, don't you, Jen?"

She jumped. "I...yes, of course."

"Okay, okay. I only asked. I thought maybe you almost told Bobby he couldn't go on the bike trip because you couldn't afford it."

"You guessed wrong. I'm not sure about it, that's all. Most boys' fathers go." She looked at her hands, winding the ring.

Peter came close and bowed over her until she was forced to raise her head. "You ride a bike perfectly well. I remember."

She remembered the times they'd all—Mark, herself and the boys and Peter—ridden through the park and picnicked. Another age. "Women aren't invited."

He touched her cheek and brushed back her thick hair. Just an attempt at kindness, so why did she tingle and ache at the same time? Why was it an effort not to close her eyes and rest a head that, if she'd allow herself the luxury of admitting her own humanness, sometimes felt too heavy?

"You've proved you can manage, y'know, girl. You're a tough one and no mistake. I'll go with Bobby. How about that?"

She swallowed so hard she was sure he must have heard. Reluctantly Jennie considered whether she had the courage to say what she should say to Peter, what was long overdue. She knew now that in the months before Mark died, he'd been too sick and troubled to see straight. It hadn't taken long after the awful scene with Peter for Jennie to admit to herself that her husband had wrongly accused his assistant of plotting again him. But could she turn the clock back on that? Even if she could put it behind her, Steven remained convinced that Peter had been responsible for precipitating the final violent heart attack that ended Mark's life. Only the night before he died, he'd ranted about "Kynaston" competing, about his plot to outshine the man who would always be his superior.

"Jennie? What do you say? Shall I pump up my own tires. I think Bobby'd be game to have me with him."

Peter was right, but she couldn't take advantage of him, not when she still owed him an explanation she wasn't quite ready to make. She patted his arm and stood up, breaking contact. "Thanks, Peter, but no. Bobby's very independent. It isn't essential that someone goes with him as long as there are plenty of other men along. He'll want to prove he doesn't need anyone."

"We could ask him."

"You're very kind, but no." Her big smile felt phony.

"The faucet's dripping."

It took a second for Jennie to register what he'd said. "Oh, yes." Plumbing was one art she hadn't mastered, and she never seemed to be home long enough to call in a professional.

Peter started to take off his jacket. "Are the tools still in the same place?"

"Yes…no. The plumber's coming in the morning."

"Okay. But if there is anything you need, call, would you? I know you've probably been holed up here trying to…well, you know. But I'm there for you, Jennie, just like I always was."

"Thank you." Surely he sensed that all he was doing was making her long to be…no, not long to be alone, but long to accept and ask him to stay. Sitting with Peter, laughing the way they used to, would be so comforting. "The last time we were together, you said you'd be back. You never came. Why?" There, she'd blurted it out. Her chest rose and fell rapidly.

Peter dropped his hands to his sides. "I think we both know the answer to that."

"You didn't deny what…you didn't say it wasn't true. You

just said you'd wait awhile, then come back. When I heard you'd gone straight from the Australian lecture tour to a big worldwide tour, I didn't expect to see you for a long time. But you've been back two months.'' She paused, her lips parted, appalled at the emotion loading her voice. What right did she have to question his actions?

"Jennie. The last time we were together, it was Mark's birthday, remember? He'd been dead six months.''

"I remember,'' she said softly.

"I knew you'd be having a bad time, so I came over. Steven told me to get...'' He shook his head. ''Bobby said you'd gone to the cemetery, and I followed you there. I didn't want you to be alone and sad.''

It had been a cold morning in the little churchyard north of the city. She'd stood, remembering how people had eulogized Mark at his funeral a few months earlier, making him sound like a stranger she'd never known. Peter had been at the service, too. The news of the death had reached him while he'd been on his way to Australia for the lecture tour Mark was to have conducted until it was decided he was too ill. Peter had rushed back, offering her his help. Then it had been easy to stand erect and refuse because she'd been so sure he was acting out of guilt.

"I was so angry,'' she said almost to herself as she remembered that wintry day when Peter had arrived at her side by the grave. "I said a lot of things I shouldn't have. But you didn't defend yourself.''

"No. I didn't feel I had to. If you couldn't trust me after all the good times we'd shared, I wasn't sure it mattered.''

"I blamed you. You must already have known that. I kept my distance from you after Mark died.''

Pain twisted his features. "Yes.''

"You know why. You know—'' Only loyalty to Mark had held her back from seeking Peter out afterward and saying those things. Why hadn't she done so, regardless? "Mark thought you had talked about him to the foundation, told them he was unfit for his job. He said he could have handled the tour if he'd been allowed more time to recover again. He thought you wanted his job right then."

"I didn't talk about him—to anyone."

And she believed him. "I know that now. Perhaps I've known it for a long time. But it isn't possible to wipe out so much bad feeling in a few minutes, is it?"

He shrugged away from the counter and put an arm around her shoulder. She resisted, but only for a moment before allowing him to pull her face against his shoulder.

"I'd like to think we could be friends again, Jennie. You and Mark were family to me when I came to this country. I didn't have anyone and, self-sufficient as I am, I do like to spend time around a few warm bodies."

Jennie couldn't help laughing. She raised her face. "Self-sufficient?" His total lack of domestic skills was legendary among those who knew him. A junk-food freak—the only balanced meals eaten by the Peter she remembered were those shared with members of his staff in their homes.

Peter appeared wounded. "I've come a long way. I discovered the Crockpot. It's great. Throw in anything, frozen or not, and *voilà*! Stew."

She laughed again. "Sounds great, all right."

Peter wasn't smiling anymore. He removed his arm from her shoulders. "I've wanted to come, Jen. There's rarely been a day when I haven't thought about you and wondered how you were."

"Mmm." The gentleness in his voice, the kindness, was too much.

"I worry about you. What do you do for recreation?"

The question turned her mind blank.

When she didn't respond, he moved closer again and looked steadily down at her. "What do you do apart from look after the house and the boys and this—" he indicated the table "—this stuff and the shop?"

"It's a studio," she said, and heard her own defensiveness. "I'm always busy. And Mark's only been dead two years. It takes time to make a new life."

"You already said that, and I know, remember?"

"I don't see why you care." And she didn't like being pinned down on the subject.

"I care because you and Mark were my lifeline when I came to the States. I'd had a lousy marriage myself. I was jaded on anything approaching permanent commitment. Watching you two made me rethink whether or not the old institution could work."

So much so that he'd decided to get engaged to Ellie...and that hadn't worked out, not that Jennie ever intended to mention the subject again.

She shifted from one foot to the other. The air between them had texture, as if it hummed with things not said. His hair was, as usual, too long, but it suited him. She ran her gaze over glinting blond streaks. He had always carried an aura of life with him, a vibrancy that filled his space and made others pale.

The silence unnerved her. "You should make the effort to meet someone else, Peter."

"I will when I've got time. Right now I'm married to the lab. The last few months have been exciting."

How familiar that sounded. "Of course. But don't let your life go by without—" What he did was none of her business. Inviting Peter here probably hadn't been a great idea. Some obstacles were too big to be overcome. She looked at her watch. "Wow, I almost forgot. Lou Ramstet invited me over for a drink. I really ought to go."

"I heard." He made no attempt to move. "Is that the extent of your social life? A drink with the neighbors?"

The questions started to feel like pointless prying. "Lou and Carl are old friends."

"So am I."

She set her teeth carefully together. Saying that he'd taken his time to try to reestablish their friendship would accomplish nothing. "Lou and Carl have been there when I needed them. Whenever I needed them. Which is more than I can say for most of the other—" She closed her eyes briefly, annoyed at what she'd almost said.

Peter looked at her sharply. "Most of the other what?"

"Nothing, really. I seem to have lost touch with most of our old friends, that's all."

"You're a beautiful woman, and bright. Meeting new people shouldn't be too hard."

"Sure." She sounded sarcastic, but couldn't help it. How typical of a self-assured man like Peter not to understand that meeting people was anything but easy for women like Jennie, who, married in her second year of college to a man who wouldn't take no for an answer, had never learned how to play the dating game. Not that she was interested now.

But Peter had said she was beautiful and bright. She colored at the thought. Receiving flattery, even if offhanded, had become a forgotten experience.

"Oh, Jennie. You and I have to put the past behind us. You need a friend, and I want to be that for you again."

There was no steadying the erratic beat of her heart. "You don't have to worry about me."

"Someone does. You don't have folks. Mark's are too far away, and anyway, parents aren't what you need."

He couldn't have any idea what she needed; Jennie wasn't sure herself. "I don't understand why you suddenly turn up worrying about me and my emotional health. What brought this on?"

He shrugged. "I've been thinking, that's all. I've been thinking ever since I was here last when Steve was so—" He cleared his throat and turned slightly pink beneath his tan.

"Rude," she finished for him, feeling hopelessly flat.

"Yes, he was that. If Bobby hadn't told me where you'd gone, I'd never have shown up at the cemetery. I had the feeling Steven was giving you a rough time, but I didn't know what to do about it."

"And now you do?"

"I should have come as soon as I got back. I was just afraid I'd upset you all over again. This afternoon, when I saw you, I knew I'd been wrong and I couldn't stay away any longer."

She didn't know what to say.

"Do you think Steven's over hating me?"

"No." Pretending would accomplish nothing. "He's still a very angry young man—angrier if anything."

"He's missing having a man around, that's all. Maybe we can do something about that."

This was amazing. Despite all that had happened, he still thought he had the power to smooth any unpleasant ripple that came his way. "I don't think you know what you're talking about."

Peter placed a large firm hand on each of her shoulders, and heat warmed her skin through tawny silk. "Yes, I do know. Please take me seriously and give what I have in mind a chance."

His eyes, so intent, held her rapt.

"I already said you're lovely. If anything, you've grown more beautiful and desirable than ever, and it's time you had a man in your life."

Her heart had stopped altogether, hadn't it?

"Are you listening to me?"

"Yes." She was listening. But she couldn't make sense of whatever messages he was trying to give her.

Peter smiled, and her stomach swooped. "You always were so gentle. Please say you'll at least give what I'm proposing a try. If it doesn't work, you can always forget it. There won't be any hard feelings."

"Peter, I don't think—"

"You don't even know him properly yet. How can you think anything?"

She frowned. "Know who?"

"The guy I'd like you to start dating."

PETER MOVED aside stacks of magazines on the couch. If he had any spine, he wouldn't allow people to look after him. "You don't have to fuss over me, Liz. Fred's going to have my hide one of these days."

"Fred isn't the jealous-husband type," Liz Meadows said, and laughed with no trace of coyness. She rammed a long pin into her untidy chignon. "Why don't you hire a cleaning lady and get in the habit of grocery shopping once a week? What would you live on if your friends didn't take pity on you occasionally? Your damn orchids?''

''There's nothing wrong with a good hamburger, or a pizza or my Crockpot stew.'' The latter was starting to bore him, but he'd never admit as much to a living soul. He settled into the space he'd made between magazines on the couch, hoisted his feet on a table and watched Liz potter into the kitchen. Killer immediately leaped onto the coffee table to sit where she could fix Peter with her ungrateful blue stare.

Liz's tuneless hum accompanied the sound of the oven door closing. Thursday was the night Fred Meadows, a veteran pharmaceutical salesman, played chess, and Liz occasionally decided to use the opportunity to perform a charity effort— bring a ''good, balanced dinner'' to Peter. She returned to the living room, shifted a gravel-filled tray of plant pots from a chair to the floor and sat down. ''You said you wanted my opinion on something.''

A mistake. Liz, unmarried until a couple of years ago, when she'd already been in her early fifties, was unlikely to see Jennie's widowhood as a problem. ''Forget it. I sorted everything out.''

Killer, who only came near Peter when she wanted food, sashayed elegantly across the room to settle on Liz's lap.

Silence settled in. A drink would be great, but Liz didn't drink. She didn't usually stay once the inevitable casserole was in the oven. Peter glanced at her and quickly fixed his attention on the scuffed toes of his propped boots. Liz was watching him with the same concentration she lavished on lab specimens.

''Don't let that cat snag your skirt,'' he said when he began to hear his own breathing.

''What's up, Peter? You left the lab early and you looked like a man with a mission.''

She should have had children. They always said good mothers read minds. ''Jennie Andrews,'' he said, clasping his hands behind his neck and scooting lower.

''Ah.'' Liz gave a gusty sigh. ''I had the feeling this afternoon that something had changed between the two of you.''

"We, we…well, to be honest, it was the first time I'd spoken to Jennie since before I went to Australia."

Liz stared. "That was…good Lord, Peter, I had no idea. Why, for goodness' sake?"

He shrugged. "I was busy, and there were things… You know some of what happened between Mark and me."

"Yes, but I assumed you and Jennie had put it all behind you."

Of course she had. Liz was one of the most reasonable women he'd ever met. "We have now. More or less." He knew that was far from true, but he and Jennie had made a start—or they had before he'd committed whatever sin she now seemed to think him guilty of. "I miss Mark sometimes," he said distractedly.

"We all do," Liz said. "I thought Jennie was doing okay, though."

"It isn't good for a woman to live alone like that."

Liz's hand stilled on Killer's back. "She isn't alone."

"Not technically. But she needs more in her life than raising a couple of boys and running a business that caters to spoiled people."

Liz muttered something he didn't quite catch, then said, "It's a shopping service, isn't it? Someone at the lab mentioned reading a little piece about it in some local rag."

He hunched his shoulders. "It's more than a shopping service, I guess. Jennie buys whole wardrobes for executives, and gives them advice on decorating, too, I think. She'd be good at that sort of thing, but I know it's only something to fill up her time because she's lonely."

"Orchids," Liz said.

"What?"

"Oh, nothing. I was just thinking it'll be a good thing when you finish building that greenhouse."

"I'm getting there. What do you think of Simon?"

"Greenbaum?"

He frowned at her. "How many people do we have at the lab called Simon?"

"He's okay."

"He's more than okay." Sometimes Liz's economy of emotion frustrated him. "He's bright and established, and—"

"Dull."

Peter stood up and paced. "Simon's quiet, that's all. Not dull. He needs an interest in his life outside work."

"Mmm. Sounds as if quite a few people do."

"Exactly. Jennie invited me to the house for coffee. I went this afternoon and tried to talk some sense into her."

"Peter! *Don't* say what I think you're going to say." Liz placed the cat firmly on the ground as if readying for action.

He stood in front of her. "Don't say what? Simon's single and the right age, and I already sounded him out so I know he's looking for someone to do things with. He likes the opera and the symphony and art shows. Stuff like that. Jennie likes the same things. They could—"

"No! Sometimes you can be remarkably naive, Peter."

"You're shouting, Liz."

She folded her hands carefully together, and her nostrils flared as she breathed in slowly. "Did you go to Jennie and suggest she date Simon Greenbaum?" Her eyes closed as if in silent prayer.

Peter's stomach made an unpleasant revolution. "Well…not exactly. I did say I had someone in mind for her. Simon's name did sort of come up, and—"

"And she told you to get lost? She must think you're mad."

"Yeah. She said just that. And I can't figure out why, damn it. She almost kicked me out." Muscles in his face and back flicked into tight knots at the thought. "She told me to open my eyes and grow up."

Liz's snort stopped his pacing. "What's so funny?"

"Oh, it's not that funny. Jennie met Simon a few times, that's all. She must have wondered where you were coming from."

"How do you know she asked me…okay, spit it out. Did Jennie and Simon have a disagreement at some time?"

"Not that I know of. But you'd better watch…you'd better be prepared…oh, dear, I'm too old for this. Simon's a nice man, and I'm sure he thinks you are, too. You'd better be ready when he asks you to the opera."

Peter stared and felt himself turn red. "He isn't...oh, hell." He gazed into space, thinking about Simon, the very capable technician, the almost-invisible member of his staff. "Oh, hell. And Jennie knows?"

"Believe it or not, most people do."

He dropped to the couch again and scrubbed at his eyes. "But not me. She was really mad at me. Told me to get out and not come back."

"She probably thought you were making fun of her or something."

"I wouldn't do a thing like that. Liz, you don't think Simon assumes I'm—"

Liz laughed, held her sides and laughed. "Somehow I doubt it. I wouldn't worry. But you probably need to do something about Jennie."

"Yeah, I sure do. She's so lovely. Feminine and gentle— well, you know—and those big soft brown eyes slay a man. Liz, help. Who can I match her up with? I don't know that many people." He saw Jennie in his mind as he talked.

"You're unbelievable."

"I can take a little abuse, if that's what you mean. I want to help her. Seeing her lonely and trying to cover up kills me."

"Well...I might have one suggestion."

"Gimme." He leaned forward. "It's got to be someone I know, though."

"Right. And all this man has to do is take Jennie out occasionally. No strings."

"No." He shook his head. "Absolutely no strings. She's the type of woman who'd get turned off immediately by anyone who came on too strong. And she's not ready for anything serious."

"So, just a platonic arrangement to lighten up a couple of lonely lives."

"Exactly. That's what I've been telling you."

"Wonderful." She picked up the phone and trailed it across to his lap. "Call and ask her out."

CHAPTER THREE

He had nerve. Jennie shoved another load into the washer and started the machine with a punch. It rattled ominously on the concrete basement floor, and she adjusted the balance. She felt a perfect fool for jumping to the wrong conclusions about Peter's intentions. She'd actually thought he was going to suggest they do something fun together, like old times. And the idea had appealed more than she wanted to admit. *Simon Greenbaum!*

She folded sheets, thinking back over Peter's visit, and began to laugh. She should be able to stay mad at him but she couldn't. Either he was so involved with his work that he wasn't aware of Simon's preferences, or he thought all she needed in the way of masculine company was a congenial and safe escort. Well, she had news for Peter Kynaston—even she didn't want to be that safe...did she? Now, that was an interesting question, and one that hadn't occurred to her recently. But the answer was obvious. She didn't want anyone at all, outside her boys. Whatever outlets she needed in addition to Steven and Bobby were very adequately filled by her work.

With a basket of folded laundry balanced on one hip, Jennie climbed the steps slowly. She was tired and it was getting late, but maybe she'd still go over to the Ramstets. The basket slipped at the same moment she heard the phone. "Shoot!" Towels fell around her feet, and she scrabbled to gather them up.

The phone rang again.

Darn, it was Thursday the thirteenth, not Friday. By the time she opened the door into the mudroom behind the kitchen, she was out of breath and the laundry was a dusty jumble.

Another jarring ring. She should have got an answering machine by now. Missing a customer call was something she definitely couldn't afford at this stage.

Running, dropping the basket on a chair, she dashed into the kitchen and snatched up the phone. "Hello...hello." With a long sigh she listened to empty buzzing for a second, then dropped the handset back into its cradle. She had to relax. True, she'd been getting business calls at night, but she should probably be discouraging people from the habit.

Getting away for an hour was definitely a good idea. With a cardigan over her shoulders, she went into the hall. "I'll be next door," she called up to Bobby as she went outside.

Carl answered her knock and led her to the glassed-in porch at the back of the house, where he and Lou liked to spend their evenings.

"Where's Lou?" The television blared with one of the game shows she was addicted to, but her well-worn blue recliner was empty.

"In the bedroom, I think." Carl, tall, thin and slightly stooped, his sparse brown hair standing on end, crossed his arms. "Will you have the usual?"

"Thanks. Light on the gin, though. I still have work to get through tonight."

"Coming up."

He didn't move.

Jennie cleared her throat. This wasn't the first time lately when she'd felt tension in her best friends' home. Apprehension cooled her skin. "Is Lou coming right out, or...?"

"She misses Jody."

The Ramstets' only child had gone away to college the previous fall. "I know."

"Sometimes—" He raised his shoulders, and Jennie saw tiredness in his gray eyes before he turned on a smile. "Oh, I don't know. It's easier for me. I've got my job, but Lou made her life around Jody...a lot of it, anyway, and sometimes she seems to be…lost? Go talk to her, Jennie. I'll make us some drinks, and we'll all cheer up, huh?''

"You bet. My day hasn't left me so relaxed, either." She smiled back at him, thinking, as she had so many times, how often the most special and perceptive people were almost invisible in their unremarkable shells.

She climbed the stairs and walked along the soft beige carpet to Lou and Carl's comfortable suite. The door stood open, and she knocked softly. "Lou. It's only me."

There was rustling before Lou said, "Hi."

"Carl sent me," Jennie said, going in to find her friend propped against a pile of green chintz throw pillows atop a matching quilt. "We decided some cheering up is in order—for all of us, but we need you."

Lou said nothing. She pressed a fist to her mouth, and Jennie moved closer. "What's up?"

Short blond hair, well cut and usually perfectly groomed, appeared mussed. Lou wore no makeup, another unlikely event for the time of day, as were the bleach-stained sweatshirt reserved for gardening and old, too-tight jeans.

Alarm sent Jennie's nails digging into her palms. She sat on the edge of the bed. "Carl said you're missing Jody. She's okay, isn't she?"

Lou nodded. "I'm uptight. I can't seem to do anything about it."

"Boy, do I know how that feels."

"How can you?" Lou lifted her chin. "You aren't fifty and useless. You've got your boys and a new business."

The anger Jennie saw in Lou's pale blue eyes shocked her. "And you've got Carl," she said quietly before she could suppress the impulse. "Jody isn't dead, only making her way. We have to let go of our children."

Huge tears formed in Lou's eyes, and Jennie instantly wished she could grab back the words. They had sounded self-pitying and patronizing, and she didn't know how she'd react when the boys left. "I'm sorry. Come on out. Carl's worried to death about you."

"Look at me." Lou glanced down, spreading her arms.

"All I think about is food. I've hardly got anything that fits anymore. Not that Carl cares. He just says I should buy new clothes."

Jennie noticed the safety pin anchoring the waist of the jeans. She didn't know if she felt more irritated than sympathetic. "You aren't fat. Most of us have to battle the bulge as we get older. Big deal."

"It'd be a big deal if you were losing your perfect thirty-six, twenty-four, thirty-six." Lou sniffed.

"I never was that. And Carl's only suggesting buying new clothes because he wants you to be happy and to know he loves you regardless...." She looked away. What a dumb thing to say.

The mattress gave, and Lou swung her feet to the floor. She put an arm around Jennie's shoulders. "I'm glad you came over. You always know how to make me feel better."

Jennie smiled, offering silent thanks that her blunder had slipped by unnoticed. "That goes both ways." She hadn't missed the open box of chocolates beside the bed.

"I'm probably going through the change. They say you can get pretty emotional. Tomorrow I'll start a diet." Lou pointed a finger at Jennie. "You're on your honor to make sure I don't cheat. Promise?"

"Promise," Jennie said, laughing. "But don't forget we're not supposed to be the svelte things we were at twenty-five. I'll do it with you. I could spare a few pounds."

Lou grunted but didn't argue.

By ten-thirty desultory conversation had been abandoned, and the three of them stared at the TV. Jennie, falling asleep over the same gin and tonic she'd nursed since she'd arrived, stirred and announced she should get back to the house. She turned down Carl's offer to see her home and walked slowly up her driveway, nose lifted in appreciation of spring's night scents. Stars shone, promising another fine day. Lou worried her. Tomorrow she'd take the time to check up on her friend.

The garage door stood open, and the Honda was still missing. So much for Steven's promises. She felt angry but apprehensive. Steven might be difficult, but he didn't usually completely ignore an agreement.

Taking the key from her pocket, she unlocked the door and heard the phone again. Maybe that was Steven. Glancing upward as she hurried into the den to answer, she saw a glow that meant Bobby's light was still on.

"Hello."

The line went dead. She couldn't believe it. Twice in one night she'd just missed a call. And why hadn't Bobby answered?

"Why didn't you get the phone?" she called, but Bobby didn't respond. He had a habit of falling asleep with the light on, and she'd figured out a long time ago that he might be afraid of the dark.

In the kitchen she heated a mug of water in the microwave to make coffee and settled down to work. The session with Mr. Gertson had been an unexpected triumph. Rather than being difficult, he'd shown enthusiasm for most of the clothes she'd taken for him to try. Then he'd surprised her by saying he'd decided to take a cruise and would like her to outfit him with resort wear. And he hadn't balked when she'd explained that this would be treated as a second commission and would require a separate consulting fee.

She pushed aside a sheaf of flyers to retrieve an envelope of cash she'd withdrawn from the bank for petty cash at the studio.

The sum was already entered in the ledger. She picked up her purse to quickly count the bills before tucking the envelope away.

That wasn't right.

Holding open the envelope inside her purse, she counted again and became very still. A chill prickled up her spine as she glanced around. The windows were shut, and she knew the front door had been locked. Nothing else appeared to have been touched.

Slowly, a sickness clamping her insides, she stood and made her way upstairs. The glow she'd seen came not from

Bobby's room, but from the bathroom. She knocked on his door but got no answer.

"Bobby?" The door swished over the carpet. He was hunched under his quilt, asleep.

On tiptoe she approached and peered down at him.

The room was cold. Moonlight spread a shaft over the shape in the bed, and she lifted her head to billowing sheer drapes...and as quickly looked back at the bed. "Bobby!" She threw back the covers to reveal bunched pillows.

Everything within her stood still. Steven? No, Steven wasn't here to go to. Hardly able to breathe, she went to the window. Outside, the roof of the mudroom sloped down to where there was a drop of only a few feet to the raised lawn in the backyard. So many times they had rehearsed this as the way Bobby would get out of the house in case of a fire. "Come on, son," Mark had said, coaching from below, "lie on your tummy and scoot till your feet touch the gutter." And it worked so well.

A pulse thrummed in her throat. Almost eleven now, and she had no idea.... Money. Steven had said he needed money, and Bobby was, as he always had been, his big brother's willing slave. An idea formed and grew into conviction. Steven must have called Bobby and asked him to get some money. Bobby had taken the missing bills and gone to meet him. But it was dark, and so late...and she didn't know where to look.

Steven wasn't a bad boy. He loved Bobby. What would make him put his brother in danger?

HE DIDN'T GET this. Jennie wasn't the kind of woman to leave her door open and every light blazing while she went out. Peter sat beside a potted plant on the front step, hands hanging between his knees, and peered into the darkness. He'd parked by the street and walked up the drive to avoid making too much noise. He needn't have bothered. Her car was gone, so she must have taken Bobby somewhere.

From what she'd said earlier, he had assumed she would stay home and work. That's why he'd become concerned when his repeated phone calls went unanswered. Surely she wouldn't leave the house open like this all evening.

He'd already considered and discarded the idea of going to the Ramstets'. Their house was in darkness.

If he hadn't let Liz talk him into asking Jennie out, he wouldn't be sitting here in the dark on an unpleasant night. He'd be at home enjoying a scotch and getting through some of the piles of research publications he never quite kept up with. He'd be comfortable, the way he usually was with his predictable and satisfying existence.

Where was Jennie? Probably dealing with some demand of the boys.

True enough, he wanted a family one of these days. Having his own kids was important. His marriage had failed because of a difference of opinion on that front, and the same issue had played a big part in the broken engagement to Ellie. But this adolescent stuff wasn't anything he felt ready to handle. No doubt his attitude would change when he'd had a chance to grow with his children through all the early phases of development.

He hadn't done so well in his relationships with women, hadn't made sure all the expectations were clear—on both sides. Still, maybe next time....

Damn Liz. It was getting colder.

The sound of an engine approached, and headlights swung into the driveway. For the first time since he'd left home, Peter gave serious consideration to what he was going to say when he saw Jennie.

Damn Liz.

Car doors slammed and footsteps crunched on gravel. "Mom, he was gonna talk to you, honest. When he called he thought you'd be home, but you weren't." Bobby's voice hissed urgently.

"Be quiet."

Peter bounced to his feet but remained in the cover of the shrub.

"I knew you wouldn't want me bothering you at Lou and Carl's and I didn't think you'd mind—"

"Don't. Don't lie to me. I can't believe you've done this, Bobby. It isn't like you."

"Steven said it was important," Bobby said, misery loading his voice. "He said I had to help him out."

"And you did it without considering you were stealing from me. And you went out in the middle of the night and caught a bus to some dive. I'd been driving around for an hour when I saw you walking. Bobby, you scared me to death."

"Mom—"

"Are you going to tell me where Steven is now and why he wanted the money?"

"I don't know. I told you that."

Peter stepped from his spot behind the bush. "Hi, Jen. I've been trying to call for hours and I got worried."

If he'd fired a rifle into the air, he wouldn't have got a more startled reaction. Jennie blinked until she located him. The glow from the doorway brushed blue highlights into the soft waves in her long black hair. Her dark eyes were huge in a pale and shadowed face.

"Hi, Peter," Bobby said in a muffled voice.

"Yes," Peter said. "Hi, sport. Sounds as if you weren't too smart tonight. Steven's still out, huh?"

Bobby nodded. "And I don't know where he's gone, honest. He took the money outside the diner, then he and Gigi took off."

Jennie appeared confused. She brushed the back of a hand over her eyes, and for an instant, Peter thought she swayed. He moved quickly to hold her arm.

"Let's go inside," he told her quietly. "You, too, Bob. You're both shaken up."

In the kitchen Jennie immediately sat at the table while Bobby hovered by the door.

"You didn't even put a coat on," Jennie said to the boy. "Look at you. A thin shirt in the rain."

"He'll be okay," Peter said, feeling out of his depth. "Boys are tough, right, Bob?"

Bobby's grateful little smile didn't improve his disheveled

appearance. "Right. I'm sorry, Mom. I shouldn't have done it."

"How about something hot to drink?" Peter said. Jennie looked at him, and he felt suddenly too warm. He smiled. "My mom's influence. Hot drinks solved everything."

"Didn't Steven say when he was coming home?" Jennie asked Bobby almost as if she hadn't heard Peter.

"No."

"I can't believe he'd do this."

"He'll be okay," Peter said, inwardly recognizing his father's attitude to crises in that comment. Smooth it over and let it go away had been Jed Kynaston's philosophy.

"You'd better go to bed." Jennie was white lipped and sounded distant.

As Bobby turned silently away, Peter longed to ease the boy's dejection. "When did you say the bike trip was?"

"Sunday."

"Okay. I'll be over to fix the tires Saturday afternoon."

Bobby gave him a glance. "That would be fine."

"Great. See you Saturday, then."

When they were alone, Jennie tipped back her head and blew out a long breath. "I shouldn't have gotten so mad at him."

"He isn't a baby." He rummaged in the cupboard above the refrigerator, where he remembered Mark keeping liquor. "There's no real excuse for dishonesty, and he knows it. But I guess there's probably some truth in all this talk about not overreacting with kids." The theory sounded good, but he was glad he only had to be a helpful bystander in practice.

"I suppose, but I've tried not overreacting with Steven, and it doesn't seem to be paying off. Anyway, none of this is your concern."

He located brandy and two glasses. "You'll work it all through. The teen years are always hard."

He shook his head. What did he know about children? He should serve up the brandy and keep his amateur psychology to himself.

"Steven's been...angry ever since Mark died. It's as if he

thinks he let him down…and me. He almost seems unsure of his identity. Most of the time I don't let it get me down because you're right—stages come and go. I just don't want him to get into any real trouble in the process.''

''Of course you don't.'' He understood what she was trying to tell him, but he didn't have anything constructive to say. He'd liked to see her smile, hear her laugh. ''Do you want to hear something funny?''

Her expression suggested she thought he had rotten timing. ''Sure.''

''You know how mad you were at me earlier?''

''Let's not get on to that again.''

''No, no. Only I've been trying to call and apologize. Liz—'' Oh, sure, tell the lady he'd had to be prompted into making those calls. ''You must think I'm a fool.''

Her gaze became speculative. She didn't answer, but straightened in the chair and crossed her legs. The beige skirt rested just above her knee, and a hint of peach-colored lace skimmed the soft curve at the back of her thigh. Beautiful legs. Beautiful figure. He'd always known those things, but in a detached way. Thirty-six was much too young for a woman like Jennie to be without the excitement of having a love life.

''Why do I think you're a fool, Peter? Supposedly?''

Heat gathered in his face. ''For suggesting you go out with Simon Greenbaum.''

She bobbed the toe of her brown pump, and the heel slid free to show her high arch in fine silky hose. His attention switched to her face, where he thought he saw a hint of amusement. But Jennie hadn't been amused by his blunder earlier in the evening.

''You may not believe this, but I didn't know he…I didn't know.''

''Sure you didn't.'' Now she did laugh. ''Everyone knows—''

''That's what Liz said, but—''

''Liz Meadows? Have you been discussing me with Liz? Why?''

Instead of climbing out of a mess, he was digging himself in deeper. "Liz came over with...she brought me some stuff and I'd just got back from seeing you. I...hell, I was still smarting a bit. She noticed I was edgy and wouldn't give up until I told her why."

Jennie made a muffled noise that got his complete and suspicious attention. She was attempting to turn a laugh into a cough.

"Look," he said, growing miffed. "It isn't that I don't know what goes on in the world. Who's going to be more aware of most things than I am? It's just that I don't take a lot of notice of the people who work for me—or not that much, as long as they do their jobs. Simon's good at what he does, and if I had known, it wouldn't have made any difference."

Jennie crossed her arms. A broad smile transformed her. Light danced in her eyes, and the dimples he remembered so well were tucked into her cheeks beside her full, soft mouth. Even if sheepishly, he had to smile back.

"You're going to have to get all parts of this story straight. Simon's a wonderful man who needs someone equally wonderful to do things with. He needs someone to share his interests outside his work. And I was the perfect choice. Isn't that what you said?"

"Well..."

"Yes, it is, Peter. But you just said you don't know the people who work for you well enough to have found out any, er, preferences? Which version should I believe?"

That I'm a blind idiot. "Okay, okay. For some reason I didn't figure it out. Satisfied?" The sooner he admitted the truth, the sooner the incident would be forgotten.

Jennie pursed her lips, but her eyes still smiled. "I think that's refreshing. A man of your age who still has some innocence. Delightful."

He'd like to show her how innocent he was. The thought sobered him instantly. This was Jennie, his old friend, and he'd better never forget it.

Searching for diversion, he drank some of the brandy he'd

poured. It burned all the way down, and he coughed, only to open his eyes and find Jennie grinning again. Damn, she was feeling superior to what must appear to be his immaturity.

"Swallowed the wrong way," he muttered, his eyes tearing.

She nodded and got up. "It was nice of you to think about me earlier, but I'm fine, really, absolutely fine."

Standing close to her again, he smelled the subtle rose scent he'd been aware of earlier. Jennie was very bright and very feminine—a perfect combination in a woman. But she wasn't fine, not at this moment. Right now she was deeply worried about Steven.

"Isn't tomorrow a school day?"

"Yes."

He checked his watch. "It's past midnight."

"I know," she said tightly, turning her wedding ring rhythmically around and around. He didn't remember the twisting habit, but he liked that she still wore the ring.

"I think you should set some limits, Jen. He won't do his best in school if he doesn't study and get plenty of sleep."

"Please—"

"Sorry if that sounds like interference. I'm only trying to help. I think Steven's taking advantage. You need someone to back you up." He probably shouldn't get involved, but caring for Jennie came naturally. He hadn't been lying when he'd said that even during his long absence from Cincinnati, he'd thought of her often and wondered how she was coping.

She began to turn away, but he stopped her and held her elbows. "Everything isn't so good around here, is it?"

"Yes, it is." Her voice broke. "Most of the time. I'm fine. We're fine. I don't need any help."

"Really? Then why are you trembling? Why is Bobby stealing and Steven staying out late?"

She gripped his arms, and her nails dug through his shirt into his skin. "This is…this isn't your problem."

He almost let her go, but she wasn't relaxing her grasp on him and the look in her eyes suggested she was far from all right. "You've already admitted being worried about Steven. Why don't we try looking for him?"

She drew in a great breath and went limp, leaned against him and wrapped her arms tightly about his body. "I'm worried, Peter. It was easy when they were younger, but they're growing up and I don't want to lose them."

There should be something sage to be said, only his brilliance didn't extend in many directions beyond test tubes. "It'll be okay. You'll see."

She raised troubled eyes to his. "It feels good to hug you. You were always so sensible."

He was good to hug. Peter smiled and slipped a hand behind her neck, holding her face to his chest again. She felt great there. While he worked to get Jennie sorted out, he'd better start deciding what to do about his own emotional life. Holding Jennie aroused sensations he hadn't experienced for too long. She wasn't the only one who needed someone special.

Jennie stirred against him, and he rubbed her shoulders. "Are you going to let me back into your life? At least a little bit? I could use a friend, too, Jen."

"You, Peter?" She put herself from him. "I always think of you as so self—"

The sound of an engine silenced her. She turned, her stance tense, and listened as a car drove into the garage. There was silence, then a slam, followed by footsteps approaching the door leading from the side yard into the kitchen.

Steven came in, head bowed. He wore a mud-smeared black leather jacket over a white T-shirt and jeans. His hair stood out in disordered spikes.

"Steven," Jennie said, going to him as if she'd forgotten Peter. "Where have you been? You promised me you wouldn't be long. That was hours ago."

"Lay off, Mom." He shrugged away from her hand and kept walking.

"That's enough." Her voice rose. "You're going to tell me exactly what went on tonight."

"I can't," Steven mumbled. "I gotta go to bed."

"Steven! Stay right where you are."

Blood pumped hard through Peter's veins. He never remembered feeling so helpless. Anything he said was likely to make things worse.

Steven looked up, obviously only just realizing Peter's presence. "What's he still doing here?"

Peter could only stare at what Jennie couldn't see.

"Don't talk like that," she said, coming to Peter's side. "Where... Oh, my God!"

Steven looked at his mother with one eye. The other was swollen shut. Blood had congealed over a gash along his cheekbone.

CHAPTER FOUR

Peter sat on the edge of his bed and flopped backward, arms flung wide. His body felt fine but his brain ached. An hour at the hospital emergency room with a seventeen-year-old yelping as if he was being murdered had reduced him to emotional pulp. But he was glad he'd been there—more for Jennie than Steven. Not that he wasn't sorry for the boy, who now had five sutures along his cheekbone to underscore a blossoming black eye.

He sat up and worked off his boots, propped himself against the headboard and dragged the phone book from a drawer in the nightstand. With the open book spread across his raised knees, he flipped through the yellow pages to the restaurant section.

"Flame and Pain," Steven had said the place was called. He sure knew more about pain than he had when he'd left home this evening—and there was no restaurant by that name.

Directory assistance told him what he needed to know. A teen club, not a restaurant, was what he was looking for.

"Yeah?" A hoarse male voice answered at the first ring, and Peter jumped. He'd been prepared to find no one there so late and to have to call back tomorrow.

"This is Dr. Peter Kynaston."

A slight pause. "So?"

Sometimes it worked. Not with this character. "I want to make inquiries about something that happened on your premises earlier."

Another pause. "You with the police? We don't serve booze. Music and soft drinks only. Strictly in accordance with the license."

"I'm not with the police." He searched for the words that might make the man less suspicious. "This is off-the-record."

"You sure you aren't with the police?"

Brilliant. He'd managed to come up with exactly what a policeman might say. "I'm calling about a friend of mine. The son of a friend of mine who was at your club. He's seventeen, about, oh, six foot, I'd say, with black hair. Fairly muscular build. Good-looking kid."

This time there was a loud gusty sigh. "You got any idea how many kids we get in here on any given night?"

"Yes, but—"

"Hundreds, buddy. They all look the same to me."

"He didn't look the same when he left," Peter said, running out of patience. "I'll make it easier for you. Remember the fight? The one when half a dozen boys ganged up on one in the parking lot?"

"Fight?" Peter could almost hear the man thinking. "I don't know what you're talking about. There's been no fight since the last time the Bengals lost to the Browns, and I can't even recall when that was."

"Think again. There was a fight last night. A bunch of boys had been drinking—outside," he added quickly as the man started to interrupt. "My friend's son found them lounging all over his car, drinking beer, and when he told them to clear out, they jumped him. His face is a mess. I'd like some help tracking down the people who hit him."

"You've got your wires crossed, buddy. There wasn't any fight here—not Wednesday night, not any night. Like I told you, I can't remember the last one."

Peter closed his eyes. "If you'd rather talk to the police, it can be arranged. And, since you don't seem to be listening, I didn't say Wednesday night, I said last night—Thursday."

The man gave a short laugh. "Why didn't you say so. Send in the police if you want to make an ass of yourself. We don't open Thursday nights."

JENNIE PLANTED her elbows on her desk and massaged her temples. There wasn't enough air in her windowless little office behind the reception area, but that wasn't the current problem. Bliss's taste in music jarred the bones...and the brain. On any other day Jennie would have complained, but the girl was doing her a favor by coming in on Saturday morning, so rap it would be.

"Are you going to work for the vampire bride?"

Jennie jumped and dropped her hands. "What?"

Bliss shuffled forward, clothes on hangers draped over her arms and dragging on the floor. "Tall, dark and—" she heaved the hangers up, hooked them on to a portable rack against one paneled wall, then pinched her nose between finger and thumb "—I'm vewy, vewy fussy, dahling. Of course, I don't weally need help, but I'm just so vewy busy."

"Bliss!" Jennie chuckled and rocked back in her chair. "Are you sure you shouldn't give the world of fashion design a break and go on the stage?" Bliss was taking occasional night classes toward her degree. When she'd worked and saved for two years, she intended to enter college full-time.

Tossing back her gleaming shoulder-length hair, she splayed her fingertips on the desk. "I'm a woman of many talents." She flopped into a chair and stretched out shapely legs encased in tight jeans. "That's the stuff from Gidding Jenny. Pretty wild."

"Resort wear," Jennie said, getting up and going to flip through the garments. "Mr. Gertson's planning a cruise to the West Indies. Actually this is fun. Makes a change, but I'm not going to make a habit of dragging everything to the customer. Takes too much time."

Bliss hitched her petite body more upright. "So, will you take her?"

Jennie smiled. "The vampire bride? You bet. I'm going to start on her in an hour or so. I did the closet session last night." She shuddered. "Valerie Willard Masters has never heard of quality over quantity. And it's all black. I mean, *all*. She waved those incredible fingernails, flapped her eyelashes and told me it was *time, dahling*. So little time that she simply couldn't waste a moment trying to run around after different accessories. With black, she just *knew* she looked her best."

"Why d'you suppose she's taking an interest now?"

"In her words, she's *planning to come out.* I gather she's so popular on the radio that she expects to be snapped up as a TV anchorwoman at any moment."

"Yuck."

"She is vivid, y'know. I'm going over to Saks in a while. I saw a stunning suit, fuchsia with black polka dots. She could carry it off. Odious she may be, but she's in the middle of things in town and I'd like to use her as a showcase."

"You sure she won't make you sign something swearing you'll never let anyone know she's got lousy taste? She'll probably want everyone to think she chooses her own clothes."

"Most women do," Jennie admitted. "I'll get around that as she comes to trust me. All she'll need is to start getting compliments."

Bliss leaned forward suddenly. "You look tired."

"Thanks." Jennie went back to her desk. "Did you run off those invoices?"

"I'm going to. That was him who called just before I left last night, wasn't it?"

Very little got past this bright-eyed girl. "Him, Bliss? What do you mean?"

A knowing smile put dimples into smooth cheeks. "H for hunk. I recognized his voice." Bliss's fine brows rose. "And I saw you talking to him on Thursday. You didn't say anything about it, so I didn't ask. You seemed a bit rattled, so I decided not to."

"That was nice of you," Jennie said dryly. "I really do think you should get to those invoices."

"Okay." With a great sigh she got up. At the door she paused. "He's someone special, isn't he?"

"The invoices." Jennie dropped her voice ominously, and Bliss took the hint.

Peter was someone special? Yes, he was. On Thursday night he'd been wonderful, with her and with Steven. She wouldn't have blamed any man in his position for walking away from a boy who'd been as surly as Steven had, but not

Peter. He'd taken them to the hospital, stayed with her while a doctor patched Steven up, then driven them home again. And yesterday he'd called from the lab to ask how they were. And it had felt wonderful, knowing that, involved as he was with his work, he had thought of them and taken time to check up. She'd been wrong about him, but thanks to his generosity, it wasn't too late to put the antagonism behind them.

Her attention centered on Steven. One thing Peter had said on Thursday made a lot of sense. Something about setting limits. But she wasn't only setting them; she would also make very sure they were adhered to. Steven was a young man who liked his creature comforts, and she clung to the hope that fear of losing them would keep him from doing anything too wild—like leaving home.

She set to work charting an average day in the life of the vampire bride—and grinned. If she wasn't careful, she'd make a disastrous slip in the wrong place. In future she would think of the woman as Valerie and nothing else. By Tuesday it should be possible to take Valerie shopping. Jennie rolled her eyes at the thought of the posturing and tantrums she was likely to endure.

Bliss knocked on the door and stepped into the office again, her face composed into business mold. "There's a lady who'd like to see you. She doesn't have an appointment, so I told her it may not be possible this morning." The expressive brows wiggled. "Mrs. Ramstet says she knows you, Mrs. Andrews."

Jennie tossed down her pen and leaped up. "Lou?" She hurried into the reception area. "Lou! Come on in. This is great."

"I'm not interrupting?" Lou, pretty and flushed in a blue linen suit, appeared faintly awed. "It was just impulse because I was shopping. But if—"

"No, no. I was going to get you down here to see the place just as soon as I was more settled." She ushered Lou into the office, wrinkling her nose at Bliss as she passed. "We'd like some coffee, please, Bliss. Can you manage that?"

Bliss made a fetching moue and dropped a hint of a curtsy.

Jennie grinned. Bliss was unconventional, but she was exactly what was needed around here to keep the atmosphere light. And, for all her zany behavior, she was efficient.

"Oh, every time I come into town I can hardly believe how busy it is." Lou perched on the edge of the chair near Jennie's desk, a navy purse balanced on her knees.

"You look wonderful," Jennie said honestly, delighted to see Lou her old self again. "That suit's a knockout."

"Are you sure?" Lou's eyes twinkled. "Is it what you would choose for me? Knowing an expert on these things can be intimidating."

Jennie pulled her desk chair around to sit beside Lou and spread her arms. "I look it, don't I?" Her jeans were thin at the knees, and an old red cotton sweater sagged about her hips. "If I don't have client appointments, I put on the first thing that falls out of the closet. It's a relief not to be dressed up all the time."

Bliss came in, set two mugs of coffee on the desk and retreated.

"She doesn't seem very old," Lou whispered.

"Old enough," Jennie said, amused. "And very good at what I need done."

"Oh." Lou picked up her mug. "I called last night, but Bobby said you were down here working."

"I was."

Lou pursed her lips. "You mustn't overdo it, Jennie. You weren't cut out to...well, you know."

"I don't think I do."

"You were meant to be a wife and mother," Lou said in a rush. "There, I've said it. This sort of thing's all right as a diversion, but women like you and I are good at other things, and that's where we belong."

Jennie contemplated her thoughtfully. "Sometimes we change, Lou. Life changes us. I'm still a mother, and I was a wife, remember. It wasn't my choice to change that, but no one asked my permission. I could have drifted, but I chose to pick up and make something of whatever talents I have, and I'm happy, really I am."

"The others were asking about you." A faint flush crept over Lou's face. "Susan was asking if there's anyone else on the horizon for you."

Getting angry had never been effective for Jennie. "And why would Susan want to know that? We haven't seen each other for ages." Not since Susan, and some of Jennie's other "friends," began to withdraw after Mark died.

Lou took a sip of coffee. "You know how it is. How those things come up. It was at the gourmet dinner club, and someone said how funny it seems not to have you there."

Poor Lou, she was too kind—and too insular in some ways—to know that she shouldn't discuss any of this with Jennie. "How nice of them to remember me." She didn't like the sick hurt this caused her. They missed her at their rotating monthly dinners, yet by avoiding letting her know when they intended to get together and whose turn it was to host next, they'd simply cut her out of the group once she was widowed. She hadn't fitted in anymore.

"Jennie? What are you thinking?" Lou sounded anxious.

"That it's amazing how we recover from things that seem like the end of the world at the time. I'm happy, Lou, really happy. I love all this—" she raised her hands "—and I like being independent. For the first time in my life, whatever happens is up to me. That's exciting."

Lou shivered visibly. "I'd hate it. And the shine will wear off for you. How's Peter Kynaston?"

Before she could compose herself, Jennie had gaped. She closed her mouth.

"You can't hold out on me, Miss Independence. Carl said he saw Peter visiting on Thursday."

"You didn't say anything about it when I was over," Jennie said, buying time.

"Carl forgot till after you went home. He said Peter brought you flowers." She settled back with a faint smug grin. "You never would tell me what happened there. Why you and Peter seemed to go your separate ways."

"He's been all over the world lecturing and raising funds for the institute." Lou was behaving as if there was something other than friendship between Jennie and Peter. "He's been back a couple of months and he came over to say hello, that's all. What he brought was one of his orchids. He raises them, you know."

"No, I didn't. He really is a handsome man, Jennie."

"Yes."

"Um, did he marry that woman in Australia?"

Jennie didn't think she liked the direction this conversation was taking. "No."

Lou wiggled forward a little. "When's the date?"

"There isn't one." Although, at this moment, she wished there was. "They've decided to call it off."

"Is that right?" The innocent widening of Lou's eyes irritated Jennie. "Peter's very successful. Carl says he sees his name mentioned as a speaker at big charity functions, and they say he's making a lot of.... Well, I don't understand any of it, but he's discovering things, isn't he?"

"I'm sure he is. Peter has an exceptional mind."

Lou looked at her hands. "Like Mark."

"Yes. Exactly." She had an inspiration for changing the subject. "Could you lend Carl to me for a little while this evening?"

"Well—" Lou set down her mug. "Um, we may be going out for a while."

Jennie frowned. It wasn't like Lou not to be immediately helpful, not that Jennie made a habit of asking favors. "Oh, that's fine. Don't give it another thought. If he'd been around, I was going to ask him to look at my kitchen faucet. I haven't passed plumbing yet, and the drip's getting to me." Getting workmen into the house was difficult, since she was never home during the day. "I'll figure out a way to bring a plumber in next week."

"No, no." Lou was bright red now. "I'll make sure Carl comes over. I'll come with him. We don't spend enough time together anymore, Jennie." She stood up. "I'd better get along. Carl will wonder where I am."

Jennie followed her out into the echoing cavern of the building. "Give Carl my love."

"I will." Lou took a few steps, hesitated and came back. "Think about what I said."

"What was that?"

"About it being time for you to think about marriage again."

Stunned, Jennie gaped. "Marriage? Good grief, I'm not thinking about marriage. I don't think I ever will."

Lou slipped the handle of her purse back and forth between her hands. "You and Mark were happy. You should want that again. We all think so."

They all thought so. And they were all wrong, at least for the moment. "Thanks for thinking about me," Jennie said, deliberately keeping her tone level. "I'm not saying a friend to do things with wouldn't be a good idea, if and when I'm not too busy to know what day of the week it is, but marriage isn't on my agenda."

Lou backed away, and Jennie couldn't decide what she saw in the other woman's eyes. "Well, I decided I should say something and I have. I hope you'll see more of Peter. There aren't too many eligible and suitable men around. See you later."

"Yes," Jennie said faintly. "Later."

PETER REALIZED he was smiling, grinning inanely, in fact. Standing in Jennie's garage, surrounded by old tires and tools he hadn't needed, his hands, face and clothes covered in black grease, he felt more relaxed and happy than he had in—he didn't remember ever feeling this good.

"It's great!" Bobby made a U-turn in the driveway and headed back, braking his bike to a squealing halt inches from Peter. "Geez, I almost forgot how to ride."

Peter refrained from asking how long the tires had needed replacing. He shouldn't have allowed Jennie to put distance between them. Her distress had been natural, and given what he knew Mark had told her, so was the way she'd vented her anger after his death. Sure, work had forced a separation for most of eighteen months, but there had been time before and after, and in the short return trips he'd made, to make sure everything was all right here. Only he'd given himself up to the hurt and limped away with his asinine wounds.

"Wanna try it out?" Bobby called.

"Sure." Peter wiped his hands on a rag and took the bike from Bobby. He pushed off, wobbling at first, then rode to the end of the driveway and back. "Nice machine," he told Bobby. "You'll be all set for tomorrow."

Bobby looked away, and Peter frowned, puzzled. For the past hour, since they'd been working together, the boy had been cheerful and obviously glad to have him around. Bobby had always been an easy kid to get along with. "Something wrong, Bob?"

"Nah." He screwed up his eyes. "Want a Coke?"

"Sure."

Car tires ground on the driveway, and Peter and Bobby turned in unison. Peter's heart lifted. He'd hoped Jennie would be here when he arrived, but Bobby told him she wouldn't be late getting home. It was already five o'clock.

Instead of the silver Mercedes, Steven's little red Honda swept up to the garage. As his brother got out of the car, Bobby went to meet him. "Peter's here," he said, and Peter didn't miss the anxiety in the voice. "He's fixed my bike, and it's so cool, Steve. We can ride—"

"Tell Mom I came back but I couldn't stay," Steven said, not glancing at Peter.

"Steve—"

"I gotta go."

Peter strode toward the Honda, arriving as the door slammed behind Steven. "How's the face," he said, bending down.

"It's there," Steven said shortly, turning the engine back on.

Peter felt a foreign surge of frustration. "Don't let me chase you off. You came back for something."

"Did I?" The boy's good eye narrowed. "I guess it wasn't important."

Peter wasn't ready for this, and he was becoming increasingly suspicious that he didn't want to be. "Do you think we could find some time to talk, Steve? Just the two of us?"

"Why?"

"Because you've got a chip on your shoulder the size of the Grand Canyon that seems to be something you blame me for. I'd like to work that out if we can."

"Why?"

Who needed this kind of grief. "No reason, Steve. Not if you can't think of one. I'm in town more or less for good now. If you change your mind and want to talk, you know where to find me."

"Don't hold your breath." The car shot backward, spewing gravel, and Steven drove back into the street.

"If the accelerator jams, he'll be airborne," Peter muttered. Clearly he wasn't cut out to deal with troubled teenagers.

"Steve's like that sometimes," Bobby said. The joy had gone out of his face, and Peter felt a dull anger with Steven. At seventeen he was old enough to have worked through the fact that his father hadn't been himself at the end of his life—and he should also have learned to curb his rude mouth.

"Don't worry about it," he told Bobby, wondering how often he took a back seat to his older brother's arrogant selfishness.

"Here's Mom."

Peter glanced up as the Mercedes swung into view. He passed his palms over the sides of his jeans and realized he was smiling again.

The car stopped a few yards from the garage.

Peter drew in a breath. He wanted to see her. He needed someone's company other than his own. That's what was happening. He was finally tired of being alone, and Jennie was a known quantity he felt he could trust.

She got out of the car, her briefcase in one hand, a grocery sack wrapped against an oversize red sweater. She closed the door with her rear, and he smiled at the unconscious action. In worn jeans and the baggy sweater, Jennie looked more like a teenager herself than a thirty-six-year-old widow. His smile faded.

"Hi, there," she called. Her hair was tied at the nape of her neck with a piece of red yarn, and she wore no makeup. And still she looked great.

"Peter fixed my tires," Bobby said. He went to take the grocery sack and the briefcase from his mother. Peter took note and decided he liked Bobby more with every moment they spent together.

"That's great," Jennie said. "Now you're all set for the ride tomorrow."

Peter noticed how Bobby hesitated again before saying "Yeah" and going into the house.

"Thank you so much." Jennie approached, smoothing back curls that had fallen loose around her face. "I don't know how I would have gotten it done in time."

"Wasn't anything," Peter said, and laughed when Jennie made owl eyes at the chaos in the garage. "Well, maybe it was a little something. I had difficulty deciding just what to use for what, but I got there. Don't worry, I always clean up after myself. Are you working every Saturday now?"

She shrugged. "Mostly. And Sundays. Aren't you?"

"Yeah, some things don't change, do they? But with me it's always the sense of working against the clock…against death in a way." When a line formed between her brows, he mentally cursed his choice of terms. "You know what I mean. Time is life in drug research."

"I know what you mean. I was married to your clone, remember…. Oh, I'm sorry, Peter. That just sort of slipped out."

He moved closer. "No need to be sorry. You're right, only I'm the clone. Mark made me what I am, not the other way around."

They looked at each other in silence, and Peter was relieved to hear Bobby coming back.

"It was nice of you to take time out to help us," Jennie said.

"I wanted to," he said with a sense of their drawing away from each other again.

She looked up and past him. "Isn't Steven here?"

Peter cleared his throat and glanced at Bobby.

"He had to go out for a while," Bobby said, avoiding Peter's gaze. "He won't be long."

"I told him not to leave the house today." Exasperation formed a white line around Jennie's mouth.

Peter could feel Bobby's tension. The boy half expected him to tell Jennie that Steven hadn't been home when he'd arrived at three-thirty and had only put in a few minutes' appearance just after five o'clock. Peter said nothing.

"What time are you off in the morning?" Jennie asked Bobby. The annoyance hadn't left her eyes.

"I don't think I am."

Peter looked at him sharply. "What d'you mean, sport? We just fixed your bike."

"Yeah, I know." Bobby slid his hands in his jeans pockets. His black hair stood on end. "I didn't get the registration over, and it's too late. They wanted it yesterday."

Jennie threw up her hands. "I signed it for you and I thought you were taking it. What happened?"

"I don't wanna go." He looked at his feet and used a toe to make lines in the dirt. "No big deal. I'll ride on my own."

Peter met Jennie's eyes and saw her confusion. "You're right, Bob. No big deal. Just a lot of kids, right?"

"Right."

"Maybe you could get your mom to take a turn around the park now."

Bobby shrugged again. "If she wants to. D'you want to come, Peter?"

He looked at the youthful face and suddenly saw it all. Bobby hadn't wanted to go with the others because he might be the only one without a father along. Peter also saw something else. Bobby was ready for a substitute-father figure. Peter didn't think he was a suitable candidate for the role.

"I'd like to come," he said. "But by the time I go home for my bike, it'll be dark."

"You could use Dad's."

A great lump rose in Peter's throat. He hardly trusted him-

self to meet Jennie's eyes, but he did anyway. Her teeth held
her bottom lip.

"That would be okay, wouldn't it, Mom?"

"Yes, yes, of course it would. If Peter wants to."

Was he going to say he didn't want to use Mark's bike
because he had a few difficult memories of his own? No, he
was bigger than that. "Okay. If I don't have to change more
tires, you're on."

By the time they cleared the houses edging the park and
started riding downhill toward the bandstand, long shadows
stretched across the grass. Giant cedars stood like sentries
along the pathways, and chestnuts spread their great branches
to form dark puddles on brilliant green. The smell of moist,
recently cut grass mingled with a hint of woodsmoke from
some unseen bonfire.

"Evening scents," Jennie called, turning to smile at him.

Peter swallowed. "Wonderful." Someone had said platonic
relationships between men and women were a myth. He didn't
want that to be true. He wanted to spend time with Jennie.

Bobby leaned over his handlebars and forged ahead. Peter
watched him go, an uncomfortable shifting in the pit of his
stomach. There were bonds to the past here, but also something new was forming. He could choose to let it happen,
encourage it, even...or he could ease away. So far he didn't
think he could make a decision.

"Ride on, Bobby," Jennie called out. "I'm going to rest
by the bandstand. You go, too," she added to Peter.

"I'll stay with you," he told her, dismounting at the bottom
of the next dip. Bobby, pedaling furiously, leaned back to
wave, then carried on.

They walked side by side, pushing the bikes, past the silent
bandstand to the edge of a small, still lake. Midges flitted over
its surface, and the wings of a firefly, at the end of its day of
life, shone with the green-purple iridescence of oil on water.

Peter took Jennie's bicycle and set it aside with his. He
dropped to the ground and offered her his hand. With her
fingers in his, she sank down, and they leaned back, shoulders
touching, against a grassy hummock.

"Don't worry about Bobby," he said, wishing he could offer more constructive advice.

"I'm not really. I think he feels badly about not having—" She turned her head away.

Peter hooked her arm through his and waited for her to turn toward him again. "That's what I think, too. I should have insisted on going with him."

"He's enjoyed having you with him this afternoon. I can see it."

"Good." If he had any sense, he'd be very careful how he proceeded from here. "I, um, I'll do something else with him soon." Well, he never had been particularly good at being careful.

"It's too bad...I'm really embarrassed about Steven's behavior. It's not all his fault, though. I should have talked it all through with him a long time ago. Now it's going to be harder."

Peter rolled his head to look into her eyes. "You intend to try to change his attitude toward me." There were black flecks in each tawny iris, and her lashes were very thick. Such a lovely face.

"I'd like to. We owe you that."

"You don't owe me anything. I'm just glad we're talking to each other again." Almost insanely grateful would be more honest. "Jennie, I think it's going to be up to me to try to reach Steven." It was coming, the moment he'd already put off longer than he should have. He had to talk to Jennie about Steven and what had happened on Thursday night—Steven's version and what Peter already knew wasn't the truth.

She'd closed her eyes as if deep in thought.

"Jennie, I made some calls early yesterday morning. We may have more trouble on our hands than we thought."

Her eyes opened, and she blinked against brightness. "With Steven?" She almost whispered. Every trace of peace had vanished from her face.

"Yes." He hated upsetting her afresh.

She sat up. "What's wrong, Peter?"

"What do you know about his friends?"

Jennie wrapped her arms around her knees. "Steven doesn't have a lot of friends. Not close friends."

"Who's this Gigi he was with Thurday night?" The anxiety he'd carried since the phone call nagged more sharply.

"A girlfriend. Gigi Burns." Her shoulder blades were bunched beneath her sweater, and Peter automatically began massaging the area.

"Did he tell you what he needed the money for?" There was no loosening of her muscles beneath his hand.

"He said he wanted it to lend to a friend."

"What friend?"

Jennie let her forehead fall to her knees. "I don't know. He gave it back to me and said the friend didn't need it after all. Does it make a difference?"

"Maybe. I'd like to talk to someone who witnessed the fight." He shook Jennie gently. "Since Steven says he doesn't even remember what the people who hit him looked like, we need someone else who does."

"Steven begged me to let it drop. He promised not to go back to the restaurant where it happened. I can't do that, but I'm not sure how to proceed."

Peter stretched out his legs and crossed his ankles. "Would you let me speak to Steven?" He wasn't about to tell her about the reception he'd got after his earlier attempt.

"I don't think that would be a good idea. Maybe I should get him to a counselor."

That sounded like a great idea, but Peter sensed she might want him to disagree. "He needs a man around. He's sensitive enough not to want to upset you too much."

Jenny eased back beside him. "Steven adored Mark. I've already told you he's still angry about his death. He doesn't want another man in his life."

"He hasn't had the opportunity, has he?"

She looked at him sharply. "No. But now isn't the time—"

"I disagree with you. Now is *exactly* the time, before he gets into any more..." He let the sentence trail off.

"Finish, Peter. I can take it. Are you suggesting Steven's just a bad kid who's bound to go wrong? He got in a fight at a restaurant. It wasn't his fault. How does that make him a candidate for juvenile corrections?"

"He...he isn't. But I think people need structure. I was the only kid of too-old parents who never planned to have children. They did their best, but they weren't there for me when I really would have liked it because they were too set in their ways. As long as I didn't cut up, everything was okay. They did what was right but nothing more. They never knew me, and I never knew them." He stopped. His background was dull history and irrelevant to this situation.

"I'm not sure what point you're making," she said, but her eyes held empathy.

"The point I was trying to make is that I was one of those kids who was totally involved in school. And I also grew up in different times. Maybe if there'd been more opportunity to get into trouble, I would have. But involved or not, I missed having a dad who gave a real damn while he was alive, and afterward I resented him because the two of us had missed out." The emotion he felt rocked him.

"Steven was close to Mark."

"Sure he was. But now when he needs what he had with his dad most, there's no one...and the surliness is coming from his feeling that he's been cheated." In the distance he saw Bobby coming in their direction.

"You can't know what's going on inside Steven's head." She didn't sound as sure as her words. "People are different. I know I'm going to have to take a hard line with him. I'm also going to have to make sure I don't push too hard or I'll lose him altogether."

Peter sat forward abruptly and caught her hand. "I think pushing a little hard is what's called for right now." He knew his attempt at a smile was thin and unconvincing. "Ask him to think very carefully about how his face got in the shape it's in, Jen."

"Why?" She pulled her hand away, and he didn't try to stop her. "What are you suggesting? That Steven lied to me?"

The tinge of red that spread over her rounded cheekbones

unnerved him. "Let's drop it," he muttered. She was level-headed and would do what had to be done without his worrying her further.

"Just like that." She gave a short laugh. "Drop it? I don't think so. You mentioned telephone calls you made. What was that about?"

He fixed his eyes on the sky, squinting. "I... Oh, I had some idea of taking the boys somewhere next weekend. I did that when they were younger. It was because I was worried and thought it might be good for them."

"That was a nice thought," she said slowly. "As a matter of fact, Carl Ramstet's taking the boys fishing for the weekend. He suggested it last month, and Steven's been kicking against it ever since. Now he seems glad to go."

Peter was quiet for a long time before he said, "When are they leaving?"

"As soon as the boys get home from school."

"Does Carl know what happened Thursday night?"

"No." She broke off a blade of grass and shredded it into little pieces. "I hope he'll understand. Carl can be a bit old-fashioned."

Peter settled his hand on the back of her neck again. "I wouldn't worry. Here comes Bobby."

"Yes. And you probably have more important things to do than talk about my problems."

He'd planned to go back into town and go over some reports. "I'm not in any hurry." This torn feeling was something new and not very comfortable.

Jennie got up, and this time it was she who offered a hand. Peter held on while he stood up, but quickly let go. He needed time to think.

"I enjoyed the ride, Peter. Thank you."

So had he. More than he would ever have anticipated. He heard himself say, "What are you planning for tomorrow?" as if his voice came from someone else. Bobby was drawing close now.

A stillness settled around her. "Work. I've got catching up to do."

"At home?"

"Mostly, I expect."

The sun had disappeared behind a cloud, and Peter breathed in suddenly stifling, moisture-laden air. If he asked to come over tomorrow, would she agree?

"Beat you back," Bobby yelled, passing on the pathway above.

Peter laughed and waved and looked down into Jennie's smiling face. He'd like her to look like this all the time— young and untroubled. "Shall we go?"

"Yes," she said. "Thanks for worrying about us, Peter. I certainly don't deserve it."

"Yes, you do. And I always will worry about you. Don't work too hard tomorrow, huh?"

"No," she said brightly. "You, either."

"I won't." He felt—disappointed? She was hardly going to invite him over.

Very suddenly she stood on tiptoe and kissed his cheek. "Always take care, buddy," she said before lifting her bike and pushing it uphill toward the path.

He followed her, mounted and pedaled behind, watching her hair blow in the breeze.

Twenty minutes later he was in his car driving into town. There was no one to go home to, except Killer. He flexed the muscles in his jaw. The lab was where he liked to be most, wasn't it? Always had been.

A light turned red, and he applied the brakes. Sitting there, he touched his cheek. *Buddy?*

CHAPTER FIVE

"Fuchsia?" Valerie Willard Masters threw her arms wide open and stretched her garnet-painted mouth into a disbelieving grimace. "Jennie, dahling, fuchsia?"

"Yes, Valerie. And I won't hear of you refusing to try it on." Jennie had quickly learned that this client responded to gentle bullying by acquiescing like a child trying to be good.

"If you insist." Valerie, standing in the middle of the room Saks had provided for showcasing the potentially significant purchases Jennie had outlined, was already stripped to her bra, panties, garter belt and stockings. All black, naturally.

Jennie hid a smile and helped her don the suit. "This is going to do wonderful things for you," she said, deliberately animated. "Only a woman with your height and figure could carry this off."

Valerie allowed herself to be zipped and buttoned into the suit and stood back before a three-way mirror, tossing the straight black hair that fell between her shoulder blades. The hair was also on Jennie's agenda of things to be changed.

"Don't you think this makes me look as if there's just *too much* of me?" Valerie asked. "Sort of polka dots forever?"

"You are five foot ten, a perfect size eight, and there can't be many women alive who wouldn't kill for your body. How could you ever look too much?"

Valerie smiled at Jennie with something approaching genuine fondness, and Jennie, although speaking the truth, knew that what she'd said would be a credit to any professional diplomat.

"Well..."

"Put these on." From the pocket of her soft gray skirt,

Jennie whipped out a pair of strikingly simple Anne Klein earrings, smooth black stones surrounded by brushed gold in simple scallops. "I'm going to show you a little trick for keeping accessories and outfits together. You'll never have to think, simply wear."

Valerie slipped on the earrings while Jennie deftly positioned a pair of black patent pumps with midheight Louis heels.

"What do you think?" Jennie couldn't help smiling. The woman was a knockout.

"I think…" Covering her mouth and giggling in a way that made her seem very young, Valerie spun around, looking at herself from all angles. "I think you're marvelous. And in future I'll never buy a thing you haven't approved."

Pure exhilaration swelled in Jennie. Over seventeen years ago she'd willingly set aside any thoughts of her own career because being Mark's wife was all she'd wanted. And she'd never regret that. But now she was so happy, so grateful that she had this special talent and that she'd found the courage to put it to work.

"What's this?" Still wearing the pumps, Valerie had already shed the suit and was fingering a dark green gown, ankle length with a filmy chiffon stole.

"Bill Blass," Jennie said, picking up the elegant creation that was split to the waist in front. "It fits tightly to the knees, then flares. You'll wear those green, watered silk shoes with the very high heels and the diamond studs you already have. Nothing else."

"Of course," Valerie said meekly, sighing as the sensuous crepe slithered into place over her body. "Just the diamonds."

Two hours later, with Valerie more than a few thousand dollars poorer, Jennie was giving a seamstress last instructions while her customer lounged in a gilt-framed brocade chair, smoking and looking dreamily at her reflection in a mirror.

"The fringe on the Givenchy must also be shortened," Jennie told the woman, who had patiently pinned, unpinned and repinned while Valerie changed her mind about just how tight or how long or short she wanted each garment. "We can't lose the line at the bottom of the skirt," Jennie added.

"So—" she turned to Valerie when they were alone "—I think we had a very good session. I would like you to have a facial and makeup evaluation."

She received a docile nod.

"And we should have a consultation on your hair."

Valerie sat up, her eyes sharp. "My hair?"

Ah, as Jennie had expected, here there would be resistance. "Only to get some advice on how to make the very best of it," she said lightly. "But there's no hurry. Next week, perhaps."

"Well, if you think so. But I don't intend—"

The door swung open and a plump blonde put her head into the room. "Ms. Andrews. There's a call for you from your office. Will you take it in here or—"

"Here would be fine," Jennie said, crossing to lift the receiver from a round cloisonné table close to Valerie's chair. Within seconds she heard Bliss's voice. "Hello, Bliss. I'm almost finished here for this morning, then I'll be back." She bowed her head and listened, her euphoria evaporating. "When did they call?"

Bliss told her that the attendance office at the high school was trying to contact her because they felt she should know that Steven had cut his last class yesterday, Monday, and had done the same today.

"You bet I should know," Jennie said shortly. "I should have been called yesterday. I'll get back to them as soon as I can."

"Trouble?" Valerie asked as Jennie hung up. The woman's vivid blue eyes held avid interest.

Jennie shrugged. "I have a seventeen-year-old son who isn't a very happy young man right now. Evidently he's been skipping classes." There seemed no point in evasion.

"Ah." Valerie tipped back her head and blew out a stream of smoke. "Didn't you tell me you were a widow?"

"Yes." Already she regretted divulging personal information.

"Mmm. You could be exactly what I need."

Jennie stared.

"How would you like to be on my show next week?"

"I'm afraid I don't understand—"

"The whole week's going to be devoted to teens. Their problems. Their parents' problems in trying to do the right thing. Perhaps you could get your son to come with you. These teenagers love to air their grievances."

"No!" Jennie said before she could stop herself. The thought of talking about what was happening in her private life in front of a listening audience of thousands turned her sick and cold. "No, thank you," she said more calmly, scrambling to salvage some of the diplomacy she'd congratulated herself on earlier. "Steven wouldn't go for that, and anyway, our problems are really very mild."

Valerie stood up and stretched. "That's what they all say, isn't it?"

Jennie knew Valerie was unmarried and had no children. The temptation to tell her she knew nothing about bringing up teenagers was quickly and mercifully squelched. "Shall we go?" She was anxious to talk to the school—and get home to check up on Steven.

"You don't want to face it all, do you?"

Jennie stopped in the act of picking up her purse and briefcase. "What do you mean?"

"The classic single woman's dilemma of the day, of course." Long, long dark red fingernails made graceful passes through the air. "The single woman parent, that is. To work, be fulfilled and eat well, or not to work, stay at home to salvage the kiddies, not eat so well…and run the risk of not being fulfilled."

LIGHT FLASHED in a million brittle bursts on exploding shards of glass.

Peter put out his hands. He was sweating. Why wouldn't his legs move? "Mark!" His voice echoed in his head, and he took a step, another, moving too slowly. "Easy, Mark. Take it easy."

"Shut your mouth, Kynaston." Mark Andrews's eyes, glittering and dark brown, stared at Peter, through him, then away. Another sweep of an arm, and more slides swept from a lab counter to the hard, tiled floor. "You're glad, you son of a bitch. You're taking my place, aren't you? Taking over everything I've worked for. When I hired you on, you were nothing. Promising, but nothing. Now you're just waiting to step into my shoes."

Peter's heart pounded. "No, Mark. That's not what I want. You're not well, that's why—"

"I'm fine," Mark yelled. But he wasn't fine. His frame looked too big for the flesh it supported now, and the once-handsome face had sunk back against its strong bones. His breath rasped. "If they gave me a few weeks to build up again, I could give those lectures in Sydney. But no. They have to be done on schedule—you made sure of that. You told them I'm failing and that you're a Sydney kid who'll do a better job."

"No. And I'm an American now." Why couldn't he reach him, make him stand still? "I'm not going because I was born in Australia. I'll talk to the foundation, make them wait till you're well enough."

"Why? So you can suck up to Jennie while I'm away? Oh, you'd like that, wouldn't you? You'd like everything of mine—my job, my wife and family. Forget it. I'm in charge around here and I always will be. And stay away from my family." Spittle clung to the corners of Mark's mouth. He threaded his fingers through the wire mesh of a basket full of vials.

Peter's stomach rose. He wanted to grab for the basket but didn't dare. "Relax, Mark. Everything will be okay."

Tears slid from Mark's eyes. "It's over. You've seen to that. Eventually they'll say Peter Kynaston was first, first in everything. He did what Mark Andrews couldn't. Broke the final barriers. Vaccines for viruses. The cancer cure. Not so easy, though. Not so easy." His face paled, the features melting together.

Peter twisted and clawed, but the basket, vials toppling,

breaking, went the way of the hundreds of slides on the floor. Above the splintering noise a scream sounded. It had to be Liz's. Peter hadn't screamed, had he?

Mark was laughing and laughing, and Peter couldn't get to him. A hypodermic, held high above the man's head, glinted. "Which batch was this for?" he asked, half-turning toward a cubicle that housed cages of mice.

"Mark, stop it!"

"Mark, stop it!" Mark mimicked Peter's accent. "Time for the definitive experiment, digger. Time for a human sacrifice."

The thud of Peter's heart deafened him. Sunlight scintillated along the little stainless-steel rapier, the deliverer of potential life...or death.

Mark's eyes were close now, hypnotic, staring down. His hand hovered an instant...then dropped.

"No! Oh, God, no!" Peter sat up, panting, and jumped as a hissing yowling streak of fur shot from behind his knees. Killer.

He'd been dreaming—no, having a nightmare. But it had been so real. And it had been an almost exact replay of what had once, on a horrifying afternoon two years ago, been reality.

Groggy, shaking, he swung his feet to the floor and sat forward on his living-room couch, holding his head in his hands.

What was wrong with him? Sure, he'd thought about the scene with Mark a few times, but he'd never done anything like this. He breathed in through his open mouth and fell back. The needle had missed, thank God. And within a week Mark Andrews was dead of a heart attack. Peter closed his eyes and realized he'd cried in his sleep.

His session at the lab last night was the reason for the flashback. All night he'd worked, feverishly goaded on by that elusive spark of something that dangled just out of reach, the conviction that he was very close to new answers. And in the midst of it all, he'd gone back to some of Mark's old notes. The strong handwriting, the wild rush of the letters carried along by the man's enthusiasm and conviction, had reached out to Peter like a tangible force, as tangible as the man had once been, and he'd started remembering.

He looked at his watch. Noon. He'd got home just before eight that morning and had fallen asleep on the couch, fully dressed, too tired to go upstairs.

Staying here was out of the question. The lab was where he wanted to be. There he was some use. He had to work, work and keep trying to finish what Mark had started. Not for Mark, but for those who would benefit, and yes—for himself. There was nothing wrong with wanting it for himself, as well.

In less than an hour, showered and changed, his hair still wet, he ran up the steps leading from Fifth into Fountain Square, opposite the Westin Hotel. A light breeze blew, but the sun was warm and bright colors were in evidence on women strolling past the cascading waters of the Tyler Davidson Fountain. He strode on, barely looking left or right, but aware of the tender green of fluttering maple leaves as he passed and the scattering of pigeons before him. Inside he still shook.

Once through the glass doors of the Dubois Tower, the soaring white walls swallowed him, and he rode upward in the silent elevator, grateful for familiarity.

"There you are, Peter," Liz Meadows said, raising her face from a microscope as he entered the lab. "I was going to call you at home shortly."

"What's up?" He didn't feel like talking, but at least here he would be forced to put any private demons aside. "I was here most of the night, so I took off to get some sleep."

By the time he'd hung up his jacket and donned a white coat, he was aware of a very pregnant interval. When he turned toward his desk, the three assistants present were standing idle. Simon Greenbaum and Kevin Thompson trained their eyes on the floor.

"Okay," Peter said, measuring the word, "did they cut our budget, or only close us down completely?"

Simon cleared his throat, and Kevin put down a micrograph

and turned around to look through the window. Dread, very real and pervasive, thundered to life in Peter.

"Nothing to do with the lab. Or not really." Liz came from behind a counter. Her hands were sunk in the pockets of her coat—the standard defensive pose, in her case.

She didn't continue.

"What, then?" Peter asked, then frowned. "Didn't Dan get back from vacation?" Dan Mitcham was the researcher next in seniority to Liz.

"He wasn't on vacation." This from Kevin, who continued to face the window with its view of a gray brick wall.

Peter shook his head. "He went on a cruise."

Liz hitched herself onto a stool and sat there, hunched. "He went to a clinic in Boston. Connie called this morning to say he's still there."

"Oh, hell!" His fist, connecting with a counter, rattled bottles. "Why didn't he say something?"

"Because he hoped he'd get good news, I'd guess," Simon said quietly, his pale ascetic features tensely closed. "Connie told Liz he's been worried for a while and they decided to cancel the cruise to make the trip to Boston."

"He's out of remission." Peter felt as flat as he sounded. "Damn, damn. What's all this for? What the hell are we doing here if we can't…" He raked a hand through his hair and tugged. The pull on his scalp hurt, but he didn't let go.

"Hodgkin's is a rough one, Peter," Liz said. "Dan's tough, though. He could go into remission again."

He began to pace, fury simmering, rising. "Don't stand around. Get to work." What had Mark said. That Peter Kynaston would blaze trails, get there first? Well, he wasn't moving fast enough.

"Peter—"

"No, Liz. I can't take platitudes. Did they start chemo?"

"They're sending him back here for that. Connie said Dan's sorry to leave you shorthanded. He hopes to be able to come back within a week. Part-time for a while, of course."

His rage was out of hand, but he couldn't help that. Good minds gobbled up by the very enemies he spent his life trying to wipe out. The advances were obvious, but today he felt he'd wasted a lot of years.

"Whatever Dan wants, he gets," he said, doing a poor job of controlling his voice. *"Why?"*

"Because we aren't there," Liz said. "One day, maybe, but not yet."

Kevin settled his long rangy frame on the windowsill and pushed his glasses up his nose. "Everything takes too long," he said.

Peter inclined his head, met Liz's lucid brown eyes, and understanding passed between them. "This hits too close," he told her.

"Uh-huh. Most of us are here because we feel less threatened where we don't have to face the reality of disease. Maybe I should say some of us, or me, anyway. It took me years to realize it, though."

She'd touched what he had never voiced before, never really put into whole thought. "Me, too, I suppose. I've always told myself research was all I wanted. But there's safety in distance. At least, there is until one of us is hit."

"We've got to get over it and go on." She slid from the stool and patted his arm. "All any one of us can do is our best with whatever comes our way."

The best. Had he done that? There was so much to do, and the struggle against cancer was always a struggle against time. Setting his teeth, he went to this desk and started poring over the notes he'd made last night. Time was a commodity he couldn't afford to waste here. He put a fist to his mouth and thought of last Saturday, of riding with Jennie, of Bobby's cheerful face, the rare peace the experience had brought. On Sunday he'd worked all day, and every few hours he'd been tempted to call and ask Jennie to have a meal with him. He should have called. Research was vital, but so was life, what you did with it, the human contacts you made. He was through wasting time...anywhere.

"I CAN'T," Jennie said into the phone. "No, Peter, not tonight."

"Okay, but would I be overstepping the bounds if I asked why?"

She could see him, his tousled sun-streaked hair, the serious green eyes. "I've got a lot going on."

"Would you have dinner with me if you didn't have a lot going on?"

"Yes." There was nothing she'd rather do this evening than have a pleasant dinner with Peter.

"What's wrong, Jen?"

He knew her too well. For several years there had rarely been a week when Peter hadn't visited the Andrewses. They had a lot of shared past.

"Need you ask?"

Moments passed before he said, "Steven?"

"He's been cutting out of school early and he won't tell me why or where he's been spending his time."

"Where is he now?"

"In his room. I was waiting for him when he showed up this afternoon, and I've told him he's grounded until I say otherwise." Not that she felt secure about her ability to make him comply.

"Does that mean you're grounded, too?"

"Of course not."

"Then have dinner with me. You can't watch him every minute of the day and night."

"I know that. It's just…" Just that Valerie's words still rattled in Jennie's mind, and Lou's comments about how children needed a parent at home…and even Peter's own remarks along the same lines.

"Just what?" Peter asked gently.

Distant bass notes from Steven's room sounded like encroaching thunder. He hadn't spoken to her since she'd met him in the driveway when he got home. There had been no attempt to deny that he'd missed some school, but no apology or promises to do better, either.

"Jennie, answer the question."

"I wish you wouldn't push me."

"Why? Because you want to say yes but you don't think you should?"

"Peter, I have responsibilities you don't have. You know perfectly well what I'm dealing with here."

He clicked his tongue before saying, "You've got to keep the upper hand."

The tawny grass cloth on the dining-room walls blurred before her stare. "I've got to go."

"Have dinner with me tonight."

"Thanks, but no. Goodbye." She hung up.

Jennie sat at the glistening oak dining table with its ten chairs. Would this room ever hold ten chattering, laughing people again? Probably not for a dinner she'd cooked. Peter had been there with the group so many times—good times. Back then, everything had seemed so simple. They would go on forever, she and Mark, in their beautiful home, with their fine sons and warm friends.

The phone rang again. Jennie studied it for a moment before answering and hoped John Astly, a client who was also an old friend, wasn't making yet another of his evening calls.

"Hello."

"When's the last time you had dinner on a riverboat?"

Jennie braced her forehead on her palm. "Oh, Peter."

"Aren't you having dinner tonight?"

"This isn't funny." So why did part of her yearn to laugh and say, yes, yes, I'll go with you?

"It isn't meant to be." The quiet intensity was there again. "Come. Please. It will be good for both of us."

"I don't know."

"It's a nice night for the river."

Jennie held the receiver so tightly her knuckles turned white.

"You're wavering. I can hear it in what you're not saying."

How right he was. "It would probably be better if you didn't pick me up here."

Peter whooped. "Good girl. Anything you say. I'll park a block from your place. In front of the house with the pink trim."

"I have to change."

"I'll be waiting."

"Peter—"

The line went dead.

Jennie went up to her bedroom and closed the door. Chewing on the inside of her cheek, she paced back and forth over her soft gray rug. Dinner on one of the riverboats would be wonderful. She couldn't hold back a smile. Despite her own dilemma, not admitting that she was flattered and that she wanted to go would be self-delusion. What could she wear?

Within thirty minutes she was dressed in navy slacks, a white cashmere sweater with a V-neck and flat shoes. She went to the window and peered down the street. Her stomach flipped. He was already there.

She left her room. "Steven!" The music still blared, and she opened his door without knocking. "Steven, turn that off."

He stared at her and made no attempt to remove the headphones that must be cutting out her voice. The noise pounding the house was intended to annoy her. She crossed to turn off the tuner and yanked the headphones off.

"Hey!"

"Hey yourself." After tossing the phones on his chest, she pulled on her lime-green poplin jacket. "I'm going out for a while. You're in charge."

He averted his face.

"Do you hear me?"

"Where are you going?"

At last, words. "Out. Bobby's doing his homework, and so should you be. I'd like you to work in the kitchen and take any telephone messages carefully. Don't tie up the line, please."

"Who are you going out with?"

He was determined to push her to the limits. And she was equally determined to hold her own. "Just do as I've told you, please."

"Are you going with *him*?"

If she allowed him to, he'd wear her down. "Peter and I are having dinner. Look after things."

"Dad would—"

"Dad would tell you to behave yourself. Peter is a subject you and I will discuss...when I'm ready." The door, slamming as she left, drowned Steven's response. She didn't have to hear the words to know what they were. And she didn't have to stay enmeshed in the snare Mark had left behind. Her mind seethed as she walked from the house and down the driveway.

Dusk had blanketed the day. Jennie made it through the gateway and halfway to the corner before she stopped. Peter, who must have seen her in his rearview mirror, got out of the car.

He waved and Jennie raised a hand. She broke into a run and reached him in seconds.

"Hungry at last, huh?" His wide, gleeful smile showed even teeth. He wore a dark gray suit, white shirt and red tie. Peter looked devastatingly handsome—and she was underdressed.

Jennie dodged his outstretched arm and got into the car. "This isn't fair," she said when he was beside her. "You wore down my resistance."

"That's right." He started the engine. "And I'm glad."

"So am I," she said, and meant it. "But I'm probably shirking my responsibilities."

"I doubt it." The car slipped away from the curb. At the crossroads he leaned forward to check for traffic, and an overwhelming sensation of happiness swamped Jennie. Every line, every angle of his face and body, was solid and familiar. She smelled his after-shave, light and clean. A powerful, reliable man who was offering her his friendship with no strings. Exactly what she needed.

"Thank you for coming, Jen." His eyes, when they settled on hers, were solemn, and clear and so green. "I did push a bit, but it was worth the effort. You'll think so, too, if you'll let yourself."

She didn't respond to the comment or to most of what he

said on the way to the Ohio. As they crossed the Roebling Suspension Bridge, the lights of Riverfront Stadium trembled on graying satin ripples beneath them. Near the riverbank, willows surrounded by water cast reflections of swaying limbs on the surface. A cool breeze brought river scents through the window.

Minutes took them across and into Covington. Only the river separated Cincinnati from the Kentucky town, but Jennie always felt the change in territory. By daylight the surrounding land even appeared greener than its sister state.

Peter, who had fallen into his own silent space for a while, pointed when the blue-and-white riverboat came into view. ''Mike Fink. Have you been there before?''

''No.'' And she was glad. Jennie had discovered the benefit of staying away from places with poignant memories.

There was no more conversation until they were parked and aboard the boat. ''We're half an hour late,'' Peter said, ducking a basket heavy with budding plants that hung from overhead.

Jennie would have stopped, but other people had walked behind them up the gangplank. ''What do you mean?'' she whispered.

''I hope they haven't given up our reservations.''

She did stop, forcing a smile for the three couples who passed. ''You made a reservation for half an hour ago?''

''I didn't think it would take so long to persuade you.'' He sounded absolutely serious, damn him.

''You're unbelievable. Doesn't it strike you that most women like at least to be allowed to pretend they're unpredictable?''

Three more people passed, and Peter painted on a phony smile to match her own. ''Don't be so touchy. It was a risk, but you're a good person, and I took advantage because I was…I wanted you to have dinner with me. Is that a sin?''

She was a ''good person''? And, without being conscious of what she'd done, there had been a moment when she'd thought of herself as a woman with an attractive man rather than just one of his friends. Were there other women in his life? She knew he couldn't have much time for socializing, and until a few months ago, he'd been traveling, but Peter Kynaston had to be aware of what a knockout he was and of his potential effect on women. Could she have become a challenge because she didn't fold at the sight of him?

"Okay, okay. I'm sorry I pressured you. My motives were pure, though."

The time came to accept defeat. Jennie gave up and led the way into the restaurant.

Seated in a curved, blue velvet booth, with Peter sitting close at her side, she kept up an aloof front only until two glasses of wine channeled relaxing warmth into her veins.

They ordered, and were served, and Jennie couldn't seem to concentrate on anything. Peter talked, and she responded. What had she said?

"Good catfish?" he asked, a sautéed frog leg halfway to his mouth.

Jennie wrinkled her nose at the morsel. "Wonderful. I could never eat those things."

"Gourmet cook and woman of the world like you? I suppose I'll have to return the chocolate-covered ants I bought for you." And he devoured the last of his meal.

Wooden-bladed fans rotated noiselessly above their heads. Jennie set down her fork and leaned back. Being here with Peter felt better than it should. For minutes on end she forgot that Steven was sulking and possibly heading for trouble.

Only for minutes. And as those minutes ticked by, a sense of waiting intensified. Peter settled back beside her, resting his head against the high seat back. The lighting was subdued. Candle flame flickered over smiling faces, and glass clinked amid the muted buzz of voices.

"Still sorry you came?"

Jennie glanced up at him. "No." She wasn't sorry, but she was apprehensive.

"Good."

She could feel him. His thigh, muscular beneath fine gray wool, was inches from hers. A big, well-shaped hand rested loosely there, tanned against a very white shirt cuff and the gleaming gold of his watchband. When Jennie raised her eyes, he looked back steadily, and she turned away, coloring.

"Coffee?"

She hadn't seen the waiter approach.

"Yes," Peter said. "And we'll have a Cointreau and a Pernod, please."

He remembered what she liked. "I shouldn't," she told him. "Cointreau's wonderful but it always goes to my head."

"It's been too long since you let something go to your head."

Like a man? Like him? Did he want her to let him go to her head? The room receded and became airless. Peter took her hand from her lap, covered it on the seat between them, and Jennie's stomach contracted.

"Cointreau?"

At the waiter's question, she started.

"For the lady," Peter said. He pushed the glass closer, and added cream to her coffee. "Still no sugar?"

She shook her head no. Tonight she was vulnerable. Peter would be amazed if he knew she was even edging around sensual fantasy with him as the trigger. For whatever reason, he was at loose ends and had turned to her because they used to have a relationship that was almost that of a brother and sister. Jennie was beginning to believe they could have that again, and it would be enough for her.

"Do you remember Dan Mitcham?"

Jennie filled her lungs. "Yes, of course."

Peter pushed his liqueur glass back and forth on the table. "He's got Hodgkin's." He stared into the distance.

Jennie bit her lip. "I know. How is he doing?" She turned toward him abruptly. "Dan was in remission. Has something happened?"

"Recurrence, damn it."

"How bad is it?" Dan Mitcham was a nice man and a brilliant chemist.

"Bad enough. Connie called today. He went to the clinic where he was first diagnosed. He'll go into chemo here."

There could be no missing the rigid set of his jaw and

shoulders, or the steel in his voice. He was angry, and Jennie understood what he was feeling because Mark's reaction had been the same.

"We're going to lick this thing," Peter said, almost to himself. "*I'm* going to lick it. One day the name Kynaston will be synonymous with cure."

Jennie touched his arm, but he didn't seem to notice. Peter had moved away from her, into another place, far, far away. Was he single-mindedly ambitious, determined to make a big name for himself after all?

"Shoot, I feel helpless." Bending forward, bowing his head, Peter rested crossed forearms on the table, and Jennie's reservations melted.

She kneaded the spot between his shoulder blades and leaned against his arm. "Peter, we all know there's a long way to go. Think of how much you've all done. And think of how far treatment has gone. Dan's no quitter. He'll come through again."

Peter turned his face to hers. "You're no stranger to all this, are you?" His eyes were so close she saw flecks of black and gold in the iris.

"Chemotherapy only gets more sophisticated," she said, and swallowed, stroking the sleeve of his jacket over his hard forearm. "You do enough work with it to know that very well. Maybe this time he'll beat the disease completely. It happens."

"Yes, it does." He put his hand on hers, linked their thumbs. "I knew I needed you tonight. Thank you for coming, Jennie."

"I…I wanted to."

"You could have fooled me," he said, but he smiled softly and tilted up his chin to look down on her.

She smiled at him. "I was on a guilt trip about Steven." Twirling the stem of her liqueur glass, she reflected before taking a bigger sip than she intended. She coughed, and tears filled her eyes.

"Okay?" Peter slipped an arm around her shoulders.

Jennie nodded. "Sometimes I think he may be reacting against my business." Her skin tightened.

"Because it takes you away from home so much?"

While he watched her, too acutely, Jennie swallowed more Cointreau, sniffed the aromatic orange scent, and closed her eyes against the burning in her throat.

When she opened her eyes, Peter still pinned her with an inscrutable stare. "Do you think that's what's bugging him— that you've changed?"

The drink was dulling her senses. "I don't think he's sure what he feels. But it's probably part of it. Only I'm not giving up everything I've worked for. In time he'll understand that he and Bobby won't be with me forever, and when I'm alone I'll need...something." She should go home and say no more.

He squeezed her shoulder. "Are you sure it isn't money? The reason you're so determined with your venture, I mean. Mark left you okay, didn't he?"

"He could have done better," she said, and covered her mouth.

"Mark?" No one feigned surprise that well. "Mark didn't spend... What do you mean?"

Peter was getting the wrong impression, and she must stop that. "I don't mean anything. There were a few bad investments, that's all. I had to make the choice between just getting by and making an attempt to solidify my financial position. I chose the latter. It'll take a while to be as good as I want it to be, but it'll happen."

His hand moved from her shoulder to her neck, and he rubbed his thumb slowly back and forth. "I'm very proud of you."

Jennie had difficulty concentrating. "Don't be until I've really proved myself."

"Bunk." He kissed her forehead lightly. "You'll never have to prove a thing for me to know what you're worth."

There was no hiding an involuntary tremor. "I think we should go home."

"I don't." But he leaned away to look at her and took a

long breath through his nose. "But I won't push my luck anymore tonight."

"Thank you." Was that what she wanted? Another swallow of Cointreau accomplished its mission. A lambent warmth suffused her. When he said he wouldn't push his luck, did he mean there would be other nights like this, with warmth and companionship? She hoped so.

"I have been considering a rather big step, Peter. Bigger than anything I've done so far." This was the first time she'd even approached sharing her thoughts on selling the house.

"Can I help you make up your mind?" He raised his own glass and regarded her steadily over the rim.

She'd hoped he'd ask. Every time she worked with the pros and cons of moving to a smaller house, or an apartment, she wished there was someone else to talk it over with. "I'd like to expand Images faster. To do that, I need more capital and the obvious place to get it is from the house."

For an instant he looked as if he thought he'd misheard her. "The house?" He laughed. "You can't be serious. You love that place."

"Yes, I do. But not so much that I couldn't be just as happy somewhere else."

Peter folded his arms and frowned. "If it's money you need, I'd be glad to invest—"

"No! Absolutely not." Her heart thudded hard.

"I know it would be a safe venture, and—"

"Peter, you don't understand. I know what I'm doing and I'm not short of money. It's just a case of deciding how to move assets around and use them to their best advantage."

Reaching for his water glass, he regarded her intently. "You always were levelheaded. But I don't think this is something you should rush into. I know I keep telling you not to let Steven run your life, but I do wonder if moving him from the home he's grown up in won't be one upheaval too many at this point."

A lump formed in Jennie's throat. Steven was hateful to Peter, yet the man brushed all that aside. "I've thought of that, too. But I have to look at the long-term picture."

"Mmm." Peter set down the glass without drinking. "I know you're good with figures, but sometimes it's nice to have someone else in on an important decision."

He couldn't know how often she'd wished for the kind of sharing he was talking about. "I know."

"Will you let me spend some time helping you work things through?"

"Are you sure you want to get involved?"

"Yes. If you're game, we'll take you home and get started right now."

He had an uncanny way of knowing what she needed. "I'd like your opinion. Yes, thank you." And the time had come to let Steven know what she was considering.

STEVEN'S SCOWLING FACE WAS the first thing Peter saw when he followed Jennie into her kitchen. "Hi, Steven," he said, determinedly cheerful, then saw Bobby before the open refrigerator. "Hi, Bob."

"Hi, Peter. I rode my bike to school today."

"That's great. We'll all have to go out again soon. You, too Steven."

Steven swallowed a gulp of Coke from a can.

"Coffee, Peter?" Jennie asked in a falsely bright voice that increased his irritation with Steven.

"No, thanks. I think we should get right to our discussion."

Her features hardened perceptibly, and he was reminded that he'd always admired her determination. "You're right. We might as well sit here." She indicated the kitchen table and sat down as if Steven weren't a glowering presence a few feet away.

"You know, another thought is a second mortgage."

Steven crossed his arms, and Bobby closed the refrigerator door with a thud.

"I considered that," Jennie said. "But we don't really need a house as big as this."

Peter felt Steven stiffen but ignored him. "It is a good investment, though, Jen. Real estate always holds its own in the end."

"What's he talking about?" Steven got up from the table. "What are you saying about our house?"

"I'm considering selling," Jennie said calmly. "The up-keep is getting to be more than I can handle, particularly the yard—"

"This is our house," Steven said loudly. "Dad said we could always live here. It's not yours—"

"Sit down, Steven," Jennie snapped. "And be quiet. Or go to your room, whichever you prefer. And remember that this *is* my house."

"What gives you the right to tell me what to do?"

"The fact that I'm your mother."

Peter clenched his hands in his pockets. For the first time in his life, he was getting a few firsthand examples of how impossible teenagers could be. He didn't like what he saw.

"Mom?" Bobby broke in, sounding anxious. "Do we have to move?"

"Not necessarily," Jennie told him with a reassuring smile. "But it's possible. Peter's offered to help me decide if it's a good idea right now."

Bobby's stance relaxed. "Oh."

"Your mom thinks you could all be just as happy in a smaller place that would be easier on her to maintain," Peter put in. "The question is, would she realize enough profit to make a substantial difference to her in investment capital?"

"It's none of your business," Steven said. "Talk to me about it, Mom, not him."

"Are we in some sort of trouble?" Bobby's voice quavered.

"No, son, no." Jennie shook her head emphatically. "Not at all. We're in great shape. I'm just trying to make the very best of what we have—for all of us."

"This is what you've wanted," Steven said to Peter. "When you didn't come around for so long, I thought you'd given up. But you were waiting till you thought we'd forgotten what you did."

A hollow silence echoed on and on in the wake of the announcement.

"Well, you aren't getting away with it. I can do whatever Mom needs help with around here. We don't need you."

Peter saw Jennie flinch. "Easy," he said, but he kept his eyes on Steven's thunderous face. "Give it up, Steven. Stop taking your disappointments out on me. I don't deserve it, and you're making your mother's life harder than it has to be."

"Because it would be easier if she had you around?" The boy circled the table but retained contact with one hand as if he needed support. "You're cozying up to Mom because... You're sick. My dad said so."

"That's enough," Jennie said. "Don't insult Peter in your father's name."

"You don't get it, do you?" Steven's face contorted and turned red. Tears stood in his eyes. "Dad told me to look after you if anything happened to him."

Peter couldn't stop himself from reaching for Jennie's hand and squeezing. "Steven, you've said enough."

"No, I haven't." Only a couple of inches shorter than Peter, the boy came to stand toe-to-toe with him. "You're moving in to finish what you started. Dad warned me."

"He warned you about what?"

"That you wanted everything he had. He said you were jealous of him because you weren't as smart."

"Steven, please." Now Jennie sounded desperate. "That's it—the end."

"He may have been right," Peter told Steven. "Mark Andrews was the smartest man I ever met."

Steven seemed to falter, but only long enough to recover and jut his chin. "You've got Dad's job."

"Someone had to take it over." Why did he feel vulnerable, as if he was missing something? What wasn't Steven saying?

"My dad said you wouldn't be satisfied until you had everything he...he loved." The boy's voice dropped. "Including his family."

CHAPTER SIX

Finally the trunk of the Ramstets' Cadillac closed with a thunk over the last of the boys' camping equipment. The fishing weekend was about to start, several hours late because Carl had been held up at the office and then Jennie had been forced to go out and replace the sleeping bag Bobby couldn't locate.

"That about does it," Carl said, smiling broadly. In a padded green vest, worn over an ancient wool shirt, and his red plaid fishing hat pulled low over his eyes, he seemed jaunty and out of character.

Bobby came to give Jennie a hug. "See ya Sunday, Mom," he said, stepping away.

She punched his arm playfully. "Just don't wear Carl out," she warned him. "Either of you." Steven, withdrawn but not hostile, had already climbed into the back seat of the car.

"I'll probably wear them out," Carl said. "Up before the birds, is my motto on these trips. Up before the fish."

Bobby groaned and shut himself into the front passenger seat.

Jennie walked beside Carl until he got in and rolled down his window. "You may have trouble rousing these two," she told him. "They think Saturdays and Sundays don't begin before noon."

"Well, they'll learn," Carl said. "Last weekend I'd played eighteen holes by noon." He waved as he switched on the ignition and backed away.

"Bye," Jennie called.

When the car moved out of sight, she walked back into the house and closed the door. She'd miss the kids, but on the other hand, two days of peace didn't sound altogether unappealing.

The phone rang as she passed the den. For one rebellious second she considered ignoring it…then she hurried to answer.

"Gone at last," Lou said without waiting for Jennie to say anything. "Come on over for a drink."

"Um…I can't, Lou. Really, thanks a million, but tonight I get to catch up on a pile of things I never seem to have time to do." She instantly felt ungrateful. "And it's all thanks to you. Really, I've needed this break for so long. Not that I don't enjoy the boys, but you know how it is."

Lou's sigh was long. "I only know how much I wish Jody was around."

"Yes, well—" If she didn't stand firm, she'd allow herself to be trapped into spending the evening listening to glowing tales of Jody's exemplary scholastic performance. "Before you know where you are, Jody will be home for the summer."

Lou sighed again. "I suppose so. What are all these things you have to do tonight?"

It seemed that she was always being interrogated. Her word was never quite satisfactory, not even to Peter. Jennie shook her head. Tuesday night had been fun until Steven's disastrous salvo. Peter had been polite before he left. He'd also said he'd be in touch, but it looked as if there could be another eighteen-month wait on that, if it ever happened.

"Jennie! Are you still there?"

"Yes. What I have to do is a lot of boring small stuff."

"Are you mad because we didn't come over on Saturday?" Jennie's mind turned blank. "I don't know what you mean."

"For Carl to mend the faucet. I only just remembered. He felt punk all weekend, and I forgot I'd said we'd come."

"Don't give it another thought," Jennie said. She had wondered why Lou hadn't as much as called.

"Jennie, I wanted to talk to you about the spring kickoff party."

Another mental void assailed Jennie.

"It's next weekend. Say you'll come."

Jennie bit her lip, realizing Lou was talking about the annual neighborhood party, the one she hadn't been invited to last year, when Maryanne and Ray Reid had hosted. After the event Lou had innocently said how sorry she was that Jennie had been unable to attend, and Jennie hadn't explained the real reason.

"Jennie, you're deliberately playing hard-to-get tonight. All the old group wants you to come. It'll be nice."

Lou and Carl might want her, but Jennie had doubts about how welcome she was with some members of the "old group."

"I'll think about it." And she wished she could get off the phone, take a hot bath while she read a magazine and paint her fingernails.

"What else do you have on your calendar for next Sunday?"

"Lou—" Getting defensive would accomplish nothing, but she hated the dig at her lack of social life. "I'll have to let you know."

"Not good enough," Lou persisted. "I need numbers."

Jennie closed her eyes. "Then you'd better count me out."

Lou moaned. "We all miss you. There's never a get-together when people don't say they wish you were there."

Sure.

"Jennie, remember our conversation when I came to your office? About how it's time you considered, well, you know."

"I remember."

"Well, there'll be one or two interesting single men at the party."

Balding hunters with paunches, roving eyes and hands and no new lines. She rolled her eyes and tapped the receiver. "I'm not interested."

After a small pause Lou said, "I saw Peter Kynaston with Bobby on Saturday…and the three of you going for a ride afterward. You looked happy."

A longer silence followed.

"Jennie?"

"It makes me happy to see Bobby happy." And that was all she intended to say. "I've got to go."

"Now you *are* angry with me."

Jennie was instantly contrite. Lou must be even lonelier than usual with Carl gone, and that was because he was doing Jennie's family a favor. "I'll come to the party."

When Lou hung up, she was giggling, bubbling with her plans for the great event. Jennie's smile lasted only until she wrote the date on the calendar. What a pushover. She should have stood her ground.

Jennie dithered, halfheartedly considering reading some of the design bulletins spread on the table. She should do some intensive research into men's sports trends. Men's sports. She stared at the wall. Now she realized what hadn't sounded quite right about something Lou had said on the phone. Carl had felt punk all weekend and had been unable to do anything as strenuous as fix a faucet? But Carl had also felt so terrific that he'd played golf both Saturday and Sunday. An uncomfortable warmth prickled over her skin. Carl wouldn't lie about a golf game—or anything else, if Jennie was right about him. But Lou…? For some reason Lou had felt she needed to make an excuse for their failure to come to Jennie's on Saturday night. Not an excuse—a lie. Was Lou, like some other old friends, starting to view Jennie as a potential nuisance?

This was ridiculous. She was being too sensitive. The uncomfortable, vaguely sick feeling didn't go away, but Jennie forced herself to decide what to do next.

Wallow in warm water and paint her nails or clean the guest bathroom…or go to bed with a book. If she painted her nails, she couldn't clean the bathroom. She didn't really want to go to bed. Much as she hated to admit weakness, she still had difficulty being alone in the house at night and tended to imagine creaks and pops until she fell asleep—often with the light on.

The guest bathroom won. She filled a bucket with soapy water, pulled on rubber gloves and hefted her burden into the hall, slopping as she went.

A soft tapping at the door jolted her to a stop, and a miniwave from the bucket sopped her tennis shoes. "Darn it," she mumbled, but her heart thudded. The porch lights had timed out, and Jennie couldn't see anything beyond the glass panels.

Still carrying the bucket, she approached the door. "Who's there?"

"Peter."

Jennie stared ahead, seeing nothing, her mind seething. A great swell of relief made her breathless. Relief and happiness. She wanted to see Peter, had been hoping for days that he'd contact her.

"Jennie? Are you okay?"

She opened the door and looked up into troubled eyes turned brilliant green by the hall light.

"Hello," he said.

"Hi." The bucket was heavy and she set it down. "I was going to clean the bathroom."

"Oh." He rocked to his heels and looked at the darkening sky. "Can I come in?"

"Bobby's not here." Peter had said he intended to do something with him. "I'm alone."

"I know. You told me about the fishing trip. That's why I came."

She felt blood rush to her face. "You'd better come in." Long ago she'd learned the danger of reading too much into what people said.

"Isn't it late for cleaning bathrooms?"

"I guess." She led him into the den. "Working outside the home all day means I have to catch up on the nitty-gritty when I can. Sit down."

He chose a brown leather chair and made himself comfortable with his booted feet on an ottoman. "You look tired."

"Not really." Dropping to the edge of the love seat that matched his chair, she flipped back her hair and tried to remember when she'd last applied lipstick.

"Your shoes are wet."

"I know."

"Take them off."

"What?"

"The shoes. Take them off."

"I…you're right." She bent over and worked at shoelaces that didn't want to budge.

"You might find it easier without the gloves."

Laughing self-consciously, she freed her hands. When her feet were bare, she frowned and tucked them beneath her. She should offer him a drink.

"I wasn't going to come here," Peter said. He looked into the empty fireplace. "I told myself I shouldn't."

His hair was more disheveled than usual. He wore a white shirt that exaggerated his tan.

"Because of what happened on Tuesday night?" She should probably have been the one to go to him. "Steven is one mixed-up kid, Peter. I'm sorry about what he said."

"As long as you don't believe there was any truth in it, it doesn't matter."

"You know I don't." But she was embarrassed by the incident.

"Thanks." He shoved at his hair, but it fell forward again as soon as he removed his hand. "How has he been the last few days?"

Jennie wound her fingers together. "Mostly like an unexploded bomb." On the last two occasions when she and Peter had been together, she'd had the sensation he wasn't saying everything he thought. Tonight the intuition was stronger than ever.

He got up and examined the leaves of a tall fichus in a wicker pot. "You need feeding, don't you fella?"

She had to ask. "Are you worried about Steven? Don't you think he'll be okay?"

"Sure I think he'll be okay. Jen—" he pulled the ottoman close to her chair and sat next to her knees "—I've been trying to decide if I should tell you about a conversation I had early last Friday morning."

She stared at him. "I thought there was something. Tell me."

His big hand covered her closed fist on her knee. "I've decided I'm making too much out of something that's not so big, but you still ought to know about it. You know how he told us he was at that dance place and got in a fight?"

She nodded.

"Well, that wasn't how he got hurt, or at least not where, because it wasn't open on Thursday night, that's all."

Her stomach made a sickening revolution. "It had to be. He said—"

"Exactly. He said. But he told a lie, and I immediately jumped to the conclusion that he was covering up something awful."

Seething, Jennie stood up. "You're right. Why else would he lie? I wish you'd told me immediately."

"Yeah, I thought you'd say that. I'm sorry. I guess this was a bad judgment call on my part."

"Damn, he's gone who knows where, and there's no way to get at him until Sunday." She went to look out into the darkness. "I've spoiled him—that's the problem. What if he's into something illegal?"

Peter shook his head. "I'm sure it's not that. The logical explanation is that he had more to do with whatever happened than he wants you to know. You said yourself he's angry. He could have mouthed off at someone bigger and ended up getting the worst of things."

Steven never used to lie. "Why wouldn't he feel he could tell me the truth?"

Peter came close and put an arm around her shoulders. His slow chafing of her arm softened the edges of her anxiety. "Could be a good sign," he told her. "If he didn't care what you think, he probably wouldn't try to cover up."

As usual he made sense. "What do you think I should do?"

"Why not let it go? I almost didn't tell you, but he's your boy. Keeping quiet didn't feel right."

She released a breath she hadn't realized she was holding. "You could be right. But I'll have to watch him more closely. And if he pulls another stunt, I'll have to react strongly."

"Right." He smiled down at her. "Feel better?"

She nodded. "Thanks for telling me. I'm sorry you had to make another trek over here to do it."

"I'm not."

Why? No, she wouldn't ask. The moment was fragile and it might break. For whatever reason a soft peace, laced at the seams with tingling awareness, had slipped over her, and she wouldn't examine it too closely. Close up, the eye, and the mind, often saw cracks in sweet illusion.

"I expect you're in a hurry to get home." Saying it took effort. "Unless you'd like coffee or something first." She didn't want him to go.

"Yes," he said very quickly.

Of course he couldn't stay. She'd already taken up far too much of his time. "Thanks again for coming." Moving out of the circle of his arm, she turned toward the door.

He caught her hand. "I thought you offered me coffee." His grin, slightly lopsided, had an impish quality but didn't disguise tired lines around his eyes.

"I thought...of course. I'll get it. Make yourself comfortable." Even with her hand in his, there was a sliding in of uncertainty.

"I'll come and help. This is my time of night for...I prefer to be doing something."

She met his gaze squarely, assessing whether she was reading the message beneath the words. Was he lonely sometimes? Did he find things to do at night to avoid going to bed alone? Although she knew he wasn't a man who made friends easily or had much time for them, she couldn't believe he had to be alone except by choice.

Straight brows raised fractionally above those intense, almost jade-green eyes, and Jennie had to look away. "Okay. Help, if you like."

At the kitchen stove they stood side by side. "I usually boil milk and make a sort of pseudo-latte. In my mind I think I'm doing my stomach and my nerves a favor."

"Sounds wonderful."

His height and breadth were a tangible force at her shoulder, more so since she was barefoot. That force produced a weakness in her limbs, an almost forgotten sense of being feminine.

"Skim milk? Whole milk?" He'd opened the refrigerator to peer inside, and the light gilded the hair on his muscular forearms and the backs of his hands.

Jennie's glance moved to his strong throat and the glow that played over the handsome lines of his face. When he tilted his head toward her, question in his eyes, she hunched her shoulders. "I could brew coffee if you'd rather."

"I'd rather have what you want." Two cartons of milk were plunked beside her, and he continued to rummage in the refrigerator as he would have two years ago. "Got any bagels?"

She couldn't contain her grin. "Some things never change. You're the only man I know who could live on bagels and cream cheese. And pizza and hamburgers, of course."

"You've got this." A box of cheese was brandished.

"And I've got bagels," she said, still smiling. "Same place as usual. In the freezer. Put 'em in the microwave to thaw, and you'll be in business."

Peter scraped a crackly bag from the freezer and moved about the kitchen, finding a knife, the plastic wrap, as only a man who knew where everything was could have done. He executed the small tasks efficiently. For a big man, he was graceful, comfortable in his body. She remembered his home in Hyde Park and the way she and Mark had teased him about its disorder. Peter, always good-natured, had protested that the house was clean and tidying up was a waste of time. She also remembered seeing him working at the lab, where he was orderly in all things. A dichotomy, fascinating in so many ways.

"Ouch!" He dropped the bagels he'd taken from the microwave and flapped a hand.

Jennie immediately grabbed his fingers. "Oh, Peter. You're hopeless sometimes." She turned on the faucet and ran water over reddening skin. "You did this with steam before."

"You remember?"

Their eyes met, and she felt a falling away inside. The

proximity, the familiarity, were chipping at her composure. "I remember a lot of things," she said, concentrating on holding him still and making sure the water was cold enough. He smelled of soap and freshly laundered cotton. She felt herself color and bowed her head. These reactions had to be the result of loneliness. Peter would undoubtedly be horrified if he could hear her thoughts.

"It's okay now." He tried to pull away.

Jennie anchored his wrist against the sink and glanced up. "It'll be okay when I say it's okay."

His smile was wicked. He brought his face closer, and she instinctively raised her chin.

"A dictator at heart, Jennie Andrews. I always suspected you were hiding your real personality behind all the sweetness."

The lift of her chin had been natural assertiveness, nothing more. His breath, clean and minty, whispered over her lips. Subtly a change had been taking place. He wasn't just "good old Peter" anymore. She was attracted to him, damn it, almost overwhelmingly attracted.

As quickly as she acknowledged the possibility, she abandoned it. Having him here felt normal, usual and incredibly good...the way it had felt when Mark had been well and had come home from work to putter in the kitchen with her.

"It'll be all right, now." She let him go and tossed a clean towel in his direction. Quickly she turned away and busied herself finishing the coffee. Peter's silence was almost tangible as he walked back and forth behind her. Did he feel her confusion? She cleared papers from the oval table, and they sat together at one end.

"Good," Peter mumbled around a mouthful of bagel.

She smiled.

"Do you put it in the window during the day?"

"Hmm?" Jennie looked at him, uncomprehending. The tendency to leap from topic to topic was almost a trademark with him, but it never failed to catch her off guard.

"The Phalaenopsis."

She frowned. "I'm sorry?"

He pointed to the orchid he'd given her. She said, "No, I didn't know I should."

"Mmm. It's okay to put it somewhere to look at during the evenings, if you want to. They're hardy. But make sure it gets some light. That window would be fine." He turned to hook a thumb toward the window over the sink. "Faces east."

"I'll remember." His serious concentration on plants had at first puzzled her, then had become vaguely irritating. Eventually she'd come to appreciate how the hobby was natural for a man whose life revolved around trying to preserve life. "How's Killer?" Now she was subject-hopping.

Peter wrinkled his straight nose. "I don't know why I bother. She hates me. Oh—" he worked his fingers into the pocket of his snug jeans "—I almost forgot. This is the food for the Phalaenopsis. A quarter of a teaspoon in a gallon of water. And don't forget to mist and water it in the morning. Foliage should be dry by nightfall."

Jennie took the plastic bag of blue crystals from him and sucked in her bottom lip thoughtfully. "Peter, maybe I shouldn't have this plant. If something happened to it, you'd never forgive me."

"What's going to happen?" He angled his face toward her sharply. "If you're worried about it, call. Anytime. I'll come right over."

Now she did have to suppress a giggle. "Thank you. I'll do my best."

Peter resumed munching and drank the milky coffee with evident relish. He finished, and Jennie tried not to move jerkily as she felt him watching her.

"Do you always start projects when you should be relaxing for the evening?"

"Not always."

"Just most of the time?" He bowed his face toward her until she looked up.

"I guess." Only when she was alone, but she wouldn't admit that to anyone.

"Why?"

Because, stupid as it sounded, she was just a little nervous as the one adult in this big house. "I'm not sure."

"I've turned into a night prowler, too. Makes Killer furious. She follows me."

"Would you like me to take her?" What was she saying? She didn't need more responsibilities.

Something close to horror entered Peter's eyes. "Oh, no...thanks, but no. She wouldn't be happy. That's her house, not mine. She lets me live there."

Jennie laughed, liking him more and more all over again. "It wouldn't be that she's good company for you, would it?"

He shrugged elaborately. "No...well, could be. I guess that's why you'd like her, huh?"

"Uh-uh. I've got enough to look after. And when you're married with children, you'll know what I mean."

A stillness fell around him. His hands, fists on the table each side of his empty plate, tightened perceptibly and remained clenched. Jennie feared she'd said something wrong, but he had said he intended to do something about marriage when he had time.

"I guess you'd like me to get out of your hair."

He stood up, and Jennie's chest felt tight.

"I'm glad you came by. I'll have to keep a closer eye on Steven, I suppose, but I don't feel so worried somehow."

"I thought you said the plumber was going to fix that."

Jennie glanced vaguely around.

"The faucet."

She shouldn't have lied about getting it fixed the first time. "You know how it goes. They get busy with big-paying contracts and have to put off small jobs."

He went to the sink, opened the cupboard below and reached inside. Jennie pressed her palms together, knowing she could stop him and send him home, but wanting him to stay for whatever reason.

With several sharp twists, he turned off the water. "This won't take long. It's time you had washerless faucets."

It was time she had a lot of things...particularly an easier home to care for. "I'll get the tools."

"No. You won't know what I need."

He was right, not that she liked admitting as much.

Within half an hour the job was done, and he packed what he'd used back into Mark's old metal tool tray. "I miss him. I know things changed between us at the end, but that wasn't his fault or mine."

The words hit her with bullet force, immobilized her in the chair where she sat. Breathing was hard.

Peter ran his fingers back and forth along the edge of the sink and picked up a wrench. "Sometimes, at the lab, I can hear his voice. He used to be calm almost all the time, but there'd be those moments when he'd let up a yell. Damn..." He faced her, and there was a sheen in his eyes. "Jen, wasn't he something?"

"Yes," she whispered. "He was really something."

"Why does a man like that die when he's got so much left to do?"

Tears sprang into her own eyes. "We don't get the answers to questions like that."

She didn't hear Peter approach, didn't sense him until he pulled her up into his arms and held her so convulsively her spine ached. But it was good, very good, and she wrapped her arms around his neck, threaded her fingers in the curly hair at his nape, rested her face against his warm, hard chest.

"Let's not slip away from each other again." He smoothed her back slowly, rocked her, rested his jaw on her hair.

"No." She closed her eyes. Beneath her cheek, the beat of his heart was steady.

She felt Peter's chest expand. "I'm sure you're working tomorrow. I am, too. Could we do something on Sunday?"

"If you like."

He laughed. "Great. Okay, we'll do something on Sunday."

She rested a palm on his smooth shirt. He looked young, boyish, and she smiled.

When he reached for her, she caught her breath. He only paused an instant before taking her face in his hands and dropping his head until his lips rested on her forehead. "Sunday," he said.

"Yes." Jennie couldn't form complete thoughts or sentences. She feared he must feel her trembling.

He caressed her hair before checking his watch. "Now I *had* better go before Lou sees me. I expect she still keeps her finger on the neighborhood pulse."

Jennie looked at him quizzically. "What does that have to do with anything?"

"Talk travels in close—" He narrowed his eyes and raked at his hair. "Well, you know."

"She's used to seeing you here, Peter." But not regularly lately, and not while Jennie was alone in the house.

"I'll call you tomorrow night." The color deepened over his cheekbones. "I'd better get along."

Without any effort to dissuade him, Jennie saw him to the front door, watched his tall, rangy frame become a hazy shadow moving down the driveway.

She shut the door.

He'd been concerned about the neighbors' opinion of them, of the conclusions they might draw. A man who hadn't considered more than a platonic relationship with a woman wouldn't flirt with such ideas.

Reluctantly she went back into the kitchen and gathered the mugs and plate from the table. She set them in the sink and picked up the tool carrier Peter had left out. What did he really want from her? What did she want from him...if anything?

CHAPTER SEVEN

Jennie rested a hand on her stomach and groaned.

"You're a lightweight." Peter laughed. "One hot dog, and you're in pain."

"One *foot-long* hot dog with everything on it," Jennie said weakly, trying, unsuccessfully, to stretch her middle in the sumptuous but confining bucket seat in Peter's car.

"Are you sure you want to do this?" He steered into the driveway in front of his house, braked and looked at her.

"I'm absolutely sure. You talked about your greenhouse all through lunch and how hard it is never to have any help with it. So, I'm going to help."

"I *didn't* talk about it all that much."

"Yes, you did. But I forgive you."

How long had it been since she was last here? Peter's big redbrick house gave the same solid impression she remembered. Her attention fixed on the two dormers that had been built beneath the apex of the main roof. "Peter's Folly," Mark had laughingly called the attic master suite, which he considered an eccentric addition to the already extensive finished space in the house.

"It's a beautiful house, Peter. Substantial. I like brick."

"Me, too." He switched off the car. "You've got to promise—no cracks about my housekeeping."

Jennie hid a smile. "Some things never change."

"Jennie?"

"Okay, okay. I promise."

Peter got out and met her on the passenger side of the car. He closed her door. "I've never built a greenhouse before and

I spend as much time tearing down what I've done as putting it up in the first place.''

"Why don't you have it done for you?" Jennie asked, holding his arm as they walked toward the house.

"Because I like to prove I can do things."

She shouldn't have needed to ask. His whole existence revolved around proving he could solve problems, just as Mark's had. Jennie halted the line of thought. She heard her own breathing, felt Peter's warmth through his denim shirt. Overhead, tree limbs trembled, their leaves sighing together in the warmth of a late-afternoon breeze.

Peter opened the door and ushered her into a slate-tiled hall. An oak-and-walnut staircase rose from one side to an open gallery on the second floor. The walls were white, as they always had been, and were still devoid of any artwork.

"No, no pictures yet," Peter said, reading her mind. "I'm scared to death of making mistakes in that area. But—" he gave one of his winning smiles "—I do know someone who could probably give me some help there."

"Oh, no." Jennie shook her head. "I couldn't take the pressure."

"I'd be just another client."

"You could never be just another client," she said without thinking.

Peter's smile disappeared. He pushed the door shut without taking his eyes from hers. "It was fun walking around town with you, Jennie," he said. "I like the city on Sunday, when it's quiet."

Jennie grew uncomfortable. While they'd walked and talked—about every inconsequential thing imaginable—there had been no tension. But it was with them now—here.

"Well." Peter touched her arm. "I've been wearing my teeth out holding nails and cursing my bad luck that I don't have a soul to help."

"There you go again. Complaining." Jennie laughed, punched his iron-hard middle lightly and watched him pretend to be winded. Tension began to ebb.

He spread a big hand over his flat stomach above the low

waistband of his jeans and assumed a hunched-over pose. "I'm in bad shape, Jen. This great house will be the end of me. Work, work, work, clean, clean—"

"Okay, Peter. Lead me to the greenhouse."

"The job's coming along nicely," he said, waving her ahead of him. "The brickwork's done, and I'm reinforcing the frames. Then there's the glass to do, and the electricity and water to finish up."

"Sounds complicated to me."

"Me, too. But I don't dwell on it," he said. And, when she was halfway along the hall, he added, "Whoa. You can't work in that outfit."

Jennie swung to face him. "You and I have to get our signals straight." She tweaked the peplum on her mauve linen suit. The skirt was slim, and her taupe pumps, with very thin heels, were pointed at the toe. "Either you're dressed to kill and I look like a bum, or vice versa." Walking all over downtown Cincinnati hadn't been the most comfortable experience she'd ever had, and she longed to wriggle her toes.

"Thanks," Peter said, pulling his shirt free of his pants. "A bum, huh?"

"You know what I mean. Anyway, all I'm going to do is hold nails."

"That's what you think." He turned her around. "You can wear one of my shirts and a pair of jeans."

She stared, clearly incredulous. "Your *jeans*?"

He frowned deeply. "Yeah, my jeans. I'll give you something to tie them on with, and then you can roll up the legs." He climbed the stairs two at a time, and she trotted behind him. She was having fun, really enjoying herself in a carefree way that hadn't happened in too long. These were stolen hours that wouldn't last and might not be repeated, but while she had them, she was going to keep right on having a good time.

When she stood in the middle of his bedroom, inches from his bed, her childlike pleasure in the moment fled. She had the sudden, strong sensation that she knew what suffocation felt like. She laced her fingers together in front of her and smiled. This was his room, where he slept. His bed. Jennie glanced around, registering nothing but the sense that she had passed over some line with Peter into a more personal facet of his existence than she'd ever entered before. Each time he glanced at her, in between rummaging through clean but unfolded piles of clothes on two chairs, she still smiled. Was there something different in his eyes, too, a wariness?

"Here we go." Tossing her a crumpled wad, he pulled a tie from a chair back. "And use this as a mooring line."

"Thank you. I'll be—"

The rest of what she said was lost as he strode from the room, shutting the door firmly.

Jennie was left with her mouth open and a wildly thudding heart. She hadn't imagined his hasty retreat. He had felt awkward with her in his room.

The jeans were useless. She gave up trying to make them work and critically assessed exactly what Peter's shirt covered when worn alone. It was fine, short but fine.

She couldn't resist taking a few minutes to look at his room. Not pry, only peek around a little. The old quilt on the big bed, multicolored and in an intricate pattern she was sure a quilting expert would instantly identify, made her smile. He'd probably rescued it from some family member and brought it here without even knowing he was clinging to tradition.

Peter's laundry caused her to grimace. Clean, but not ironed, it made mountains on the chairs. He needed someone to take care of him...or force him to take care of himself. The bathroom was huge, carpeted in the same kelly-green rug as the bedroom. A huge black Jacuzzi tub, raised and surrounded by a wide border of kelly-green and black tiles, had a dip for a headrest, and an inflatable pillow rested there. Jennie glanced quickly at the other end of the tub. Of course it would be made with matching headrests.

She was taking too long—and his scent lingered here. Touching her mouth with fingers that, ridiculously, trembled, she backed away. After-shave, a comb, a razor, a damp towel draped over the shower door. The intimacy she felt here raked like sensual claws along her nerves. Peter had said two years could be a long time. But it wasn't long enough to give her an excuse for the yearning these ordinary masculine things caused.

Leaving her clothes in a tidy pile on the bed, she opened the door—then looked at her feet. Her shoes would look ridiculous, and bare feet were out of the question around nails. Thongs, very large ones, lay under a chair. Jennie picked them up and carried them downstairs and through the house to the kitchen.

The chaos caused a wince. A charming and functional room, its skylights and a wall of glass brought light in to bathe golden wood; the walls were tiled in shades of cream and coffee. Jennie preferred this kitchen to her own because it was a cook's dream, or would be if anything had been put away recently and if Peter didn't insist on cramming plants into any spot where sun was likely to hit. She pushed open the arched door to a trellised deck, stepped over the boots Peter had been wearing and went into the garden. Here, any suggestion of disorder vanished.

Jennie positioned her feet in the thongs and flapped precariously along a winding path through lush plantings. She followed the sound of hammering to a clearing next to the brick wall surrounding the property. The size of the half-completed greenhouse amazed her. It was huge, big enough to hold at least three cars.

The hammering persisted, but she couldn't see Peter. "Hi!" She raised her voice and jumped when he popped from behind brick that rose as high as his waist. He didn't say anything, and she switched her weight from foot to foot. Evidently he was already absorbed in what he was doing.

"This is incredible," she said, hoping to sound flippant. Turning her toes in, she crossed her arms around her middle. "You could rent out the house and live in this thing." The shirt stopped several inches above her knees, and she felt vulnerable.

His steady, unsmiling gaze was unnerving.

Peter made a guttural noise. She peered at him more closely—and grinned. No wonder he couldn't talk. He really did hold the nails in his teeth. In one hand he brandished a wooden strut, in the other a hammer. He mumbled again, and with finger and thumb, Jennie removed the nails from his mouth.

"The jeans didn't work?" He looked from her knees, now clamped together, to her feet. "Very fetching, as they say. Don't break your neck in the fancy footwear."

His attention returned to the greenhouse, and she was aware of her stomach making a dip. Disappointment. She actually wanted him to show more than a friend's interest in her. Jennie straightened, let her arms drop and pointed her toes deliberately forward. Why should she be disappointed when she didn't want another romantic involvement?

"Nail," Peter said, holding out a hand without as much as glancing at her.

She dropped one into his palm, and he went back inside the structure. "Why does it have to be so big?" she asked, following him.

"Formula," he said, going to his knees. "First you make sure you're absolutely sober." He squinted up at her, shading his eyes against the sun's low rays. "Got that?"

Jennie shook her head slowly. "Nope. Doesn't mean a thing to me."

Dust rose from the wooden floor as he dropped to sit and draped his forearms around his legs. "Make sure you don't touch a drop of booze. Then sit down and imagine the biggest greenhouse you could ever need. I mean *ever*. Then multiply the size by three and be prepared to build the next one in, oh, two or three years."

"You can't be serious." Either her imagination was out of control, or his eyes were trained on her thighs where they probably showed a clear outline through the thin cotton shirt. She didn't move a muscle.

"Suit yourself, girl." He wiped the back of a hand over his forehead. "It's the honest way I figured it out. My dad didn't tell me much, but he did give me his greenhouse formula."

"Your father liked to raise orchids, too?" This was the

closest to a story about a family tradition Peter had ever mentioned.

"He liked to garden. And he raised palms and yucca." The hand shaded his face, but Jennie couldn't shake the sensation that Peter was examining her, inch by inch. "Come on. You volunteered to help, and the light's going to start failing soon. Let's move it."

He did move it, rapidly getting to his feet and turning his back on her. There was something...

"I never knew my father," Jennie said.

Peter, bending around a stud, glanced at her. "I didn't realize that. I knew both your folks were dead."

"Dad was killed in a sawmill accident a month before I was born. That was in Oregon. My mother moved when I was around two—to Chicago and then various other places. She was diabetic and never looked after herself. She died when I was twenty-one."

"Funny, isn't it," Peter said. He faced her and perched on what would become a window rim. "At least, I think it is. We tend to want our children to have whatever we think we needed and didn't get ourselves. Don't you think that's true?"

"Yes. It's frustrating when it doesn't work, though."

Peter swung the hammer between his knees. He was grimy now, with sawdust in his hair and on his chest, where his unbuttoned shirt clung to patches of sweat. Jennie liked looking at him, being with him like this. With Peter there was no need for subterfuge or posturing.

Quiet and calm settled. Peter raised his lucid eyes to hers, and she wondered what he was thinking. A shadow moved over his face, and Jennie glanced at the sky where a cloud, driven by the breeze, slunk across dimming blue. When she returned her attention to Peter, light followed the shadow, shone gold on his jaw, the dimpled groove in the hollow of his cheek, the upturned corners and clear lines of his mouth.

Jennie jiggled the nails in her hand, searching for something to say. "You seem to be forever adding to this place, Peter. Inside or outside."

"Yep. Sort of a compulsion, I suppose. In the back of my mind there must be a need to create permanency here."

It had never struck Jennie that Peter might not feel secure. She laughed uncomfortably. "We seem to be going in opposite directions with our homes. You're going up, and I'm planning to scale down."

His stare became unfocused. "I've always wanted children," he said, more as if speaking to himself than to Jennie. "The original idea behind the master suite on the third floor was because... Oh, I don't know. I kind of thought it would be nice to have plenty of space even when...if I did have kids."

"Sounds logical." Jennie found herself a spot on the low wall and hitched herself up. "I never thought I'd want to give up our house. And I may not do it, but it sure makes sense."

"I think it's a bad idea," Peter said abruptly. He returned to work with a fresh flurry of energy. "Families need to belong somewhere. I often think that's a problem in this country—no place to go back to that's always been there. You know, a place where you've got roots."

When he talked like this, he created doubts she didn't want to confront. "That's all very well if life doesn't throw you any curves, Peter. I'm on my own now." She moved closer with the nails and quickly added, "I wouldn't have chosen to become a widow, obviously. But I like what I've done with my options. I like the independence."

He paused but didn't turn around. After a few moments he said, "Good. I'm glad you've got what you want."

Jennie felt...disapproval? Sometimes she forgot Peter was Australian and had some of the stereotypical attitudes the males of his culture were reported to have toward women's roles. He probably didn't think she should be happy making her own way.

She continued handing him nails. There were times when she didn't enjoy being alone, but she wouldn't admit that, not to Peter. His silence now, the unapproachable wall his broad back had subtly become, filled her with defiance.

An hour went by. The day's brilliance began to dim, and

although Peter appeared not to notice the rapid drop in temperature, Jennie shivered. Wood dust clogged her nails and clung to her skin.

"Nail."

She slapped one into his hand. "I'm getting good at this." Even if her nose was starting to run. "Scalpel? Retractor? Swab? Can I interest you in a suture?"

"Just keep the nails coming."

He was so intent on whatever he became involved with. At the lab she knew the technicians respected and admired him, but they also regarded him as driven, just as Mark had been. Jennie hunched her shoulders. Peter had never made a secret of the fact that his ex-wife had tired of his preoccupation with his work. Living with dozens of orchids might have become wearing, too, and falling over all the other debris Peter seemed to create almost without moving from one spot.

"That's it," he said, standing and flexing his legs. "The light isn't so good anymore. Can't see what I'm hitting anymore either and I need my fingers."

"And I *don't* need pneumonia," Jennie said, sniffing.

"Ah, grief. Why didn't you say something?" Rapidly he packed away tools in a metal case. "You'll catch your death, girl. I always get carried away—you know that."

With a hand on the back of her neck, he marched them along the path and into the house.

On one kitchen wall an incongruous clock featuring a pink neon cat, its tail clicking away the seconds, showed seven-thirty. "I'll run up and change," Jennie said.

"No. You'll want a shower before you put your suit on. I'll give you a coat to wear home over the shirt." He loped into the hallway as if there were no question of argument, and she trailed along to watch him piling logs into the living-room fireplace.

"Warm up and have a drink," he said. "In that order. Shove everything off this chair and get close to the fire."

To refuse would be ungrateful, and she didn't want to, anyway. She did as he asked, stacking books and magazines on the floor with as much nonchalance as she could muster. Peter was undeniably a slob.

He was also accustomed to being alone. For stretches of minutes he seemed to forget that he had company.

The fire was roaring when Killer put in an appearance. Slinking from the hall and bypassing Peter without a glance, she sat at Jennie's feet and allowed herself to be stroked.

Peter got up, grumbled unintelligibly in the cat's direction and left the room.

Jennie slid back in the chair. He might be afraid to buy paintings, but he had great taste and color sense. All the right things lay beneath the disorder in this room. Rough white-plastered walls wouldn't have occurred to most people, but they created airy space. Modular sectional furnishings in beige, glass-topped tables through which rich shades of burgundy glowed in rugs scattered over pale wood were all beautiful. Jennie rested her head and mentally removed clutter. A vague notion to at least tidy a few spots was scuttled by Peter's return.

"Sorry to be so long." He'd obviously accomplished the feat of taking a shower, combing his hair and throwing on clean clothes in less than ten minutes.

"It's okay. But I should be going."

"Not yet. You're having a drink." He paused en route to the cart. "Are you hungry?"

"No, thank you."

"I'll get some cheese and fruit in a minute."

He didn't appear to notice her discomfort. Did he notice *anything* about her? She'd once been an accepted fixture in his life and appeared to have slipped easily back into the role.

"Gin and tonic?"

He remembered.

"Just tonic, I think. I've got things to do when I get home."

"You won't lose your head on one drink."

"No, but—"

"Tonic won't warm you up." He eyed her critically. "You looked pinched."

"Thanks."

"Brandy." It wasn't a question.

Jennie whistled soundlessly and let him give her the drink he'd decided upon. One of the better things about being single again was that, most of the time, no one presumed to know best what she wanted or needed.

After ten minutes spent with only Killer for company, she was presented with a plate and offered a tray of fruit and sliced cheese. She took several pieces. Peter's face showed serious concentration that might have been amusing were she not growing increasingly uncomfortable with silence.

He poured himself a drink and settled, cross-legged, beside Killer, who promptly wrapped herself around Jennie's feet as if desperate to put even a few more inches between herself and an adversary.

"What do you think of the greenhouse?"

Jennie, her mouth full of cheese, swallowed several times. "Lovely."

"You should have one at your place."

She stared at his bowed head. Moisture beaded his hair and dampened the collar of his gray shirt. "Why would I want a greenhouse?" And had he forgotten she was thinking of selling?

His broad shoulders rose and fell before he took a long swallow from his glass. "If you want to be happy for a few hours, get drunk. If you want to be happy for a weekend, get married. If you want to be happy all your life, be a gardener."

She laughed explosively, choking on a sip of brandy that burned every millimeter of her esophagus.

"You can laugh," he said, turning an unconvincingly serious face up to hers. "That, girl, is an old Chinese proverb, and I'll tell you it's a true one."

"If you say so. I think you're thinking up sneaky ways of getting that second greenhouse without using your garden."

"Caught," he said, smiling.

Swirling the liquor in his glass, he settled his elbows on his thighs.

Ticking. Another clock, this one an elegant brass piece, rotated inside a glass dome.

"How are things going at the lab?" She almost stopped breathing. Those words used to be her reflexive evening greeting to Mark.

"Fine. I try to forget work on the weekends."

The response startled her, and she didn't believe him. Firelight moved over his profile, the rigid and uncharacteristic downturn of his mouth. He had become perfectly still, staring into the flames. She would be left to guess what was really on his mind, but whatever series of experiments he was involved with were there—she knew the signs too well.

"My orchid's doing well."

"Mmm. Do you mist it?"

"I bought a spray bottle—"

"And you do it in the morning?"

"Yes."

"Good. When the blooming's over, I'll store the plant here for you. I'm going to give you Waikiki Gold next. You'll like that."

She'd like not to feel as if they were making conversation. "Thank you." The lighthearted ease of their afternoon in the city had waned.

"More brandy?"

"No, thank you." What she'd already drunk caused a warming in her limbs, a relaxing of muscle, but one drink had always been about her limit.

"What time is Carl planning to have the boys back?"

Jennie stirred and sat forward. "Any time now, I'd think. I should be there."

Instead of getting up, he offered her a hand, and she automatically laced her fingers in his.

"Thanks for a lovely day," he said. "You're good for me, Jennie."

Unsure what to say, she concentrated on the pressure from his powerful hand, the corded tendons in his muscular forearm. It felt so good to be with him.

"Do you know how much it means to me to spend time with you again?"

Thoughts tumbled over each other. What she wanted, knew

she wanted, collided with what she felt—that she didn't want to face a time when she and Peter might drift apart again. But he would move on toward what he wanted—a wife and his own children. Jennie would continue to follow her newfound path.

"Jennie, we've gotten over…we're all right now, aren't we?"

She rarely cried, but her eyes filled now. "Of course we are. And I'm very glad." And very confused.

For seconds he turned their joined hands this way and that, stroking their palms together. How could he not know how sensual the touching of their skin was? Jennie could only let herself feel and watch. What would he say if he knew how many times she'd visualized his face, his lean and very male body, since they'd last been together? She swallowed, vaguely disoriented. Until this moment she hadn't allowed herself to acknowledge that she was becoming preoccupied with him.

He met her eyes. Jennie ran her tongue along her bottom lip, and the intent green gaze flickered to her mouth and back.

"We enjoy each other. That's what I want, Jennie. More time for us to enjoy."

"I—" This was dangerous. She must not make a fool of herself by letting him see she was torn in her famous quest for independence. "You've always been very kind." Removing her hand, she smiled.

Peter didn't smile. His gaze moved fleetingly over her before he turned to the fire. She saw a muscle in his jaw tense.

Enough warning signals. Regardless of their individual goals for the future, it would be so easy to respond to each other physically, when they were both lonely and…and, yes, attracted to each other. They weren't kids. That attraction was something they didn't need to talk about to know it existed.

"What are you thinking about?"

Jennie started. She hadn't felt him look at her. "Oh, nothing, really." Smoothing the shirt, she got up, dislodging Killer, who flew to a corner as if wounded. "I want to get back before the boys do."

He turned to see the clock. "You've got time. Would you be more comfortable taking a shower before you go?"

No, no, no. "I really must go. I'll borrow that coat, I think. Would you mind getting my things? I don't walk so well in these thongs." And she didn't want to go back into his bedroom.

Without a word Peter left, to return minutes later with her shoes in one hand, her dress draped over the other arm. Her hose and lacy white slip trailed. Jennie turned hot. With as much nonchalance as she could muster, she took the clothes and rolled them up. There was no choice but to switch the thongs for her shoes.

In the hall Peter helped her into a tan raincoat, insisting she needed it to keep warm.

They walked to the Lotus, and he helped her in. Peter got in, and the low-slung car swept quietly from the driveway to the street to pass through gathering darkness toward Eden Park.

Jennie kept her arms tightly wrapped around her bundle of clothes. There could be no mistaking the tense awareness she felt between them, an electricity neither was prepared to face head-on. She could almost hear him thinking, as she was, that they were in danger of passing over that intangible line where friendship turned into something much more. Just how dangerous would it be if that happened—for both of them, or at least for Jennie?

"I used to fish," Peter said. "Deep-sea, out of Cairns. That's northeastern Australia. One of the jumping-off spots for the Great Barrier Reef."

Jennie glanced at him, grateful for any subject that would break the awkwardness. "I'd like to see the reef."

"You'd love it," he said, the light of a passing car washing over his face, throwing the lines into clear, handsome relief. "Maybe I'll be able to take you sometime."

Doubtful, Jennie thought, not without longing. The idea of being with Peter in the sun, carefree on foreign and fascinating waters, held more magnetism than it should. But even she could fantasize, couldn't she?

"Looks like the wanderers have returned," Peter remarked when her house was in sight. Every light blazed, as was the pattern when the boys were home alone.

"I hope they've had a good time," Jennie said. And she wished she didn't want so forcefully, not to have to leave Peter.

"I'll come in and say hi."

Instantly her insides flew into spasm. "You'll need to get back home."

"I've got time."

Short of making a big deal out of Steven's illogical dislike of Peter, there was no excuse she could come up with to say no.

Just outside the gates, Peter drew the car to the curb and switched off. "Do you mind if we wait a few minutes before going in?"

Jennie pressed her arm to her middle against a tightness there. She shook her head.

"You had a good time today, didn't you Jen?"

"Yes," she said quietly. "You know I did."

"I'm...very fond of you."

She could hardly breathe. "I'm fond of you, too, Peter."

"I wondered if we could make a kind of a pact. Only if you want to, of course." He swallowed loudly enough for Jennie to hear, and she took courage from knowing he was as anxious as she.

"Tell me about this pact." She raised her face to his.

Peter hesitated, then slowly ran a forefinger down her temple and cheek. He stroked back her hair and rested his hand on her neck, his thumb moving gently back and forth on her jaw. "I'm not sure how to put it. Could we start by saying we'll try spending some time together—more time together? And could we promise to be honest if we feel it isn't working?"

Jennie could hear her own heart. They'd already admitted how different their goals were. Was this a proposition that they move toward a physical relationship with no permanent strings attached?

She couldn't simply refuse. There was potential trouble here, but the draw he held for her was strong enough to make the risks seem worthwhile.

"Jennie? What are you thinking?"

"That I should probably say no and run like hell, only I'm not going to. I can't."

Peter laughed, tipping back his head in the abandoned way she loved. "Lady, you just said what I've been thinking ever since I decided I was going to have to ask the question. But I knew I'd ask it, anyway. Good. I like your reaction. Good buddies we'll be. When one of us wants out, the other won't die of a broken heart, right?"

"Right," she agreed, but she wasn't laughing.

"Shake—" He leaned closer. "No, we won't shake on it. If you'll let me, I'd like to kiss you instead."

Jennie looked into his eyes, glanced up at the glinting hair that fell over his forehead, down at the dimpled groove in his cheek and on to his sensual, slightly open mouth. Even her blood seemed to have stopped moving. She closed her eyes and said, "Yes."

He bowed over her, his lips coming so close she felt his light breath. Jennie squeezed her eyes more tightly shut. This was Peter—it was all right. Or wasn't it all right because it was Peter?

Their mouths met softly, not with passion but with an infinite sweetness that made her tremble. Peter pulled her closer, holding her firmly but gently against him while he played the kiss on, moving his lips over hers, touching his teeth to her bottom lip in a suggestion of deeper possession. The tip of his tongue slipped to the corner of her mouth before he drew back his head and smiled. Again he bent toward her to rest his cheek on hers while he stroked her hair.

"Thank you, Jennie," he whispered.

"Thank you." She spread her fingers over his neck and jaw, ran them over his cheek.

"Let's go and see those boys of yours."

Jennie roused slowly from the drugged sensation he'd invoked. "I'll go alone."

"No, you won't." As he spoke, he opened his door. "If we're going to make good on that pact, other changes will have to be made around here, and we might as well get started."

She kept her arms around her clothes, grateful for an excuse not to hold his hand when they'd be confronting Steven. There were definitely changes to be made in that area, but she'd rather approach them from a position of strength.

The garage door stood open, with both cars inside. The boys weren't in the kitchen and didn't answer when Jennie called.

"Listen," Peter said. "They're in the backyard."

What Jennie heard was Steven's voice raised in anger, and she sighed.

"Hey," Peter said, giving her a quick hug. "They're just having a sibling-type argument. Don't look for trouble. You change, and I'll go see what's up."

"I don't think—"

"Well, I do." He turned her around and gave her a playful swat on the bottom. "Go. Or you'll have questions to answer about why you're coming home with me in that getup."

Jennie grimaced. "You're right. But don't take any guff from Steven. If he's rude, walk away and—"

"I'm capable of looking after myself, Jen," he told her, the amusement in his eyes coming as a gentle reproof.

"Yes." How right he was, Jennie decided. She only hoped she was just as capable.

PETER STOPPED when he reached the path leading to the back patio. Both boys were intent on their task. Or Bobby was intent while Steven watched and delivered scathing epithets about his brother's lack of skill. The task in hand appeared to be the mutilation of several fish.

"Get the head off first," Steven said loudly.

"Why don't you?" Bobby rotated the globby mess beneath his hands and tried valiantly to do as he'd been told. The knife he used looked suspiciously like Jennie's silver carver.

"Want any help?" Peter sauntered forward, deliberately smiling when Steven turned around.

"We've got it," Steven said, but Peter noticed a lack of the boy's usual bravado.

"Hi, Peter," Bobby said, rubbing the back of a forearm over his eyes. Both he and Steven were grubby and crumpled.

"Mom's not here," Steven said, his eyes characteristically narrowed. The changing colors and sutures on the right side of his face did nothing to improve his appearance.

"She's upstairs changing," Peter said. The time had come for a new strategy. "We've been working on my green house."

Steven stared, his mouth mutinously set.

"Mom was helping with that?" Bobby grinned. "I'd like to have seen her."

"Next time you'll have to come, too."

Steven's wall of dislike was still firmly in place, so Peter concentrated on Bobby. "Is that a bluegill?"

"Yeah. The others are crappie. We didn't get any bass, but we had a ball, didn't we, Steve?"

"If you say so."

"You sure I can't help?" Peter persisted. "I used to fish myself."

"We know what we're doing," Steven said.

"Oh, sure." Bobby made a face at his brother. "What's with the 'we'? I don't see you doing anything, and it was you who told Carl we could manage."

"What was I supposed to say with Lou carrying on about how late we got back and how she needed him at home?"

Bobby tossed down what Peter was now certain had to be a silver carving knife. "Well, you do it."

"Hold on, sport." Peter took his trusty Swiss Army knife from his back pocket and flipped open its well-worn blade. "Let me have a go."

Bobby stood back while Peter sawed away the head and tail and neatly slit and laid open the bluegill's body. "Steven," he said over his shoulder. "Take your mother's good knife in and dispose of the evidence before she sees it. There's a good chap.''

In the following moment's hesitation, he expected the boy to refuse.

"Where's it go?" Steven said to Bobby. "You got it out."

"In the buffet in the dining room," Bobby said, hanging so far over Peter's hands that he could hardly see what he was doing.

"Oh, hell," Steven muttered. "That's the good stuff, you idiot. She'll have a cow." He snatched up the knife and headed for the kitchen door.

Peter spared a satisfied glance at his retreating back. Evidently he still cared what his mother thought about some things. A good sign.

"This knife isn't really right, either," he told Bobby. "Much too small. But it's sharp and it'll do. Here, slip down behind the backbone and pry it loose."

Bobby eagerly did as he was told, standing back to hold the fish's skeleton aloft. "Did it." He slid another fish toward him and went through the steps Peter had shown him.

Footsteps let Peter know Steven had returned, but he pretended to concentrate on what Bobby was doing. "How was the camping?"

"Great," Bobby said, looking up with a flushed face. "We had a fire both nights. It was cool."

"Did I ever tell you about the time I went camping with a mate and woke up—"

"With a kangaroo sitting on your belly." Bobby guffawed.

"Yes, well, I guess I did tell that story."

Steven inched in closer to Bobby. "Let me have a go," he said, his face firmly kept down.

"Sure." Ever good-natured, Bobby handed his brother the knife. "Head and tail first."

"I know," Steven automatically answered, and did a creditable job. He slit open the belly, then hesitated.

Peter reached around him, covered his right hand and showed him how to slip the knife behind the backbone. "Ease it up," he said. "Like this." They worked together, Peter guiding Steven, deliberately anchoring their shoulders together.

"Good show!" He put distance between them. "You two are naturals at this. The three of us should go out some time. Would you go for that?"

"You bet," Bobby said, grinning.

Steven dragged the last fish toward him.

"How about you, Steve."

The boy pulled his shoulders up inside his sweatshirt. "I don't know. Maybe."

Maybe? Peter didn't make a sound, didn't smile. Playing it cool was called for in these moments of minute triumph.

A slight sound made him look up. Jennie stood in the kitchen doorway. Their eyes met, and she smiled before backing silently away.

Peter drew in a long breath. Jennie could come to mean a great deal to him. She already did, but not in the way he was beginning to feel he wanted.

"This okay, Peter?" Steven said.

"Great." He hardly looked at the fish.

The possibility for disaster loomed larger and larger. Should he try to head it off, or march ahead, praying they wouldn't all end up bloodied? Instinct warned him he'd probably forfeited his choice.

CHAPTER EIGHT

This was a mistake. She'd known it was a mistake even as she'd allowed Lou to bully her into going to the wretched neighborhood party.

Jennie glared at the jumbled heap of clothes on her bed. Nothing felt right for the occasion, and the unexpected warm spell wasn't helping. She'd just have to call and say she couldn't make it.

She sat amid the confusion, staring at the phone. If she was honest with herself, she'd admit that the main problem was Peter. They'd had lunch once during the week, spoken several times on the phone, but she wanted to spend more time with him. And today would have been their day together if it hadn't been for Lou's famous party. Could she call him and say she was free after all?

"Mom!"

Steven. He'd left to study at a friend's house less than an hour ago. Wrapping her robe more tightly about her, she went to the top of the stairs. "Hi. What are you doing back so soon?"

"I need to talk to you, Mom." He was calling from the direction of the kitchen, and she couldn't see him.

Jennie took a deep, apprehensive breath. "Give me a few minutes."

Among that heap on the bed there was at least one outfit that would be fine. She would find it and she would go to the party, even if only to put in an appearance.

The dress she decided on was white piqué with black polka dots. Small buttons closed a tight bodice with a low, scalloped neckline. A full skirt and black belt did wonderful things for her small waist and her legs. The bodice could be a little low.... She wouldn't change one more time. Quickly, trying not too successfully to put longing thoughts of a relaxed afternoon with Peter out of her mind, she pulled her hair into a very high knot off center from her crown, leaving wisps of curls loose around her face.

She must hurry. Three was when she was supposed to be there. Dinner, a barbecue, would be started at five. Three had already come and gone.

Low-heeled fabric shoes, also white with black dots, made her feel young and comfortable. Her makeup was fine, and she looked...not so bad for an old lady. She smiled. She might be old, but lately she'd been feeling happier and more sure of herself by the day.

For a last instant before setting out, she stood before a full-length mirror on the back of her bedroom door. How odd to be going to a party on her own. Peter came into her mind again. She saw his fine eyes, the way he shrugged his big shoulders inside his shirt, the fit of his jeans on lean hips, his long, long legs. What would he think of her outfit? She felt herself color and lowered her head. Peter wasn't a man who seemed to notice such things. And he'd accepted her refusal of his invitation for today without argument. He seemed comfortable with whatever happened between them. She chewed her lip. This was what she wanted, someone fun to do things with who didn't want to own all of her...wasn't it?

"Mom!"

"Coming." A small black purse was the last thing she grabbed before speeding out and trotting downstairs.

"Geez, Mom, what took so long?" Without as much as a glance in her direction, Steven marched back and forth, looking repeatedly at his watch. "We gotta get going."

"You look very nice, Mrs. Andrews." Gigi Burns's pale, serious face turned up to Jennie from the spot where she sat cross-legged on the floor.

Jennie, not expecting to see the girl, cast a hard stare in Steven's direction. He appeared oblivious.

"Thanks, Gigi. Er—" She'd almost made the automatic

response that Gigi looked nice, too, but the girl, in tight pale blue jeans and a too-large white shirt that looked suspiciously like one of Steven's, appeared drawn.

"We wanted to let you know we're going to the jazz concert in Eden Park." Steven braced his feet apart and hooked his thumbs into his pockets.

Jennie frowned. "You went over to Robbie's to study. What happened to that?"

"Something came up."

"What?"

"I told you. The jazz concert." He didn't just sound truculent; anger simmered in him.

"Your grades could use some work."

"Why? I'll graduate."

A churning anxiety gnawed in her stomach. "Steven, graduating from high school isn't supposed to be the zenith of your ambition."

"Cut the big words, Mom. We—"

"Don't speak to me like that." She glanced at Gigi, whose blue eyes were wide in a rapidly flushing face. Why on earth would Steven do this in front of a stranger?

Jennie leaned against the island in the center of the kitchen and regarded her shoes. "I'm due at a party next door. I don't appreciate your springing things on me. You know that."

"Gigi needs a break...." He broke off, and when Jennie stared at him he turned his head away. "We both do."

The door from the side yard opened, and Bobby came in. He wore his new jeans and topsiders with the oversize lime-green-and-black shirt he'd wheedled her into buying. Dressed for an occasion. Jennie frowned again.

"Look." Steven dropped his voice to a normal pitch. "There's no big deal here. A nice little outing. We've already invited Bobby and afterward we'll go out for chili. Think about it, Mom, the nuisances off your hands for most of the day."

"You are not nuisances to me." She resented the tactics he used, his attempts to put her on the defensive. "I'm not sure this is a good idea."

Gigi got to her feet, pushing straight, waist-length blond hair behind her shoulders. "We'll be careful," she said, and Jennie thought, not for the first time, that the girl seemed too serious and perhaps too sad for a sixteen-year-old. "We'll stay together."

"Why is it so important?" There was an air of desperation here that tied Jennie in knots. "Why not go downtown? There's a food fair on."

"We don't want to go to a food fair!" Steven's shouting was becoming a habit. "There's a reason why.... We *like* jazz, okay? Simple as that. Why are you making such a big deal out of everything these days?"

Jennie raised a brow at his tone, but maybe she was too protective. Sooner or later she'd have to start letting go. "Okay. Go. But be careful."

"We will," Gigi said quietly. "We'll be very careful."

Jennie's eyes traveled to the rolled-up sleeves of the shirt, and she drew in her bottom lip. Barely visible on each arm were purplish bruises.

"I've never been to a jazz concert," Bobby said, grinning.

"No, you haven't," Jennie said slowly. "Stay close to Steven and Gigi."

"Sure."

Gigi's pretty face had grown closed, and she put her arms behind her back. She'd noticed Jennie's glance.

"What happened to you, Gigi? The bruises." From the corner of her eye she saw Steven move toward the girl, who shook her head slightly.

"Gigi—"

"It's okay, Steve. Your mom already knows."

"I already know what?"

The blue eyes didn't meet Jennie's. Gigi giggled nervously. "Steve did it. He was trying to stop me from getting hurt."

"Gigi!"

"It's okay, Steve," Gigi said loudly. Bright pink had spread to her neck as well as her face. "When those boys attacked Steven that night, he was afraid I'd get in the middle.

He grabbed my arms and pushed me out of the way. That's all. It doesn't hurt.''

A nasty slow thudding pelted Jennie's temples. "Two weeks ago? At the teen club?''

Gigi smiled. "That's right. At the club.''

AT FOUR O'CLOCK, having watched Steven and Gigi drive away in the Honda with Bobby in the back seat, Jennie locked the front door and walked over to the Ramstets'.

Voices, laughing female screeches, came from the backyard. Jennie went around the house. Steven had promised they'd be back around ten, and she'd be waiting. If only Gigi hadn't lied about whatever happened on that Thursday night.

"Jennie!" A big, sandy-haired man with pink skin held together by ruddy freckles bore down on her. "How the hell are you? Another five minutes, and we were coming to carry you here if necessary.''

She smiled at Hank Simpson with all the enthusiasm she could muster. A district sales manager with the same electronics firm where Carl was an engineer, Hank was a decent man despite his overly hearty manner. "Hi, there, Hank. Good to see you. Where's Eileen?''

He waved pudgy hands. "Somewhere around.'' His laugh moved a big belly, and Jennie couldn't avoid a thought about his health. "How're the boys? You should bring them over. It'll be time to get the pool in order soon. They always liked that.''

"Yes, they did. Thank you.''

Carl worked over the barbecue coals, sweating slightly, an obviously new red-and-white-checked apron tied around him. On the front, Cooks Do It Better was embroidered in black. A not very original gift from one of the guests, Jennie supposed. She should have brought something.

"Hi, Jennie,'' Carl said when he saw her. "We were getting worried about you. Nice of the weather to cooperate, huh? Lou's in the kitchen. We'll eat out here.''

Ray Reid saluted her with a beer can and showed his perfect white teeth. Wings of gray at his temples slashed through black curly hair, and his height had become camouflage for extra pounds. "Good to see you, Jennie," he said.

"You, too." She hovered, unsure what to say or do. Today she was very aware that she and Mark had been the youngest of the group. Yet she was the first left alone.

"Well—" she backed away, sidestepped "—good to see you. There must be something I'm needed for in the kitchen."

In the distance a group threw horseshoes, and she heard their alternating cries of triumph and frustration.

"...Steven. Boys can be a handful without enough supervision," were the words she heard as she stepped through the open door into the newly renovated burgundy-and-gray kitchen. "She'd better be on the—"

"Hi, Jennie!" Lou yelled as if drowning out deafening noise rather than the one belonging to Maryanne Reid, who, Jennie had no doubt, had been talking about her.

"Sorry I'm late," Jennie said with a smile that cost her too much. "All this sun threw me off. I guess it's time to put away the winter woollies."

"How are you, Jennie?" Maryanne of the violet eyes and permanent moue batted heavily mascaraed lashes in slow doleful sweeps. Unfortunately she didn't have enough height to carry the spread of recent years, and her pink floral shirtwaist dress strained at the seams.

Jennie wet her lips and realized with irritation that she was nervous. "I'm fine, thank you."

Maryanne came closer and took Jennie's hands in hers. Diamonds glittering on her fingers matched those in her ears. Jennie noted that Maryanne had decided to keep her shoulder-length hair platinum at any cost.

For seconds the woman gazed into Jennie's eyes before she said, "Oh, Jennie, you don't have to cover up with us. I'm one of your oldest friends, remember. How are you really?"

Nervousness gave way to irritation. "I'm wonderful, really I am." For Lou's sake she wouldn't tell this phony to get lost.

"We're eating outside," Lou said, sounding flustered. She wore a fluorescent purple muumuu bought in Hawaii several years previously. Jennie disliked the dress, but Lou appeared comfortable and that was all that mattered.

"I suppose the little business helps," Maryanne continued, undaunted. "But that kind of thing can't fill all the spaces, can it?"

Jennie kept her mouth firmly closed and turned it up in a smile.

Maryanne sighed. "You always were so brave. Oh, I almost forgot, did you talk to John Astly?"

"Maryanne." Lou looked up from tossing a green salad, and the hint of warning in her voice surprised Jennie.

"I didn't see John or Marcie," Jennie said of the Astlys. She had seen John a few days earlier, when they'd had a wardrobe consultation.

"This is fate," Maryanne said, hands fluttering. "Don't you think so, Lou?"

Lou's mouth formed a shush that Jennie obviously wasn't supposed to see, and Maryanne deepened her moue in response.

Whatever the coded conversation was about, Jennie had a feeling she was the object and that she'd be less irritated if she didn't hear. "I'll carry these out," she said, seizing a tray of glasses.

"Marcie left John," Maryanne said, stepping into Jennie's path. "What do you think of that? She's filing for divorce. After all he's done for her. Can you believe it?"

Jennie didn't like the gossipy tone of this conversation. "I'm sorry to hear that."

"Well—" Maryanne shrugged and didn't meet Jennie's eyes "—men will be men. We all know that. I'm sure it was the only time he went astray. Anyway, Marcie's already got someone else."

Jennie almost said "Good for Marcie." John might be a customer who had once been part of her social circle, but he'd always been slightly too familiar. When she'd last seen him, he'd suggested they have lunch, and Jennie had gracefully slid out of the situation.

"Talk to him, Jennie," Maryanne said. "He's really depressed."

Sure. Depressed because he'd played around and it was costing him. "I really don't know what I could say to him." She didn't add what she was sure they didn't know, that John was a customer and she didn't believe business and personal relationships mixed particularly well.

"I'm sure you'll think of something." Maryanne swept a glance to Jennie's feet and back. "It might be worth the effort. The right kind of man isn't available too often."

Isn't available? Jennie looked for Lou's reaction, but her face was bent over the salad as if her task took great concentration. Jennie moved purposefully past Maryanne and escaped to the blessedly wide outdoors. *John Astly?* Both Maryanne and Lou had said in the past that Marcie was a blind fool if she didn't divorce him. Jennie couldn't figure out why they would try to push her at him.

Even as she thought, John appeared from the direction of the horseshoe pit. He waved and broke into a trot, drawing close as she set the tray down on a red-and-white-checkered tablecloth atop the picnic table.

"I thought I saw a gorgeous vision arrive."

Before she could get out of his way, he gathered her in his arms and planted a kiss on her mouth. She stood still, eyes wide open and staring, until he released her.

"Will you look at you?" he said, holding her shoulders and standing back to survey her, inch by inch, as if they hadn't spent two hours together a week ago. "I swear, Jennie, you get sexier every time I see you." Boyishly handsome, California-blond and muscular, John expected women to melt in his presence. Jennie felt frozen. She would have expected their business dealings to make him more circumspect.

"Nothing to say?" He tilted his head and allowed a lazy, suggestive smile to hover at the corners of a too-beautiful mouth. "You always were quiet. It's part of your mystery. But you know that, don't you, baby?"

Jennie took a step backward. "I hear Marcie left you. You didn't mention it at our last meeting."

"A guy doesn't like to whine." He wrinkled his nose. "I can't pretend I don't feel bad, though. It wasn't what I wanted, but *c'est la vie* and all that. I've been thinking about you. I really think you can go places with your venture." With one blunt forefinger he quickly traced the neckline of her dress to the cleavage between her full breasts. He laughed when she knocked his hand away.

Jennie looked around. Their position effectively blocked her from anyone else's view. "I bet they could use your help at the grill," she said tightly. "Or maybe Hank would let you go over and swim in his pool. He said something about getting it ready for summer, but it should still be pretty cold."

He shook the fingers of one hand. "Ouch. Still prickly, are we? The time comes to reevaluate positions, baby. You're alone and so am I. From where I'm standing, it seems it's easier for me to do something about that than you. Think about it. We could have some good times." He leaned closer. "And—if I can see it's worth my while—I can throw a lot of business your way."

"Hi, Jennie. Lou told me you were out here."

Peter's voice jarred Jennie to her toes. Relief overwhelmed her.

"Am I interrupting something?"

He must have gone to the front door and come through the house. Jennie wondered how much of her exchange with John he'd overhead.

"What a lovely surprise, Peter," she said, a cool eye on John. "You weren't interrupting a thing. John's a client of mine. We can have any necessary discussions during work hours, can't we?"

"If you say so," John said, not quite hiding truculence. "We've met, haven't we?" he added to Peter.

Peter, less than informally dressed in an old blue striped shirt and worn jeans, rested his weight on one leg. "Have we? I don't remember." The unspoken message was that he didn't want to remember.

"Did you say hi to Carl?" Jennie clamped a hand on Peter's forearm, urging him away. She didn't like the combative gleam in his eye and was certain he'd heard at least something of John's attempted advance.

"No," Peter said as they walked away from John, silent and watchful now, and moved in the direction of the barbecue. "Let's make it fast. The atmosphere isn't healthy around here."

Jennie bit her lip. So he had heard.

"Hi, there, Peter," Carl hailed as they drew close. "Didn't expect to see you. You've been missed around here." He turned hamburger patties and slathered on thick sauce.

"I've been away," Peter said noncommittally. "Actually I can't stay. It's good to see you. I'll just have a few words with Lou and cut out."

Jennie's stomach turned. She went with him toward the house. "What are you doing here?" Not that she cared—she only wanted to be with him.

"I came because Lou said you were here. She got a message to me on my call forwarding. I was working at the lab. Why didn't you say this was where you were going today?" He halted, his hands deep in his pockets. "I thought you were making an excuse when you said you weren't free."

"Why would I do that?"

Peter looked down at her. "Because you didn't want to spend time with me."

"Oh, Peter." She held his forearm and smiled. "I didn't tell you I was coming here because I didn't think to. And I've been furious all day because I'd *wanted* to be with you but I'd already agreed to come."

"You're sure?"

"So sure you wouldn't believe it," she told him, not caring that she sounded as vulnerable to him as she felt. "But I don't understand why Lou didn't tell me she was inviting you."

"Neither do I." They walked slowly, arm in arm, toward the kitchen.

"You imagine things." Lou's voice came to Jennie clearly.

"In a dress like that?" Maryanne Reid responded. "I don't envy you, Lou. At least the rest of us don't have her parading her assets right next door."

Jennie stopped and glanced down at herself. Peter had stiffened at her side and taken her hand in his.

"Jennie's too busy with her boys to be thinking about another man in her life," Lou said, and Jennie silently thanked her friend.

"Is that why you made the sudden call to her doctor buddy?" Maryanne laughed. "Jennie's a man's woman. And I warn you—she's always had a thing for Carl."

Jennie couldn't seem to make her body move.

"Carl's fifteen years older than Jennie," Lou said, and Jennie recognized the breathy quality that meant tension. "Being a friend—helping out with little things—that's what people do for someone they care about."

Little things, Jennie thought, like taking half an hour to fix a faucet.

"Let's go," Peter said quietly. "Now."

"I can hardly wait," Jennie told him. "Let me get my purse."

Moving swiftly, she entered the kitchen and turned to leave just as quickly. "Sorry. I can't stay for dinner." She was down the steps when Lou caught up. "Tell Carl I'm sorry."

"What is it? Why are you leaving?" Lou looked frantically from Jennie to Peter.

Jennie glanced at the sky.

"You know how it is with these men's women, Lou," Peter said. "They can hardly wait to get a guy on his own."

CHAPTER NINE

Peter dropped into his seat, closed the door and gripped the steering wheel. He probably shouldn't have said what he had to Lou. And Jennie was probably about to tell him as much.

She made a choking noise, and he turned toward her. "Are you okay? Look—maybe I shouldn't—"

Her hand came down on his forearm, and she leaned against him. "Did you see her face?" She laughed and wiped away tears of mirth. "Oh, I'm rotten. But Lou had it coming. How could she be so stupid?"

The laughter was infectious. Peter tilted his head against the headrest and grinned. "I thought you were going to give me hell for picking on your neighbor."

"I am, I am. As soon as I can stop laughing. I'm so glad you came. You can't know how I felt back there."

He had a pretty good idea. "The man you were talking to, the one leaning all over you, was the other woman in the kitchen his wife?"

Jennie shook her head. "Uh-uh. That's John Astly. He and his wife are in the middle of a divorce. Actually he's become a client, which may make things awkward."

Peter opened his mouth to say he'd rather she told the guy to get lost, but whistled through his teeth instead. "You'll deal with it. Maybe you should let him know business is booming and you can do without him if he doesn't want to operate on your terms."

"Unfortunately business isn't quite that booming. And I can't afford to risk ending up with a big bill that could be difficult to collect."

Jennie definitely wouldn't appreciate his offering to do the collecting for her. "Give yourself time to think it through. Is there anything you have to do now, Jen, or could we spend some time together?"

"I kind of thought that's what we were going to do."

He smiled at her. "That's one of the problems I have with you. You never speak your mind."

They laughed together and he started the car. "Is it okay if we take a run back to the lab? I was in the middle of something when I got Lou's call and I'd like to finish."

"This is the man who doesn't work on weekends?"

"Okay, make fun of me." He checked over his shoulder and pulled away from the curb. Sunlight scintillated along the still-warm hood of the car, and trees lining the street cast dappled shadows on gleaming black. "I won't be long. Afterward we'll grab a bite to eat."

"Sounds fine." She settled lower in her seat and folded her slim hands in her lap. "Lou called, and you came right over because she said I'd be there?"

"Nah. She mentioned my main addiction—hamburgers. That's what got me."

She rubbed his arm. "Of course. Thanks anyway, Peter. The fact that Lou did call you may make it easier for me to get over what she did to me today—or what she didn't do, I guess. She didn't stand up for me the way she should have."

"Try to forget it."

"I am."

His spirits lifted as he drove. Jennie had that effect on him—made him feel in touch with the best of the real world. Research had been all of his life for too long. He'd lost count of the number of times Liz, and other people he'd admired before her, had warned him of the evils of not making friends. He would turn into a classic example of the absentminded professor, become an insular boor and develop a variety of objectionable habits. He wasn't going to be or do any of those things, but neither would he ever be a gregarious joiner. One friend would be enough, a best friend and lover....

"Can you believe how hot it is?"

Peter kept his eyes on the road. "No." A friend who was a lover, a wife, and children of their own. His spine felt locked. He was mentally testing Jennie in a role she showed no interest in occupying. And Jennie already had a family—and a new career she'd let him know was the intended center of her future.

"Are you okay, Peter?"

He ran his tongue over dry lips. "Sure. Of course. Where are Steven and Bobby today?"

"At a jazz concert." Her tone suggested she wasn't thrilled.

Drawing closer to the city center, they turned south on Race Street. Glare bounced from plate glass windows, and Peter took his sunglasses from the dash. "You mean the concert they advertised for Eden Park?"

"That's the one. I wasn't keen on the idea, but Gigi assured me the three of them would stay together. I'm beginning to realize how fine a line we walk as the parents of teenagers. No limits, and they run wild. Too many limits, and they run wild. I'm praying I'm somewhere in between."

Peter slid on his glasses. "Steven's still seeing Gigi?"

"Yes. I think it's pretty serious between them. As far as I'm concerned, they aren't old enough, but she really is a nice girl. I like her." She hesitated. "Peter, she's got bruises on her arms. Big ones as if she'd been grabbed hard."

He parked, but didn't immediately open his door. "You sound worried."

"I am. When I asked what she'd done, she told me it happened the night Steven got hurt. She said he'd done it when he pushed her out of the way when the other boys attacked him."

"And?"

"This supposedly occurred outside that club, Peter. The one we know wasn't even open."

"Hell." He picked up her hand and rubbed it. Her fingers were cold. "Y'know, it could be that they were in the parking lot, anyway. Maybe we misunderstood that they were saying they'd actually been to a dance there.''

"You know we didn't.''

"It's too late to make an issue of that now,'' he told her. "Whatever happened will probably be a mystery for good, as far as we're concerned. Let's get to the lab and then eat. I'm already starving.''

He had his own key card to the building. As they rode the elevator and went into the lab, he felt the usual comfortable sensation of coming home.

"I've been reviewing some early papers on cancer-causing genes in viruses,'' he said. "Interesting stuff.''

Jennie walked across the room, realized she'd unconsciously risen to her toes and tried to relax. Peter continued to talk, more to himself than to her. He didn't seem to consider that she might find coming here difficult. The last time had been over two years ago, and with Mark.

"The coffee's still on,'' he said. "Pour us both some, will you?''

She did as he asked, moving between the long steel counters topped by shelves crowded with bottles. Next to microscopes, gas valves shone and trailed lengths of tubing for burners. Orange cursors blinked on computer terminals that were never turned off. All so familiar.

Peter accepted his coffee while jamming a micrograph into a viewer. "Dated, but a good shot,'' he murmured, tapping at photographed clusters of cells with a pencil. "See how HIV thrives in the vacuoles of a macrophage? It's hidden from the immune system there.''

"Mmm.'' Jennie wandered away. She had no idea what he was talking about and knew that he didn't need any response from her, anyway.

Angled across a corner of the room, the same couch from Mark's time sagged between old oak tables stamped with white rings left by endless cups and mugs. Jennie perched on the couch and routed through a heap of magazines.

"Good, good.''

She looked up to find Peter smiling at her across the room. "Relax and enjoy yourself while I get through this."

An hour later, having given up on the very technical selection of reading material, Jennie went to a window and looked out at a royal-blue sky. The only sounds came when Peter got up to retrieve data from a computer or to make an entry.

She turned and sat on the sill. With his blond head propped on a fist, he skimmed over sheets of paper, making rapid notes.

And Jennie slipped back in time.

She'd been here before, sat on that couch and waited before, sometimes when she and Mark had been on their way out to dinner and he'd suddenly remembered something he *had* to finish, or when she'd been at the house alone for too long and decided to drop by and surprise him.

If Peter's hair were dark, he could *be* Mark. The fast-moving hand, the total preoccupation, even the set of wide shoulders, were more familiar than Jennie wanted to recognize.

Yes, in many ways, Peter was a repeat of Mark. It wasn't so strange that she should be strongly drawn to the same type of man twice.

She crossed her arms. The room was chilly. In the two years since she'd been widowed, it had been easy to remember only the good from her marriage, but everything hadn't been so rosy. There were many times when she'd felt abandoned. Jennie frowned, feeling guilty that, even now, she should allow self-pity to creep in over something that was finished. But could she handle the same frustration again? She'd better make up her mind.

"What are you thinking about?"

Peter's voice startled her. "That you're very like Mark in some ways," she said without thinking.

"Is that a fact?" He set down his pencil. "How's that?"

"Oh, I don't know." She spread her hands. "It's quiet here and it makes me remember things. I used to feel jealous of this lab. Isn't that ridiculous?"

"Why jealous?"

"Because it was first with Mark. He loved me, but—"
What was she saying? What was the point after so long?

"He had important things to accomplish," Peter said.
"They take time. You have to understand that we often feel
desperate because we know we may never reach our goals."

"And those goals are more important to you than anything
else? More important than living, breathing people?"

He seemed to consider, getting up slowly and coming toward her. "What we do is intended to help living, breathing
people, as you put it. But what I accomplish here will one
day be what I'm remembered for. Doesn't everyone want to
produce something worthwhile? To actually complete the
most important things they start rather than leave ends for
someone else to tie up?"

Somehow they'd moved from Mark to Peter, as if the two
were, in some way, one. "Not everyone cares about mass
recognition. You do." She would not think about, would not
mention that Mark had been forced to leave the very ends
Peter was tying now.

He frowned. "I'm not sure we interpret recognition in the
same way, but yes, I do want what I do to count to a lot of
people."

She stood up and smiled at him. "This is getting too deep
for me. I really should think about getting home. I want to be
there when the kids get back." And she didn't want to continue the conversation.

"Okay," Peter said, but his eyes had sharpened, grown
speculative. "We'll grab a burger as we go, if you like."

She was about to refuse but didn't feel like trying to cover
for her sudden change in mood. "That would be great." This
experience hadn't been a waste; her tinted glasses had been
stripped away where Peter was concerned. Whatever their involvement was destined to be, she'd better be prepared to take
second place to his professional ambition.

When they walked past the foaming, illuminating waters of

the fountains in the square, Peter took her hand and turned in the opposite direction from where the car was parked.

"It's only seven," he said. "I know this fantastic greasy spoon burger stand close to Yeatman Cove. We could wander over there to eat and watch the barges go by."

She had time. "I wonder why 'greasy spoon' sounds like 'gourmet' on your tongue."

Peter chuckled and laced their fingers together. "I feel it's my duty to make sure you don't miss out on important cultural experiences. All those balanced meals can't be good for you."

The city had emptied, and their footsteps were an affront to peace—Peter's a solid, measured thud on the sidewalk, while Jennie's lighter steps sounded in double-time between.

They passed the post office in Government Square and turned down Main Street toward the river. Ahead loomed the dome of Riverfront Stadium.

"Do Steven and Bobby like baseball?"

The breeze had become a wind, and Jennie shivered. "Yes. They like...used to like to go to the games."

Peter drew her to a halt. He took off the jean jacket he'd taken from the car when they went into the lab and put it around her shoulders.

"You'll be cold," she said.

Instead of releasing her, Peter held the sleeves of the jacket and pulled her closer. "I'm not cold."

She felt him watching her. "This—" she had to swallow "—whatever's happening with us wasn't something I'd planned on, Peter."

"Neither had I."

Her skirt whipped against his legs. "Doesn't work, does it? Being buddies?" She rested her hands where his belt met the smooth fabric of his shirt—and felt the lean, warm flesh beneath.

"I doubt it. But we can keep on trying, if you like." Holding both the jacket sleeves in one hand, he stroked back her tossed hair with the other, and breath caught in Jennie's throat.

"What are we really saying here?"

His thumb moved along her jaw to the point of her chin. "Ah, Jennie, you'll always say what's on your mind, won't you? A man could never play guessing games with you."

Jennie looked up at him. His gaze was intense, the lines around his eyes and mouth sharply defined. "Earlier you talked about time, and how we never seem to have enough of it to do all the things we want to do. I guess I've always thought playing games took too much time away from the important stuff."

She knew he was going to kiss her. His lips parted slightly, and his attention flickered from her eyes. Very slowly, very gently, he brought his mouth to hers. His kiss was light, a softly stroking caress of skin on skin, a careful brushing that offered so much but demanded nothing.

The jacket was forgotten. Peter put his arms around her, pulled her to her toes as he bent, totally absorbed. His hands heated her back through the thin cotton dress, and his lips on hers seared every other part.

He raised his head. "I want us to have a chance together, Jen. D'you think that's possible?"

Jennie sighed and sought his mouth once more. This time some of the restraint was gone, replaced by hunger that made her ache. Peter framed her face with his hands and ran his tongue along her bottom lip. When Jennie opened her eyes, it was to find that his were tightly closed in a face drawn rigid by emotion that needed no translation—desire. Her womb tightened, and she drew in a sharp breath.

Peter planted tiny kisses across her cheek to her ear and buried his face in her hair. "If you say you want it, I'll try to back off."

She heard her laugh as if it had come from a stranger. "You know that won't work."

He nuzzled her jaw up to press his mouth to her neck. His hands moved up her sides and spanned her ribs. When his fingers made contact with her breasts, he instantly edged down, pulling her to him once more.

Jennie felt the start of tears. Peter wasn't a man who would push. She couldn't tell him that with every nerve in her body she longed for him to touch all of her.

"Maybe we'd better get those hamburgers." His voice was thick.

"I'm not hungry. But you're probably right."

They made it as far as the first of Yeatman Cove's grassy lawns before turning to each other again. This time Peter shook his head and rested his brow on hers. "This could either turn out to be great or one hell of a mess," he said.

Jennie eased his face up. "I know. We can't work it all out tonight, Peter." But they could kiss, again and again, if she had her way. And she showed him with her mouth, and her hands, how much she wanted to touch and be touched by him.

"God, we're never going to eat." He drew back, breathless and somber, and added, "And we don't care, do we?"

"Nope." They strolled across redbrick paving to sit where they could see the lights of the river traffic.

With their hands joined atop his thigh, Peter stared ahead.

Jennie felt the flexing of firm muscle beneath her hand and absorbed an unnerving jolt of physical awareness.

"At the lab you said I was a lot like Mark."

"I meant as far as the work goes." And now she wished there wasn't a tiny part of her that felt disloyal to Mark for being with Peter. If they continued to see each other, she'd have to get over that.

"You said you sometimes felt jealous of the lab because you saw it as Mark's first love when you wanted that place with him."

"I said that, yes."

"Were you telling me that—" He turned his head away.

Her stomach clenched. "Telling you what?"

"Forget it. I was being presumptuous…or maybe wishful would be more accurate."

"Say it."

He shifted to face her so abruptly she flinched. His arms went around her. "Were you thinking about how it might be between us if…'' Crossing his wrists behind her neck, he threaded his fingers into her hair. ''Were you saying you thought we might be able to love each other.''

His frankness stunned her. She tried to bow her head but he propped her chin with a thumb. ''I don't know,'' she said, and knew it was a lie. ''How can you ask me something like that?''

He kissed her again, with gentle intensity made more unbearably sweet because she could feel what restraint cost him. ''I can ask you—'' he said against her hair ''—because I'm wondering the same things. We don't have to have all the answers now, Jen, but the questions won't disappear unless one of us decides to back away.''

Jennie looked into his eyes and reeled from the impact of his effect on her. *She could love him.* ''We never talked about the accusation Steven made to you.'' The intimacy spinning them together was overwhelming, and she wasn't ready for its implications.

''No.'' He pulled her head into the hollow of his shoulder and settled her against him. ''I think he'd like to put it behind him, Jen. I got that feeling last Sunday.''

''With the fish?''

''Mmm. It wasn't much of a victory, but I did see a crack in him. It's hard to let go of a grievance—real or imagined— when you're a passionate seventeen-year-old.''

Jennie nodded. ''I hope you're right. He's so angry all the time.''

''Mark said those things to me, too, you know.''

She held very still. ''What things?'' Mark had sworn Peter didn't know the full extent of his boss's suspicions.

''A week or so before he died, Mark accused me of wanting to reap the glory from his research. But you knew that.'' He waited, and when she didn't respond, continued, ''He told me to stay away from you and the boys. He said that if I did, he'd never tell any of you that I had designs on you.''

Jennie felt sick. She tried to sit up, but Peter held her fast. ''He told me what he thought,'' she said softly. ''And he told me he'd never confront you. Supposedly he was warning me what a shark you were. He told Steven, too. I wish he hadn't.''

"He loved you, Jen—more than his work, whatever you think. When he got so sick, I think he lost perspective, on everything, and he wouldn't let anyone help him. He went inside himself, and the rage at what was happening to him turned to irrational hate. He was sick and I wasn't. I was going to carry on with his work. So I became the focus of his hate, and somehow he became convinced I'd try to step into his shoes with you, too.''

He expelled a long breath that seemed to drain him. His arms became heavy around her. Jennie lost track of time as they sat silently, leaning on each other. She knew their thoughts ran on a single track: there was a chance that Mark's fears could come true.

"Peter—" she straightened "—what exactly happened with Ellie? Or is that something I shouldn't ask?''

"I don't mind.'' He faced the river but kept one arm around her shoulders. "We—or I—made the mistake of not making what I want out of a marriage clear. Ellie's a pediatrician, a very good one. I always assumed that meant she was crazy about kids.''

Jennie looked at his profile. The corner of his mouth turned down. "Isn't she?''

"Other people's. Her own would interfere with her career.''

"And you couldn't have worked a way around that?'' She was really asking if Peter had loved Ellie.

"No,'' he said flatly. "And I don't have any regrets. Neither does she. It sounds trite, but it was just one of those things that sounded like a good idea at the time. There wasn't any real...passion.''

Jennie swallowed. Peter's eyes met hers, and again she had the sensation that their thoughts followed the same course. Could there be passion between them? She thought so. But for how long when it was clear that they might never be able to reconcile the hopes and dreams that drove them?

She stood up and offered him her hand. "Come on. Where's your famous hamburger stand?"

Peter hauled himself up, smiling. "Gone," he said ruefully, hooking a thumb over his shoulder. "That's where it used to be."

"Why didn't you say something?" Jennie planted her fists on her hips. "I could taste that burger."

"I'll take you somewhere in town."

"No, you won't." She dragged him, grumbling, behind her. "We'll take potluck at my place."

Immediately the spring was back in his walk, and a happy breath expanded her lungs. He really did want to be with her. She would take and hold that idea for as long as she could. Whatever came next could be dealt with.

From time to time on the drive home he turned his wonderful quiet smile on her. They spoke little yet she felt a bond between them that made her wish she need never leave him.

"Here we are," he said when he swept the car into her driveway and stopped in front of the garage.

"I hope you like tuna," she said.

"Are you sure it's okay?" His eyes asked her to insist that he stay.

Jennie grinned. "Would I serve you bad fish?"

"Very funny."

She smiled at the alacrity with which he sprang from the car and swerved around the hood to open her door. When he was happy, he looked so young.

Lights showed through the glass panels in the front door. The boys must be home. This time Jennie didn't feel apprehensive at the thought of Peter and Steven coming face-to-face. Her son couldn't be allowed to dictate what she did with her life. And, as Peter had noted, Steven showed signs of relaxing with him.

She unlocked the door and led the way into the house.

"I'll get the tuna out," Peter said from behind her. "I take it we're having sandwiches."

"You've got it. Yet another of those balanced meals I serve around here. It's already mixed."

She pushed the kitchen door open with her shoulder and put her keys back in her purse.

"Hi, Mom." Bobby sat on the counter near the sink. "Hi, Peter."

"Hi," they replied in unison.

Jennie slipped Peter's jacket from her shoulders. "How was the concert?"

"Not so hot."

"Crowded, I'll bet," Peter said, advancing into the room.

Jennie glanced at him and saw that he mirrored what she felt: sudden, intense apprehension. Bobby's hunched back and puckered brow spoke more than any words. Something was wrong.

"Where's Steven?"

"I don't know."

Cold slicked over Jennie. "Isn't he here?"

When Bobby's dark brown eyes finally met hers, she drew in a sharp breath. He looked...scared. "Bobby, what—"

"That guy shoved Gigi around."

"What guy?" Despite the rapid banging of her heart, she kept her voice steady.

Bobby tilted his head to one side. "The guy Gigi's mom lives with."

"I didn't know she lived with anyone but her husband."

"They're divorced. She's got a boyfriend and he's mean. Steve says he pushes Gigi's mom around, too."

"Take it easy, Jen," Peter said, coming to her side as he must have felt and seen her distress. "Bob, try to tell us exactly what happened. As quickly as possible."

"Okay." He wiped a hand over his eyes. "Steve and Gigi were worried about Gigi's mom. That's why they wanted to go to the concert. Mrs. Burns found out this guy had gone with someone else and she was upset, so she went looking for him. Gigi was afraid that if she found him, he'd get mad and hit her. That time when Steve wanted that money it was for Gigi to give to her mom. She'd borrowed it from Dan while he was out and Gigi was afraid he'd...well, I guess she got it back before he came home.

"Anyway, today Gigi asked Steven to help her. I think he asked me to go along so you wouldn't think anything was up."

Jennie felt sick. "And you three found both of them."

"Uh-uh. The guy found us and he pulled Gigi off behind the rest rooms and shoved her around. He told us to get lost and took Gigi with him."

"He took Gigi home? So where is Steven?"

"Aw, Mom." Bobby slid to stand on the floor.

"Bobby," Peter said, "please just tell us."

"Steve said this Dan is a pervert who gets his kicks pushing women around. He sent me home on the bus."

"Oh, my God." Faintness washed over Jennie.

"I'm supposed to tell you not to worry." A moist sheen showed in his eyes. "Mom, I'm scared. Steve said he was going after Dan. He said he was going to get him."

CHAPTER TEN

Jennie hit the telephone redial button for the third time. She and Peter had driven over to Gigi's house and found no one at home. Then, with Bobby suggesting places to check, the three of them had toured one area after another, trying to locate Steven. Deciding that someone should be where he would expect to find them, Jennie and Bobby had returned home while Peter continued to search. Now it was almost midnight, and the Burnses' number had been busy for half an hour.

Jennie hung up. "I'm going over there again. If the phone's busy, they've got to be in."

"Don't, Mom. Steve won't be there, and you don't want to run into that guy."

"If he isn't there, where is he?" It wasn't a question she expected Bobby to answer. A rising tide of panic sent her pacing back and forth.

"Mom—"

"It's okay." A capable mother didn't go to pieces when the going got rough. "Get to bed. I'll wait for Steven. He'll show up eventually." If only she felt as certain as she sounded.

"I'll wait with you." He squared his shoulders, and Jennie hid a smile. This wasn't the family baby anymore, and he wanted to make sure she understood as much.

"Thanks, but you've got school in the morning. I'd feel better if you got some sleep."

Finally he gave up arguing and went upstairs. Jennie was grateful not to have to be careful what she said or what she showed. After watching the clock for another half hour, she dialed the Burnses' number, and her heart rolled when the receiver was picked up at the other end.

"Hello."

She didn't recognize the woman's very soft voice. "Hello. Mrs. Burns?"

"Yes." A sniff. Either Gigi's mother had a cold or she was crying.

"Is Gigi there?"

There was a pause before the woman said, "Who is this?"

"Jennie Andrews. I'm Steven's mother."

"What do you want with Gigi? She's asleep."

"Um—" Care was essential. "Did Gigi mention where they went after the concert?"

"She came straight home. Goodbye."

"No! Wait." Jennie pinched the bridge of her nose. "I, er, I know Gigi went home but—"

"I can't talk to you now."

"Please—"

The line went dead, and Jennie slapped down the receiver. She pounded her fists on the counter. When she got hold of Steven, he'd find out how sick she was of his antics. No more catering to a spoiled brat.

She would not cry. How could she blame him? If he was spoiled, it was partly her fault. Please let him be safe. All she wanted was for him to walk through the door in one piece.

The kitchen began to irritate her. She went to sit in the den, where the driveway was visible through the windows.

Peter had been wonderful. Not judgmental, just solid and willing to do whatever he could to help. She wished he'd come back and have Steven with him.

Watching for headlights began to hurt her eyes. Folding her arms against a steady trembling, she went into the hall and upstairs. He could have come home and fallen asleep while they were all out searching.

Steven's room was empty. Rock posters glared eerily in the red light he insisted upon. Edges of photographs, most of

Gigi, curled around the frame of his mirror. The unmade mattress he slept on—the bed had been disposed of one day while Jennie was out—spilled sheets and blankets and a twisted heap of clothing onto the rug.

"Oh, God." Jennie lowered herself to the mattress. "Come home, Steven. I'll never complain about this mess again. Please come home."

He could be lying injured somewhere...or worse. With her throat so dry it hurt, Jennie retraced her steps to the den and picked up the phone again, finally ready to do what had been Peter's first suggestion. Fifteen minutes later she hung up, despondent. Too soon, the police had said. Sure, they'd get in touch with her if a boy matching Steven's description turned up. *Turned up?* Did they mean as a body?

Lights swung into the driveway.

Running, scarcely able to breathe, she rushed into the hall and threw open the front door. "Steven!"

"It's me, Jen." Peter, walking slowly, sounded apologetic.

Jennie leaned against the jamb and waited until he climbed the steps and took her in his arms. "I can't find him. I'm sorry." He urged her inside and shut the door. "We'll have to call the police."

"I already did. They said it's too soon for them to do anything."

Peter cursed under his breath. "Listen. You're worn out. Try to rest somehow and I'll keep going."

"Keep going where?" They moved, side by side, into the kitchen. "He's going to come home, Peter. I know he is."

"Of course." But Peter's voice lacked conviction.

"You probably shouldn't be here when he gets back," Jennie said in a rush. "You've done everything you can, and it'll be best if I deal with him myself."

He gave her a long, hard look. "You think I'll make things worse?"

"I didn't say—"

A muffled click electrified her. Creaking, squishing followed...someone tiptoeing in tennis shoes.

"Steven?" Jennie dashed into the hall in time to see him starting upstairs. "Get down here." Her clenched teeth scraped together. He must have seen the light shining through from the kitchen and decided to try to sneak in via the front door.

"I'm tired."

The next upward step he took was his last. Jennie lunged to grab the sleeve of his jean jacket and jerk him off balance. He stumbled and half fell beside her.

"Hell, Mom. What d'you think you're doing?" With a shrug he pulled free of her grasp and jammed his hands in his pockets.

"In the den."

She heard the sound of another door opening and closing, and leaned against the bannister. Peter was leaving. After all he'd tried to do, she'd let him go thinking there were parts of her life she wouldn't share with him.

"That's Peter," Steven said. "I saw his car. Why was he here?"

"He was with me when I got home." Not that she owed any explanations.

"So he knows—"

"There are things you don't want any of us to know, aren't there, Steven?"

"I'm tired."

The lines were being drawn, and she didn't intend to be on the losing side. "So am I. Move."

With his head down Steven scuffed into the den and flopped into a chair.

"You look awful," Jennie told him.

"I don't care."

"Why did you deliberately not do what you promised to do? Why did you send Bobby home alone, then stay out half the night? Where have you been?"

"Out."

Jennie rolled in her lips, willing herself to choose words with caution. She sat opposite Steven. His hair stood on end around an unnaturally pale face, and his black eye, turning to shades of green and purple now, showed starkly. Jennie wouldn't let herself look at the wound on his cheek. He stared at her, his hand over his mouth, and she pushed aside the impulse to go and hold him.

"Bobby told me about Dan, or whatever his name is."

"My brother the narc."

"What did you expect him to do?" Leaning forward, she held out a hand. "You send him home alone, and he's supposed to invent some excuse for you staying out for hours without anyone knowing where you were? Steven, I called the *police*. Do you hear me? The hospitals would have been next."

"I hear you." He rested his head back, tilting up his chin. "Why'd you have to do that? Are they gonna come asking questions?"

"No. And that's not the point. The point is that you worried me out of my mind."

He turned his face away. "You don't understand."

"Maybe not. But only because you won't let me understand. I'd like to *help* you, Steven." She looked for some sign of reaction and found none. "We have to deal with whatever you're mixed up in because of Gigi. If this is the kind of thing you'll do if you continue to see her, then we'll have to re-evaluate the friendship."

Steven jumped to his feet. "Gigi's my girlfriend. You can't do anything about it?"

"What does that mean?" She stood and faced him, every nerve in her body on alert.

He mumbled something unintelligible.

"There's something wrong at Gigi's house, isn't there?"

"It isn't your business."

"It is if it affects my son. Gigi's mother has a boyfriend, right?"

"Yeah."

"Dan?"

"Bobby's got a big mouth." But Steven's own mouth trembled. The toughness was beginning to fray.

"And this Dan pushes Mrs. Burns around...and Gigi?"

"Maybe."

Jennie saw the sheen of tears in his eyes.

"Look, Mom. I should have let you know where we were, okay? Things got a bit heavy, is all, and we needed to get away on our own."

He was trying for peace. Jennie went to touch him, but he stepped away. "Will you at least tell me what happened tonight?"

"It's a mess," he said, walking to stare through the window. "His name's Dan Wallace, and he lives over there. When he drinks he gets mean. Mrs. Burns was upset because he went to the concert without her. Something about him having some other woman he sees. I don't know all the stuff. Anyway, Mrs. Burns said she was going to find him, and Gigi was scared he'd hurt her, so we went to try and bring her back."

"Only this Dan found you." At least he was talking to her, and as he did, his shoulders dropped. The fight was seeping out of him. "I saw the bruises on Gigi's arms. Did he do that?"

Steven shrugged. "She doesn't want me to tell anyone. If I do, she says she'll deny it."

Jennie scrubbed at her face. Her eyes felt full of grit. "This is the kind of thing you read about. I don't know what to do, Steven—or what to say."

"There's nothing. But thanks." He turned around, and the exhaustion in his face twisted her insides. "Bobby probably told you I followed Dan. He got a head start on me. By the time I got there, he and Mrs. Burns had gone out and Gigi was alone. Mom, she was so scared."

"We should do something, Steven," Jennie said. "We could—"

"We can't do anything. The authorities won't touch that

kind of situation if there aren't any complaints. Gigi won't make any because of her mom.''

"Where did you go when you left Gigi?"

"I didn't leave her till later. We went to a diner. Then I took her home and came here."

"What happened when you took Gigi home?"

"She went in through a back window like she always does." His eyes slid away.

"I see." She was afraid she saw too much. "I suppose she sneaks out to meet you a lot."

"Some. Can I go to bed now?"

"I'm worried. You wouldn't—" She closed her mouth. Suggesting that he might have considered running away with Gigi was foolhardy. "Steven, I don't want you to go to Gigi's house again."

His chin came up defensively. "I'm not a kid. I can go where I like."

The last thing she wanted was to put him on the defensive again, but backing down could be disastrous. "As far as I'm concerned, you're my minor son, and that means what I say goes. I think we should see a family counselor. We need—or I think *I* need—some professional advice."

"I won't go."

And she probably couldn't make him. "We can talk about that. But Steven, from now on I want to know where you are—all the time."

"Good luck," he said through gritted teeth. "Keep pushing, Mom, and you'll never know where I am again."

Jennie swallowed but kept her eyes steadily on his. "What does that mean?"

"Work it out. I'm going to bed."

SHE'D ALLOWED him so close, only to push him away again. Peter closed the garage door and strode into the house, yanking his shirt buttons undone as he went.

The bony streak he fell over before he could turn on the lights hissed and wailed as it cannoned away. What was it with him and females? He couldn't even inspire trust in the damn cat?

When the lights glared over his messy kitchen, Peter winced. Even he couldn't put up with this.

By the time he reached the bedroom, he'd removed his shirt and unzipped his jeans. He hopped, first on one foot, then the other, and his clothes landed in a heap on the floor before he located a pair of cutoffs and a sweatshirt. Physical labor was needed here, something to keep his mind occupied, and since he couldn't do anything outside in the dark, he'd be domestic until he was tired enough to sleep.

Forty-five minutes later, on his knees with soapsuds up to his elbows, he allowed himself to stop for breath. The score from *Dangerous Liaisons* blasted forth at an ear-splitting level. He liked it that way.

The kitchen already looked better. Two weeks' newspapers disposed of, canisters lined up, counters washed and buffed, dishes shuttled into the now-running dishwasher—not bad. But the floor was a challenge, and he'd been forced to resort to a scrubbing brush.

Sitting on his heels, he rotated his neck. *He was falling in love.* Was he mad? Today at the lab, Jennie had given him yet another indicator that nothing permanent was likely between them. He rubbed a hand over his face and cursed when soap got in his eyes. "Hell!" Scrambling, one eye squeezed shut, the other almost so, he hauled himself to the edge of the sink and flushed out the soap.

A tap on his shoulder almost ended his life. He threw himself around with so much force that his bare feet shot from beneath him on the wet floor. Spread-eagled—his rear stinging—he peered up at Jennie, who immediately bent over him.

She said something he couldn't hear, then shouted, "I rang. The door was unlocked." Her windblown hair framed her face like black silk.

She was still dressed in the black-and-white dress that hugged her breasts and accentuated her small waist, and the sight of her turned his mouth dry.

Peter got up and trod carefully across the floor and into the hall. When he'd turned off the disc player, he returned and found Jennie where he'd left her, beside the sink. She looked pinched, anxious. Like him, she must be trying to decide where to go from here.

"Did you do something to your eyes?" she said.

He restrained himself from gathering her into his arms. "I was scrubbing the floor and I got soap in them."

"Ah." She nodded, holding her lip between her teeth. "I guess I'm not the only one who occasionally does housework at night...when they can't sleep."

He crossed his arms over his shabby middle. The gray sweatshirt had shrunk in the wash. It rode higher in the back—above his waist—than it did in front, and one short sleeve hung loose at the shoulder, where the seam had ripped. When he'd flushed his eyes, water had sprayed over his chest. Peter rubbed at the wet spots, trying to decide what to say.

He could imitate her usual method for dealing with conflict and blurt out everything that was on his mind. But he'd be jumping the gun. And he couldn't be sure she wouldn't be horrified and refuse to see him again.

"I had to come, Peter." She sounded breathless.

"Why?"

"Don't make this harder."

Why *was* he reacting like this? "It's kind of late, Jen. We had a long night. I don't mean to be rude, but—"

"But you will be, anyway?" She looked at the toes of her intriguing polka-dotted shoes, and Peter had his hands full not touching her. "I'm sorry if I hurt your feelings," Jennie said.

"What makes you think you hurt my feelings?" That was it, wasn't it? He'd felt they were working side by side, as one, then she'd shut him out. And he was hurt.

"You're pouting."

"I'm *what*?"

"Pouting. Offended. Being difficult." She puffed out her cheeks. "I was hasty. I was so worried about Steven that I didn't think before I spoke, so you're going to make me suffer for it...even though I've apologized.''

He felt his face heat. ''I'm a little old for that sort of behavior, don't you think?''

''You said it.''

''Oh, so now *I'm* supposed to feel guilty?'' Typical of a woman. Manipulating the situation to put the male on the defensive.

''No, you're not. You're supposed to say you understand me. And that you forgive me.''

He chewed his lip, assessing her. She looked tired, vulnerable and very, very appealing. They had a long way to go to wherever their joint path was meant to lead, but they'd already come quite a distance. Jennie Andrews had become important to him.

''Well.'' She threw up her hands. ''That's it. I'm not groveling. If you want to stay mad, stay mad. Let me know if and when you feel like coming out of your sulk.''

Peter rubbed his hands over his face and shook his head. ''You're unbelievable. You have the makings of being a nuisance in my life, but I still like you.''

''Gee, thanks.'' She approached and plucked at the sodden front of his shirt. ''There's nothing a woman enjoys more than being told she's a potential nuisance. You should get out of this before you get pneumonia.''

He laughed and plunked his hands on her shoulders. ''You, my dear, know better than that old wives' tale. What happened with Steven?''

''The same as usual. I said all the wrong things, and he got angry.''

''I'm sure he got angry, but I doubt if you said *all* the wrong things. Want to talk about it?''

''That's why I came.''

He pulled the sweatshirt over his head and tossed it aside. ''And I thought you were here because you were worried about my tender feelings.''

Jennie gathered up the shirt and looked around, but not

before running her gaze over him. Pink rose in her cheeks. "I was. Where's the laundry?"

"Through there." He pointed to the laundry room off the kitchen.

"Try to get into the habit of putting things where they go as soon as you're through with them. It'll save you from these horrible middle-of-the-night cleaning sessions." She went through the door to the washer and dryer, and he winced at her exclamation.

"Peter," she said, quickly returning. "You've got to get organized."

"Yes, I know. And I will. Let's go in the sitting room and talk."

Jennie followed him, keeping her eyes on his back. Well-defined muscle in his shoulders and biceps moved smoothly. His body tapered to slender hips, where ragged cutoffs rode perilously low. Dark golden hair covered his powerful legs. She raised her attention to a point above his head and went to sit at one end of the couch.

The kitchen banter had been a useful tool to overcome awkwardness, but sooner or later banter must be set aside and reality confronted. Since they'd come together again, there had been a rapid change in their relationship.

"Thanks for coming, Jen."

She turned. Peter stood behind the couch, feet spread, hands on hips. He met her eyes and smiled. "I had to," she told him. "You were wonderful tonight."

"I did what I wanted to do. Shall I light the fire?"

"Not for me." He was probably cold. Putting on a shirt would solve that problem, but she'd rather he stayed with her as he was. "On second thoughts, yes, light it."

With his usual economy of movement, he crossed the room and heaped paper and wood into the grate. When flames shot up the chimney, he rested on his heels, rubbing his hands on his cutoffs.

Pushing backward, he sat on the rug. "Do you have to get back soon?"

"Before too long. Steven and Bobby are asleep, but I need some rest, too."

"What did Steven have to say?"

She explained about the concert, Dan, how Steven had spent time with Gigi later and finally her own fear that Steven might decide to leave home.

"And you feel helpless," Peter said after a while. "I guess that's a parent's lot with this sort of situation."

He was right, but she couldn't bring herself to agree. "I'm going to insist we get some family counseling."

"Did you mention that to Steven?" Firelight sent light and shadow over his body. When he turned to toss in another log, the simple twist of his spine, the ripple of sinew over his ribs, brought her heart into her throat.

"He said he wouldn't have any part of it." What was the particular trigger that caused her to be drawn to Peter, to every little thing about him?

He faced her, cross-legged, a deep frown drawing his straight brows together. "You aren't going to push it, are you?"

"I probably can't. But I'd like to try."

"Maybe you should give him space and show you trust him to do the right things. If you try to force counseling, you may really end up driving him away."

Exactly what she was afraid of. Hearing Peter voice that fear didn't help.

"You're thinking I'm out of line making suggestions when I've never had any kids, right?"

Jennie stretched out her hands, and he held them. "Something like that, but that doesn't mean I won't consider what you say. I wish I didn't have to think about it at all for a while."

"Then don't," Peter said. "Today was special. Despite the crises."

"Yes, it was. I didn't want it to be over."

"It doesn't have to be."

She looked at their joined hands. Peter's thumbs moved in circles.

"Jennie, you could stay with me." He pulled until she slipped to kneel on the floor before him.

"You know I can't do that." She suddenly felt anxious. Peter was letting her know that he wanted them to be lovers.

"Whatever you want is the way it'll be," he said. "I won't pretend I'll be happy if you walk away from me, but...I'm not a saint. I want you and I'm going to try every way I can think of to make you want me, too."

She didn't have to tell him she already wanted him. What she needed to say, but didn't know how, was that wanting wasn't enough—an affair destined to go nowhere wasn't right for either of them.

"Jennie?" He bent forward and cupped her chin. "Say something. You already know things have changed between us. You've become very important to me."

Very important. What did she expect—a declaration of love? She didn't want that, did she? In a way, earlier he'd spoken of the possibility that they could come to love each other. But love came in different forms and it could be temporary. It could also leave someone hurt.

Peter ringed her neck loosely with his hands and studied her face. "You aren't the only one with a lot of questions, Jen. Or a lot of reservations. But you wouldn't be here if you didn't feel anything at all for me. You could have waited and called tomorrow—or decided to let me be the one to make the next move."

And she had no words to deny what he said. Jennie's heart sped, and intense warmth swept over her. She slipped a hand behind his head and fingered his hair. "When I left home, I told myself I was being polite and decent—coming to apologize for being short with you. But you're right—I could have done that by phone."

He didn't smile. His eyes flickered from hers to her mouth. Jennie could hardly breathe. She leaned toward him and kissed him softly. The touching of their mouths was light, but every nerve in her body jumped.

"Oh, Jennie, Jennie." Peter sighed. He gripped her waist, keeping his mouth on hers while he got up, lifting her into his arms. Cradling her against him, he laid his cheek on hers, and she felt the rapid beat of his heart. They were caught, trapped by desire that held more danger than either of them was sure how to handle.

Jennie put her arms around his neck and tilted her face up to his. In his eyes she saw question. He was weighing how she would react if he pushed for them to be lovers.

"Can you at least stay awhile?" he asked.

She closed her eyes and kissed him with trembling lips, afraid to speak.

He sighed deeply and let her feet slip to the ground. "You're special to me," he murmured, holding her close. "More than that. I'm not sure when I realized how much I want to be with you. Maybe about ten seconds after I saw you walking toward me that first afternoon."

His self-conscious laugh made her smile. "True confession time. I asked you for coffee, then convinced myself you wouldn't come. I was disappointed, Peter. But then you did come, and I was so glad."

"But we didn't expect this, did we? At first I told myself I had some notion of playing matchmaker for you with some other noble and suitable candidate. We know—"

She silenced him with her mouth, and this time their lips parted. Still the kiss was restrained, but the tentative meeting of their tongues sent pure fire into Jennie. She made herself draw her head back. "We know that was a cover, right?"

He looked deeply into her eyes. "We do now. I sure didn't then."

His hands tightened around her waist. Her breasts touched his chest, her hips, the solid muscle in his thighs. "I'm really nervous about this, Peter. That sounds wimpy, but it's true."

"And it's wise." He glanced at her mouth again. "But I can't seem to keep focused on the potential problems."

"Or the fact that we're a very unlikely couple."

His hands shifted to her arms, rubbed steadily from shoulder to elbow and back again. "I think we make a terrific couple. Can't we just keep on going from there? We don't have to plan the rest of our lives." He spread his fingers on her cheek, ran them down to rest in the hollow above one collarbone.

"We don't—" She had to say it aloud. "We don't want the same things. If we go on from here, we're likely to make each other very unhappy eventually." She might form the rift that would drive them apart now. Jennie wasn't ready for that.

He was waiting for her to finish.

"I'm not sure about anything," she said.

"You're not sure you want to be with me?"

She drew in a breath and held it. This was it, the time to get in and take the consequences or get out and begin the process of trying not to miss him every hour of every day.

"Jennie." He nuzzled her brow with his chin. "Tell me what you're thinking. Whatever it is, I can take it…. No, I probably can't, but I'll try."

"I want to be with you." Her hands were flattened on his chest. She tried to push away, but he held her fast. "But I don't have many illusions, Peter. I'm past that stage. I know that sooner or later one of us is likely to have to say we need to go a different way." She meant she knew that eventually he'd decide *he* had to go a different way.

"Can't we take it a day at a time? Isn't what we feel for each other enough for now?"

Was it? For him, maybe. The visit to the lab reared in her mind, what he'd told her about the importance of his research. What mattered most to him was that he be remembered for his work. She knew from experience that men like Peter could decide at any time, even as they held a woman in their arms in the night, that there was that desperately important something that called them to another place. And they went, always with the distracted, apologetic pleas for understanding, the promises that they wouldn't be long. Sometimes the absence was very long, and even if it wasn't, the knowledge was left behind that the woman they'd held and loved couldn't keep them longer than they wanted to stay.

"Jennie, what do you say?"

Trying to avoid his eyes wouldn't help. Slowly she trailed her fingers over the hair on his chest, paused to rub a thumb over one flat nipple and watch it contract. Jennie kissed him there and he trembled. The skin at his sides was warm, smooth, then rougher when she enfolded him and reached around to the dip in his spine. Glancing up, she saw him grit his teeth. The muscles in his jaw jerked.

There wasn't enough air in the room. "I don't think I have a choice."

The slow rise of his chest, the heated concentration in his eyes, said everything. She thought she could feel his soul, his heart, reaching for her.

His gaze moved languorously from her eyes to her mouth to her breasts. Jennie moistened her lips—an instant before Peter covered them with his own. Blood pulsed through her. He kissed her softly, moving in whispering grazes over her sensitized skin, teasing his way past her lips to slip a light and burning path just inside.

Her skin was on fire, stripped to the nerves.

"If it's going to happen that we can be together—" his throat moved convulsively "—really together, we'll both want it to be exactly right."

Jennie smiled at him, but her mouth quivered. "Yes. If. And that can't be now. Maybe not for a long time."

"Where am I going to get the patience to wait?" Peter pressed his mouth to her throat. Raising his face, he studied her, then bowed his head to kiss the swell at her neckline.

Her legs felt boneless, and she knew she should leave.

Softly, spreading his fingers, Peter covered her breasts and returned to possess her mouth once more. This kiss was deep, demanding, and Jennie hesitated only an instant before returning his ardor. His fingers curled beneath her bodice, brushed back and forth along the lacy edge of her bra.

With her breath coming in gasps, Jennie drew away. Peter immediately dropped his hands. A pulse beat visibly at his temple. Jennie put two fingers there, tilted her head, telling him with her touch, her eyes, that she didn't want to do what she must—leave him now.

"When?" he asked simply, his voice barely audible.

She shuddered. How could she answer, she wondered, her heart hammering. "One day at a time. You said that."

"Yes, but I won't be able to wait forever." His nostrils flared. The green of his narrowed eyes was flinty. "Not that I'm worried."

"I guess that's good," Jennie said speculatively. "Do you want to share what makes you so sure of me?"

Peter brought his mouth close to her ear, and she felt the merest touch of his tongue. Jennie couldn't contain her little moan.

"Does that answer your question?" Peter whispered.

CHAPTER ELEVEN

"I waited till Carl left for the office and went straight over to the house," Lou said from the doorway to Jennie's office. "You'd already gone, so I decided to come here."

Bliss, hovering in the background, gave an apologetic grimace.

"It's okay, Bliss," Jennie said. "Don't hold any calls. And Valerie should be coming in. If she does, please interrupt this."

Lou, apparently oblivious of just how unwelcome her visit was on a Monday morning, settled herself in a chair. "I'm really up to my eyes," Jennie told her. Eventually she would work her way through the negative feelings she had for her old friend, but now wasn't the time to make a start.

"Carl believed me yesterday when I said you went home because you were feeling ill. I tried to call you several times, but you didn't answer. And I sneaked over. You weren't there."

"No."

Lou crossed her legs. "I had to tell Carl you'd gone to bed."

"Why did you have to?"

Lou flapped a hand. "Well, you know, so he'd think you were at home."

"Why did he have to think I was there?" She wasn't making this easy on Lou, but so far the other woman hadn't said anything to make Jennie feel kind.

"You wouldn't want him to know what Maryanne said about you."

"I don't give—" A wild surge of anger engulfed Jennie. "The only thing that matters is truth. If I'm not guilty of any of the things that were said about me, why should I feel defensive? Anyway, Carl isn't the type of man to take notice of malicious gossip." And Lou was as guilty as Maryanne.

Lou pouted and wiggled as if settling more comfortably in her chair. Jennie longed for her to leave.

"Maryanne felt terrible, you know."

Jennie raised her brows. "Really?"

"She didn't mean those things she said."

"Ah, Lou." Jennie sighed. "Sure she did. For some reason she, and other people who were supposed to be my friends, don't like having a single woman around. What she said was pretty vicious."

"You're making too much of it." Lou fiddled with a button on her jacket.

"Maybe. But Lou, she said I was after Carl." She felt her color heighten. "You and Carl are my oldest friends. You know what kind of woman I am."

"I'm sorry—"

"Do you have any idea how I felt?" She hated this.

"It wasn't my fault, Jennie. I didn't have any part of it."

"You didn't…" Lou had tried to deflect that suggestion, even if not strongly enough. "Why did you try to push me at John Astly?"

"It was Maryanne's idea." She looked perilously close to tears. "I shouldn't have gone along with it."

"No, you shouldn't." Bringing up the incident of the lies over the faucet wouldn't help. The sooner this was all forgotten, the better, although Jennie found it hard to imagine that she could ever be truly close to Lou again.

"Can we forget about yesterday?"

"In time." Saying she wouldn't remember what had been said would be a lie. "You and I don't have to talk about it again."

"Maryanne mentioned wanting to get the old group together for coffee so we can—"

"No. Don't talk to me about it again. And tell Maryanne to relax. The husbands of the world are safe from me."

"We could just have coffee and—"

"I don't want to sound rude, but I must get some work done. You and I will get together again. I'll call you later, okay?"

"All right." But there was reproach in Lou's pale eyes. More mending would be necessary between them, but not now.

The intercom buzzed, and Jennie leaned forward. "Yes, Bliss?"

"Call for you on line one."

Jennie picked up the phone and noticed with irritation that Lou had ceased her leave-taking motions and showed signs of settling in.

"Hello, this is Jennie Andrews."

"Good morning, Jennie Andrews." Peter's voice soothed and excited her at the same time. "How are you?"

"Fine. You?" Why didn't Lou go?

"Lonely. And tired. I've been at the lab since six."

She hadn't left him until almost three o'clock. "Why?"

"Can't you guess?"

Jennie met Lou's interested eyes. "I'm working, Pe— You should probably go back home and get some sleep."

"You've got someone there."

"Yes."

"Not the odious Astly?"

She grinned. "Definitely not."

"Okay, okay. I can take the hint. How about lunch?"

"I'd love to, but I can't today."

"And I can't go a whole day without seeing you."

Her heart began to race. "Could we discuss this later?"

"We certainly could. That was what I was hoping you'd say."

"Um—"

"No. Don't say a thing. I can tell it's difficult there, so I'll do the talking. One question. I'd like to take Bobby and

Steven to a baseball game. I guess there's a lot of rivalry between the Reds and the Dodgers?"

"I wouldn't know." What she did know was that Peter was making an effort to reach out to Steven and Bobby. The happiness that should bring was tinged with apprehension.

"Well, according to Liz there is. Anyway, L.A. comes to town in a couple of weeks, and I thought I'd ask if the boys want to go, then get tickets."

"I'm not sure—"

"Trust me for once, Jen. Steven will come around. You'll see. Talk to you later."

He didn't give her any more time to argue.

"You went out with Peter yesterday, didn't you?" Lou asked as Jennie hung up. "And that was him, wasn't it?"

The questions caught Jennie off guard. "Er, yes."

"You two are starting to see a lot of each other."

So, that had been noted. "Peter's a good friend." The fact that Lou had called him yesterday meant she'd been keeping a close eye on who came and went from the Andrewses' place. "I was surprised you invited him to the barbecue."

"It was a spur-of-the-moment thing." Lou blushed. "But why not? He used to come over when Mark was alive. You said he'd been away, so I thought it would be nice to let him know that he's always welcome in our home now that he's back. I wish you'd both stayed."

"Let's not get into that again."

Lou's eyes shifted away. "You two always got along so well."

Jennie looked thoughtfully at Lou. "Yes, we did—all three of us."

"Is there…is there anything different between you and Peter?" She had the grace to blush again. "I mean, he does seem more than—"

"Does he?" How long would she be able to keep the new twist in her relationship with Peter a secret, Jennie mused.

"He never did get married again?"

"No. That's over."

"I thought so," Lou said, smiling smugly. "I just knew it in fact. Are you two...well, you know?"

"No, I don't know." She wouldn't evade direct questions, but neither would she volunteer information.

Lou smoothed her shiny blond hair. "You can be so close-mouthed, Jennie Andrews and I'm not going to play your games any longer. In two weeks, that's the second weekend in May, Carl and I are having a dinner party. We'd like you and Peter to come."

Jennie bit back the temptation to ask why she hadn't been invited to come on her own or why she'd been excluded from other gatherings the Ramstets held. They spent time with her, had her to dinner from time to time, but never with the old group.

"Well?" Eagerness transformed Lou's pretty face. "You'll come, won't you?"

It wasn't in her heart to be cruel. "I really can't speak for...oh, the second weekend in May?" The weekend of the possible trip to the baseball game. "Peter said he might be busy that weekend."

"Darn." Lou visibly lost animation. "Let me know if he is free. I can always adjust at the last minute."

No suggestion that she was welcome on her own. How could Lou be so crass?

"You do know he's perfect, don't you, Jennie?"

Frowning, Jennie sat straighter in her chair. "Why is he perfect?"

"Don't pretend you don't know what I'm saying. Encourage him. He's exactly what you need."

Jennie glanced sharply at Lou. "How do you mean?"

"You know. Someone of your own to look after you."

Irritation flared. "I don't need someone to look after me."

"Every woman does," Lou said in a conspiratorial tone. "And if you and Peter got together, it would be perfect. You wouldn't have to rely on others anymore."

The words fell like stones on Jennie. "I'm self-sufficient.

And that's the way I intend to stay. I don't rely on other people.''

"Nooo, not for most things. But there are times when a woman can't manage on her own.''

"What kind of times?'' She willed Lou to be honest.

"You wouldn't have to worry about things breaking down around the house, or doing the yard.''

In other words, for all her declarations of undying friendship, for the past two years Lou had harbored her own pile of resentment against Jennie.

"Jennie, you couldn't do better than Peter. It isn't easy to find a good man when—''

"Please forgive me, Lou.'' She stood up. "I've got an appointment.''

"Now you're angry.''

Jennie longed to say that she adored Carl as a friend and a good man, but nothing more. "I'm not angry, only—yes, I am. I don't like the suggestion that I'm a nuisance to other people.''

"You *aren't*.''

Silently Jennie led Lou through the reception area. "I'd like you to bear in mind that I don't need a man to take care of me. I didn't choose to be single at this time of my life, but I'm managing extremely well and I intend to go on that way.''

"Jennie—''

"Goodbye, Lou.''

THIS WAS another of Liz Meadows's brilliant ideas: to spend time with Steven and Bobby. Peter sat in Jennie's kitchen, waiting for Steven to get home. Bobby, who sat on the opposite side of the table, watched Peter, who had run out of things to say.

Liz should be the one here sweating. He'd left the lab in time to meet both boys when they got home from school, invite them to a baseball game and, if possible, to have a few private words with Steven. By the time Jennie got home, he'd hoped to have everything more or less smoothed out so that he could take her somewhere and talk about something much closer to his heart. Only it was five-thirty, Steven hadn't arrived yet and Peter was afraid Jennie might walk in first.

"Is Steven always this late?"

"Mostly," Bobby said.

"Is he involved in sports, or something else at school?"

"He's supposed to be in track, only—" The boy wrinkled his brow. "He's in track."

Peter decided not to push that. "So your mom usually gets back first." These were the questions he should have asked as soon as he'd arrived.

"No. She's real late most of the time."

And the tone suggested Bobby didn't like spending so much time alone.

The door to the side yard opened, and Steven walked in. Raindrops glistened in his dark hair, and his sweatshirt clung to his shoulders.

"Hi, Steve. Peter's here," Bobby said.

Steven dropped his schoolbag and gave Peter an unsmiling glance. "Yeah. Where's Mom?"

"At the office, I expect," Peter said. He resisted the temptation to get up. "Come and take the weight off your feet."

Steven sauntered to the refrigerator, rummaged inside and surfaced with a Coke and a plate bearing half a cheesecake. These he set on the table while he found a fork. He slumped between Bobby and Peter. "So, what are you doing here without Mom?"

He hadn't expected this to be easy. "I came to see you and Bobby."

"Since when?" The cheesecake grew rapidly smaller.

"I used to come by a lot," Peter said. "We both know what changed all that and we can talk about it, just the two of us. What I wanted to ask first is if you boys would come with me to Riverfront."

"Who're we playing?" Bobby leaned forward, his eyes bright.

"L.A. It'll be in two weeks, if you're interested."

"We're interested, aren't we, Steve? Geez, yeah."

Another wad of cheesecake entered Steven's mouth. "Depends," he mumbled. "Don't know what Gigi and I'll be doing then."

Peter relaxed slightly. The immediate reaction was better than he'd hoped for.

Bobby's shoulders had dropped. "Yeah, we don't know what we'll be doing then."

Peter looked speculatively from one boy to the other. "Well, think about it."

"You can go, Bob," Steven said. He swung onto the back two legs of his chair and rocked. "You don't have to do what I do."

"Maybe Gigi would like to come, too." What the hell—anything in the name of peace.

Steven made a clucking noise.

"You could ask her, Steven," Bobby said, evidently sighting fresh hope.

"I could."

At least Steven was sitting close enough to breathe the same air as Peter without showing signs of wanting to throw up.

Peter made a decision. "You and I will go anyway, okay, Bobby? I'll get four tickets in case Steven changes his mind. I can always give any extras away."

Steven's chair returned to the floor with a crack. "What about Mom?"

"She hates ball games." Not that he was wild about them.

"You know her pretty well, don't you?" Steven said. He took a long swallow from his Coke.

"Yes. Your mother and I've known each other for a long time. That's no secret."

"What day will we go to the game?" Bobby asked. He jiggled, clearly nervous. The even-tempered member of the family always had to play punching bag for the rest.

"Saturday. We could have a barbecue at my place, then go in the evening." He didn't mention that there would be a doubleheader. Regardless of how good the cause was, he could only take so much.

"That would be great," Bobby said. He eyed Steven. "Remember Killer, Steve?"

"Yeah. Okay cat."

"She hates me," Peter said flatly.

Steven laughed. "Why do you keep her, then?"

"Habit. You know how that goes. You kind of put up with things you don't know how to change. Anyway, she's part of the scenery, and I'd probably miss her."

"Maybe I'll come, too," Steven said, closing one eye to peer into the murky interior of his pop can. "Gigi won't want to. She's like Mom."

Peter carefully kept his expression bland. "Your choice. Want to give me a call when you're sure?" He fished a card from his pocket and slid it across the table. "Use the lab number or the one at home, whichever works."

"Yeah." Steven picked up the card and read it. "I've been thinking about things."

"Want to talk about them?"

Bobby got up. "I'd better do my homework. Mom loses her wool if I get behind." In other words, this apparently happy-go-lucky boy had a nose for potential conflict and was making his escape.

"Go for it," Peter said.

When the door closed behind Bobby, Steven resumed rocking on the back legs of his chair. "Mom said I had no right to be rude to you the way I was that time."

"You were angry. You still are. And you've got a right to that." Peter could feel the change in the boy. He could also feel how tenuous his own position was with him. "It's tough losing your dad."

"He said you wanted his job and you've got it."

"Someone had to take over. You understand that."

"Yeah." He buried his face in his hands for a moment. "But...you don't know how it was. He changed a whole lot and he said it was your fault."

"Steven—" Peter risked pulling one of the boy's arms to the table and holding it there "—was it my fault your dad got Parkinson's?"

"No." Emotions, mostly uncertainty and confusion, flitted across his handsome face. "But he said you were driving him and talking about him to the foundation. Then he had the heart attack and died, and—"

"And, because you're human, you wanted someone to blame. I was convenient. Do you honestly believe I wanted those awful things to happen to your dad? He was my friend, and I admired him more than any other man I ever knew."

A glistening sheen covered Steven's eyes, and he tipped up a face that rapidly turned red. "I just don't want to feel so bad about it anymore."

"Then don't." If he didn't know Steven would never allow it, Peter would hold the boy. "Forgive your father for leaving you when he had no choice, and start trying to forgive me for being the one to take his place."

"Dad said you were sweet on Mom." Steven sniffed and looked around.

Peter pressed a handkerchief into his hand. "I always liked your mother. But there was never anything more than respect and friendship between us, Steven. I swear that."

"But there is now."

Peter ran his tongue over his teeth, momentarily at a loss for words.

"She likes being with you."

He couldn't even enjoy the announcement. "And I like being with her. But we're still good friends who enjoy each other's company." Not that he had any intention of allowing the situation to remain so simple for much longer. "Your mother cares deeply what you think. That means she needs to feel that you don't disapprove of me."

"You'll do whatever you want to do. My opinion won't matter."

"Maybe, maybe not. But what about you and I giving each other another chance?"

Steven looked directly into his eyes. "I don't know. Maybe. I'd like Mom to be happy. She doesn't think so, but I care what happens to her."

A lump rose to Peter's throat. This was a flash of the boy he used to like so much. He wasn't sure how much he trusted this new development to last after such strong opposition, but he was prepared to take a chance.

"I wouldn't do anything to hurt Jennie," Peter said quietly. "Does that stand for anything?"

Steven bowed his head. "Yeah, I guess. Did she say anymore about selling the house?"

"No. I wouldn't worry too much about it now." Peter felt strongly that Jennie shouldn't totally uproot her sons, but had deliberately avoided the subject.

"We've got enough money," Steven continued. "She can make the business grow without selling, can't she?"

Peter felt uncomfortable. "I don't know too much about your mother's finances. I'd guess it'll come down to her deciding how quickly she wants it to grow."

"I sure hope she doesn't—" Steven stopped, cocked his head toward the door. "What's that?"

Scuffling sounded on the gravel outside. Peter frowned. "Probably an animal."

Another noise came—a whimper—and Steven leaped to his feet to fling open the door.

Sitting against the jamb, huddled in a ball, was a girl about Steven's age with long, damp blond hair fanned over her shoulders and obscuring her face.

"What the—" Peter strode behind Steven, who had already knelt beside the girl and brushed back the cascade of hair. "Let's get her inside."

At first Steven didn't respond. The girl let him raise her face, and Peter's jaw clenched. "Oh, Gigi," Steven whispered. Red marks that would become bruises marred her face, and her lower lip was split. She brought unfocused eyes in Peter's direction and started to cry soundlessly, the tears coursing down her battered cheeks.

So this was Gigi. Steven gathered her in his arms and half dragged, half carried her inside.

Peter knew better than to try to help. "Who did this to you?" he asked.

Gigi shook her head, and Steven, setting her on a chair, went to his knees and held her. Peter noted the proprietary way he cradled the girl. Jennie had been right—this had moved beyond an average teenage crush situation.

As Gigi leaned into Steven, her white shirt worked above her waist, and Peter drew in an angry breath. More red marks.

Another sound outside the door stilled them all.

"No," Gigi moaned.

Peter looked at her sharply. "Is someone after you?"

The girl shook her head again.

Before Peter could make a move, Jennie came in backward, shaking an umbrella. "Ugh. It's horrible out there."

"We've got a little crisis, Jen," Peter said quietly, and she spun around. "Steven's friend, Gigi, appears to have had an accident, but she won't tell us what happened."

Jennie looked from Peter to Steven and Gigi. "What—"

"Jennie." Peter shook his head at her, approached the girl and bent over beside Steven. "Did you come here on your own, Gigi?" Peter smoothed back her hair and examined her face.

"Yes. On the bus. I want Steven."

"Steven's right here," Peter said, meeting Jennie's eyes again for an instant. "Who did this to you?"

"No!" Gigi pulled away.

"I see." He wasn't going to get far while she was this uptight. "Well, my car's out front. Let's get you to the emergency room."

"I'm not going."

"Steven," Peter said quietly. "Gigi needs to be checked over. The cut on her lip may require sutures."

Steven nodded. His skin had assumed a gray-white tinge. "Gigi, come on, I'll go with you."

"I can't."

"Open the door, Steven," Peter said, and he lifted Gigi into his arms. She was fragile, almost weightless. "Bobby's doing his homework, Jen. Let him know we're leaving."

She snatched up her purse and ran into the hall. "Bobby, we've got to go out," she called.

He came to the head of the stairs, saw Gigi in Peter's arms and opened his mouth.

"We don't have time to talk now," Jennie said. "Stay here. If anyone calls asking for *any* of us—you haven't seen us. You understand?"

Bobby nodded, his face screwed up, "Yeah, I got it."

Without waiting for instructions, Jennie ran outside and squished into the back of the Lotus. Steven piled in beside her, and Peter settled Gigi carefully in the front passenger seat.

Once on the road, he didn't waste time before resuming his questions. "Someone hit you, Gigi, didn't they?"

"Uh-uh." She sounded as if the inside of her nose was swelling.

"What, then?"

"Nothing."

"You don't turn up on someone's doorstep, bruised and battered, if nothing's happened to you."

Gigi huddled closer to the door.

"What's your mother's boyfriend called?"

"Dan Wallace," Steven responded. He leaned forward to rub Gigi's neck. "It's okay, Gi."

Peter met Jennie's eyes in the rearview mirror, then returned his attention to the road. "Did Dan hit you?"

"No."

"Why did you go to Steven's house?"

The girl gulped. "B-because I h-hurt?"

"Why didn't your mother help you?" Peter knew he was relentless, but he was also frightened for this girl.

"Sh-she isn't home?"

"Is Dan home?" He made his tone neutral.

The hesitation was slight but unmistakable. "N-no."

Again Peter's gaze flitted to the mirror, and Jennie shook her head slightly. She probably thought he was being too hard.

"At the hospital they'll ask how you were injured." He leaned into a sharp turn. "What are you going to say?"

A stifled sob, and another, filled a pause. "I...fell downstairs." Gigi rolled her forehead against the window. "No one was home to help me."

Peter grunted. "And you sustained multiple contusions on your face? You didn't attempt to cover up?"

"No."

"You'll have to do better than that. Using your arms to save yourself is instinctive. Unless you can pretend you hit your face on every baluster on the way down, no one's going to believe your story."

There was a pause before Gigi said, "Those things on the stairs. What do you call them?"

"Balusters?" Peter asked.

"Mm-hmm. Those. That's what happened. My face kept hitting the b-balusters. A-and my hands were in m-my pockets."

PETER STOOD in the middle of the hospital corridor, his hands on his hips. "You know she's lying," he said. "I gave her that story about the balusters, and she used it like a parrot." A nurse glanced at him in passing, then looked back.

Jennie had just come from being with Gigi while her lip was stitched, and now Steven was sitting in the cubicle. "She's afraid of that man. I'm sure of it."

Peter stopped pacing between the gurneys and wheelchairs that lined the walls and stood in front of Jennie, big and ruffled—and clearly frustrated. "Why didn't I keep my mouth shut? She'd probably have tripped herself up."

"None of this is your fault, Peter." How like him to feel responsible, even when he was almost totally unconnected with what had happened.

He rammed a hand into his hair. "She wasn't convincing," he said through gritted teeth. "But as long as she won't say what really happened, there's nothing any of us can do. I did make that call, by the way.''

Jennie swallowed. "Call?" She glanced nervously at a doctor who passed. "I told you I'd try to find out what, if anything, can be done in cases like this. The answer is nothing. Not without a complaint.''

"And she won't make one." She rested a palm on his chest and stroked distractedly.

Peter squeezed her shoulders in his powerful fingers. Even when he was still, energy emanated from him. Though he was tired, and angry, Jennie felt his strength. She put her hands at his waist beneath his jacket. What she needed—what they both needed—was to be alone with each other.

"How long before she can leave?"

"Lois Burns has to show up and sign papers. She's still not answering the phone, so it'll be half an hour even if she gets home in the next few minutes.'' Jennie didn't relish confronting Gigi's mother.

"Steven will stay in there?"

"They said he could until she's released. I only hope he doesn't say anything inflammatory to Mrs. Burns. It wouldn't help.''

Peter turned her around, draped an arm around her shoulders and started for the swinging exit doors at the end of the corridor. "Don't worry, he won't. Right now Gigi's making sure of that, poor kid. Hell, I feel helpless.''

"Me, too. Where are we going?"

They leaned against the wall as two medics rushed a loaded gurney over shining tile.

"Out of here," Peter said when they could move again. "We're in the way. Let's find a bench in the fresh air. Steven will find us.''

In the courtyard the wind was blessedly cool on her heated skin. Even the misting drizzle felt heavenly.

"No benches," Peter said, opening his coat and pulling her inside. "Come on.''

With their arms around each other, they hurried to a concrete planter beneath an overhang. Perched side by side on the rim, they enjoyed a moment of stillness, and Jennie turned her face up to Peter. Rather than release her, he wrapped her more intimately to him. "We're going to have to step back from what's happening with Gigi and her mother. There's nothing we can do to help now."

"You're probably right." A gust slapped drizzle into their shelter, and Jennie brushed moisture from her eyes.

"We'll be there for Steven—and Gigi. There are other issues to deal with…like you and me. I've missed you today, Jennie."

"We were only—" The air rushed from her lungs. She pressed her face into the hollow of his shoulder. "It was only last night, Peter."

He groaned softly. "Too long ago." His fingers wound into her hair. "Jennie, there's something I want to ask you. I've been rehearsing since this morning."

Despite her concern over what was happening inside the hospital, Jennie's insides quickened.

"Something's come up. I've been asked to go to Vancouver, British Columbia, next Saturday."

Jennie turned her face up to his. "How long will you be away?" She shouldn't feel anxious, as if she couldn't bear for him to be gone.

"Just two days. Fly up on Saturday, back on Sunday. I've got a dinner lecture to give on Saturday evening. The rest of the time would be free. Jennie, I want you to come with me."

CHAPTER TWELVE

Jennie clutched his sleeve. "Oh, Peter, this is something."

A bus from Vancouver's city center had brought them across Granville Bridge. The bridge spanned the glistening blue waters of False Creek, an inlet gouged between downtown Vancouver and the larger spread of the city's business and residential areas.

"Some people say this is the most beautiful city in the world," Peter said as the bus wound down an off-ramp connected to Granville Island, a triangular blob of teeming activity sprouting from the inlet.

The throng exiting the bus carried Jennie forward, and Peter grabbed for her hand. She laughed at him over her shoulder, and he felt a catch in his throat. The wind that whipped her hair brought a moist sparkle to her dark eyes and color to her cheeks. In a tangerine-colored blouse and white pants, with a white cardigan tied by its sleeves around her neck, Jennie looked lovely. To Peter she was the most exciting woman he'd ever met.

"Come on, come on," she said, tugging at him. "We don't have long, and I see places to *buy* things."

Peter laughed and broke into a run. In seconds Jennie was dragging on his arm. "Slow down," she begged breathlessly.

"Make up your mind." He wrapped an arm around her shoulders, and she half fell against him. "I didn't know you were into buying things."

"Are you kidding?" She made owl eyes at him. "What do you think I do for a living? I'm the one who first said 'shop till you drop.' Let's go into the market."

He would gladly go anywhere with her. The stirring she caused with the slightest touch or glance wore down even his disciplined control. They'd left their bags at the hotel and rushed out. Peter thought yet again how much he would rather have stayed there.

"Watch it!" He pulled her from the path of a barrow heaped with vegetables and pushed by a red-faced man puffing from exertion. "If I'm going to live, we'd better eat soon." Neither of them had eaten the two airline meals served en route, and lunchtime had come and gone several hours ago.

"We'll eat," Jennie said, but she forged purposefully ahead toward a warehouselike building that housed a public market. "If we don't look now, we never will."

Once inside open, hangar-sized doors, rows of handcraft stalls caught her eye, and Peter smiled indulgently. Her happiness caught him, and he gladly allowed it to carry him along. After the restraint between them on the journey—Jennie had spoken little and reminded him with every worried glance out the plane window that she'd been reluctant to come—her change of mood made him exultant.

"Look at this." Jennie broke away to pick up a plastic sculpture of what looked like a drinking glass, half-filled by a stream of Coke supporting a tilted can. "Doesn't it look real?"

"Mmm. It sure does." If she looked at him closely, maybe she'd think he was merely restraining his enthusiasm.

"Don't you think Steven would love it?"

He felt his smile solidify. All week she'd used her sons as an excuse to avoid committing to this trip. He'd finally got her to agree that they were old enough to look after themselves for a couple of days, but they obviously continued to fill her mind.

"Peter?"

He took the piece from her. "It's definitely Steven. Give it to me and pick something out for Bobby."

Her smile broadened, and he congratulated himself grimly

for picking the reaction that was bound to please her most. "How about the midair spaghetti with the fork in it?"

Jennie considered. "No...no, I don't think so."

Peter stood at her shoulder and settled a hand on her neck. He wanted her alone. Was that wrong? He wanted what he couldn't have: Jennie without a past with another man.

"Maybe we should get him something completely different," she said, leaning farther over the table.

He had to make a decision. Either he accepted the situation, complete with teenage kids and a woman who'd come to treasure independence because she'd never had it before, or he had to give up and separate himself.

"I've got it!" Jennie turned around, grinning and brandishing the frozen effigy of a flattened catsup bottle, the squeezable variety, its top flying off amid splattering red globs.

Peter pulled out his wallet. "Who thinks up these things?"

"I think they're fun," Jennie responded, working money from her purse. "I'll get them."

"This is my trip," Peter argued.

"And the gifts are for my children. Why should you pay?"

There was no possible response.

With her treasures wrapped and dangling from her wrist in a plastic bag, she slipped her arm through his, still smiling.

"Maybe I'd have liked to take something for Steven and Bobby," he said mutinously.

"Then the gifts are from you, too. Okay?" Her open untroubled face disarmed him.

"Okay." Unable to restrain himself, he bent to kiss her.

"Oh, Peter, I do..." She stopped, her lips parted, a startled look in her eyes.

"You do what?" he asked gently while his heart pounded. *Love you.* Was that what she'd almost said?

Reaching up on tiptoe, she flattened a hand on each side of his face, mindless of the lumpy bag trapped between them. "Thank you for making me decide to stop treating my sons like little children. I'm so glad to be here with you."

The bustle around them receded for Peter. Raised voices, laughter, color, the scents of flowers and spicy food and the drifting tarry odors from the waterfront outside became a blurred backdrop against which the two of them were all that was clear and sharp.

Jennie's fingers, cold and soft, moved over his ears to tangle with his hair. And it was she who placed the next kiss, pressing their mouths together, darting her tongue so quickly to meet his that he might have imagined the intimacy.

Sighing, her eyes closed, she let her heels meet the ground once more and settled her brow on his chest. Dully, Peter became aware of the bumps of passersby.

Resting his cheek atop her head, he rubbed her back. "We're becoming a spectacle," he whispered.

"Who cares?"

"Not me." And in that moment he had the answer to his question. He could no more sever from Jennie than willingly give up his life. He'd take whatever they could have for as long as they were given to share each other.

"I want to buy you something," she said, squaring her shoulders. "What would you like?"

"Lunch."

"Don't be so predictable. One of these days I'm really going to take you shopping. A completely new image. I've already thought about it."

"You have?" He didn't mind the idea at all. "Are you saying you don't like my wardrobe?"

"I love it. But if you could see most of the men I dress, you'd understand how much I'd like to get my hands on you."

Peter plopped his forearms on her shoulders and leered suggestively. "That, love, can be arranged."

She blushed so charmingly he chuckled. "I think we'd better move on."

"But I want to find something for you."

"We'll look as we go," he said with no intention of doing any such thing.

They'd almost made a complete circle of the stalls when Peter saw an earring display. Miniature origami fans in subtle shades, faintly dusted with glitter, fascinated him, and he moved closer.

"I suppose you'd wear these with an evening gown or something," he said to the artist.

The thin woman pulled a purple woolen cap lower over long dark hair. "Or something," she said, returning her attention to a glue gun. "Wear 'em with a swimsuit if you don't plan to swim."

"I'll take those," Peter said, pointing to groupings of three fans—torquoise, pink and lavender.

When the purchase was boxed, wrapped and paid for, he put it in his pocket.

Jennie, her arms crossed, frowned at him. "They're pretty. Who are they for?"

"I thought I'd take them to Liz," he said airily.

"Oh." She was too circumspect to say that Liz, with her tweeds and brogues, would probably think he'd lost his mind.

Emerging into sunlight, they wandered on past pottery shops, fiber-art displays, handmade-toy vendors and, scattered between, the open doors to ships' outfitters.

Ahead, backed by the jumble of downtown skyscrapers on the other side of False Creek, hundreds of ships' masts bobbed and jiggled.

"Food," Peter said, sighting a restaurant. "Can we eat, please ma'am?"

They passed through the restaurant to find outside seating beneath bright umbrellas spread along a busy dock.

Jennie ordered a Mai Tai. "It seems like a vacation thing to drink," she said defensively when he looked questioning.

"You're right. Make that two. I'll also have the burger."

Jennie chuckled. "What a surprise. Bagels and lox for me, please."

She sank back into her chair, and reflection replaced humor.

He'd probably be happier not knowing, but he had to ask. "What are you thinking about?"

"The fiasco with Gigi last weekend."

"I thought we'd made a pact not to think about it."

"I can't help it, Peter. If I were honest, I'd admit I'm mostly concerned about Steven being dragged into something awful. Does that make me an unfeeling monster?"

"It makes you a normal parent."

She thanked the waitress who delivered their drinks and pulled out the little paper umbrella speared into a chunk of pineapple. "I keep trying to put it out of my mind, but everything rushes over me. Am I spending too much time away from home, Peter?"

Whatever he said was unlikely to be what she wanted to hear. "You mean being here with me?"

"Well, yes."

"Steven's seventeen and Bobby's fifteen. They don't need you to hold their hands anymore." Now he was committed. "I don't think they *want* you to hold their hands. If they need anything, you're always there for them."

"I'm not today."

He swallowed rising annoyance. "We've already beaten this to death. If they need anything, they'll contact the Ramstets or Liz. And we're only going to be gone two days."

"I know." She turned her hand palm up on the table, and he laced their fingers together. "Sorry."

"Jennie, I don't have any right to tell you what to do, but for what it's worth, I really do think you need your business. Kids grow up and go their own way. When they're gone, if you haven't made a life separate from theirs, you're left with nothing."

"You're right."

"And I think that if you trust your kids and believe they're basically sensible, you get the best out of them by giving them some freedom."

Jennie squeezed his fingers more tightly. "In other words, you believe I should loosen up, particularly with Steven?"

"Yes, I do. As I told you, when I talked to him, I was impressed by his maturity. He had the guts to tell me he thought he'd made some decisions about me based on emotion, and was coming to terms with his father's death.''

"He told me the same thing.'' She drank some of the Mai Tai. "Did he call you?''

"Uh-huh.'' He would have told her all this on the plane if she hadn't been so closed. "He got through to me at the lab and said he'd like to go to the baseball game next Saturday.''

Jennie smiled broadly. "Maybe it'll all be okay, huh?''

"Maybe.''

"Anyone who thinks the toddler stage is tough hasn't dealt with teenagers.''

"I wouldn't know.'' Saying that he'd like a chance to watch a baby of his own grow into an adult was definitely out.

The arrival of their meals was a welcome diversion. Peter ate and eyed snow-capped mountains so close to the city that their peaks seemed to sprout from tall glass buildings.

"Peter,'' Jennie said suddenly, "this is wonderful. I feel free. I haven't felt like this in…I can't remember when I did.''

He set down the hamburger. "You're like a yo-yo. One minute you're worried about everything back home. The next you're crazy about being here.''

"Being here with you.'' Immediately she lowered her eyes.

Peter swallowed. He wanted her so badly he could hardly think of anything else anymore. This thing with Jennie was physical, but so much more.

Jennie was looking at him, waiting.

"I'm crazy about being here with you, too.'' Telling her what he believed they could have together would be easy. What held him back was that then he'd have to risk putting his reservations into words.

WHATEVER WAS on the television didn't matter. Jennie watched pictures, saw mouths move—and assimilated zero. The sumptuous hotel suite with its rich shades of royal blue and gold had registered as they arrived, but made little lasting impression. Another stroll of Granville Island, an extra hour stolen to delay their separation while Peter attended the fund-raiser, had made them late. They had arrived back at the hotel with barely enough time for him to shower and change for his dinner lecture.

She perched on the edge of a love seat in the sitting room, her white cardigan draped over the arm. Once the door of the suite had closed behind them, Jennie's assurance had fled. Her flight bag hung from a hook in the bedroom, near the vast bed—unpacking would seem so calculated.

The sound of the shower stopped. Jennie pursed her lips in a soundless whistle and fastened her eyes unseeingly on the television screen.

"Jennie, love, I'll be about three hours." He was moving into the bedroom. "Do you feel like going out to eat? There are some good restaurants in the hotel, or you could take a cab somewhere. Shall I call down for recommendations?"

"No." She sounded ridiculously shaky. "I think I'll have room service." She thought she wouldn't eat at all. One bite of food would probably make her sick.

"Are you sure?" He came through the archway, wearing tuxedo pants and shrugging into a snowy white shirt. A golden gleam warmed the solid outlines of his muscular chest and flat belly.

"I'd rather…" An indrawn breath collided with her words. "It's been a long day. Maybe I'll get an early night." Now she felt utterly stupid.

"Oh?" Peter approached, putting in cuff links. The shirt caught up over one powerful shoulder, and his feet were bare, his hair still damp. He was something, and she felt like an unpopular teenager who'd been invited out by the school's number-one jock.

Peter stood over her, adjusting the shirt, threading studs, tucking in, zipping…all slowly and all while he riveted her repeatedly with his all-seeing eyes. "Are you telling me you're going to be asleep when I get back?"

She shrugged her shoulders and noticed his glance flickered

to her breasts and away. He was a subtle man—sexy, sexual, utterly masculine, but understated in every approach he made.

"I might drift off. I'm one of those people who needs a good seven hours."

"Do what you want to do. I'll understand." He sat on his haunches and, with one finger, traced the side of her face, drifted a breathtakingly sensitive line down her neck and along the edge of one lapel to the shadow between her breasts.

She caught his hand, held it to her lips, then set it firmly on his knee. "You're going to be late."

"You sound like...my mother," he finished, but there was a speculative glint in his eye. "Jennie, I hope you won't be asleep when I get back."

She propped her chin on a fist. "Does this feel like an assignation?" Her wretched predictable blush arrived on cue. "I mean, does this trip seemed contrived?"

He stood up and slid back suspenders over his shoulders. Jennie spared a covetous stare. Jeans and boots might be his preferred garb, but he wore formal dress with such nonchalant panache.

"Jennie," he said at last, "this *is* an assignation."

She shuddered and hunched up again. "Don't put it like that."

"Sorry. How should I put it? Jennie Andrews and I just happened to be in Vancouver, British Columbia at the same time. So we decided to cut costs by sharing a room?"

"Don't make fun of me."

"Ah, my love." He bowed over her, tipped up her chin and kissed her with a thoroughness that left her gasping. "I'm not making fun of you, only showing you there's no way to pretend we didn't come here together." Pausing, he slipped a black tie beneath his wing collar and tied it expertly. "And I think we came because we want to be together, or am I wrong?"

"No."

"Good. That's solved, then." He left, to return with his hair somewhat tamed, his jacket over his arm and a frown in place as he studied a black satin cummerbund. "I hate these things." His glance was hopeful.

Jennie immediately got up and turned him around. She fastened the buckle at the back of his trim middle, then reached to smooth a wrinkle at the shoulder of his shirt. Her hands lingered there, and she stroked the smooth fabric, feeling heat from the well-toned muscle and sinew beneath.

Peter became still. "I'm glad you're with me, Jen."

"I'm glad to be here," she said, meaning it fervently. "We've said it so often it must be true." Putting her arms around him and resting her cheek on his back was so natural. He covered her hands, holding her close, and for seconds they stood, immersed in each other. They could have something special, a oneness of mind, body and spirit—Jennie felt the tentative seeds of that now.

Reluctantly she released him, somehow certain that he would never move away willingly. "Go, Peter. I'll be here when you get back."

"Awake?"

"Maybe," she said airily.

"I'll hope, then." With a last lingering look, he grabbed his lecture notes and strode from the room.

After an hour Jennie decided she couldn't continue to behave like an adolescent. She ordered dinner and unpacked what little she'd brought by the time her meal arrived.

Another hour slipped by. The quiche had tasted good, and the wine, of which she had only intended to drink a glass. Three had definitely been a little excessive, but at least they had dulled her jitteriness for a while. When the clock showed ten-thirty, every nerve in her body tensed.

She took a quick shower, pinned her hair to keep it dry, smoothed lotion into her skin and splashed on some of the light-scented toilet water she loved.

Pale lavender satin? Good grief, why had she chosen that? Full-length but split to the hip at one side, backless and plunging from a halter neck, between her breasts to the waist in

front, the gown looked deliberately sexy. Who was she fooling? That's what she had intended when she packed it.

She dared a peek into the mirror and immediately looked
away. Her nipples showed clearly, and the satin clung to her
body.

With an unpleasant twisting inside, she remembered the
diaphragm she'd obtained before taking the trip. Hastily she
fished the container from her toiletry bag. She looked at herself in the mirror again and thought of Mark. What she was
contemplating wasn't disloyal. Mark was dead and she
wasn't. The time had come for her to live again.

A key turned in the door.

Rushing, she threw back the spread, slid between cool
sheets and flipped off the light.

"Hi, Jennie. Going to sleep now, huh?"

Feeling silly, she turned on her back and put a hand over
her eyes. "Sort of."

His jacket slung over his shoulder, Peter came to stand
beside her, looking down in the subdued illumination from
the bathroom. "It's raining. Can you hear?" His low voice
mesmerized her.

"I do now."

"Go to sleep. I'll be as quiet as I can."

Sitting up, she turned the lamp on again and moved to kneel
on the bed. She wrapped her arms around her middle.

Peter's lips parted. His eyes moved over her face, her shoulders and down—and Jennie tingled with their passage as if
he had touched each spot with lingering fingers.

He tossed the jacket aside and tugged his tie undone. "You
are very beautiful."

"So are you." She bowed her head. Even the right words
escaped her. Everything felt wrong.

"Thank you. Lie down and I'll cover you up. You'll probably sleep better if I use the couch."

"No!" Swinging her feet from the bed, she caught his
hand. "I'm behaving like a fool and I don't know why. I'm

here because I want to be and now...now I don't know what to do anymore.''

''Sh.'' He put a finger to her lips. ''I understand. I never was very good... Hell, Jennie, how are we supposed to say all these things? The feelings are there, but I'm not sure of all the right words.''

Jennie held out her arms, and he came to her. Held tightly with her face pressed to his chest, he smoothed her hair with shaky hands. ''We'll take this very, very slowly.''

All she could do was hug him ever tighter.

''We'll lie together, Jen, listen to the rain and be glad of each other's warmth. I'm tired of being alone, and there's no one else I want to be with but you.''

Tears sprang into her eyes, and the strangled noise from her throat brought no shame. ''Hurry up, Peter. Come to me.''

She stayed where she was, watching while he undressed. As tense as he must be, he remained graceful in every move he made.

Quickly he slid off suspenders, removed studs and pulled his shirttails out. ''You're sure—''

''Yes.'' Scooting backward, she reached the far side of the bed.

Peter paused in the act of pulling the shirt from his pants and leaned over the bed to pull the covers to her waist. His eyes held hers steadily, then he drew away again. He shrugged the shirt from his shoulders and arms. Muscles rippled. Golden hair covering his chest narrowed over his **belly**.

''I'm not sure I'm tired,'' he said.

''Neither am I.''

Lamplight delineated the finely toned beauty of his body. Jennie's breathing quickened. He stepped out of his pants and shoes, stripped away his underwear and socks. His laugh surprised her.

''What's funny?''

''I'm just an old outbacker at heart. Uncivilized. I never did own a pair of pajamas.''

Fiery heat swamped her and she lay flat. Her awkwardness

forgotten, she'd calmly watched him shed his clothes. "It doesn't matter."

The bed dipped and she turned her head away. He switched off the lamp, but light from the street threw a silvery wedge over the bed.

"How did the speech go tonight?"

"Very well. Only my mind had a tendency to wander." Peter was also on his back, and Jennie was aware of them, side by side, staring at the ceiling. Rain beat a steady tattoo on the windows. "I kept wondering what you were doing up here."

"I was wondering what you were doing," she told him. "And getting scared about your coming back." She laughed awkwardly.

"I know. I was half-afraid I'd get up here and find you'd left."

Jennie rolled toward him. "You knew I wouldn't do that."

His hands were behind his head, and the eerie light caught in the curving lines of his mouth, the square angle of his jaw, and played over his chest. Tentatively Jennie set her hand where his breathing moved his body, and she felt an answering jolt of tensed muscle. He didn't lower his arms. Slowly, lightly, she played her fingers back and forth in springy hair, took a single finger to trace its line to his navel and beyond. She spread her hand on his belly and let it rest there.

"Jennie," Peter murmured, turning to her, "you know what's happened to me, don't you?"

She raised her head and caught the glitter in his eyes.

"I've fallen in love with you."

Her heart seemed to stop. Sighing, she pressed herself to him and kissed his shoulder, his neck and finally his mouth.

His hands roamed down her back and up her sides until his thumbs rested where her full breasts weren't completely covered by satin. "Peter," she murmured, straining against him. Solid pressure nudging her belly sent blood pulsing through her veins.

Peter's firm mouth, his tongue, ranged gentle, then demanding over Jennie's, delving deep…and she gave back her own passion with trembling force.

Straightening, he removed the few pins she'd forgotten to take out of her hair and allowed it to fall about her shoulders. Then his face was buried there, his breath warm on her neck. "I never want to stop touching you."

She reached for him, but he held her away.

"Peter—"

A quick kiss silenced her, and he ran his hands from the halter at her neck downward over tingling flesh until Jennie moaned. But she kept her arms at her sides. With infinite care Peter brushed aside the provocatively split bodice to lay her breasts bare. She heard his breath catch. He stroked, surrounded, lifted the soft weight of her, and she dropped back her head. Peter made her feel beautiful and desirable, and utterly vulnerable.

His lips, closing over a nipple and sucking it into his mouth, brought a cry to her lips. He took his time, lowering her to her back, bending over to lavish attention on every inch of exposed skin. Gentle pinching between finger and thumb, the nip of his teeth and flick of his tongue, threatened to crush Jennie's last shreds of reason.

When she could wait no longer, she pulled him down beside her and pushed him onto his back, curled over to press her magnetized flesh to the rough hair on his chest and rub until they were both gasping.

A cry, half a sob, escaped Peter. He eased the halter from her neck and down her arms. His grasp slid over satin to cup her bottom. Their bodies molded together like one.

Control wavered and fled. Peter worked the nightgown down until he could lean over her and pull it away. Returning, he foiled her efforts to wriggle, pinned her and kissed the backs of her knees, her thighs, planted his open mouth on her hip and slid his tongue to the hollow at her waist.

"Peter, please!"

She felt him smile before he carried on, relentlessly mouthing his way to the underside of one exquisitely sensitive breast. He claimed her nipple and moved to the other breast before Jennie writhed, pushing him from her to catch breath.

He laughed, deep in his throat, and she laughed with him.

A breath in time, and he was touching her again with his mouth, his hands, his body. But he was waiting for her. Jennie opened her mouth in a great, draining sigh. Peter was waiting for a sign from her. Without it, whatever it cost him, he'd go no further.

Jennie didn't want to wait any longer. Reaching between them, she touched him delicately, then surrounded smooth, ready skin and reveled in Peter's groan.

"I want you," she told him, easing back and urging him over her. His hand slid deftly down her belly and between her legs, testing, but she stopped him. "I want *you*, Peter."

"Love." The word jarred from his lips. "My love. You belong to me."

DESPITE LOWERING CLOUDS and a hint of drizzle, brilliant Windsurfer sails across English Bay dazzled the eye.

Peter turned up the collar of his tan parka. "Feel like walking into Stanley Park? I can't remember the last time I went to a zoo. Probably in Sydney."

"That'd be great." As long as they were together, she didn't care where they went. And something to divert her mind from the troublesome circles it had been running this morning would be welcome.

"Are you warm enough?" He turned her toward him, eyeing her face critically. "Here, button your collar." But he did it for her and tightened the string running through her hood. The inevitable, pulsing awareness followed, and he kissed her softly, lingeringly.

"Peter, we aren't going to get anywhere if you keep this up." She smiled, certain they would probably both rather be back in bed if the maid's intermittent tapping hadn't driven them out.

As soon as they strolled on, she remembered what he had said last night. *You belong to me.* Why that? Why the need to declare possession of what had been freely given? How soon would his evident fascination for her wear off now that she was no longer a challenge? The questions circulated unceasingly, but they could never be asked aloud. And behind them nagged the reminder of Mark's warning about Peter.

She was being ridiculous. The old misgivings couldn't be allowed to resurface now.

"How about some hot chocolate?" Peter said as they came to a stall. "And a hot dog?"

"Yes," Jennie said. She didn't remember ever being so hungry.

While he stood at the stall, she perched on a wooden piling and looked out over the water. Jennie loved him. That shouldn't make her feel so sad, but she was a realist and the odds against them were too high. She couldn't give up all she'd worked for to be the kind of wife he'd expect. And he wanted something else she wasn't ready to even consider giving him—his own child. Jennie pressed her lips together. All these concerns were irrelevant. Marriage wasn't in their future.

Peter came to sit on another wooden piling and handed her the hot dog and chocolate. The wind intensified, gusting their parkas against their bodies. Peter laughed, his teeth so very white against his tanned skin. "I love this. It makes me feel wild."

He made her feel wild. "It's great."

Children scampered over grass liberally scattered with sand blown up from the beach. Jennie gave Peter a surreptitious sideways glance, and her stomach contracted at his delighted smile while he watched the play. He obviously wanted a child of his own. A baby was definitely the last thing she wanted at this stage in her life.

"Finished your hot dog?"

Jennie nodded and let him take the paper and napkin. He rolled them into a ball with his, set down his cup and took several running steps in the direction of an open garbage can. Hopping on one foot, he turned and executed a toss behind his back. "Basket!" he yelled triumphantly as he sank the shot. "Ah, when you're good, you're good, my girl. Aren't you lucky to have a prize like me?"

She chuckled. "Very lucky."

He returned and sat beside her, held her hand and stuffed it with his into a pocket. "This feels right, doesn't it?"

"Yes." Her heart lifted. Today, now, she could let go and enjoy the moment.

"Jennie, we are making progress together, aren't we?"

She smiled at him. "Yes, of course we are." Why shouldn't she hope that what they'd found could last?

CHAPTER THIRTEEN

He was glad they were almost a day late getting back, because he'd enjoyed every extra hour spent in Jennie's company— even if they had been delayed in airports.

"Hurry!" She sprinted ahead of Peter toward a side entrance into the basement of the Terminal Building. "Can you believe this? The middle of the afternoon already. I hope Bliss has everything under control."

"She will have. I'll use your phone to check in with Liz, then get out of your hair."

Coincidentally he had a meeting upstairs with the foundation in an hour. First he wanted to make sure there were no developments at the lab that he should be aware of, then grab a cup of coffee and gather his thoughts about the reception he'd received in Canada.

"I feel thoroughly irresponsible," Jennie said breathlessly, running up steps to the main level.

Peter caught her as she reached the top and pulled her to a stop. "You didn't make the planes late, did you?"

"Of course not. Come on—"

"So you're not irresponsible because you're late, are you?"

"Well...no." She smiled and kissed his mouth lightly. In a red linen suit and matching high-heeled pumps, she looked wonderful. No one would guess she'd spent the night sleeping against his shoulder in an airport lounge.

Arm in arm, they walked the rest of the distance to Executive Images. Peter read the sign and glanced at the woman beside him. She was bright as well as beautiful.

"There you are, Mrs. Andrews." Jennie's pretty assistant

was on her feet before the door closed behind them. "I was worried about you. Steven called first thing this morning and said your plane had some sort of trouble."

"Yes. But I'm here now. What's going on?"

Peter watched, strongly aware that he was seeing the flip side of Jennie. This was the businesswoman who lived in the same body with the funny, sexy lady he'd come to love.

"Good grief, *everyone* wants something." She riffled through a stack of memos. "It's a good thing I didn't have any outside appointments today."

"As soon as you can, you'd better contact Mr. Perez. He's in conference at the Westin for the day but he'll be back in his office at four-thirty." Bliss got up to look over Jennie's shoulder. She tapped a pink sheet. "And this guy's from the *Enquirer*. Potential new client."

"Newspaperman?"

"Yes. He's just published some sort of novel, and the publisher's sending him on tour, so he's got to change his image." Bliss raised her brows. "Valerie recommended you."

"Good. Oh, Peter! I'm sorry. Bliss, this is Peter Kynaston."

"I know." The girl grinned broadly. *"H."*

Peter looked inquiringly at Jennie, who sucked in her cheeks and narrowed her eyes at Bliss. "You wanted the phone, Peter. Go ahead. Bliss, I don't suppose you heard from Valerie."

"I forgot. She came in. She brought a picture of this, um, unusual dress."

"Unusual?"

Peter picked up the telephone but didn't punch in the numbers. Jennie frowned as she talked and made notes on the memos at the same time. She *was* very involved with Images.

"She says she'd like you to consider switching it for the green she was supposed to wear to the governor's ball. It's strapless and made of cotton lace. You can see through it."

The exasperated expression on Jennie's face made him smile. Bliss had her full attention.

"Who was it by?"

"Um. I'm not sure. It was black."

"Argh!" Jennie threw up her hands. "I can't leave her alone for a moment. Did she buy it?"

"No. She said she wanted your opinion." Bliss poked out the tip of her tongue, evidently deep in thought. "She wouldn't do a *thing* without your approval, she said. *Erez.* That's who it's by, and she left the picture."

"Good. Where is it?" To Peter, she said, "Valerie Willard Masters is the radio announcer. She's quite a challenge. Where's the picture, Bliss?"

"I filed it."

Jennie went to a cabinet and flipped through hanging files. "Not here. Where—" Her head came around slowly.

Bliss cleared her throat. "V for vamp—"

"For Valerie," Jennie cut in, and they both laughed. "You're incorrigible."

Peter shook his head, baffled but glad Jennie made time to have some fun in her work. He tapped in the lab number and listened. "Not ringing," he said, and tried again.

"Oh, sorry." Bliss touched his arm. "The phones are out of order. They have been since about noon."

"Blast." Peter looked at his watch. "I'd better run out to a pay phone."

"There's one on the corner of Fourth," Jennie said, pre-occupied.

Business had to be taken care of, but so did his need to know he'd be with her again. "You'll want to spend the evening with the boys."

She gave him her full attention and said, "Yes," but he saw the subtle suggestion of anxiety in her eyes. Like him, she wasn't ready for them to part. The knowledge gave him all the confidence he needed.

"How would it be if I pick up something for dinner for all of us and stop by on my way home?"

"Any excuse for pizza or hamburgers." But her smile was soft and happy.

Backing toward the door, he held up his right palm. "This is purely an act of humanitarianism. You'll be too tired to cook."

"Okay. Great."

Bliss, grinning, cleared her throat. Jennie glanced around as if she'd forgotten the girl and turned pink.

"I'll get Chinese food from—" The door opened against Peter's arm, and Liz Meadows, white hair awry, her mouth set in a grim line, poked her head into the office.

"Am I glad to see you," She addressed Jennie before noticing it was Peter she'd used as a doorstop. "Peter! Thank God. This was my last ditch. I thought I was going to have to stand in for you upstairs without managing to reach Jennie."

Peter's skin prickled. He urged Liz fully inside and shut the door. "What's the matter?"

"The phone's out here."

"Yes."

"Why did you want me, Liz?" Jennie asked, then she dropped the pile of memos on the desk. "Steven and Bobby."

"Everything's all right," Liz said in her best smooth-it-all-over tone. "I wanted to give you the rundown before you saw Steven, is all. That, er, what's her name? The woman who lives next door?"

"Lou Ramstet," Jennie said. Every trace of color had left her face.

"Yes, that's the one. The school got hold of her, but evidently she wasn't able to help. Something about not being able to reach her husband. Not that I know what her husband had to do with it."

"Liz," Peter said, "please, just spit it out."

"Yes, yes." She plunged her hands into the pockets of a brown check blazer. "When this...Lou, said she couldn't help, the school called me—Bobby told them to—and I went over to the police station. No, sorry—the juvenile detention center. Anyway, I took Steven home, and everything's pretty much sorted out, so don't worry."

For seconds the only sound in the room was the hum filtering in from the mall.

"I don't understand," Jennie said slowly.

"You mustn't get upset," Liz said, looking worried herself. "Evidently he was picked up at the Greyhound terminal with a girl. Gigi?"

Jennie nodded.

"A neighbor of the girl saw Steven leaving with her late this morning and called the mother. Mrs. Burns, I think. All the details aren't important. I went straight over to the center, and they said that since there were no charges, Steven could go. You'll probably have to talk to them tomorrow."

"What did he *do*?" Jennie's voice rose, and Peter went to her side.

Liz rubbed the space between her brows. "As far as I can gather, Gigi wasn't in school today. Steven went to her house and talked her into running away to California." Liz's eyes went to the ceiling.

"California!" Jennie sat heavily on the edge of Bliss's desk.

"I think he knows it wasn't the wisest thing to do."

Peter settled a hand on Jennie's shoulder. "Calm down. Getting upset won't help."

"Easy enough for you to say." She shrugged away and stood up. "I'm going home. Bliss, you're in charge here, and I don't want any calls at home. Can you manage?"

"Don't worry about a thing."

"Jen, I have a meeting upstairs or—"

"I know you do." She gathered her purse. "Liz, I'll talk to you later. I'm so grateful to you for being there."

"You don't have your car," Peter said. He felt a coldness, a slipping away. "I'll run you home."

"It isn't necessary. You've got things to do, and I can get a cab."

"Jennie," Liz said, catching her arm, "you know what's been happening with this girl and her mother. Steven shared some of it with me. He was afraid for Gigi. That's why he did it, to try to get her to safety.''

Jennie scarcely seemed to hear. "This is my fault," she said. "If I'd been where I should have been, I would have known what my son was doing."

"WAIT, JENNIE!" Carl Ramstet reached her as she paid off the cab driver. "Lou just told me about Steven."

She didn't want to talk to anyone *but* Steven, least of all the Ramstets. "Everything's under control, thanks."

"So Lou said. She said everything was sorted out by the time they called her. Otherwise she'd have gotten in touch with me. I could have taken care of things."

"Yes," Jennie said, feeling stone-cold. Poor, silly Lou. Lying, and not well, because she was afraid of her husband getting close to Jennie. "Thanks, Carl. I'd better get in."

The sight of Lou trotting in their direction turned Jennie's stomach, but she couldn't be rude in front of Carl. "Hi, Lou."

"Hi. Carl, Ray Reid's on the phone."

"That can wait," Carl said. "Jennie, you'll probably have to go in and talk to the authorities. At least, I think that's the way these things work."

"I suppose so." She was tired and wanted no more than to be alone with her sons.

"Let me know, and I'll go with you. Helps to have an extra pair of ears hearing what's said."

"Thanks, but I don't—"

"Ray's on the phone," Lou repeated shortly. "And I'm sure Peter will be available if Jennie needs any help. Right, Jennie?"

"I won't need help," Jennie said, turning away. From here on she'd keep her priorities straight and turn to no one for anything.

"Good luck," Carl said from behind her. "Don't forget we're here for you."

"I won't."

"Carl," Lou whined. "Come *on*."

Jennie hefted her flight bag over her shoulder and walked up the driveway. A desire to cry came and quickly fled. Some things forced a woman to be strong. One was responsibility. Another was the need to make decisions. She had to put Steven and Bobby first, at least for the next few years. That meant her own needs and desires might have to go on hold. She narrowed her eyes against a mental picture of Peter.

In the house an unnatural silence greeted her. She dropped her bag and kicked the shoes from her aching feet.

"Mom?" Bobby came from the den.

Jennie opened her arms, and he walked into them, hugged her as he hadn't for a very long time. "A mess here, huh?" she said.

"Yeah. Steven's upstairs asleep. He's wiped out."

She set her jaw grimly. "I'll go up."

"Do you have to right now? He didn't look so hot. I could make you something. Coffee, maybe, or tea."

She opened her mouth to refuse, but changed her mind. "Sounds like a great idea. Tea. I'll come with you." Bobby was always the buffer. Something else she'd have to fix.

He went into the kitchen and clanked around, putting on the kettle, knocking mugs together. His anxiety showed. He was afraid she'd change her mind and the inevitable unpleasantness would start.

Jennie took off her jacket, hung it over a chair and sat down. "Steven didn't go to school at all today?"

Bobby put a mug in front of her. "I guess he went, then cut out when he found out Gigi wasn't there. The police contacted the principal and Mr. Halen called me in. He phoned Lou, but she said she couldn't do anything. So I had them call Mrs. Meadows at Peter's lab. She's neat. Steven said she was great at that place. She told the policeman or whatever he was that he was being an ass." Bobby bent his head, reddening.

Jennie grinned and felt a welcome lightening of her spirits. "Good for Liz."

"Yeah. Then she brought Steven home and she came back

to the school and got me, too. She told me everything was gonna be fine.''

Jennie silently blessed Liz. ''It is. And remember, none of this is any fault of yours. But I am going to have to sort things out with Steven.''

''He said you were gonna be real mad.''

''Try not to worry. I'll only do what has to be done.''

''Mom, are we gonna have to move?''

She bit her lip. Bobby's dark eyes were troubled. ''Don't think about that. Right now I'm only concerned with making sure you and Steven are all right. I may never sell this house.'' But she had heaped one more insecurity on her children because of her own blind ambition.

The thud of familiar footsteps surprised her. She swung around to see Peter coming through the hall, bulging white sacks in his hands. ''Door wasn't locked,'' he said. He smiled at Bobby, dropped the spicy-smelling bags on the table and ruffled his hair. ''How're you doing, sport? Short meeting, Jen. The head honcho had something else he was in a hurry to get to, and my business was straightforward. Brought dinner, as promised.''

''I'm glad you and Mom are back.''

Bobby's feelings for Peter didn't need an interpreter. Already the boy was including the man in a family portrait. Jennie tried to put aside the confusion that thought induced.

''Did you talk to Steven?''

''No,'' she told him. ''Bobby and I were talking first.'' Their eyes met, and she was the first to look away. He had to feel the strain that had sprung up between them, but she couldn't deal with that now.

''I guess this is all about me.''

They hadn't heard Steven approach. He came into the room and sank to sit on the floor, his back against a cupboard. His sweatshirt and jeans showed signs of having been slept in, and there were red lines from the pillow on his face. ''I blew it.''

''Do you want to tell me what happened?'' she asked carefully. Overreacting wouldn't help. "Liz said you were going to California. Why?"

"We were going to get married," he said almost inaudibly. A violent blush washed his face.

"Oh, Steven."

"You wanted to get Gigi away and keep her safe, didn't you?" Peter said.

Jennie raised her face but bit back the temptation to tell him this was none of his business.

"Dan beat her up that night when he knocked her down the stairs," Steven said. "Just like you thought. He tried—" he raised his shoulders "—if he hadn't been so drunk he'd have…you know."

Jennie closed her eyes. "Why didn't you both come to me? I'd have figured out something if you'd been honest."

"You can't do anything without a complaint. I told you that."

"Take it easy, Jen," Peter said.

"I'm doing what's best here," Jennie said shortly. *Why* hadn't she followed her own instincts and stayed where she belonged last weekend? "So Gigi's back in the house with that man."

Steven shook his head. "No. Mrs. Burns kicked him out."

"She did?" Jennie inhaled a great, relieved breath. "Are you sure?"

"Yeah. Gigi said there was a big row and her mom told him to get lost."

"Thank God," Peter muttered. "The woman's got guts. Usually they don't break out."

"Break out?" Jennie frowned at him.

"Change the pattern," he said. "Battered women tend to stay in abusive relationships."

"I know," she said irritably. Her agitation kept building with Peter as its focus. She didn't know why, or how to deal with the force of her antagonism. "Steven, what were you going to use for money? How did you think you could support yourselves in California?'' She couldn't grasp what her child had intended to do.

He let his head fall back against the cupboard. ''I closed out my savings account. When we got there, we were going to find jobs. There's always work in restaurants and stuff.''

''How do you feel now, Steve?'' Peter asked. ''Pretty beat?''

''Yeah. And kind of a fool.''

Jennie looked at her hands.

''The motive was okay,'' Peter said. ''Remember that. It's never wrong to want to help someone. Only next time, trust the people who love you. Ask for advice, right, Jen?''

''Of course.'' Of course he was right, logical and trying to support her. But she must have time to think things through. ''Are you hungry, Steven?''

''I'd rather sleep.''

''Can't tempt you with a little sweet-and-sour pork?'' Peter offered Steven a hand and hauled him up.

''Thanks, Peter, but I'm wiped out. I didn't sleep last night because I didn't dare call Gigi with that guy in the house. And I've been worried about her all week. Her face is a mess.''

''Was it Dan who hit you?'' Peter asked. He held Steven's shoulder. ''The night you said some other boys beat you up?''

''Yeah. He told me to stay away from Gigi and hit me. Only Gigi didn't want me to say anything because of her mom.''

Jennie felt her own overwhelming deluge of exhaustion. ''Don't think about it anymore tonight. Go on up to bed. We'll talk some more tomorrow.'' She wanted to sleep herself, to blot everything out.

''Yeah.'' Steven smiled crookedly at Peter and started for the hall. On the way he stopped beside Jennie. ''Sorry, Mom. It was a dumb stunt.'' He kissed her cheek and quickly left the room.

Jennie, fiercely blinking back tears, listened to his footsteps on the stairs. ''I'm so tired.''

"Would you find some plates, Bob?" Peter said. He took white waxed cartons from the bags he'd brought. "Eat a little, Jen, then get to bed yourself."

She wasn't hungry, but she nodded. "Steven seems to have gotten over his anger with you." For some indefinable reason she wasn't sure how she felt about the change.

"He's a good kid. He loved his dad and wasn't ready to let go."

"And you think he is now ready to forget Mark?"

Peter, in the act of spooning food onto plates, looked at her strangely. "You sound angry. With me?"

"No. Why should I be? I was just making an observation." But that was part of it, a sadness that Steven had abandoned his unshakable belief in Mark. Which made no sense. She was too tired to think straight.

"Steve's over all that," Bobby said quietly. "He told me about the things Dad said about Peter. Steve knows Dad was sick and upset."

Peter stared at Jennie until she had to look away.

The phone rang, and Bobby picked it up.

Peter gently rubbed Jennie's cheek with the backs of his fingers. "What is it, Jen?"

"Nothing." She covered his hand, turned her face to kiss his palm. *She loved him.* "I'm mixed-up."

"This is for Steven," Bobby said, running past. "I'll go get him."

Peter sat down beside her. "You aren't sorry about the weekend we spent together, are you?"

How could she explain what she didn't fully understand?

Peter put a plate in front of her. "Eat, then get some sleep. We'll all think more clearly in the morning."

"He could have been on a bus heading for the other side of the country." Jennie wasn't hungry. "They could have said he'd kidnapped Gigi or something. What do they do to someone his age for things like that?"

"I don't know. But it didn't happen."

"If I'd been here—"

"If." Peter leaned back, and his broad chest expanded. "If you'd been here, he might have done exactly the same thing. You can't keep an eye on him every minute of the day for the rest of his life."

"You don't—" A dull thump sounded, then engine noise. "Was that our garage?" She got to her feet.

Peter stood more slowly. "Stay here. I'll check."

"I'll check myself." Hurrying into the hall, she collided with Bobby. "Did you hear that? I think someone took one of the cars."

"Peter," Bobby said, ignoring Jennie. "Steve's doing something dumb."

"What?" Jennie heard her own voice, shrill and rising.

"That was Gigi on the phone." Bobby trembled visibly. "She said Dan's over there. He's broken into the house and he's got a gun."

"Oh, my God." Jennie's skin sprang tight and cold. "Have they called the police?"

"I don't…yes, Steve said they had."

Peter was already opening the front door. "Steven went over there, is that what you're saying?"

"Yes. Gigi said she and Mrs. Burns were locked in the bedroom but they could hear Dan banging around and smashing things. Steve heard him shouting, so he ran out of here."

Jennie's heart thundered. She stepped into her discarded shoes. "Bobby, I've got to go after him. Will you please sit by the phone—"

"You stay here, too," Peter ordered. "I'll go."

Jennie pushed past him. "Steven's my son."

"I want to come," Bobby said, his voice cracking.

"Please do as you're told!" She couldn't lose control. "I need you here, Bobby. Understand?"

He nodded.

Peter stopped her as she turned toward the garage. "It'll be quicker to take my car," he said.

She was beyond arguing and, as determined as she was to

deal with this her own way, she was glad to have Peter with her.

The Lotus slipped rapidly through the darkening streets. Jennie gave directions, and Peter followed them without comment.

She looked out of the window, numbed by what was happening. "Can a seventeen-year-old boy be in love?" she asked.

"I think Steven's in love, you know that?"

"Yes," she said, and closed her eyes. Maybe he wouldn't have gone looking for someone to love if his mother had been more available.

"Ah, hell," Peter muttered.

They'd arrived at the end of the street where the Burnses lived. Jennie swallowed acid. Blue and red lights flashed on police cars that formed a barricade. People stood in clusters, watching. Most must have come out of their homes and chosen to move behind the blockade, where they could watch in relative safety.

Peter parked the car. "Stay here," he said, getting out.

Jennie immediately joined him on the sidewalk.

"Please get back in the car, Jennie."

"No." She attempted to walk past the police cars and was stopped by an officer. "No one goes in there, ma'am."

"I have to." She wound her fingers together, looking around for Peter. He was nowhere in sight.

"You'll have to wait," the policeman said.

Jennie shivered. She hadn't picked up a coat, and the linen suit didn't keep out the evening chill.

She would get to Steven...she had to. Where was Peter? She flattened to some bushes and crept forward. A searchlight, flinging its white light over the houses, stopped her.

The next sound she heard was a gunshot, then there was another. Her own cry reverberated inside her head before men in uniform, bending as low to the ground as possible, started to run. "Someone's hit," a voice called in the gloom.

"Oh, no." Jennie ran, too, close to the hedge, unnoticed in the surge.

The blinding light illuminated the house.

"You! Get back now."

She'd been sighted. Slowly she edged a few steps away until she saw the man return his attention to the house. Lights shone in an upper window.

"...exactly who's inside?" A whisper came from Jennie's right. "Two women. The suspect's in there, too, and some kid who slipped by—damn, the inspector says another civilian may have just slipped in. Male. By the back door."

Some kid...another civilian. Male. Steven and Peter were both in that house with a man carrying a gun. And she could only watch and wait.

"Wallace! Dan Wallace!" A deep voice over a bullhorn destroyed the enforced silence. "We know you're in there. Come out or we're coming in."

Jennie sank to the concrete. They would get killed. She tried to pray, but couldn't think straight.

Again a shot rang out.

"Damn it all," one of the nearby voices growled. "The bastard isn't giving up."

Then there was a chorus of exclamations. The front door opened, slammed wide, and Gigi stumbled down the steps, followed by a plump blond woman who could only be her mother. Lois Burns sobbed loudly while her daughter did no more than subside onto the lawn and put her head on her knees.

"I've got to go in there." Jennie's mind saw only Steven and Peter lying wounded...or dead. "Let me go!" She fought a policeman, who swept her back and held her fast.

"My son's in there. And my...my friend."

"There's nothing you can do."

"Please—" She stiffened in his steely grip. Two officers came out of the house, a man between them. They held his arms behind his back, and he yelped and cursed at every step.

Jennie stopped breathing.

"Hold on," the policeman said quietly to Jennie. "This may be what you're waiting for."

There was no mistaking the big man who came through the front door next. He walked slowly, obviously trying not to jar the heavy burden he carried.

"Let me go." With strength born of fear, she broke loose and dashed toward Peter.

She stopped short. Shouts roared in her ears. "What's happened to Steven?"

"He's been shot."

CHAPTER FOURTEEN

Jenny paced, looked up at the clock in the too-familiar hospital corridor, and paced some more. "What's taking so long?"

"It'll be all right," Peter said. He sprawled in a chair, his jacket and shirt splattered with blood—Steven's blood.

She was jumpy. Steven had regained consciousness by the time the aid car got him to the hospital, but his face had been ashen and he'd trembled steadily.

Peter's face was no less pale and had an added gray tinge. His eyelids drooped above purplish slashes of fatigue.

"Why don't they tell me how he is?"

"Because they're busy working on him," Peter said with more asperity than sounded natural. "Sit down, Jen. You're making me nervous. More nervous."

She crumpled then, sat beside him and covered her face. "I haven't even thanked you for going in after Steven. Thank you, Peter, from the bottom of my heart."

He shrugged. "At least they've got that crazy in custody."

"I feel sorry for Gigi's mother. She must have cared about him for some reason."

Peter shifted, his eyelids closing and opening again as if weighted.

"Now she's got to testify against him," Jennie continued. "I know Gigi wanted to be here with Steven, but who knows when the police will be through with her."

"Yeah. I still have to put in time with them."

A doctor appeared from the treatment area, hands in pockets, stethoscope slung around his neck, weary eyes speaking of a long night's duty.

Jennie was instantly on her feet and in motion. "How is he?"

"Shaken up." He spoke more to Peter than Jennie, but she let that pass. Probably thought Peter was Steven's father. "The scalp wound is pretty deep. Later we'll tell him he's lucky his skull's so thick. Not tonight. He isn't ready for jokes."

"Doctor, was that the only wound?" Peter asked, rising slowly. "I didn't have time to check him over."

"That's all. And it was enough. He lost a lot of blood and he's a bit weak, but the young spring back faster than the rest of us. Give him a couple of days complete rest, and he'll be ready to go out and find more trouble."

Jennie didn't miss the resigned note. "He isn't a boy who goes looking for trouble," she said. "The man Steven's girlfriend's mother was involved with threatened their lives. He was trying to intervene."

"I see. Brave kid."

She hadn't thought of that.

"He is a brave kid," Peter agreed. "I went in through the back door of the house, and when I got up to the landing, where the guy was holding a gun on the women, Steven was about to leap in front of the gun. I wasn't quick enough to stop him, but the guy did fall over me when he turned to run."

"Oh, Peter." She wrapped her arms around his middle and hugged. His hand went to her hair and rested heavily there.

"When can we take him home?" Peter asked.

"In a few hours. Once we're sure he's stable. A couple of days at home afterward, and if he feels up to it, he can get back to school." He smiled. "I'd worry about him feeling conspicuous over the shaved patch on his head, only he'll probably enjoy being a hero. You'll be able to go in shortly."

When they'd been waiting ten minutes, Jennie heard multiple footsteps approaching. First she saw Bobby and held out her arms. He buried his face in her shoulder. "Mom, how's Steve?"

She rubbed his back and eased him down beside her. "He's going to be okay. There's a scalp wound and he's lost blood, but he should be back in school in a few days."

"Geez, I was scared when you called."

"Hello, Jennie."

She realized for the first time who was with Bobby. The Ramstets stood watching with twin expressions of trepidation.

"Hi," Jennie said. Bobby must have called them. "Thank you for bringing Bobby. I'll get him home."

"Is Steven really all right?" Lou asked. Her eyes were puffy as if from crying.

"Yes," Jennie said. Bobby had gone to sit on the other side of Peter, and Carl stood over them all, his hands clasped behind his back.

"Jennie," Lou began, "about when the school called...."

"Not now."

"No, of course not. Not now."

Carl swung to the balls of his feet and back to his heels, frowning deeply. "Are they going to have to keep Steven?"

"No. We...I'll be able to take him home in a few hours." She felt Peter shift at her side. He'd noticed the correction. He couldn't know how utterly miserable and confused she felt...or how guilty.

Tentatively Lou patted Jennie's hand. Tears stood in her eyes. "You're my friend, Jennie. I love you. Sometimes things, well, sometimes..."

"Let it go." There were no reserves of strength left, nothing to draw on for extra compassion.

"Yes, you're right. We've got other things to think about now. More important things."

Jennie leaned back against the wall and closed her eyes. "Forget it. I understand." And she did in a way. She had enough hang-ups of her own.

"Well." Carl cleared his throat. "We probably shouldn't have come, but we were worried."

Jennie avoided Lou's eyes. "I'm glad you did. I'll be talking to you both in a few days. For a while I want to have time to decide some things on my own."

Again she felt Peter move.

"Would you rather we left, then?" Lou asked.

"Thanks for coming." Jennie managed a smile. She and Lou would make their peace eventually.

"We'll go now, then," Lou said softly. "But you call if you need anything. Anything, mind you."

"I will."

Relief softened the worry lines on her friend's face. "Jennie, you're so important to me."

Jennie didn't trust herself to speak. They subsided into silence for several seconds.

"Come on, honey," Carl said to Lou. "Should we take Bobby back with us, Jennie?"

"No, thank you. We'll both wait for Steven."

When the Ramstets had left, each casting glances over their shoulders, Peter stood up and looked down at Jennie. "I thought you were going to put that party behind you. You obviously haven't."

"That's not all of it," she told him. "Not nearly all of it. But I don't care now. I've got important things on my mind."

"Did you have to be so unkind?"

She folded her arms and turned her face away. "Peter, I'll always be grateful for what you did tonight."

"But?"

How could she explain? What were the words to tell him she thought she loved him but she wanted to slow down, back off and be sure before going forward?

"Jennie, are you dismissing me?"

"Not dismissing. No. It's just—"

"Would you rather I left, too?"

She looked at him now and could scarcely breathe. His face was closed.

"Okay. I get the message, not that I understand it. Don't forget you don't have a car."

"I can always—"
"Get a cab. Yes, I know."

THIS PAST WEEK RANKED among the most miserable of Peter's
life. He swept up Jennie's driveway and parked in front of
the door. He could see her in the den, shelving books. Despite
her not very inventive excuses for avoiding him since Monday
night, and his own vows to forget her, the truth was that there
was nothing he wouldn't do to beg, borrow or steal some time
alone with her. He'd groped toward this Saturday, grateful for
his original idea to take Jennie's sons to Riverfront. This
would be his best shot at getting her to confront their differences.

Taking advantage of her apparent obliviousness to his presence, Peter wrapped his arms around the steering wheel and
watched. She moved fluidly, standing on something he
couldn't see to shift volumes around, bending, showing her
maddeningly appealing derriere to best advantage and reaching so that her shirt stretched over the voluptuous curve of
her breasts.

Peter leaned back and rested his head. In five days he'd
played more mind games than could possibly be healthy for
a man dedicated to logic.

He loved this woman. That much needed no more examination. She was avoiding him, and his wonderful logic had
quickly worked out the most obvious reason for that: she
blamed Steven's difficulties on the time she and Peter had
spent together recently. And that's where he could blow holes
in *her* logic. Kids didn't always need help to get into bad
spaces, and this particular fiasco had sprung roots a long time
ago.

Jennie's guilt was a mountain-sized stumbling block. In addition to what had happened between them, she was undoubtedly questioning the time and energy she'd poured into her
career.

Peter didn't know exactly how to help her work through
the doubts, but he was going to try.

Then there were one or two hang-ups of his own. And he and Jennie would have to look at those in bright light. His record as a failure in relationships intimidated him. Another failure wasn't something he'd risk. That meant the next time had to be for good. Then there was the question of children...his own. He and Jennie had never discussed the subject, but he didn't need words to get the message that she was probably closed to the idea.

That left a final decision for him: if he and Jennie decided their lives were meant to be spent together, would he eventually resent the substitution of another man's sons for his own? He wasn't sure. What he did know was that he wasn't now, and might never be, ready to give up Jennie. And he had come to care for Steven and Bobby in a special way.

Yesterday he'd been lucky enough to time a call when Jennie wasn't at home. He'd reminded Steven and Bobby of the ball game and had made arrangements to pick them up. It had been agreed that the barbecue be put off. There had been no mention of involving Jennie in the plans, and he'd sensed that the boys were as aware of the tension as he was.

Enough of playing the voyeur. He got out of the car and mounted the steps. Before he could ring, the door opened and Bobby offered a wide smile.

"Hi, Bob." Peter liked the boy more with each encounter. He had a subtle sense of humor not always evident in his position as shadow to a more forceful older brother.

"Hi." Bobby's lowered voice reinforced the notion that Jennie might not be expecting Peter. "Is this really it? We're going to Riverfront?"

"You betcha. The Reds playing the L.A. Dodgers—would I let us miss out on that?" His heartiness almost caused him to cringe.

He went into the house with Bobby at his heels and met Jennie in the hall. Her automatic smile changed to a frown. "Hello, Peter."

"Where's Steven?"

"In the kitchen eating, where else? Since about Wednesday he's been stuffing down food almost every waking minute."

"He's a growing boy." He held himself rigid. The longing to reach for her was almost more than he could contain.

"Why did you want to see Steven?"

He made himself laugh. "It's Saturday. Did you forget the ball game?" Turning to Bobby, he shrugged elaborately. "*Women.* They just don't get their priorities straight."

"Yeah," Bobby said, but his eyes were anxious.

"I'm not sure Steven's up to it." Jennie crossed her arms, and Peter noticed signs that she might not have done any more sleeping than he had this week.

"Sure he is, Jen. He's back at school." His conspiratorial wink at Bobby brought an uncertain smile. "Hope it's not inconvenient that I'm early. I thought we could spend a few minutes together before I take off."

Steven wandered to join them, a half-eaten sandwich in his hand. Apart from a shaved patch on his head where a livid scar showed, he looked completely fit. "Gigi wanted to come," he said, and quickly added, "I told her she wasn't welcome."

"Not in those words, I hope," Jennie said tartly.

"Nah. I told her we were gonna pork out on hot dogs. She hates 'em. I'll take her some place tomorrow."

If Peter had to guess, he'd say Steven and Gigi would turn out to be a teenage duo who lasted the rigors of a long court-ship.

"Are we gonna win tonight?" Bobby yelled. "Yeah, we're gonna whip their—" He closed his mouth and flushed.

"You bet," Peter said, swallowing his mirth. "Those Dodgers had better keep an eye on their wickets."

"Wickets?" Steven screwed up his eyes.

"That's cricket, Peter," Jennie told him. "You just made a little slip, right?"

"Right." He wished this were going to be a cricket match. That was something he could really get up for. "Steven, why don't you and Bobby go get ready?"

Taking his hint, they both went upstairs.

"You had forgotten the game," Peter said when he was alone with Jennie.

"I've had a lot on my mind."

"So have I."

Jennie averted her face. He couldn't stand this distance between them.

"We don't have long," he told her. "Can we try to talk?"

"If you want to."

"No." He held out his hand, and she hesitated before holding it. "We both have to want whatever happens from now on."

They walked into the den. He pulled her down beside him on the couch. "Steven's problems had nothing to do with you and me...with our spending time together."

Her head was bowed, and dark hair fell forward to hide her face. "Yes, it did. In a way. I've been too involved with what *I* wanted to realize how serious things were for him. And if I'm not careful, Bobby will be getting into situations I'm too busy to notice. I won't allow that."

He had to be patient. "Are you saying everything's over between us because you can't have your own life *and* be a parent? Jen, millions of people do just that."

"What exactly are you asking of me?" She held his hand more tightly. "I know what you want. You've told me how important having your own children is and you must know that would be a huge step for me. So I guess you want us to go on having an affair."

He pulled his hand away, anger swelling within him. "I told you I loved you. That hasn't changed."

She was quiet.

Peter smoothed back her hair, and she looked at him. He felt himself drawn closer. Her soft mouth parted. Moisture glistened in her troubled eyes. But there was no invitation there, only doubt. She doubted him, after all they'd shared.

"You told me to give Steven more freedom," she said quietly. "And look what he did with it."

For an instant he wasn't certain he'd heard correctly—or interpreted her meaning accurately.

"The thought of me selling the house bothered him. Too much for him to even communicate how he felt."

Peter found his voice. "Are you blaming *me* for everything?"

Jennie pressed a fist to her brow. "I'm saying I've allowed myself to be swayed because of my own wants."

"I didn't tell you to sell the house."

"You didn't say I shouldn't."

Anger mounted. "It wasn't my place. I did tell you I wasn't sure it was a good idea to uproot the boys now."

"You're a lot like Mark."

He fell back on the couch. "Where did that come from? What does it have to do with anything?"

"I don't know. I'm muddled up. But I know there are things I don't want to repeat."

"Name them."

She pressed her hands to her face. "Like playing second-fiddle to a man's career."

"I thought it was your children's welfare that was standing between us."

"It is…oh, it's everything."

She subsided into silence, and Peter could only stare at her. He felt her struggle, and the part of him that could still think clearly wanted to reach out to her. But his pride had taken enough.

Jennie turned toward him, and their eyes met.

"What are you thinking?" He wanted her to say something, anything that would give him hope.

"That I love you."

"Oh, Jen." He felt first formless, then incredibly powerful. Overcoming her slight resistance with ease, he pulled her into his arms and settled her face against his shoulder. "We'll be okay. You'll see."

Footsteps approached, and she pushed away. "No, Peter. One of us has to be strong. Take the boys, please. They're looking forward to this. Then do yourself a favor and think. Really think.''

"Why?" He stood up, his heart pounding. "Why are you making this so damn difficult?"

Jennie sighed. "You kind of answered that, didn't you? I'm making it difficult. I'm the one who has to do all the accommodating and I don't think I can—not anymore. I'll have enough to do cleaning up the mess I've made already."

"But—"

"It won't work."

Steven put his head around the door, and Jennie said, "Make sure you've got a key in case I'm not home when Peter drops you off."

JENNIE SAT on a ladder-back chair beside a small, round rosewood table near the living-room window. Over the years this had been the space least used in the house, and here she felt less drawn into memories.

She wanted Peter. But how could she be sure they could work out anything together that wouldn't end in disaster?

The distant ringing of the doorbell twisted her nerves. The only people she wanted to see wouldn't be ringing the bell.

The ring came again, and several minutes later, again.

Giving up, Jennie walked slowly through the hall and opened the door to confront Lou.

"I know you're alone—I was watching when Peter—"

"Please, Lou. I'm tired and I was resting." And she wished the woman would stop her perpetual surveillance.

"This won't take long." Lou walked into the house and closed the door. "We can stand right here. I've just got to say what I've got to say and get it over with. Then you never have to talk to me again if you like. I wouldn't blame you."

Jennie softened. "Come in and sit down."

"No. I don't think I should. I've got some apologizing to do, is all. And I can't wait any longer." She tilted up her chin. "I'm so ashamed."

"Please don't be." Jennie felt suddenly sad and embarrassed.

"I don't understand why everything got out of hand for me," Lou said indistinctly. "Suddenly I was so jealous I thought I'd go mad. I was almost convinced you were after Carl."

Awkwardly Jennie patted Lou's hand.

"I don't expect you to forgive me completely, not now. But at least I can be honest about what's been going on in my head and say I'm sorry."

"It's all right," Jennie said. Her throat ached.

"It's obvious, I suppose," Lou continued as if Jennie hadn't spoken. "With Jody gone and too many hours to myself, I imagined things. Gaining weight didn't help, or feeling plain. But I shouldn't have taken that out on you. You've been through enough."

"Lou," Jennie said, putting her arm around her shoulders. "It's all right now. Forget it. I'm going to."

"I'm upsetting you. You want me to go away."

"I want you to let us both get over this and go back to being friends."

"You mean it." Hope softened the worry lines on Lou's face. "Jennie, you're so important to me, and I've been such a fool."

They fell into silence for several seconds.

"I'm only going to say one more thing, then I'll go."

Jennie raised expectant eyebrows.

"Make the best of a good thing. And I mean Peter Kynaston. If he isn't a man in love, then I've never seen one, and it's you he's in love with. And you're in love with him. Do something about it." With that, Lou hurried out into the night and closed the door behind her.

"Mom? Can I come in?"

Jennie turned over in bed. She'd been in bed, wide awake, for hours. "Sure, Steve. Can't you sleep? Does your head hurt?"

"My head's fine, but I can't sleep."

She sat up and switched on the bedside lamp. "Come sit by me."

There had been a time when Steven's night visits had been routine—in the first few months after Mark died. Then he'd started drawing away from her. Jennie patted the mattress. She wanted the closeness back again.

He sat down and ran a hand over ruffled hair. "I've been awful lately."

This was turning into a night for apologies. "You've had some hard decisions to make."

"Yeah. And I managed to make 'em all wrong."

"You didn't set out to mess up, Steve. None of us does. It just happens sometimes."

"D'you like Gigi?" His neck, bent forward, looked oddly vulnerable.

"Yes, I do." But she hoped these two kids had learned that they had plenty of time to make the biggest decisions of their lives.

"I thought you did." He turned his face toward her. "Bobby and I had a great time at the ball game."

Jennie swallowed. "You already told me. I'm glad."

His dark eyes impaled her. "I came to a lot of wrong conclusions about Peter. He's something."

"Peter's special." She had to look away.

"So why are you trying to turn him off?"

"How do you know that's what I'm doing?"

"I'm not a kid. You made sure he dropped us off without coming in tonight. And you're having us take all the telephone calls so you can say you can't talk to him."

Jennie smoothed the sheet. "You don't understand."

"I guess I don't if you say I don't. But I sure hope Peter isn't going to stop coming around. You get kind of… Who *does* like it when the people they like keep dropping out?"

"Steven—"

"Peter asked me to give you this when you had a quiet moment." He reached to drop a small box into her lap.

Jennie picked it up.

"Hey," Steven said, "all of a sudden I'm tired." He got up, and Jennie heard him say "Night, Mom" as he closed the door.

She lifted the lid and smiled. The fan earrings he'd bought in Vancouver, supposedly for Liz, and a note:

Jennie: I intended to give you these when we got back from Vancouver. Then everything went crazy. Then there never was a right time. I bought them because they were part of a special moment with you. Here's to decisions. Let's hope we make the right ones.

Love, Peter.

SHE COULDN'T LAST another day without talking to him.

"Hold my calls, Bliss." Jennie closed her office door and picked up the phone. Sunday had come and gone, and Monday, and Peter hadn't called. Why should he? The next move was up to her.

She pressed each button deliberately. There was still time to change her mind.

"Hello." Liz Meadows's voice.

Lou thought she and Peter were meant for each other. Steven and Bobby were crazy about the man. Was she being pushed into trying for something against her own will?

"Hello!"

"Ah, yes, hello. This is Jennie Andrews." No, she wanted him, on whatever terms she could have him. "May I please speak to Peter?"

"Hi, Jennie. Liz here. Peter's out."

"Oh." She felt overwhelmingly disappointed. "Never mind."

"Jennie! Don't hang up. How are you?"

"Fine."

"Peter's not."

Jennie squeezed her eyes shut against a sudden headache.

"He's pretty down, but I guess you know about that."

"I'm sorry."

A tapping came as if Liz was using a fingernail on the receiver "He's gone for an interview. I hope you'll get in touch with him soon...very soon."

"Why?" Jennie held the phone with both hands. Liz was trying to tell her something. "What's wrong."

"If Peter takes the job, he'll be leaving us. The position's in Germany."

CHAPTER FIFTEEN

Germany

Darkness was seeping through the last remnants of day, streaking the sky above Peter's house with smoky bands bled through by the sun's last red embers. Jennie's schedule had made it impossible to come earlier. She'd driven directly from a client's home and now she wasn't sure she should have come at all.

She idled the Mercedes's engine at the curb. She hadn't tried to call him again and she'd heard nothing from him. Liz couldn't have had a chance to pass on the message that Jennie had phoned, or, if she had...

Slowly she drove into the driveway.

The Lotus was there.

Jennie parked and got out, letting the door swing shut. She straightened the skirt of her green-and-white striped suit and smoothed her hair. The garage doors stood open, and banging came from inside—and the steady, soft beat of music.

She advanced hesitantly, conscious that her narrow skirt beneath an exaggerated peplum forced her to take small, hip-swinging steps.

Peter bent over a workbench at the back of the garage, still dressed in the well-fitting gray suit slacks and white shirt he must have worn for his interview. His jacket and tie were slung over the handle of a lawn mower, and Jennie automatically winced at the prospect of oil stains. Then she smiled. Love was a weird, dangerous pest that could make a woman crazy—even about a man's bad habits.

Jennie watched him work, his shoulders moving as he lined up pieces of wood, making a frame of some kind. Along a windowsill at the back of the bench, where a window had been built to extend out and accommodate shelves, orchids that were not in bloom crowded one another. He had no shortage of interests. But these things weren't human. They didn't return all the warmth, and the love, he had to give.

It was Killer who gave away Jennie's presence. The cat streaked from a shadowy recess, leaped in front of Peter and deposited herself at Jennie's ankles.

Peter turned and saw her—and ran the handle of the hammer slowly back and forth between his fingers before setting it down.

Whatever happened, his would be a face Jennie had no hope of forgetting. Peter walked slowly toward her, wiping his hands on a rag. His eyes were clearly green, even in semishadow, and the fine cut of his nose, his cheekbones and square jaw pleased her deeply, as did his wide mouth with slightly upturned corners. But it wasn't his handsome face, the big well-made body with its power to stir her, that touched her deeply in the moment. In those unforgettable eyes lay gentle kindness—and a flicker of resignation, perhaps.

"How are you, Jennie?" He tossed the rag aside.

"Fine...not fine. All muddled up."

He stood a few feet to one side of her, facing out toward the encroaching darkness, his arms crossed. "I'm sorry to hear that."

"You went for an interview."

"Yes." He glanced sideways, into her eyes.

"Is it okay that I dropped in?" She became warm.

"It's okay. You look wonderful."

If she touched him, would he reject her? "Thank you. So do you."

"I don't feel so wonderful." A step brought him to her side, but he stopped in the act of reaching for her.

Being so near and continuing not to touch him was impossible. Jennie settled a palm on the side of his face, stroked him carefully, ran her hand around to his nape. A muscle jerked in Peter's jaw, but he watched her face—and kept his arms at his sides.

Jennie slipped her wrists lightly around his neck and nuzzled her cheek to his. "Whatever you want for yourself, I want too, Peter. You're my best friend."

He drew in a ragged breath. "You called the lab and spoke to Liz." His hands settled at her waist.

So he had gotten the message. "Yes."

"You called for me. Why?"

"I can't remember now." She felt foolish.

Peter moved slightly, held her more firmly. The music continued to play from a radio balanced on a shelf, and Peter began to move with it, to sway their bodies gently together.

Jennie looked up at him, lips parted...and he looked steadily back.

"How was the interview?"

He wrapped her against him, and they turned as one. "It was only a formality. The job's mine."

Her heart and stomach dropped. "Oh, Peter." Helplessly she buried her face in his shoulder.

His hands, steadily chafing her back, were warm through thin fabric. "It's for a year."

"Then you'll come back."

"That would be the plan."

Jennie raised her face. Instantly Peter's lips, making gentle contact with hers, achieved their magic. Her breath trembled, mingled with his. Her eyes flickered closed, opened again to find his tightly shut. They could have worked things out. He'd shown he was willing, only she'd shied away and forced him to find a way to get on with his life—alone.

"You must have had something to say to me," he said, still very close to her mouth.

"It doesn't matter now."

"There are a few things I'd like to say to you. Even though they don't matter now." Peter rubbed his knuckles up and down the sides of her face and pushed his fingers into her hair. "I'd like you to know some of the things I've...things I'd thought through before you came to your decision about us.

"There was a time there when I wondered how good a father I'd make to a couple of teenage boys—" He settled a thumb on her mouth to silence her response. "But I came to the conclusion that I was cut out for the job. I'd have been a late starter, is all, but I'd have been damn good."

"Peter—"

"Then there was the problem of more children." He smiled as he interrupted. "You know, if you'd suddenly decided you wanted nothing more than to have another baby, that would have been great. But the biggest thing was that I discovered that what I really didn't want to do without was you."

Jennie realized she was trembling steadily. "I thought about it all, too. Lots of women have babies at my age and then go back to work. I've always loved babies. They seemed like something from the past, is all, something I'd never have again because I was alone."

"But you wouldn't have been alone, Jennie. We'd have had each other."

"I know that now." If he was angry, this would be easier. "Peter, blaming you for my decisions about Steven was wrong. I felt guilty and inadequate, and I was lashing out while I looked for answers. But he's going to be okay. You were right."

"Maybe I should have kept my mouth shut. You'd have worked it all out on your own."

Slithering softness around her ankles startled Jennie before she remembered Killer. She tried to laugh. "You already have a kid here. Are you going to keep your house?" Her voice sounded funny and her throat hurt.

"Oh, yes."

A small flare of hope made her heart beat faster. "I'll take Killer for you. After all, she does like me."

"Why would you do that?"

She glanced at him and quickly away. "While you're in

Germany. She might not get along with the renters, and you wouldn't want her mistreated.''

''I'm not going to Germany.''

Jennie spread her hands on his chest, putting space between them. ''What?''

''I'm not going. I turned the job down.''

''Why?''

''I told them I was flattered but that I had unfinished business here. Both personal and professional.''

''Peter...'' She had to hold on to him for support. The little jerk beside his mouth didn't go unnoticed.

''I really would like to know what you wanted to talk to me about earlier.''

Jennie took a very deep breath. ''Oh...oh, I'm not sure.''

''Try to remember.'' He watched her intently.

What exactly had she intended to say? The truth was she hadn't known, then or now. ''It was probably something completely off the wall.'' Sometimes instinct was the key. ''I might have been going to ask you to marry me.''

Peter grinned, tipped back his head and laughed.

Jennie smiled uncertainly. ''Pretty dumb, I guess.''

Without warning he stooped and swept her into his arms. Heading for the house, he continued to laugh.

''What?'' She pulled his face down. ''What are you laughing at?''

''Please, ma'am.'' He paused, his face serious. ''Would it be all right if I took you to my room? I'd kind of like you to lie with me and chat about a few things.''

''Like what?''

''That must mean it's okay.'' He kicked open the door and strode into the hallway.

As he started upstairs, Jennie tugged at his collar. ''Peter, *what* things do you want to discuss?''

''Ah, nothing much. Stuff like how things are done. Who's supposed to ask whom, and what. Marriage proposals and the like.''

She squirmed, but not too much. "We've reached the age of supposed equality. The old rules are out the window."

Peter sighed, set her down on a step and leaned over her. "Ask me again...properly."

Jennie shook her head and smiled. "Peter, I love you. Will you marry me? Please?"

"Mmm." He nodded slowly. "I love you too. Okay. Yes."

A MAN LIKE MAC

Fay Robinson

For my mother, who was fearless

And for Tom Woodward and the late
Robert Mount, who taught me that heroes
sometimes come with wheels.

Acknowledgment

My deepest appreciation to Paralympics gold-medal
winner Shawn Meredith, respiratory therapist
Steve Patton and rehabilitation specialist
Lynn Carpenter-Harrington for their help with
research. Any errors are mine and not theirs.
Thanks also to the many disabled people and their
spouses who were willing to answer questions.
And to the staff at East Alabama Medical Center in
Opelika, Alabama, for the guided tour of the
trauma center and the smelling salts.

PROLOGUE

September 27

"TELL ME YOUR NAME!"

The demanding voice lurked at the edge of her consciousness, an intruder who prevented her from slipping into the welcome comfort of a pain-free sleep.

She struggled to keep her eyes open. She wanted to see the annoying person attached to the voice, but her eyelids felt heavy, too heavy to lift for more than a few seconds, and the enormous sun that hung in the air a few feet above her face blinded her.

Impossible. Her muddled mind tried to make sense of it. The sun couldn't be so large or so close, yet it was there each time she opened her eyes. Dark figures danced around it to a music that was eerie and frightening, that pulsed in rhythm to the fiery pain in her right side.

What were they doing to her? Who were these people whose hands roamed her body? They hurt her. They made her cry out as they poked her chest and stomach, as they slid their hands downward along her legs.

"Tell me your name!"

A man's voice? She licked her cracked lips and tasted blood. The smell of antiseptic fouled the air and stung her nose and throat.

"Hurts," she cried.

"Where does it hurt?"

"Everywhere."

The voice pressed closer, just above her face. "Do you know your name?" This time she was certain the voice belonged to a man, but what man hated her so much to inflict this kind of pain? She opened her eyes and saw him, a green shroud covering his body and bloody bandages on his hands.

"Please...no more. Don't hurt me anymore."

"Honey, it's okay," said a soothing female voice at her ear. "You're in the emergency room. We're going to help you."

Emergency room? Images floated through her head, but they were indistinct, as if she were looking at them through frosted glass.

Hands moved along her legs and feet, touching and squeezing, sending pain shooting through her whole body. She screamed in protest.

"Stabilize and splint that leg," the man said. "That's all we can do for now." He leaned down. "My name is Dr. Tatum. Can you tell me yours?"

She tried. The name was so close she could almost touch it, but it toyed with her memory, scooting away just when she thought she had it.

She concentrated as hard as she could to clear her mind. The name revealed itself first. Then a flood of childhood memories poured out to overwhelm her. Her father. Her mother. Euphoria and pain. Love and anger.

"Keely. My name is...Keely Wilson."

"Keely Wilson, the runner?"

She nodded before he even had a chance to finish, an automatic response to a question she had answered thousands of times. *The runner.* The phrase defined not only *what* she was, but *who* she was. Over the years people had referred to her that way so often, the words were no longer a description but an extension of her name. Keely Wilson, *the runner.*

The doctor told a nurse, "Call Dr. Vanoy back and tell him the patient is an Olympic runner with a serious orthopedic injury. And make sure the pulmonologist knows she has a pneumo."

Serious orthopedic injury? Panic seized her. Details of the accident suddenly hit her. She'd been in the third hour of a slow run in midtown Atlanta. A car hadn't stopped at a red light and struck her as she crossed an intersection.

"Do you have family we can call?" the doctor asked.

She was an only child. Her mother lived a few miles away in Buckhead, but Keely hadn't seen her in months. Since the divorce seven years ago that had caused her father's fatal heart attack, she and her mother hadn't had much to say to each other.

What was there to say? With her betrayal, Liz Wilson had destroyed their family and caused the death of the most important person in Keely's life. Never would she forgive her mother for that.

"No, no one. I have no one."

The doctor pulled down his mask and took off his visor. She guessed he was in his late fifties or early sixties, nice-looking for an older man, but his face was much too grim.

"Will I be able to run again?" she asked.

"I don't know. Let's wait and see what happens."

His words held a glimmer of hope but his expression told her the dark truth. Not only didn't he believe she would run again, he didn't believe she would live.

She closed her eyes. Reaching deep inside herself, she grabbed hold of the strength that had seen her through more than one tragedy. Maybe this thing she possessed wasn't strength at all but pure stubbornness. Hardheadedness, her mother called it. An inability to ever give in, even when the odds were against her.

Not once in her amateur or professional career had she quit a race. Now she faced the toughest one of all—a race against death.

Calm replaced fear. Determination replaced sorrow. For twenty years she had struggled to become one of the world's elite athletes. While she might be worthless at everything else, racing was something she knew how to do.

And there was something else she knew how to do, something that, despite the grim line of the doctor's mouth and the sorrow she saw in his eyes, told her everything was going to be okay.

Keely Wilson knew how to win.

CHAPTER ONE

April

I NEED YOU.

No, Mac corrected himself. That wasn't what she'd told him. Old fool that he was, he had allowed his heart to trick him into hearing what he longed to hear, instead of what she'd really said.

I need your help.

Yes, that was it. She needed his *help*. Nothing more than that.

He'd been so overwhelmed at hearing from Keely after all these years he had let old feelings eclipse reason. Her sultry voice on the telephone, her soft pleading that he help with her rehabilitation, had distracted him. When she'd broken down and cried, his normal good sense had crumbled. He'd been willing to promise her anything just to make her feel better.

Had he been rational, he would never have agreed to this meeting, but he'd hesitated just long enough to wonder what it would be like to see her again in the flesh, rather than having to be satisfied with her photo on a magazine cover. That hesitation had done him in.

Now, he realized, and with deep regret, they would both pay a high price for his weakness, because he couldn't give her the thing she wanted most—to run again. No one could. And telling her in person was going to be ten times harder than doing it over the phone.

He shifted and did a few more lateral raises on the exercise machine, feeling the tautness of stress in his shoulders and back with every movement. A touch of vanity and a choking dose of insecurity had brought him to the athletic department's weight room to meet her, rather than having her sent to his office.

Normally he was neither vain nor insecure about his looks. Having had thirty-nine years to reflect on them, he considered himself in that gray area between handsome and ugly, somewhere around "passable." But today, for this woman, "passable" was inadequate, especially considering how much he'd changed in the six years since she'd graduated from college and they'd last seen each other.

With nervous fingers, he combed through his hair. He started to wipe the sweat from his face and put on his shirt, then thought better of it and tossed away the towel. He wanted to look like he was working out, instead of sitting here, waiting for her.

Although it galled him to admit it, he wanted her to see him without his shirt. The rest of him might be questionable, but he had put hundreds of hours into building the muscles in his chest, arms and shoulders. If he was going to give in to his stupid vanity, it only made sense to show off his assets. His defects were glaringly obvious.

The crowd in the weight room had thinned with the ringing of the eleven-o'clock bell, but twenty or so faculty members and students without a class the next period had lingered to work out, making Mac suddenly question the wisdom of this location for his meeting with Keely. He hadn't considered her feelings. She might not want anyone to know she'd asked him for help.

"McCandless, you're an idiot," he mumbled to himself.

Now it was too late to correct his error. She entered the room surrounded by student admirers she'd collected on her way up to the second floor. They bombarded her with questions.

"Are you recovered?"

"Are you competing in the Sydney Olympics?"

She answered the questions patiently, but the tightness around her mouth told him she was fighting pain. Her left leg appeared unstable, although seven months had passed since her accident. She favored the leg when she walked, favored her entire left side, and that worried him.

The beautiful skin he remembered as bronze from outdoor roadwork was sallow, a visible reminder of the trauma she'd sustained from the accident and the months away from training. The huge blue eyes, once so bright and full of life, reflected her weariness.

No way was she as far along in her recovery as she'd led him to believe.

"Hi, Coach," she said, smiling softly. "I'm so glad to see you." The hand she extended felt weak when he shook it. He could have pulled her off her feet with a simple tug.

"I'm glad to see you, too, Keely."

Her gaze left his face to creep with excruciating slowness across his upper body, then slid downward. Feminine admiration lit her eyes and left him feeling almost dizzy.

"You look terrific." Her words seemed genuine. "Fit. More handsome than ever."

"And you're still beautiful."

"Well…older."

"So how come it doesn't show?"

Her smile widened, showing her dimples, making his heart constrict.

"I should have come much sooner, Coach. I'd forgotten how charming you can be."

"Call me Mac." He was twelve years older, and while that had probably seemed like a lot to her at seventeen, he hoped it didn't seem like much to her now at twenty-seven.

"Okay…Mac."

The young people had crowded closer and were grinning, obviously enjoying the exchange between their coach and his famous former student. Mac cleared his throat; it was enough to make them scurry out the door to class.

He motioned to the other end of the padded bench. "Do you want to talk here or would you rather go to my office for privacy and some quiet?" The noise of machines and the grunts of bodies straining for perfection surrounded them. The air, he suddenly noticed, also reeked with the smell of sweat.

She eased without hesitation onto the weight bench facing him.

"Here's fine. Feels like home to me. Besides, I've found it's impossible to keep anything private anymore. Ten minutes from now I'm sure some sports reporter will have discovered I'm here. Figuring out why will take about another two seconds."

He nodded, understanding.

"The receptionist told me on my way in that you're now the athletic director. From assistant coach to A.D. in such a short time? I'm very impressed. Do you still teach?"

"Oh, sure. Sport Management and also undergraduate classes in Adaptive Physical Education. At a small university like this, it's not practical for me not to teach. And I like teaching. I still coach, too, although my duties have changed."

"I can't believe how out of touch I am. I've been meaning to visit, but my schedule's so tight it's hard to even get home to Atlanta more than once or twice a year. Still, I feel bad that I've let so much time go by without dropping in. The drive from my mother's house to Courtland only took a couple of hours."

"Hey, don't worry about it."

"I'm glad I have the chance to thank you in person for the flowers you sent while I was in the hospital and your sweet note. Hearing from you meant a lot to me. I was feeling pretty low at the time with the rehab and the pain, and the doctors so discouraging about my future th-that hearing…"

Her voice cracked and her bottom lip trembled. An awkward silence descended between them as she struggled not to cry. She fingered the car keys in her lap, looking at them, instead of him.

Watching her, Mac struggled with his own emotions. The ache inside him, the one he'd carefully controlled since meeting this woman ten years ago, threatened to overwhelm him now and make him do something foolish. He could imagine his arms reaching out to hold her, his face against her own as he reassured her everything was going to be all right.

But he couldn't tell her everything was going to be all right because it wasn't. And he couldn't hold her, because if he did—even once—he would never be able to let her go.

"I'm sorry," she said in a near whisper, finally looking at him. "I detest weepy women, but I seem to be one of them lately. I'm fine and then without warning I feel like I'm going to fall apart."

"You sustained terrible injuries. Your emotions need to heal just like the rest of you."

"People keep telling me that, but everything's taking so long."

"Like your rehab? I can see you weren't straight with me about that when you called."

"Yes, like my rehab. I shouldn't have lied and I'm sorry, but I thought if I could only talk to you in person I could convince you things aren't as bad as you might have heard. I'm not healed, but I really am feeling much stronger physically. A few weeks ago I couldn't walk without crutches. Now, I'm getting around fine."

Mac bit back his comment. She was fooling herself.

"I understand I have a long way to go before I can run again or get back to a level where I can compete, but with you coaching me and supervising the rest of my rehab, I can do it. I know I can."

She sounded so certain that Mac wanted to believe it, too, but what she wanted was impossible. The thick package of medical records, X rays and progress reports he'd insisted she have her doctors send him told the horror story. He had read and reread them, praying for something that would back up Keely's claim. He never found it. She *might* run for pleasure, but she'd never be able to compete again at a national or international level. Her career was over.

"Your doctors don't seem to think it's physically possible for you to run again," he reminded her.

"Those doctors don't know what they're talking about! They didn't think I'd live, but I did. Then they told me I'd never walk again, but you notice I walked in here without any trouble. So I have no reason to believe they're right when they say I can't run.''

"And your current trainer? What does he think?"

"Former trainer," she corrected. "We had a difference of opinion about my chances for a full recovery so I fired him."

"I see."

She leaned forward, her face taut with determination. "Mac, no one understands me the way you do. You know what I'm like when I set my mind to something, how relentless I can be. You know I'll give this everything I've got."

Yes, he knew. She had more heart and talent than any student he'd ever coached, had always put running ahead of everything else, including her personal life. She would focus every breath, every hope, every moment on getting back her career. And when she failed…she would have nothing left.

Unless *he* gave her something.

"What will you do if you try your best and it's not enough?"

"That won't happen."

"Keely, you have to consider the possibility. All the grit in the world won't matter if your body's physically unable to do what you're asking it to do. Believe me, I know."

"Are you saying I can't ever run again?"

Well, there it was. He had prayed she wouldn't put it to him quite so bluntly. He didn't want to give her false hope, but he didn't want to crush her faith, either. She would need that faith, and much more, to get through the long months ahead. Her rehabilitation had only just begun.

"I didn't say you couldn't," he answered, hedging. "If it turns out, though, that you can't get back to the same level as before your accident, you need to be able to accept it and go on with your life."

"If I can't run I don't have a life, and that car might as well have killed me."

"You don't mean that."

"I *do* mean that. Mac, being a runner isn't just something I do, it's what I am. I get up in the morning so I can run. I go to bed at night so I'll feel rested enough to run. I eat only what I know will help me run faster and longer. These legs—'' she grabbed her good thigh with one hand for emphasis ''—are what make me Keely Wilson. They're all I have.''

"Keely, life is more than running, and you're more than just a set of legs. You're bright. You're a hard worker. You could retire and—''

"I'm not retiring! I'm going to run again and I'll do whatever it takes to make that happen.''

Mac rubbed the back of his neck in growing frustration. She was determined to try this, and no argument he could make was going to change her mind.

Her iron will was a curse, as well as a blessing. She couldn't accept that she had a permanent physical problem, wouldn't accept that her career was over until she exhausted every chance to save it. In doing that, she'd push herself to the limit. She could end up even more severely injured unless a qualified trainer guided her.

The reality was, *he* was the most qualified for the job and they both knew it. His credentials in rehabilitation were as good as anyone's in the country. He had also coached Keely during her four years in college. He knew her strengths and weaknesses.

"Please, Mac, don't say no. Maybe the doctors are right and it will take a miracle, but all I'm certain of is...without you I don't have any chance at all. Please. I *need* you.''

He groaned, knowing now what he should have known the instant she walked into the room. It didn't matter if she didn't have a chance of ever running another race, much less winning one. It didn't matter if she couldn't run three feet without falling on her face. He was going to help her, anyway.

"All right, Keely, I'll oversee the remainder of your rehabilitation. If, after that, I think you can do any serious training, I'll help you. But I have a major condition you'll have to agree to, or the deal's off.''

She let out a breath in relief. "Oh, anything. I'll agree to any condition you make. Thank you. You won't regret this.''

"I hope you're right about that. Let's go to my office and work out the details. I need access to a telephone."

She stood to follow him. He grabbed his towel and slung it around his neck, then reached out and grabbed his wheelchair, pulling it closer. He started to transfer but Keely shrieked, attracting not only Mac's attention but the attention of everyone working out around them.

He froze at her expression of horror.

"My God! What happened to you? Why are you in a *wheelchair?*"

Exercise machines around the room were turned off one by one. Conversation stopped. Silence wrapped itself around them, and he felt its smothering embrace. He prayed for a giant hole to open up and swallow him, but nothing happened.

Everyone waited for his response. He could feel their eyes boring into him.

Finally he found his voice. "I assumed you knew. There was an accident and I can't use my legs anymore. I'm paralyzed."

SHE WAS GOING to throw up. The nausea was moving up her throat, and Keely fought it with every bit of strength she had left.

She hung her head over the sink in the women's washroom and commanded her stomach to stop its roiling. Already she had humiliated Mac in front of his students and some of the staff of the athletic department. Getting sick would be another insult to him. She couldn't do it. Wouldn't do it.

But as she thought about him, about his useless legs, misery overwhelmed her. She hobbled to the small couch against the back wall and put her head between her knees.

Paralyzed! How? When?

Next to her late father, she admired Mac McCandless more than any man she'd ever known. At one time she'd even imagined herself a little in love with him, as most of his female students probably had. That rugged face, those eyes the color of expensive chocolate, had driven her to distraction whenever she was close to him. As a coach, he was as gifted as anyone in the business.

Now he was paralyzed. Dear God!

The door to the rest room opened and a woman walked in. Keely straightened. "Hey, hon, are you gonna be okay?" the woman asked. "Mac's about to go crazy outside worrying about you."

"I'm okay. I just needed a minute to myself."

"Do you want me to get you some water? A cold drink?"

She shook her head. The woman plopped down on the edge of the couch facing her. She was shaped like a basketball, and Keely had to turn sideways and slide all the way to the back to give her room.

"I heard what just happened. The story's all over the building."

"Oh, no!" Keely put her hand to her stomach as another wave of nausea hit her.

"Name's Miriam Ethridge. I've been Mac's secretary for the last five years."

"Did he send you in here to check on me?"

"Yep, he's pretty frantic. You scared him when you nearly passed out in the weight room."

"The shock of seeing him...you know, like that."

The horrible moment flashed back to her. Oh, no, she'd screamed! She'd seen the wheelchair, realized it was his and let out a loud awful scream, as if suddenly confronted by a monster.

"Mac will never forgive me for this. I humiliated him in front of all those people."

"Honey, what that man's been through the last few years would've killed anyone else, but he hasn't let it beat him, so I don't think a bit of insensitivity from you is gonna be lethal. As soon as he could get around after he got hurt, he was right back at work as if nothing was wrong, showing people that he was still the same man. And he *is* the same man. They don't come any better than John Patrick McCandless, in or out of a wheelchair."

Keely wanted to ask what had happened to him, how Mac

had been injured, but she didn't know this woman. She already felt uncomfortable discussing Mac with a stranger.

Miriam patted her on the arm with a chubby hand. "Pull yourself together and come on out. He's not as patient as he likes people to think. I won't be able to keep him out of here much longer."

"I can't go back out. I don't know what to say to him."

"Oh, I think you do. You just have to find the courage to say it."

COURAGE. SHE DIDN'T HAVE much of that lately. Her courage was in a constant battle with self-pity, and more often self-pity won. But Miriam had stood and walked to the door, leaving Keely no choice but to gather what little courage she had left, ease off the couch and follow.

Mac was in the hall in his wheelchair. His demeanor was calm and his complexion was no longer flushed from embarrassment, but those dark expressive eyes of his told her he was in pain. Regret, as sharp as the blade of a knife and just as deadly, pierced her heart.

"Feeling okay now?" he asked.

"Y-yes." The quaver in her voice made her statement seem false and ridiculous.

"Maybe you should lie down aga—"

"No, I'm okay." *Please,* she wanted to shout, *don't fuss over me! Don't be nice to me!* His concern only made her feel worse, because she knew she didn't deserve it.

With extreme effort she tried not to look at his legs or the black and chrome wheelchair, but a force stronger than her willpower *made* her look. The chair was bad enough, frightening, but seeing him in it put a horrible pain in the center of her chest.

She had come here expecting to find the Mac McCandless she remembered, the man who liked to run with his students, the man who had so loved to dance that at the graduation party for her class he spent the entire night whirling one partner after another around the floor. A physically perfect Mac.

Confronted with *this* Mac, she didn't know how to act or what to say.

Miriam coughed, breaking the silence. Keely's eyes snapped upward. She turned scarlet, realizing she'd been staring at his legs, trying to detect any change in them. Were they misshapen under those sweatpants? Scarred like hers because of some horrible accident?

"If you don't need me anymore, I've got errands," Miriam said, giving Keely a warning look as she walked away.

Mac suggested they go to his office. Once there, he cleared off a place on his couch and told her she could lie down if she needed.

"No, I'm fine now. Mac, I'm so sorry about everything, about coming here today without understanding...the situation. I feel terrible about what I did, how I reacted."

"Don't. I'm as much to blame as you. I assumed when you called you knew. I should have made sure."

"What happened to you? Why are you in a wheelchair?"

"I got shot a few years back. The bullet hit my spinal cord."

"Shot? Who? How?"

"I walked into the middle of an argument between a man and his girlfriend, not realizing the guy had a gun. We struggled, the gun went off, and I got hit right below the waist."

"When was this?"

"Four years ago this fall."

She thought back to that time, remembering where she'd been: France, Spain, England. Four major marathons and a string of personal appearances had kept her out of the country. She'd hardly had time to read an international newspaper, much less keep up with the Georgia news. But that was no excuse. Had she stayed in better touch with Mac after graduation as she'd intended, he could have told her about the shooting himself.

"Can you walk at all?"

"No, and I never will."

The thought was too horrible to even contemplate. "I'm so sorry."

"I've accepted it. Things could have been worse."

He ran his hand roughly through his hair. The strands of gray at his temple hadn't been there six years ago, and the deepened lines around his mouth and eyes added a maturity that was also new.

"Keely." He shifted in his chair. "After this... misunderstanding, it might not be a bad idea for us to rethink our coaching arrangement."

Slowly, she nodded in agreement, but depression overwhelmed her. Hope drained away.

When she'd had her accident and the doctors told her she wouldn't run again, a solitary idea had planted itself in her brain and refused to leave—Mac McCandless could help her. She'd fed on that notion, using it to sustain her during the agony of physical therapy. She had called it up and clung to it at night, when the pain had gotten unbearable and hopelessness had nearly defeated her.

But now... What was left for her now? Mac wasn't going to help her. She had nowhere else to turn.

"I can't blame you for not wanting to coach me anymore," she told him, determined not to make him feel bad about it. "I've acted like an idiot today."

"I don't remember saying I wouldn't coach you."

Her pulse quickened. "Are you saying you might still be willing?"

He hesitated. "Before I decide that, I think the bigger question is, are *you* willing? You had a pretty strong reaction to my disability. Given what you've been through the last several months, it was understandable. But—and this is a pretty big but—my paralysis isn't going to change. A month from now, six months from now, I'll still be in this chair. Can you handle being around a paraplegic?"

"Yes."

"Don't be so quick to answer. If you can't keep yourself from getting sick or feeling like you're going to pass out every time you look at me, the days'll get pretty long."

"Mac, I'm sure," she countered, desperation rather than confidence guiding her answer. "Please, will you help me?"

As HE SAT ON HIS PATIO late that night, polishing off another beer, Mac wondered how he'd talked himself into taking on a project that was doomed before it started. Keely was hoping for a miracle, and he didn't believe in miracles. After nearly four years of asking for one every night and waking up every morning still paralyzed, he'd finally gotten the message and stopped asking.

No, miracles weren't his department. He couldn't deliver. Knowing that, knowing that if he did this she'd probably blame him or even hate him when she failed to get her career back, he'd still been stupid enough to agree to coach her.

He was crazy. Hell, they were both crazy. A runner who couldn't accept that she would never run again and her gimp coach stupid enough to help her try. The problems were enormous. She couldn't even look at him below the waist without turning green.

Where was he going to find the time to coach her?

He was already overworked.

How could he keep her from hurting herself?

She had no patience.

But the biggest question, the one that had been consuming him since that first telephone call: *How could he keep himself from falling in love with her again?*

CHAPTER TWO

May

LIZ WILSON WATCHED as her daughter stuffed clothes into a suitcase. "I can't believe you're going through with this," she said, no longer able to keep quiet.

Keely sighed and latched the bag. "Mother, please don't give me a hard time. You promised."

"At least wait until you're feeling better. Surely six months won't make any difference. In the fall, when you're more completely healed, then you can move to Courtland."

"I can't afford to lose the training time. I'm already deconditioned."

"But—"

"No, it's settled. I've rented a house. I've already enrolled in graduate school. Support my decision, please."

"Sweetheart, you know I support you. I'm thrilled you're going back to school, but you don't have to move halfway across the state to do that. You can stay here."

"Getting out of the city where the air is cleaner will help me recover faster. You know the smog bothers my lungs. Besides, Coach McCandless is there."

True, Liz thought, somewhat consoled. A nice young man that John McCandless. Polite. Responsible. Liz was sorry to hear he was now in a wheelchair.

Keely opened another suitcase and limped to the dresser to begin emptying it. Liz doubted she'd ever walk normally again.

"What about the commercials you're doing? Didn't Ross

Hewitt negotiate some new ones for you? I don't understand why you don't wait until after you've completed those.''

"I'm not doing any new commercials. The sportswear company dropped me as their spokesperson.''

"Dropped you? Why?''

"I guess they decided no one wants to wear gear endorsed by an injured runner with ugly scars all over her arms and legs. I don't make a pretty picture anymore.''

"Don't be ridiculous! You're as beautiful as ever.''

"And you're slightly biased, I think.''

"What about your contract? They can't simply cancel it, can they?''

"Ross made them pay it off. He bought me a company with the money.''

Liz couldn't have been more shocked. When had this happened? Keely had never mentioned it. "You own a company?''

"Uh-huh. Coxwell Industries in Miami.'' She crammed shorts into another suitcase and threw running shoes in on top of them.

"What does it do?''

"Makes custom linens for hospitals and nursing homes.''

"A big company?''

"No, more like a small business. Only fifteen employees.''

"But textiles? Why?''

"Because I have a patent for a fabric I developed a few years ago while trying to come up with racing clothes I could wear in extreme weather.''

This was news to Liz as well. "And...? she prompted, wanting to know the rest of the story.

"And...it turns out the finished fabric also makes a perfect covering for trauma victims because it helps regulate body temperature and reduces shock.''

"Sweetheart, that's wonderful!''

"It's no big deal, Mother. The lab I hired did most of the work because I didn't have the skills. And the medical application thing...I only stumbled on that by accident.''

"But it was still your idea.''

"Yeah, but Ross is the one who saw the potential for using it outside sports. He's convinced me to go into limited production with the stuff and test the market."

"When did you make this decision?"

"I don't know. Two, three months ago."

"And you didn't tell me?"

Keely shrugged as if she hadn't thought of it or, worse, hadn't considered her mother important enough to be told.

Wounded, Liz sat on the bed and busied herself by trying to straighten out the chaos created by her daughter's haphazard method of packing. Communication between them had been minimal for years, at times nonexistent, but Liz had worked hard since Keely's accident to correct that. Insisting she come home to recuperate had helped.

Liz believed she was making progress, as much progress as Keely allowed her to make. Her daughter's pain over the divorce was so deep-rooted Liz didn't know if she'd ever be able to overcome it.

"Will you let me visit you?" she ventured to ask.

Keely stilled momentarily, obviously surprised by the request, then recovered sufficiently to counter Liz's attempt to get close to her. "You'll be too busy with what's-his-name to do much visiting, won't you?"

Touché, Liz thought, but she wasn't going to let her daughter beat her that easily. "I'm sure I can find the time. Perhaps I can bring Everett with me. I'd like the two of you to know each other better."

"One big happy family," Keely said sarcastically.

"Everett is a good man, and I care about him. I wish you'd make an effort to get along with him for my sake."

"Please, don't start this. Not today."

"Not today. Not yesterday. Not tomorrow. When?"

"Mother, if we talk about this we'll only argue, and I don't want to start arguing ten minutes before I leave."

"Neither do I, but I'd rather argue than have you push me away. You don't talk to me or share your life with me. You refuse to share in mine. We're becoming strangers. Is that what you want?"

"No, of course not."

"Then why can't you at least try to be tolerant of my relationship with Everett?"

"I'll say goodbye here. No need for you to come out to the car."

"Keely, don't do this."

"I have to. I appreciate your letting me stay here these past few months and everything you've done to help me get back on my feet. I really do. But I have to go on with my life now."

"You could have a life in Atlanta with me."

Keely stared at her in disbelief. "That wouldn't work and you know it. We'd be at each other's throats all the time, yelling and fighting like..." She looked away.

"Like your father and I did? That's what you were going to say, wasn't it?"

"Yes. And I couldn't go through that. Not again."

She made her way slowly to the window and called to the gardener to come inside for the last two suitcases, then picked up her billfold and keys and limped to the door.

"Please, Keely! It's been seven years," Liz cried in desperation. "How can you continue to hate me for divorcing your father when you know it was better for all of us?"

She hesitated, then turned. "Mother, don't say that or even think it. I don't hate you. I know you had some problems, some differences of opinion, but I can't understand how you could kick Daddy out. I certainly don't hate you for it, though."

"You act like it sometimes. You've put up a wall between us, and no matter what I do, I can't seem to get past it. Little by little you've shut me out of every part of your life, as if you're trying to...to punish me."

"I haven't."

"Yes, you have. At least admit it to yourself, if not to me."

Keely stood quietly for a moment. "I'm sorry. I don't mean to shut you out, but I'm not sure I know how *not* to."

"You might start by forgiving me."

"I want to, it's just..." She shook her head. "I can't help

wishing things could have been different between you and Daddy—that you'd somehow worked things out so the last months of his life could've been happy. You claim to have loved him. But when you love people, you don't give up on them.''

Her daughter's words cut deeply. For seven years Liz had allowed herself to shoulder the blame for the breakup and she longed to tell Keely what had really happened.

But to do so would destroy the only thing her daughter had left of the father she adored—good memories. And she couldn't do that to Keely or even to Spence, not with him dead and unable to defend himself.

So instead of telling her the truth as she wanted to, Liz kept silent. Keely would never believe her, anyway.

Liz watched from the window as Keely somberly walked to her car with the aid of a cane and climbed in. "You're right," she whispered, saying to herself what she wished she could openly say to her daughter. "When you love people, you don't give up on them. And I'm not giving up on you."

KEELY WAITED until she was a safe distance from the house before she let the tears flow freely. She pulled over to the side of the tree-lined street, turned off the engine and wept until there were no tears left to shed. The purging was long overdue. The pain had been festering for years, just waiting for the right time to come spewing out. The intensity of the release, however, surprised even her.

Her father had meant everything to her. He'd been her first coach, but most importantly, her best friend. The divorce, then his death from a heart attack less than two months later, had ripped a hole in her life, and that hole kept getting bigger, no matter how many times she attempted to repair it.

In truth, the hole had almost always been there; it had started as a tiny crack one winter night when she was five and had awoken in the dark to the frightening sound of her parents' raised voices in the next room. The words were unclear, but their tone was unmistakably angry.

After that, many more arguments had followed to widen the crack.

"Why do you and Mother fight?" Keely had asked her father one day with a child's innocence.

"Because your mother likes things her way."

For a child who worshiped her father and had little in common with her mother, that had been sufficient explanation.

Later it was clear they fought for exactly the reason her father had said. Her mother liked to be in charge. When she wasn't, the people around her suffered.

But knowing the reason for the unhappiness in her family had done nothing to alleviate the pain Keely felt every time her parents screamed at each other. Only running had done that. What had started as a way to escape the house during their verbal wars quickly changed to a lifeline for her, a means of self-therapy that could help her endure.

She used to convince herself that if she made it around the block without stopping, everything would be all right when she got back home. When around the block wasn't enough, she ran a mile, then five, then more. The silly superstitious ritual had given her some sense of control over a situation that was beyond her control.

Her parents stayed together twenty-three years, until their differences finally tore them apart. How it had worked that long, Keely didn't know. They were terribly mismatched. Her mother liked expensive clothes, fine wine and elegant dinners. She came from old money and was a patron of the Atlanta Symphony Orchestra and the Alliance Theater Company.

Her father had been a simple insurance salesman, happy in a pair of shorts from Wal-Mart. He'd loved beer, hot dogs and sports of all kinds. The Braves hadn't played at home without his being in the stands.

Different politics, different friends, different interests. Her parents were as far apart as two people could be. Keely wished they'd called it quits long before they did, although the breakup, when it had finally come, had been terrible. Her father's death on the heels of it had devastated her.

Her mother was to blame for the divorce. To her father's

credit, he had at least tried to find some common ground. Her
mother had refused to give an inch.

Your mother likes things her way.

Her father's words explained everything.

THE HOUSE SHE'D RENTED in Courtland was larger than she
really wanted, but size hadn't been her first priority. She had
needed something in an area with quiet streets, a house with
no steps or difficult areas to trip her up since she was walking
no better than a child in her first pair of shoes.

With Mac's help she'd found a great house in an older
neighborhood about three miles from campus. Airy, with
plenty of glass to let in the sunlight, it had a big tub in the
master bathroom. The pool, though, had sold her on the place.
Anytime she felt like taking a swim, she could step out the
back door.

Well, almost anytime. Mac had given her specific instructions about the use of the pool and threatened her with un-
specified consequences if she disobeyed. The man could be
downright dictatorial at times.

And he could be a saint. When she arrived, several burly
young men had been lounging on her steps, saying "Coach"
had given them orders to unload her car and carry everything
into the house. What little furniture she owned, in storage
since the accident, had also arrived, and she supervised its
placement.

Now it was dark and after eight, and she sat at the kitchen
table making a list of things she needed to do this week.
Picking up the portable phone, she dialed Mac's number again
to thank him for the help, but as with the previous calls, there
was no answer. She quickly hung up before the machine
clicked on. One message was enough.

Was he out with friends? With a woman? Even men in
wheelchairs dated on Saturday night, she supposed. She
guessed they even got married, although she was pretty sure
Mac hadn't.

Did he have someone special in his life?

"No, Keely, don't start this," she warned herself out loud. Mac's personal life was none of her business.

A WOMAN WASN'T KEEPING Mac's body occupied but definitely his mind, as he raced lap after lap around the track. He was desperate, and exercising to exhaustion was the only antidote he could think of.

It wasn't working. The desire to drive to Keely's house was as overwhelming now as it had been hours ago. The last month had been hard, waiting for her to move to town some of the worst agony he had endured. But it was nothing compared to what he was going through now that she was here and he was trying to stay away from her.

Ever since three o'clock had rolled around—when she was due to arrive—he'd fought the urge to stop by or call her. He wanted to see her, talk to her, hear her laugh. He wanted to say something witty so she'd smile really wide, and her dimples would appear.

Maybe he should go over there just to make sure she got moved in okay. No, that was a bad idea.

He hit the push rings on his racing wheelchair with a hard even stroke. Her training and school would throw them together enough hours; he didn't need to invent reasons to be with her.

Finally having achieved the exhaustion he'd been seeking, he gave up and drove home. The light on the answering machine blinked, indicating three messages. The first and second were from women he dated occasionally. Both wanted to know where he'd been the last month and why he hadn't called. The third was from the object of his misery.

"Mac, it's Keely. Sorry I missed you. Just wanted to thank you for sending over the help this afternoon. I really appreciate it. You're sweet. Bye."

The last of his resolve drained away at the sound of her voice. He took out the piece of paper in his wallet where he'd written her new number and dialed it. She answered on the second ring.

"Hi, it's Mac. Sorry it took me so long to get back to you."

"That's okay. I really didn't expect you to call me tonight."

She sounded strange, so he asked, "Did I wake you?"

"No, I was up. I'm trying out my big bathtub. Mmm, it's wonderful."

He hung his head as his mind created the picture: Keely naked, that incredible body slick with soap.

"Did you get moved in?"

"Uh-huh. Thanks to you. I can't thank you enough for providing all the help."

He could hear her moving in the water, and he closed his eyes in an attempt to block out the image the sound created. He could almost see the droplets beaded on her breasts, her face flushed from the heat, her hand moving across her skin.

"Are you feeling okay?" he managed to croak out.

"I'm feeling fine. Better emotionally than I've felt in months, as a matter of fact. Can we start on a light exercise program this week?"

"Don't push it. We need to do a full evaluation of your condition first. Get settled in with classes next week. After that, I'll work out a program with your doctors."

"Oh, all right."

"Hey, cheer up. I've got something to keep you busy. I'm doing roadwork with a few of our wheelers tomorrow afternoon, and I could use your help."

"You want me to help with wheelchair racers?" He could hear the tension in her voice, could almost hear her mind clicking away, trying to find an excuse to get out of it. "I don't know anything about wheelers."

"You don't need to. I only need another pair of hands. You're on my way, so I'll pick you up at about a quarter to two."

"But I'll be useless."

"No, you won't. And this will be good experience for you. As Coach Stewart's teaching assistant, you're going to have to work with all the athletes, even the disabled ones, so you might as well jump in and get your feet wet."

"Okay, then. I'll try my best."

After they hung up and Mac started to think about what he'd done, his smile of triumph faded. This was only her first day in town and already he'd found an excuse to call her. And to spend tomorrow with her. He glanced at his watch. Actually he hadn't lasted a whole day. Only about six hours.

He sighed deeply and shook his head. He was never going to make it through the next few months.

CHAPTER THREE

"WHO ELSE NEEDS sunscreen?"

Male hands shot upward at Keely's question. Mac groaned and his best friend, Alan Sizemore, who sat next to him on the track, chuckled.

"I may be wrong, but I think she's already put sunscreen on half those jokers with their hands up," Alan said unnecessarily, just to needle him.

"Sizemore..." Mac warned under his breath, but he doubted it would do any good. He should never have told Alan he'd once had feelings for Keely. His second mistake was inviting her to come here this afternoon, when he knew Alan planned to train with them. Never one to miss an opportunity to taunt him, Alan had been in rare form from the moment they'd gotten out of the van.

"Who's next?" Keely asked the students, oblivious to the turmoil she was about to create.

Wheels clashed and elbows jabbed as the six young men scrambled in their racers for the front position. Ben, a senior from Athens, pushed forward with amazing agility to crowd out his teammates; he was moving faster than he had in any race. Mac and Alan watched the drama from several feet away, Alan with an amused look, Mac with an uncharacteristic scowl.

Watching the guys hit on her didn't bother Mac. He'd expected that. But watching her touch them was driving him nuts.

What was going on? When she looked at *him* in his wheelchair, she got sick to her stomach. So how come she could slather lotion on *these* guys in wheelchairs—guys she'd never met before—and not so much as blink an eye?

"Here you go," she said, leaning over to offer Ben the bottle of lotion.

She had dressed in loose-fitting blue shorts cut high on her thighs and a matching top that was little more than a couple of straps and a swatch of cotton across her breasts. It was a typical running outfit, worn for comfort and not to entice, but on Keely's perfect body, enticing as all get-out. From their low vantage point in the three-wheeled racers, the men were treated to a constant view of those incredible legs of hers. Long, supple and perfectly formed, they seemed to go all the way up to her throat.

"Man, oh, man," Alan muttered as the back of her shorts rose to expose even more of her legs.

Five heads cocked so five sets of eyes could get a better look at her backside.

Ben asked Keely to help him with the lotion. "My hands aren't working right today," he complained. "Always takes them a while to loosen up."

"Are you telling me the truth?"

"Really, I can't do it by myself." After the lie he gave her his "poor cripple" look, the one they'd probably all used a hundred times to get attention from women, the one Mac had used himself more than once.

The other guys exchanged grins behind her back.

"Seems to me that someone with enough dexterity to race a wheelchair ought to be able to put sunscreen on himself," Keely told him. Squeezing some into her palm, she smoothed it across Ben's shoulders and down his arms while every man there watched with undisguised longing.

"You suppose that guy's as sensitive on his upper body as you are?" Alan wondered out loud. Then he added with a devilish twist, "Probably more sensitive. Yeah, I bet he is. If she rubs him just right, she's liable to make that old dead pecker of his stand up and salute."

Mac could only growl a response.

Keely had finished applying lotion to the last man and was

carefully making her way over to them with the help of the cane Mac had insisted she use for a while.

"Oh, goodie," Alan said. "Here she comes."

"Embarrass me in front of her, and I'll beat the crap out of you."

Alan just grinned.

Keely stopped in front of them. "Hi."

"Hi, beautiful," Alan said. "Any fatalities over there when you started rubbing on sunscreen? Do we need the paramedics?"

"Did they really need help or am I just exceptionally gullible?"

"You're exceptionally gullible," Alan told her. "But don't feel bad. Guys in wheelchairs are experts at hitting on women, so you never had a chance."

"I was afraid they were conning me, but I wasn't sure."

"That's standard operating procedure. The first things you learn in rehab are how to hit on women and how to get laid. We call it Rehab 101."

She reddened, but she laughed. "Oh, Alan, you're terrible. I don't know when to believe you."

"That's easy," Mac said. "Never believe a word he says."

He called to the students to put on their helmets and gloves, then picked up his own.

"Is there anything else I can do?" Keely asked him.

"No, not right now. We'll pull out in a minute." He told himself not to bring it up, but he couldn't help himself. "You seem to be getting along okay with the guys. No queasy stomach?"

"No. Funny, isn't it? I feel comfortable with everyone out here."

"Not everyone."

The smile left her face and her eyes filled with regret. "No, not everyone."

"Why do you think that is?"

"I can't explain it. Maybe because I knew you before you got hurt. I'm not sure."

Alan looked at Mac, then at Keely, then at Mac again. "I think I missed something here."

"Never mind," Mac told him.

"Is the university funding this program?" Keely asked, deftly changing the subject.

"The university provides minimal training, but nothing for racing, since it's not a recognized sport here. I'm working on corporate sponsorship, but right now we sponsor ourselves. You have to understand that a bunch of crippled guys racing wheelchairs isn't exactly what businesses want when they hire an athlete to represent them."

"I do understand. Aztec couldn't wait to drop my sports-wear contract after my accident."

"I'm sorry."

"Oh, don't be. I was never comfortable with it, anyway. Now I can concentrate on getting back in shape and not be distracted."

"Your shape seems fine from where I'm sitting, doll," Alan said, wiggling his eyebrows, "but don't tell my wife I was looking at it."

"Is this one of the lines you learned in Rehab 101?"

"Absolutely. But it's Rehab 102 I really want to excel in."

"Oh, and what's Rehab 102?"

"Get Mac to show you," he said slyly with a wink. "He teaches the class."

THE ROUTE TOOK the wheelers through the oldest part of campus, where the buildings predated the Civil War and sat among the magnolia trees like graceful elderly ladies. Keely rode in the front seat of the van, while graduate student Dean Averhardt, Mac's teaching assistant, drove.

Ahead of them, Mac led the men in a tight line. His arms flexed as he worked the wheels, and his body stretched forward until every muscle in his back showed, a truly awesome sight. Watching him, Keely had to keep reminding herself to breathe.

He was wearing only a black spandex unitard that left most of his upper body uncovered, black gloves and a black helmet that allowed a glimpse of his hair on the sides and back where it was cropped close.

His muscles were taut. His skin had the patina of rich polished wood, and like the surface of a finely made table, it tempted you to reach out and run your fingers across it. How was it possible to be physically attracted to a man, yet repulsed by his physical condition? She had struggled with the answer all day.

"He's really good, isn't he?" she said to Dean. He knew immediately that she was talking about Mac. No one else came close to having his endurance or speed. While the others labored, Mac seemed to race effortlessly.

Dean answered without taking his attention from the road. "People have started calling him the Terminator because, when he races, he dresses all in black and he wipes out the competition. He's unbeatable in the shorter distances. Nobody can touch him when he wants to win. Just wish we could get him to want to win more often."

"Why doesn't he?"

"He didn't tell me this, but I think he feels bad competing against his own students in road races."

"When does he turn forty? He can race as a master then and be out of their division."

"November, I think."

They passed through an intersection that marked a change between city and country, where smooth asphalt turned into coarse gravel pavement, and condominiums gave way to thickets of pine and pastures of green spring grass. Cows the color of the red Georgia clay lifted their heads to stare or call out an occasional greeting as the athletes streaked by.

"Do you like working with the wheelers?" Keely asked.

"To be honest, I hated the idea at first, but Mac can be pretty persuasive when he thinks you ought to do something. Part of my graduate study is adaptive sports for the temporarily and permanently disabled, so Mac felt this would be good practical experience. And it is. I'm glad he convinced me to do it."

"Will you teach me about the physical needs of the students?'' Keely asked. "If I'm going to help out, I want to learn as much as I can so I don't do something stupid."

Dean snickered. When he glanced at her his pale eyebrows were lifted in amusement.

"Uh-oh," she said with dread. "I've already done something stupid, haven't I?"

"Not stupid, just funny. And the guys are to blame for tricking you into it, so you shouldn't be embarrassed about it."

"Tell me, Dean."

"Well, a couple of them have said they're supersensitive on their shoulders and chests since their accidents, and apparently that's common among people with spinal-cord injuries. Areas not affected by the paralysis become almost like sexual organs. And when you stroke them—"

Keely held up her hand to stop him. "I get the picture."

"It's really kind of funny when you think about it."

"Oh, hysterical," she said dryly. "I don't know when I've heard anything quite so funny."

CHAPTER FOUR

BY THE TIME they returned to the track, Mac's hair was lank and oily and his body was covered with enough dust and road grit to fill the bed of a pickup. The sweaty odor wafting from him wasn't something he wanted Keely to have to deal with, so he transferred from his racer to his wheelchair and pushed up the hill with the rest of the guys to the athletic complex. He took a quick shower while Keely waited in his office talking to Dean.

He was in the dressing room trying to get his feet into some old loafers when Alan rolled up and popped him in the head with a towel. "Bring Keely over to the house tonight and we'll throw something on the grill. You know Vicki's going to freak when I tell her about you two. She'll want to check Keely out—make sure she's good enough for you."

Mac looked around to see if anyone had overheard. Thankfully the others were still in the shower or getting dressed on the other side of the wall in the student area. "There's nothing to tell about me and Keely. We're not involved like that, Alan." Giving up on the shoes, he tossed them back in the locker.

"Okay, there's nothing to tell, but you know I'm going to tell it, anyway, so you might as well bring her to the house to meet Vicki and get it over with. C'mon, buddy. We can grill some steaks or chops."

"I'll pass. Having Vicki interrogate her and embarrass me isn't my idea of a pleasant evening."

"She won't if I tell her not to."

"Yeah, right." Asking Alan's wife to mind her own business was like asking Alan to keep a confidence. Both were impossible. The minute Alan told her about Keely, Vicki was going to be all over him asking him personal questions and wanting to know if he was involved with Keely romantically.

He closed the locker and patted his pocket for a comb, belatedly realizing it was in the storage compartment of his van with his wallet. He ran a hand through his wet hair to get it off his face, but dark strands fell in his eyes each time he raked them back.

"If you won't come to the house, then invite Keely over to your place," Alan suggested. "Vicki and I will leave you alone so you can have some privacy. Fix dinner, open a bottle of wine, light a few candles and," he added just to goad him, "show Keely your tattoo."

"Very funny."

Why Alan got so much pleasure from reminding him about his stupidity, Mac didn't know. Getting a tattoo was just one of several outrageous things he had done after his injury, but it was the most permanent. The shock of suddenly finding himself unable to walk or maintain an erection had pushed him over the edge.

He had gone a little crazy, drinking too much and trying to prove his manhood in a variety of insane ways: skydiving, white-water canoeing, orally satisfying Courtland's female population. That last one had earned him a nickname that three years later still had women leaving messages on his answering machine for "Mouth" McCandless.

The ultimate insanity had occurred one night when he and Alan had driven to Columbus, Georgia, to a grimy little place called the Hole in the Wall near the Army's Fort Benning. Countless beers later, the party moved to a tattoo parlor and they'd both come away with souvenirs of their foolishness. Fortunately the tattoos were small and located where they couldn't be seen by just anybody. Born to Raise Hell, Alan's groin proclaimed. Mac had a hissing coiled snake about two inches long on his hip.

Alan, with his usual irreverence for everything, thought the experience amusing, but Mac cursed the tattoo every time he took off his pants.

"So, are you going to ask her to your place tonight?" Alan's question drew him back into the conversation.

"I already have." Alan's delighted grin faded to a scowl when Mac added, "I'm working out a conditioning schedule for her, and we plan to go over it."

"Ah, man, are you nuts? You don't invite a beautiful woman you're crazy about to your house and then talk business. And I *know* you're crazy about her, regardless of what you say. When she's around, you're like a hungry dog with his eyes on a T-bone."

"Alan, she needs a friend right now, not a relationship."

"How do you know that? Maybe a relationship with you is exactly what she needs."

Mac dismissed the idea immediately. "She came to me because she needs a coach, not a man in her bed. Besides, she isn't attracted to me. The sight of me turns her off."

Alan rolled his eyes in disbelief. "I don't buy that for a minute."

"I'm not kidding. My disability freaks her out. That's what we were talking about on the track earlier. She's uncomfortable with my chair and me. Didn't you notice how she avoids looking at my legs or even touching my chair?"

"I was too busy looking at *her* legs to catch it. She admits she's turned off?"

"Not in those words, but yes."

"So, use a little of that McCandless charm. Spend some time with her when it isn't part of her training. Romance her."

"No. She's struggling through a tough time because of her injury, and the last thing she needs is me hitting on her."

Alan popped him hard with the towel again, doing more damage to his hair. "There you go, getting into your self-sacrificing mode. You always worry about what everyone else needs. What do *you* need? Do you ever think about that?"

Yeah, he thought about it, but he was afraid to think about it very seriously. What he needed and what he could have were too far apart.

Now, what he *wanted*—that was an entirely different matter. Immediately his mind drew her picture: blond hair, big blue eyes, coltish legs. He had a weakness for women, but Keely Wilson made him weak to the point of near-helplessness.

His heart had been in jeopardy from the instant he'd first laid eyes on her more than ten years ago. Telling himself it was just an older man's infatuation with a younger woman, or a strong case of lust, hadn't done a thing to lessen the ache.

Now as then, he had to keep his feelings in check. She was emotionally vulnerable; she trusted him to help her, and he wasn't going to betray that trust by doing something stupid, like making a move on her.

"I've got to go. She's waiting for me." He bundled his dirty unitard and jock together and put them in the net sling under his chair, then pushed toward the door.

"Hey," Alan called. Mac stopped and turned the chair to look back. "How much of a chance does she have for a come-back?"

"No chance at all."

"You're kidding. Then why did you agree to coach her?"

"When the doctor walked in that day and said you'd never walk again, do you remember what you did?"

Alan chuckled. "That wasn't one of my better days."

"You called him a few choice names and threw a water pitcher at him. The minute he left the room you tried to get out of the bed and walk. You fell on your ugly face."

"We both did, my friend. Remember our great escape attempt? We decided we were gonna blow that place, but neither one of us could even get our underwear on, much less escape."

"We had to fall on our faces a thousand times before we finally accepted that we wouldn't walk again."

Alan nodded slowly, understanding what Mac was getting at. "And letting Keely fall on her face is the only way she's going to really accept not running again."

"I think so. If she doesn't take her best shot at a comeback, she'll spend the rest of her life wondering if the doctors were wrong and maybe she just gave up too soon. I care about her. I don't want her to have any regrets."

Alan pushed over, looked at him squarely and asked, "Just how much *do* you care about her?"

Mac sighed in resignation. He had spent the afternoon denying to Alan that he still had feelings for Keely, and years denying the truth to himself. "More than I should."

"Go after her if she's what you want."

Mac laughed bitterly. "Yeah, right. I'm sure her idea of the perfect man is a paraplegic in a wheelchair. A guy who can't get it up and can't hold his bladder half the time. What kind of life would she have with me?"

"Much better than the one she'd have without you," Alan said pointedly.

AS SOON AS MAC LEFT the building, Alan raced to the pay telephone and made a call to his wife. If Mac wasn't going to do what was in his best interest, Alan would do it for him.

Vicki answered, and the bloodcurdling scream of a child echoed in Alan's ear. "What in the blazes is goin' on?" he asked.

"Murder, mayhem and madness," Vicki said calmly. "The usual."

"Well, tell them to be quiet. I need you to get some things together and take them over to Mac's before he gets home."

"Hey!" she yelled at the kids. "Take it to the backyard. And, Savannah, quit tormenting your brothers. You know that's my job." Several minutes and threats later, she turned her attention back to Alan. "Okay, they're tying up J.P. and preparing him for sacrifice, so I'm free. What do you need me to do?"

"Don't you have a pan of that potato-casserole stuff Mac likes so much?"

"I think so. Want me to heat it up for him?"

"No, I want Keely Wilson to heat it up for him. And not just the casserole."

"Who? What are you talking about?"

"Hold on to your panties, woman. Have I got a story for you."

CHAPTER FIVE

"THIS IS IT," Mac said. "Don't expect anything fancy."

Keely looked through the windshield of the van at the small lots and plain but charming houses of Mac's subdivision. People were walking or working in their yards, and the kids were playing up and down the quiet street the way they probably did in her older more upscale neighborhood on a Sunday afternoon.

"I like it," she said with honesty.

In the middle of the next block he pointed out where Alan and his family lived. Mac's place was directly across the street in a small house with white vinyl siding and green shutters.

A child's bicycle blocked the entrance to Mac's driveway. Grumbling, he parked on the street. "I've told Savannah a million times to watch where she leaves that thing."

"Savannah?"

"One of Alan's kids."

Keely moved to the lift door in the center of the van's side panel and waited her turn to descend. "How many kids do Alan and Vicki have?"

"Three. Bay Alan's thirteen, Savannah's seven, and John Patrick just turned two."

"John Patrick? They named him after you?"

"Yeah," he said, grinning.

"Something tells me you don't mind that too much."

"No, J.P.'s a great kid. Real sweet. All the kids are when they're separated, but together they're like wild animals. I guarantee you've never seen anything like it."

"Are they that bad?"

His expression of horror made her smile. "Real terrors.

Especially Savannah. Even I can't take it when they get wound up, and I'm used to coping with screaming kids.''

''Oh? Why are you used to screaming kids?''

''Because I raised four of them.''

HIDDEN BEHIND THE CURTAINS of her living-room window, Vicki Sizemore watched what was going on across the street and wondered what Mac and the woman were saying. Vicki was dying to get a good look at her.

''Putting the bicycle in the driveway so he couldn't park in the garage was pure genius,'' she told Alan.

He had poured himself some tea in the kitchen and was just pushing through the door with the glass held between his legs. ''I have my moments.''

''I wish she'd hurry up and get out. Oh, wait, here she comes. She's about to step on the lift.'' When the woman moved from the interior of the darkened van into the sunlight, Vicki sucked in her breath. ''How old is she?''

''Twenty-seven. Twenty-eight. Something like that.''

Vicki conceded that was old enough. ''Maybe I should pop over there and pretend I need to borrow something.''

Alan quickly nixed that idea. ''He won't like it that I asked you to fix the food. If you show up at the door, he'll kill us both.'' He rolled up next to her at the window and peeked out.

''But I can't tell what she really looks like,'' Vicki muttered.

''She's cute,'' Alan said. ''Mac was drooling all over himself. Of course, we all were.''

Vicki reached down and playfully backhanded him for including himself. ''I'll bet she's stuck up if she gets that kind of attention.''

''Nah, didn't seem like it. She made a real effort to talk to all the guys and get to know them. Whenever Mac or anyone needed anything, she was right there offering to help. Although Mac did say she has a problem being around him now that he's a gimp.''

''She *what?* Why that hateful little—''

"Now, hold on. Don't get all bent out of shape. I started thinking about it on the drive home and it's a good sign. We had eight or nine guys out there today, plus me and Mac, but Keely didn't have a problem with anyone except him. I watched her laugh and fool around with the wheelers, even the amputees, and she wasn't put off by any of them."

"So?"

"So that tells me she's not turned off by gimps, but by *Mac* being a gimp. And she wouldn't get turned off by Mac being a gimp unless she cared about him."

Vicki's eyes narrowed. "You may have a point," she said slowly.

He nodded. "Look at it this way. Did you get upset when Mrs. Arnold down the block fell and broke her hip? No," he answered for her. "You felt bad because she's a nice old lady, but you didn't get upset, right?"

"Right."

"Yet when Mac got that tiny little cut on his finger making J.P.'s rocking horse, you almost had a stroke. Why?"

"Because I love him and I can't stand to see him hurt."

"Bingo!"

"So maybe I ought to wait until I meet her to decide whether she needs her eyes clawed out."

"That's my girl."

Alan put his tea on the end table and patted his lap. Vicki reluctantly gave up her snooping and sat. She rested her head on his shoulder and sighed deeply. "I'd hate it if he got hurt when he's been through so much already. Do you really think he's in love with her?"

"Sure seems like it."

"No wonder he's never gotten serious about anyone. He's been pining away for Keely Wilson all these years."

"Not pining away, but I think when he saw her again he realized he still had feelings for her."

"I'd give anything to be a fly on the wall in *that* house tonight...."

"Yeah, me, too. Nothing we can do about it, though."

As if he'd suddenly thought of something, his whole body jerked.

"What's the matter?" she asked, alarmed.

"What's that I hear?"

Vicki listened, then shook her head. "I don't hear anything."

"Exactly. No screaming. No crying. No fighting. What's wrong?"

She relaxed and laughed. "Bay Alan went to the movies with the Cooper boy, and Savannah and J.P. are next door helping Miss Agnes bake brownies. They won't be back for an hour or so."

"Wait a minute. You mean we're alone in this house for the first time in months and we're wasting it on Mac's love life? Get nekkid!" She giggled as he frantically whisked her top over her head, then pulled off his own. He jerked down the zipper of her cutoff jeans and thrust his hand inside.

Thirty seconds later Vicki didn't give a damn what was going on across the street. Mac was on his own.

"I DIDN'T KNOW you had children," Keely said. The blood rushed to her face. They made their way through the garage to the side door.

"I was talking about my three younger sisters and my brother. I raised them."

"Oh, brothers and sisters." The relief was instant, but Keely didn't like feeling it.

"I was twenty-two when our parents died, and the court allowed me to have temporary guardianship. After a year, when I proved I was able to take care of them, they awarded me permanent custody. Of course, the kids are grown now and scattered all over the country."

"You raised them by yourself? But you were so young."

"I couldn't let them be separated, and no one in the family was willing to take in four kids, three of them teenagers. Jilly, my oldest sister, was seventeen, so she was a big help with Brand. He was ten at the time."

"Still, it must have been hard."

"It was, particularly when I was also trying to go to graduate school and work, but I'd do it again in a heartbeat if I had to."

"I remember Brand. He visited you at the track one time when he was on leave from the Marines and got the entire women's team in trouble for gawking and flirting."

He chuckled. "I forgot about that. None of you could keep your eyes off him long enough to do any work."

"He was gorgeous," she said in self-defense. "And he was your brother, which made him that much more attractive to us, since we all had terrible crushes on you." He looked at her with genuine shock. "Oh, surely you knew! We almost swooned every time you spoke."

"I find that very difficult to believe."

"Believe it. I had the worst case of lust for you when I was a senior."

Rendered speechless, he stared at her with his mouth open.

"All female students lust after their coaches," she said quickly, trying to make light of it.

"I didn't know that."

"Oh, sure. Happens all the time."

The door from the garage opened into a laundry room, and he waited for her to go first. Right inside on the floor, blocking the way, was a large covered basket with a note taped to its handle.

"Someone's left you a present," Keely said, stepping back so he could reach it. He put the basket in his lap and pulled off the note. As he read, he made a noise in his throat she wasn't sure how to interpret. "Problem?"

"No, no problem."

Through a second door was the kitchen. Mac put the basket on the table and began emptying the contents. "Alan and Vicki sent over dinner. Potato casserole, salad, bread."

"That was nice of them to do that for you."

"Ah...it's not meant for only me."

He took out two candles, a bottle of wine and a small bunch of multicolored zinnias that looked like someone had just snipped them from a flower bed.

"The dinner is for two," he said unnecessarily, "if you'd like to join me. We don't have to light the candles or use the flowers if it makes you uncomfortable."

Her inner voice warned that she was moving into extremely dangerous territory. By staying, she could be asking for problems she was ill-prepared to handle.

She had once felt a tenderness for this man that strayed beyond the boundaries of a normal student-coach relationship. She was struggling now with conflicting feelings of attraction and revulsion, feelings she didn't understand and couldn't seem to control. Having an intimate dinner, even without the candlelight, would only complicate things.

"How about it?" he asked. "I can't eat this all by myself."

He had the most expressive eyes. They said he really wanted her to stay for dinner, and not because he needed someone to help him eat all this food. He wanted to be with her. The knowledge played havoc with her insides.

"The flowers are beautiful," she said, nodding. "I guess it would be a shame not to use them."

ACROSS THE DINNER TABLE soft candlelight illuminated Mac's face. He had changed into a pale-blue shirt that brought out the few strands of gray at his temples and emphasized his dark hair and eyes.

Some men grew less handsome as they got older, but age had increased Mac's appeal a thousand percent. The tiny lines around his mouth, the slightly weathered skin, added something immensely attractive.

When she was in undergraduate school and he was her coach, they'd sat like this over lunch in the cafeteria many times and discussed her training. And like those days, Keely was in real danger of losing her heart again.

"...gradually add weight-bearing exercises until you've strengthened the soft tissues..."

Her thoughts wandered from the conditioning program Mac was outlining to the shape of his lips as they formed the words. They really were nice lips. Perfect. Enticing. She wondered if they felt as good as they looked.

"...in the biomechanics lab..."

He turned a page in the black vinyl binder in front of him and the fabric of his shirt whispered across his skin like the seductive melody to a song, making Keely nearly moan in harmony.

Mmm, he had wonderful arms and an exquisite chest. Even his neck was sexy.

"...put you in one of those pink ballet costumes and give you a beehive hairdo and red fingernails..."

She had to get her mind back on work and away from those fine taut biceps and those— *What* had he said? Beehive hairdo? Red fingernails?

He'd stopped talking and was grinning playfully.

"I'm sorry," she said with chagrin, hoping she hadn't communicated her thoughts. "I was, um, thinking about something else. What were you saying about joint stress?"

"Forget joint stress." He put aside her progress binder. "Let's wait and go over this later in the week. We have plenty of time, and I think what you need right now is to relax for a change—forget about running and everything that goes with it."

The irony of his words amused her. She hadn't been thinking about running at all.

"How about some wine?"

"I don't usually drink."

"Half a glass? You're no longer on medication, so a little won't hurt you."

"Yes, I think I will."

He poured them each half a glass and she took a sip.

"More casserole? Salad?"

"No, thank you. Everything was wonderful. Thank Vicki and Alan for me when you see them." She paused. "Are you good friends with them?"

"The best. Alan and I met in rehab, so we went through some rough months together. They moved him in as my roommate a few weeks after he broke his neck."

"How was he injured?"

"He fell asleep at the wheel and hit a tree."

"I noticed his hands and arms don't work exactly right, but that doesn't seem to hinder him."

"No, not much slows Alan down. He has a lethal sense of humor, and you never know what he's going to say or do, but he's the best friend you could ever hope for and a great neighbor. I convinced him and Vicki to move here from Valdosta when a job opened up at the college, and I've never regretted it."

"He's on the faculty? He doesn't seem like the college-professor type."

"Oh, don't let that good ol' boy redneck routine fool you. Alan's smart as a whip. He's really *Dr.* Sizemore and is a highly regarded researcher in microbiology."

"Is Vicki disabled?"

"No, she's able-bodied."

Able-bodied. Keely made a mental note of the correct terminology. She wanted to remember it.

"What does she do?"

"Makes gowns for the sorority and fraternity formals, bridesmaids' dresses, majorette costumes, things like that. She must be pretty good at it. She complains of having more business than she can handle. I think she's even made a couple of wedding dresses."

"Must be nice to be so talented."

She started to get up to clear the table, but he stopped her. "Sit here with me a little while longer and let's catch up. We really haven't had a chance to talk today about how your house is working out. Is it as comfortable as it looks?"

"Oh, it's terrific. I love it." She pushed her plate aside, then folded her arms and rested them on the table. "How long have you had this house, Mac?"

"About two years. I have all the space I need and the changes I showed you make things easier for me."

She could see how they would. He had given her a tour before the meal and she'd been intrigued by the way he'd redesigned the house to make it more practical for someone in a wheelchair.

"It's comfortable," Mac said. "I could use more room

when Brand and the girls come at the same time, but that doesn't happen too often so it's not really a problem.''

''Where are your sisters and brother living?''

''Brand's in Wisconsin. He's a computer specialist with a company that designs product packaging. Jilly's an artist and lives in Santa Fe, and Megan and Christine are both in California. Chris works for a travel company and Megan teaches high-school English and French. The girls are all married and have kids, which means I don't get to see them as much as I'd like.''

And that saddened him. She could tell by the tone of his voice. ''I'm sorry you're so far apart. You must miss them.''

''I do. I never thought we'd be this spread out and it's not what I'd planned for us, but they have their own families and careers, and that's the way it should be. I can't expect them to rearrange their lives for me.''

But he had rearranged his life for them; Keely was certain of it. When his parents had died and he'd brought his sisters and brother to live with him, it must have caused an immense change in his life. Twenty-two, responsible for himself and four children...

How many men would have done what he had? None she could think of. The few men she knew or had dated tended to be focused on their careers like her, caught up in their own lives and oblivious to everything else. Mac wasn't the least bit self-centered. He went out of his way to help his students, to help his family, and he didn't seem to expect anything in return. He valued their happiness, but surely he had dreams of his own that weren't tied to other people.

''Did you always want to be a coach?'' she asked. ''You've spent most your adult life making sure other people achieve their dreams. I'm curious about what you want for yourself.''

''I'm happy being a coach.''

''I know you are, but did you ever want to be something else?''

''As a young man, sure. I was a runner like you, and I dreamed of being a world-class athlete, but I quickly set my sights on being a good coach, instead. I've never regretted it."

"But why did you change your mind and go into coaching? If you wanted to run, you should have done it."

"I had responsibilities that made it impossible for me to even think about something like that."

"Raising your brothers and sisters interfered with your plans, didn't it?"

"Yes, but I'm not complaining, because having those kids around was the best thing that ever happened to me. I got my chance to be a father."

His only chance?

He rolled back from the table and pushed to the coffeemaker on the counter. "Do you want some decaf?"

"No, but you go ahead." She watched him fill the pot at the sink and get the can of coffee from the refrigerator. She wondered whether it was proper etiquette to ask him if he needed help, but after a minute, she saw that he didn't. He measured coffee into the filter and poured in enough water for two cups, then pushed back over to the table to wait while it brewed.

"When I was young, I was a lot like you," he said, continuing his story. "I had my life mapped out, I wasn't responsible for anyone but myself, and I couldn't imagine anything stopping me from going after what I wanted. Then my folks were killed and the kids came to live with me. Suddenly I was responsible for five people. I had to face the reality that my life had changed and that my goals would have to change, too."

"But don't you have *some* regret about not fulfilling your dream?"

"Honestly? Yes, but I can't waste my life grieving over lost dreams any more than I can waste my life grieving over being in this chair. I meant it when I said I'm happy doing what I'm doing. I'm a good coach. At least, I think I am."

"You're a great coach. And apparently you're also great at other things," she added, remembering what Dean had told her that afternoon about Mac's ability to wipe out the competition when he raced. "I heard about your nickname."

He had just taken a sip of wine and still had the glass to his lips when he suddenly choked and lurched forward, spraying wine everywhere. He dissolved into a coughing fit and grabbed his napkin to put over his face.

"Mac? Are you okay?"

He nodded rapidly but was still unable to talk.

"Do you want some water?"

He shook his head.

He didn't seem to be in any danger, so Keely left him alone to catch his breath. After a minute he recovered enough to talk, but when he did, his words didn't make sense. They held a tone of desperation that confused her even more.

"Who told you about my nickname?"

"Dean. He says you're really good."

Mac's expression said he was horrified to hear it.

"He had no business telling you something like that! I swear things have changed. After I got hurt I was really messed up about being in this chair, and I thought I had to go out and prove my manhood. You understand that, don't you?"

Her forehead wrinkled in confusion. Why was he so upset about being nicknamed the Terminator by other racers?

"Mac, I don't get it. Why does this bother you so much? They gave you that nickname because of how good you are. You should be proud they recognize your talent."

He gave her an incredulous look. "Proud of being called the Mouth by women who are only interested in me for oral sex?"

His words were such a shock that at first she didn't react. And then understanding hit her. The Mouth? Oral sex? She was barely able to contain her laughter and her body shook with the effort. Against her will, her gaze slid to his mouth. So, she wasn't the only one who thought it luscious.

"Why, Mac McCandless, I didn't know you could be so naughty. I was talking about wheelchair racing, not oral sex."

"Oh, hell!"

She grinned. "Something tells me I just figured out what Rehab 102 is."

CHAPTER SIX

MAC COULDN'T SLEEP that night for thinking about the stupid thing he'd done. The next day at work, he was irritable and distracted, causing Miriam to remark more than once that he must be coming down with something. A cold, she decided, and fussed at him for not taking better care of himself.

The word raced out in record time, even for the athletic department. Almost immediately, containers of chicken soup and homemade remedies to promote healing began showing up on his desk: garlic pills, licorice candy, a lemon-and-whiskey concoction to swab his throat. Purple-onion cough syrup he wouldn't have taken even if he *did* have a cold.

"What did you do, hire a skywriter?" he asked Miriam. "I'm being overrun by female witch doctors trying to cure me with voodoo remedies."

"I just mentioned to a couple of the women that you were sick."

"I'm not sick," he repeated for the hundredth time.

He had to leave before the women in the building drove him nuts. He grabbed his cell phone from the desk, stuck it in the chair sling and headed down the hill to the track, where the men's team had started drills.

As he pushed up, Scott Madison, a junior and one of the best sprinters Courtland had seen in decades, shot out of the starting blocks a fraction of a second before the pistol, setting off a chorus of curses from the coaching staff and a bellowing reprimand from the head coach, Doug Crocker.

"You've got bricks for brains, Madison. You pull that stunt one more time and you'll never run for my team again, and I mean scholarship or no scholarship. You got that, hotshot?"

"Yes, sir, Coach."

Madison had no more false starts, but later, while the runners were doing drills, the young man again earned Crocker's wrath with his sloppy form. "Madison, get over here!" Crocker threw down his clipboard and chewed out not only Scott but the other runners in the line. Mac watched from the apron of the track with Dean.

"Man," Dean said, shaking his head, "Scott's still got serious problems. Crocker's likely to kill him before the day's over."

Or at the very least demoralize him, Mac thought.

He shifted in his chair to relieve the pressure on his backside, wishing he could do something to relieve the uneasiness in his chest about this whole situation. Technically he should stay out of it. As athletic director, he was no longer just a coach responsible for the women's track team, but an administrator in charge of a multimillion-dollar operation and twelve sports.

He was supposed to let his staff handle the majority of the coaching duties while he ran the department and supervised rehabilitation. If Scott had problems, it was Crocker's job as coach of the men's team to correct them.

Mac found it hard, though, to do nothing while a young man with Scott's potential slid deeper into trouble.

He let out a shrill whistle and gave Crocker a hand signal. Crocker glared to let him know he didn't appreciate the interference.

"If looks could kill..." Dean said with a chuckle. "He's never going to get over you getting the A.D.'s job, instead of him."

"Yeah, well, he can look at me any way he wants as long as he does his job."

The staff and teaching assistants believed Crocker's hostility resulted from Mac's promotion two years ago, but Mac had felt the beginnings of it long before that, from his first day back at work after his injury. Everyone had been uncomfortable with him in the beginning, even Miriam. Eventually, to his relief, they'd started treating him just like before. All except Doug Crocker. His wariness had never gone away. His anger over the promotion had simply changed it into something more destructive.

Crocker obeyed Mac's hand signal but with clear resentment, scowling as he sentenced Scott to leave the group and run laps. Experienced runners like Scott considered laps an indignity, but Mac had found them to be a much more effective punishment than Crocker's verbal abuse.

"Here comes something much better to look at," Dean said, and Mac turned his head toward the gate. Using her cane, Keely slowly made her way in their direction. She waved and Dean waved back.

Mac didn't know what to say to her. All day his mind had replayed last night's dinner with Keely, confirming what an idiot he was. The Terminator. He hadn't known the other wheelers called him that. She'd laughed at his mistake until she'd cried.

"Dean, get a racer out of the shed and a pair of gloves for me, will you?"

"Sure," he said, jogging off.

Keely reached Mac. "I burned down our neighbor's workshop when I was eleven," she said.

"What?"

"Mr. Johnson left his cigarettes out there, and I sneaked in and tried to smoke one, but I dropped ashes into some sawdust and the floor caught on fire. To this day, that poor man believes he started it by leaving one of his cigarette butts smoldering."

Mac didn't say anything else, wondering if there was a point to her strange story and if it was forthcoming.

"That's one of the worst things I've ever done. I've always been afraid people would think badly of me if they knew, so I've never told a soul, not even my dad, and he was closer to me than anyone."

Ah, he was beginning to understand.

"We're even now. I know your deepest darkest secret and you know mine. So you don't have a reason to be embarrassed about what happened last night. You don't have to apologize again or feel uncomfortable around me. Actually, I think trading personal secrets like this might make us blood brothers or something. What do you think?''

His gaze covertly skimmed her figure-hugging shirt and shorts. He couldn't imagine her as his brother, but the "or something" part sounded intriguing.

"Why don't you sit down and get off that leg, and we'll talk about it?"

"No, I didn't come to stay. I just wanted to drop by for a second and see if you were okay. You ended the evening so abruptly I was a little worried.''

"I was an idiot, not only because of what I said, but how I acted after. I'm sorry.''

"Oh, no," she warned instantly. "No apologizing. Friends need to be able to say stupid things in front of each other and not worry about it. Right?''

He tried not to smile, but he couldn't help himself. "Right.''

"Good. With that settled, I wonder if I can talk you into coming over one night this week.''

"Did you want to finish reviewing your schedule?''

"No, I had the pool filled this morning and by the end of the week, the water should be warm. I wondered...is it possible for you to swim?" She turned a little red and added quickly, "If you can't swim, that's okay. We can just lie by the pool being worthless.''

"I can swim, but I choose not to. I'm not exactly graceful getting in and out of a pool.''

"Oh.''

"But I'm great at lying around being worthless.''

"Then please come. I'd really like you to be the first guest in my house. We can have a late supper on the patio. I make a low-fat vegetarian lasagna that I guarantee you can't tell from the real thing. It smells so good it'll make your mouth water.''

She was trying to tempt him. As if he needed tempting. His mouth was already watering, thinking about that body of hers covered only by a wet bathing suit. Would it be a one-piece suit? Blue like her eyes? Modest or daring? The real thing would probably be nowhere near as exciting as the one he'd just created in his mind.

"Sounds great. How about Thursday night? I should finish here about six."

"That's perfect."

After she left, Mac put on gloves and transferred to the racer Dean brought him. He waited until Scott came around the track, then pushed out to join him in his laps.

They did five laps, neither one speaking, settling into an easy pace that Mac purposely dictated. On the sixth lap the kid couldn't stand it any longer.

"Why are you taking my laps with me, Coach?"

"Your laps? These are my laps."

Scott glanced down at him with a confused expression on his young face. At twenty, he was technically a man, but today he seemed about fifteen, a scared and desperate fifteen.

"What did *you* do wrong, Coach?" he asked.

"Allowed myself to forget the most important part of my job."

"What?"

"That I'm supposed to be your friend, as well as your coach. Now, how about telling me what's bothering you. I can't help if I don't know what's wrong."

THE SUIT WAS RED, one-piece and fit Keely like she'd been melted and poured into it. Mac watched her swim, his serene look a deceptive cover for the battle between honor and desire raging within him. Honor wanted Keely to stay concealed in the water. Desire kept thinking up excuses to entice her out of it.

He checked his watch and smiled to himself. Finally he didn't need to fabricate an excuse to end her swim. "Hey," he called out. "Time's up. You've been in there over an hour, and that's long enough for today."

She swam to the side. "Fifteen more minutes?"

"No, I don't want you to overdo it your first time in. Now

hit the deck. And be careful coming up those steps. Hold on to the rail.''

"Oh, Mac, I've hardly gotten wet."

"Don't 'Oh, Mac' me. And don't try to wheedle me into letting you stay in there, because it won't work. Come on out."

"Slave driver," she muttered, but she carefully climbed out and limped past him to retrieve her towel, impishly flicking water at his head as she walked by. "Dictator."

The towel retrieved, she limped back to him and began to rub her body briskly. Mac tried not to stare, but his gaze was drawn to every place the towel touched—the slender throat, the long supple arms, the legs that seemed to go on forever.

Casually, so as not to be obvious, he picked up his shirt and placed it strategically across his lap. The erection would fizzle in a moment. It always did.

"You're making progress," he told her. "Your limp seems less pronounced than it was even a few days ago."

"You think so?"

"I can tell a difference."

"So can I, actually. You're taking good care of me." She wrapped the towel around her waist and tied it in a knot. "And now it's time for me to take care of you. I'll get you some ointment and bandages for those hands. I know they have to be hurting."

"They're okay. They don't need bandaging."

"I think they do. Let me see them."

He lifted his palms. Constant training this week had worn holes in his gloves and rubbed his hands raw. This afternoon, when he and the wheelers had run a twenty-mile point-to-point, both hands had bled.

"I'll put something on them when I get home," he told her.

"But I have everything here. The longer you wait, the greater the risk of infection."

"I don't need..." He stopped, realizing it wasn't such a bad idea. "Okay. Thanks."

"Be right back."

While she was in the house, he transferred from the lounger to his wheelchair and positioned a patio chair nearby.

She returned a few minutes later carrying a duffel bag stuffed with bandages, ointments and wraps. "Here you go."

She tried to hand him the bag, but he refused it. "You'll have to wrap them for me. Sit here."

Panic spread across her face as she noted how close the patio chair was to him, to his wheelchair.

"Keely, you only have to touch my hands, not my legs. Surely you can do that without feeling sick."

"Did I say I couldn't?"

"No, but you're thinking it might be a problem. The second you thought you had to touch me, you started grabbing your stomach. Look at your hand."

She jerked away the hand that had unconsciously gone to rest against her middle.

"You need to deal with this for your own sake. And mine. Knowing you're afraid of me…it hurts me."

Her face twisted with pain. "Please, don't be hurt. I do feel more comfortable around you than I did. Really."

"Then show me."

The challenge issued, he said nothing more, just waited. Was he doing the right thing? He hoped so. A misstep now could intensify her fear and ruin everything. But he wasn't asking much of her, only to touch his hands. If she couldn't do even that, there was no hope she'd ever get past her revulsion.

Slowly she eased into the chair, careful not to let her knees brush against his, careful not to let her feet touch the foot plates of the wheelchair.

That's my girl. Keep going.

He leaned forward slightly and held out his hands. "A little ointment and some flesh strips and you'll be finished in five minutes. No big deal."

The deepening lines on her forehead marred her perfect face and showed her turmoil. Her hands shook as she removed what she needed from the bag on her lap. Gingerly, fearfully, she placed a dab of ointment on his skin. With soft hesitant circles she rubbed it across one of his palms.

Mac sat quietly and savored the small victory. Her fingers didn't caress or entice, didn't attempt to make him feel good or even try to soothe him. Her fingers touched only what they had to touch. And they touched only because he had given her no choice.

But it was enough.

For now.

CHAPTER SEVEN

June

KEELY UNOFFICIALLY continued to help with the wheelers after classes began in June and put in two hours every day as a teaching assistant to one of the other coaches, helping her with the freshmen runners. She enjoyed the work, but watching the students train was a daily reminder that she was doing little toward her own training.

She walked every day and did deep breathing exercises to improve her lung capacity. But even the next-door neighbor's little poodle, who had started escorting her on her walks, moved faster than she did. She found it depressing to walk with something that had legs only six inches long, could stop and relieve itself on every tree and still beat her back to the house.

Mac kept telling her she had to go easy on herself, but it was tough to hold back when she had such a passionate need to run. Her body was changing, adapting to this new slower way of life, and she was losing ground with every passing week.

She was getting fat, for one thing. Not only had she gained back the nine pounds she'd lost because of the accident, but she'd added two more this month. And for the first time in years, she had a normal period, with bloating, cramps, the craving for chocolate, all those horrible things she had avoided for most of her life.

"Wonderful!" her mother said when Keely mentioned it during one of their Sunday-afternoon phone conversations.

"You're excited I'm having cramps?"

"I'm sorry, darling, but you know how I've always felt about your excessive exercise. Pushing your body like that is unnatural. You'll want a baby some day and at least now you know your body is capable of it. By the way...how's that nice John McCandless doing?"

"Not getting ready to give you a grandchild, if that's what you're hinting."

"I was just asking about the man, Keely, not suggesting you have a baby with him."

"He's paralyzed, remember?"

"Some paralyzed men father children, don't they?"

"No," she said, but then she remembered Alan's two-year-old son. The child had been conceived *after* Alan's accident. Obviously some paralyzed men could father children despite their injuries. "Well, I guess some can, but that doesn't mean Mac's one of them."

"Has he told you he can't have a child? Is he able to have sex?"

"Mother! I haven't exactly quizzed the man about his sex life. Things like that don't come up in the course of normal conversation."

"I'm surprised you aren't curious. He seems nice. He's educated. You should let him know you're interested before someone else snaps him up."

"Whoa! I didn't say I was interested in Mac. I've *never* told you I was interested in Mac like that."

"If you're not, you should be. When's the last time you had a date?"

Keely gritted her teeth. She reminded herself to remain pleasant. Her mother meant well, but she didn't understand that a relationship, with Mac or any other man, wasn't in her plans. Relationships wasted energy. And they never worked for her, so why put herself through the torture? She'd be better off if she *never* fell in love and *never* got married. Her parents' divorce had taught her that lesson.

"Mother, I need to go," she said, yawning loudly. "I've got a test and I need to study."

"You're still not sleeping at night, are you?"

"A few hours, but I usually catch a nap at lunchtime. Don't worry about me."

"I wish you'd go see someone about why you're afraid to sleep."

"I don't need to see anyone. I'm fine. I have my nights and days mixed up is all. Look, I hate to cut this short, but I really do need to study. I'll call you later."

"When?"

"Before the end of the week."

"I'll be expecting it. I want you to call at least once a week from now on. I'd phone you, but I get your answering machine and you don't always return my call."

"I'm sorry. I've been busy trying to get back into the routine of school and I forget. I'll call at least once a week from now on."

"Promise?"

"Yes, I promise."

VICKI SIZEMORE wasn't known for her patience. After waiting three weeks for Mac to introduce her to Keely, she decided she wasn't waiting any longer.

When he answered his phone, Vicki didn't bother to identify herself or go into a lengthy explanation of why she was calling. He knew.

"Keely. My house. Wednesday night after the game."

The Wildcats, the wheelchair basketball team Mac and Alan played on, had an exhibition game to raise money for the rehabilitation hospital. Some of the men, their wives and girlfriends, were coming to the Sizemores' home afterward.

"Tell Keely I've followed her career and want to meet her if you don't want it to look like a date."

"When have you ever seen her race?"

"Never. But I won't say anything if you won't."

"I keep telling you, we're not involved. We're just good friends."

Vicki snorted. "You're spending nearly twenty-four hours a day with the woman, and you can't tell me that's all business. Call and invite her or I will."

"All right, I'll ask her. But I'm not promising she'll come."

"She'd better come. If you can't convince her, I'll take matters into my own hands."

She listened to him sigh loudly and grumble an obscenity she'd never heard him use before. "You're interfering in my life, Vic. You realize that, don't you?"

"Don't thank me, sweetie. You'll make me blush."

"MM-MM-MMMM. I love these games. All those half-naked men sweating and grunting. Makes me hot!"

Vicki's latest outrageous comment made Keely bite her lip to avoid laughing nervously. The woman was one of a kind. She talked dirty. She was loud and blunt. If she didn't like someone, she didn't pretend she did. Frequently she'd commented on the way someone looked or talked, although her own Southern drawl was atrocious, and her hair was a bright and fiery red that drew stares.

Keely had liked her immediately.

Certainly part of her appeal was the affection she obviously felt for Mac, but beyond that, Vicki Sizemore had something that made you want to look past her crudeness.

"Y'all won't mind me delaying the barbecue an hour while I jump Alan's bones, will you, girls?" she asked, and this time Keely couldn't help herself. She chuckled.

"We don't mind waitin' if you don't mind us watchin'," the woman on the other side of her said, and everyone giggled. Keely thought the woman's name was Sandy. She'd been introduced to so many people today she was having a hard time keeping everyone straight.

From the moment she had arrived, however, she'd realized the women were all friends. They shared a camaraderie that sprang from their similar situations—loving men with spinal injuries.

Vicki motioned for everyone to lean closer. "I heard a great joke the other day. Wanna hear it?"

Of course they all did.

"Why are men like parking spaces?"

"Why?" the women echoed.

"Because the good ones are taken and the rest are handicapped."

Everyone howled with laughter except Keely.

Vicki promptly poked her in the ribs. "Oh, lighten up, sweetie. If you're gonna hang around with crips, you've gotta keep a sense of humor and not be sucking up your drawers every five minutes over something somebody said."

Keely was pretty positive she had never once sucked up her drawers, but she got the gist of what Vicki was saying. Not that it made any sense. Fifteen minutes ago they'd all been indignant because Sandy said a waiter at a local restaurant was rude to her husband because of his disability. Now they were laughing at an insensitive joke.

When the others walked over to get soft drinks, Vicki tried to explain the difference.

"Look, it's like laughing *at* somebody versus laughing *with* somebody. We joke around and that's okay because we don't mean any harm. And we're all like family, so nobody's gonna get their feelings hurt. But that waiter was deliberately mean and we don't tolerate that. Understand?"

"I guess," Keely said, but she didn't, not entirely. *She* was an outsider, and yet Vicki had gotten on to her when she *hadn't* laughed at the joke.

Keely took advantage of the other women's absence to ask Vicki to match the wives and girlfriends to the players.

"Okay, you know Sandy's married to Dave. He's the one with the mustache. Pam is married to Kevin, the guy with the glasses and kinky hair. Beth Ann, the teeny one with the short-short haircut, is dating Stanley. Felicia and Curtis, and Patsy and Byron are the black couples. Curtis is easy to remember. He has that silver patch in his hair. Now Lisa…"

"I know Lisa. She's going with Chris, the young guy Mac just added to the wheelers, so I've talked with her at practice."

"That just leaves Mike and Bailey," Vicki said, pointing out the two remaining men. "They're both single and didn't bring anybody."

"Which is which?"

Vicki laughed and shook her head. "You're so funny."

"Why? What did I say?"

"Bailey's gorgeous, he's available, he's hit on you twice today, and you didn't even bother to learn his name. I guess that means you've got it bad for somebody else, huh?"

She grinned, making Keely roll her eyes. No matter how many times Keely insisted she wasn't dating Mac, Vicki wouldn't believe it. "You're determined to throw me and Mac together, aren't you?"

"You're already together, sweetie. You just won't admit it. And if it makes any difference to you, I approve, although Alan will make me eat crow over it because I didn't believe for an instant that I'd like you, and he said I would."

"You didn't think you'd like me? Why?"

"Because Alan told me about you being put off because Mac's a gimp, and I figured you were one of those uppity you-know-what women who think they're too perfect for a man in a wheelchair."

Keely winced.

"But I've watched you with him today," Vicki said, "and what I see is a woman with real problems and no idea what to do about them. You're attracted to him, but you don't want to be. And you're a little afraid of him, which bothers you more than the attraction because *that* problem he's aware of. He's still clueless about the attraction. So, my new friend, I've decided not to pull your hair out but to help you, instead."

"Vicki, you're reading this all wrong. Mac and I have known each other for a long time, sure, but I've never thought of him as more than a good friend."

Vicki just grinned.

"Honestly," Keely said. "But I'll concede you're right about my being afraid. And it makes no sense."

"That problem will disappear when you work through the other one."

"I'm not sure I understand."

"You will."

The gymnasium crowd gave a loud, collective gasp, and Keely quickly turned her attention to the court. The Wildcats were losing by two points to the Rebels. Two players had tumbled to the floor.

By the time Keely muttered, ''Oh, no, Mac,'' he was back in his wheelchair and rolling down the court again at breakneck speed.

Vicki patted her reassuringly on the leg. ''Relax. He's fine. They fall all the time.''

''They don't hurt themselves?''

''Nah, it hurts us more than it hurts them.''

Keely had tried to act unaffected, but every time someone slammed into Mac or Mac slammed into someone else, she felt it. ''I guess I didn't expect this game to be quite so physical,'' she admitted.

''Did you think because they're in wheelchairs they'd be less competitive?''

''I guess I did.''

''They're men, honey, muscle and testosterone. And they're just itching to ram each other. Putting wheels on them just makes them rowdier. They can race faster and hit each other easier. You think *this* is bad, you should watch a game of quad rugby. 'Murder ball' the guys used to call it, and that's a good name for it.''

''Couldn't be any worse than this.''

Vicki laughed. ''Hon, I'm talking about a full-contact sport with wheelchairs slamming into each other at high speed. Alan and Mac really get off on it.''

''How can you watch Alan when he does this kind of stuff and not worry?''

''I didn't say I didn't worry. That man's been worrying me to death since I was five years old, and I don't suppose when I'm an old woman it'll be any different. But I've learned not to be obvious about it.''

''You knew Alan as a child?''

''Oh, yeah, love at first sight in kindergarten for me, but he was stubborn, so I had to do some persuading.''

''What did that involve?''

"I wrestled him to the ground, pinned his arms behind his back and forced him to say he'd be my boyfriend."

Keely smiled, imagining what that must have looked like.

"Even then, he resisted," Vicki added. "He's still got the scar on his shoulder where I bit him."

"How old were you when you got married?"

"Eighteen."

All these years married to the same man. Loving him unconditionally. Raising children together. Vicki had done things the right way, and Keely admired her for it.

She supposed it was unfair to compare her mother's situation to Vicki's, but she couldn't help it. Liz Wilson had bailed out on her husband and her marriage. Vicki had stayed with Alan even through a crippling injury.

"Aw, ref, you're outta your mind!" Vicki yelled loudly. Keely smiled.

No, Vicki Sizemore was definitely not like Liz Wilson—or anyone else Keely had ever met.

CHAPTER EIGHT

THE MEN WERE BATTERED, bruised and lost the game, but it didn't appear to Keely that their spirits had been dampened any. One had a busted lip, another a scratch across his face where someone's fingernail had raked him during a scuffle over the basketball.

Mac had gotten an elbow in the eye in the last quarter, and it was still a bit red. Keely tried to put an ice pack on it when they got to Vicki and Alan's, but Mac insisted the only cold thing he wanted was a beer.

"Here you go," Vicki told him, getting a beer out of the refrigerator and tossing it to him. "Keely, I have juice, tea, bottled water or beer. Which would you like?"

"Water would be great. Thanks."

Alan called out from the backyard for Mac to come and help him cook the ribs and to bring them all another beer. Vicki put some ice, beer and soft drinks in a small cooler and set it on Mac's lap. "That should hold everyone for a few minutes."

"Thanks. Hey, where's the portable phone? I want to call and see how track practice went."

"On the patio."

"You're calling Coach Crocker?" Keely asked, surprised.

"Hardly."

Mac had never mentioned his problems with Crocker, but Keely had seen how hostile the coach was to Mac, and everyone in the athletic department knew the two didn't get along. Dean had filled her in on some of the details. Crocker had expected the athletic director's job when Mike Collier transferred to Georgia Tech, but the job had gone to Mac, instead.

According to Dean, a resentful Crocker had convinced himself it was because the university wanted someone disabled in an administrator's position so they could boast of being an equal-opportunity employer. He called Mac the "token cripple" behind his back, although Keely suspected Mac knew.

"Dean covers practice and he'll fill me in on how things went," Mac explained. "Normally I don't worry about it, but I have a student who's in danger of losing his scholarship and I want to see how he did today."

"Bad grades?" Keely asked.

"Bad judgment. But he'll get over it with some help."

Mac headed out to the backyard to join the others. Keely stayed behind at Vicki's request to help slice tomatoes.

"He's a special guy, isn't he?" Vicki asked.

"Yes, he is. I don't think I've ever met anyone quite like him."

"I just love him to death. He's too nice sometimes, but I guess there are worse flaws in a man." Vicki put her at the table with a plate, a knife and the washed tomatoes, then walked back to the counter where she'd been mixing potato salad. "By the way, when you have questions about stuff, I'm available anytime. All you have to do is ask."

"Stuff?"

"With Mac. Crip stuff." She shot Keely a grin over her shoulder and added, "And sex stuff. You know—how he does it."

Keely almost sliced her finger with the knife. "Mac's sex life is none of my business. I told you earlier that he and I aren't involved romantically. And we're definitely *not* planning to have sex."

"Uh-huh. Well, I want you to know that the day you decide to, you can come to me with questions. Even though the traditional stuff is sometimes out of the question with a para or a quad, sex can be terrific as long as you understand what they can and can't do. I don't want you to get scared off because you don't know what to expect. How much they can do depends on the location of the injury and how bad it was."

"Vicki—"

"Now Alan can still get it up, even though he has problems higher up on his trunk than Mac. But Mac's injury is in a different place and was more concentrated, so—"

"Oh, please, I *don't* want to know this."

They were interrupted by the shrill scream of a child from the adjacent living room, where the Sizemores' oldest son, Bay, was baby-sitting the others. Vicki didn't bother to walk to the doorway. "Savannah, whatever you're doing to J.P., stop it this instant."

"Yes, ma'am," came the reply. The screaming ceased almost immediately.

"How did you know she was the one bothering him?" Keely asked, chuckling.

"Experience. This morning I found him with lipstick on and Savannah trying to put him in a dress. Honestly, I don't know where that child gets her streak of mischief."

Keely thought it was pretty obvious. All three were physical miniatures of their parents: redheaded and freckled. J.P. had soft baby curls in shades of copper like his father. Savannah and Bay had their mother's flaming hair. They also had their parents' personalities, in addition to their looks.

"What were we talking about?" Vicki asked.

Keely quickly brought up a subject less threatening than the one they'd been discussing prior to J.P's scream. "I was about to ask you about Mac and Doug Crocker. Weren't they friends once? They seemed friendly when I was an undergraduate student."

"Not close friends, but friends," Vicki agreed, "and Mac's been really hurt by Doug's attitude. He's made multiple attempts to mend the relationship, but Doug doesn't respond. So Mac's quit trying. Now they just tolerate each other."

"I can't imagine anyone believing Mac didn't deserve that job. He's so good with his students."

"Doug's six years older and he has more tenure than Mac or any of the other coaches, so he thinks he should have gotten it. Plus, he was working with the men's team, which he thought was a more prestigious job than working with the women."

"But he has such a grating personality and the A.D.'s job involves ninety percent public relations. Doug would have alienated everybody the first week."

"That's exactly what Alan says. He can't stand the guy, either, although his friendship with Mac probably has a lot to do with that."

"Will Mac and Doug work it out, do you think?"

"I doubt it. Some people just have hate in their hearts and nothing can change that. Like that woman Mac got shot helping. She never bothered to thank him, even testified he shouldn't have interfered. Can you believe it?"

"I can't imagine anyone doing that!"

"The jerk was trying to bash her skull in with the butt of a gun. If Mac hadn't jumped in, he probably would have killed her."

"Mac told me he didn't know the guy had a gun."

"Oh, he knew all right."

"Then he lied to me. I wonder why."

Vicki wiped her hands on a dish towel and sat down across from her at the table. "Don't be upset. Despite how well-adjusted he seems, he still has trouble dealing with what happened to him. He tends to downplay everything."

"What he did was pretty courageous."

"I think so, but he doesn't. People made a big deal over what a hero he was, but when he was lying in that hospital, dead from the waist down and facing life in a wheelchair, he didn't feel much like a hero. He still doesn't. And I'm not convinced he's completely accepted his condition."

Keely nodded slowly. She could certainly identify with that.

"You know," Vicki continued, "the sad part is that Mac got hurt for such a stupid reason. I get furious when I think about how that woman supported her boyfriend. I just want to find her and tell her what I think of her. But then I tell myself she probably got what she deserved by staying with a man who beats on her."

"What happened to the man?"

"He got a three-year suspended sentence for assault and had to pay a fine for carrying an unlicensed pistol."

"He didn't go to jail?"

"Not a day."

"That's so unfair!"

"Ironic, isn't it? The only one who's paying for what happened that night is Mac, and I guess you could say he got a life sentence."

"YOU TURNED PRETTY QUIET all of a sudden tonight," Mac said as they made their way down the walkway to Keely's patio door. "Didn't you enjoy the barbecue?"

"Yes, very much."

Mac waited until they were in the kitchen to ask, "What was it about my friends you didn't like?"

She looked at him oddly. "I liked your friends. As a matter of fact, I liked them very much."

"Then what's the matter?"

"Nothing's the matter." She went to the refrigerator and opened it. "How about some fresh juice? You don't have to go yet, do you? It's still early and I'm dying to open the housewarming present you brought me."

The package sat on the kitchen table where he'd deposited it when he'd picked her up for the ball game.

"The present can wait. Something *is* bothering you and I want to know what."

Mac was determined to get to the bottom of this. She'd seemed fine after the game and even animated and unafraid when she'd met the other guys on the team. He'd believed she was having a good time. Then suddenly she'd gotten quiet.

"Did someone say something to hurt your feelings?"

"No, no one said anything. Your friends were very nice and I enjoyed myself." She got a tray from the cabinet and put the pitcher and two glasses on it. "Let's drink the juice on the patio where it's cooler. You'll like this mixture. I added a secret ingredient that gives you a boost. I've been experimenting with creating my own energy drinks, and I've come up with one I think is pretty unique." She started to walk to the door, but he rolled in front of her.

"If Bailey said something out of line, tell me and I'll kill the guy. I noticed he cornered you a couple of times."

"Bailey?" She seemed confused, then she chuckled. "Oh, Bailey. He flirted a little, but I wasn't offended."

Mac took the tray from her hands and set it on the counter. "Then who did offend you?"

"No one offended me." Seeing he wasn't going to give up, she shrugged, deciding to explain. "When we were alone in the house, Vicki told me more about the day you got shot. She said you knew the man had a gun."

A knot formed in Mac's throat. "And now you're hurt because I lied to you about that."

"No, not hurt. Well, a little, I guess. Why didn't you tell me the whole story?"

"I didn't think you'd care."

The minute he'd spoken, he realized he'd said it badly.

"Now *that* hurts me," she said.

"I didn't mean it like that. I meant, when you asked about my injury we'd just seen each other for the first time in several years. The last thing I wanted to do was bore you with the details of my stupidity."

"Stupidity? Mac! Trying to disarm that man was incredibly brave."

"No, what I did was incredibly stupid. Don't blow it out of proportion."

Agitated, he ran his hand through his hair. Man, he hated this, hated the look people got in their eyes when they heard what he'd done. He wasn't brave. He'd reacted without thinking that day. One minute he'd been walking to his car and the next minute he'd found himself in a desperate struggle to get the gun.

He couldn't remember the time in between, couldn't remember any conscious decision to intervene on the woman's behalf. Suddenly he was on the ground with the man and they were both rolling like a kicked soda bottle, the wrong end of cold steel pressing into his stomach.

"I'm sorry I barked," he told her.

"Don't apologize. What happened to you is very personal, and there's no reason you should feel obligated to tell the story to just anyone."

"You're not just anyone, Keely."

"No, I'm your friend. And that's why I've felt so strange about this. I felt you needed to know what Vicki told me tonight, but I hated to bring it up. And while we're clearing the air, I think I ought to tell you that I asked Vicki about your relationship with Doug Crocker. I wasn't being nosy, but there's so much speculation among the staff it's impossible to know what to believe."

"Crocker has major issues with me."

"Because you were promoted over him? Or because of your disability?"

"Both, probably. I don't know for sure. I've never been able to get anything concrete out of him."

And Mac regretted that more than he could say, not only because it kept them from resolving their hostilities, but because of the gossip they generated.

"Can we not talk about this?" he asked. "I try to leave problems at work and not let them intrude on what little free time I have."

"Okay, enough depressing talk for tonight." Keely wagged her finger at the package on the table. "Besides, I can't stand it any longer. Are you ever going to let me open that gift? You're cruel to bring it here and then tell me I can't open it."

"I'm trying to teach you patience."

"Fat chance of that and we both know it." She picked up the drinks tray and set it on his lap. "Let me change clothes and I'll be out in a second. Then you can show me what you brought."

Mac took the juice out to the patio, then went back for the flat rectangular package he'd picked up earlier in the day.

Keely walked out a few minutes later, wearing an oversize T-shirt that went to her knees and hung precariously off one shoulder to reveal an expanse of creamy skin.

She liked to be comfortable. That was one of the first things he had discovered about her, and she hadn't changed in the past ten years. She wasn't an exhibitionist, but she wore as little as she could get away with and still be decent.

She wouldn't wear a dress if she could wear pants. She didn't wear pants if she could wear shorts. And he suspected she probably removed the shorts and everything else when she was alone.

Judging by the nipples that strained against the T-shirt, underwear wasn't high on her list of priorities at the moment, either. She'd obviously shed her bra. But surely she had something on under that thing. Shorts. Something.

"I hope you like it," he said, handing her the package. "I had a hard time deciding what to give you."

"You didn't have to give me anything." Her eyes glowed with childish glee. "But I'm glad you did. I love getting presents."

She flipped on the outside lights, then put the gift on the patio table and tore into the paper, as eager as a six-year-old on her birthday. She gasped with delight when she saw the large framed photograph of her and her father embracing. "Oh, Mac, this is wonderful!"

He'd thought long and hard about an appropriate gift, deciding it should be something personal but not too personal. Cleaning out a file drawer a few weeks earlier, he'd run across an old media guide for the women's track team. This photograph from Keely's freshman year had been used on the cover. The university archives still had the negative, so he'd borrowed it and had a local photo store make an enlarged print.

Keely touched her fingers to the glass, as if she could touch her father's face beneath. "I remember this. It was taken after my first conference title. My dad ran out on the track to hug me when I crossed the finish line. This is most thoughtful thing anyone's ever done for me."

"So you like it?"

"I love it. Thank you!"

She leaned down, and for a moment he thought she might

hug him, or better still, kiss him on the mouth. But all he got
was a quick peck on the cheek.

Pulling back, she smiled at him softly, but then her sweet
expression turned to—God help him—longing. He had never
expected this and it stunned him, weakened his resolve.

He'd had a hard enough time resisting her when she
thought of him only as her coach and friend. But to see passion in her eyes, to know that a part of her didn't fear him
but desired him as a woman desires a man, stripped him of
all reason.

He reached for her. "Keely..."

Abruptly, she straightened and backed away. She picked up
the photograph. "I should put this inside before the dew ruins
it." She fled through the patio door before Mac could stop
her.

He expelled a breath in frustration, understanding suddenly
what had eluded him before. She wasn't afraid of him. She
was afraid of *wanting* him. A relationship was a threat to her
running plans.

His chin dropped to his chest. If his adversary had been
another man, he'd know how to fight for Keely's heart, but
it wasn't a flesh-and-blood person. She was in love already—
with being the best runner in the world.

"How do I compete with your dream, Keely?" he wondered out loud. Sadly, he realized that was a fight he could
never win.

CHAPTER NINE

August
Pensacola, Florida

KEELY PRETENDED that night on the patio had never happened. To Mac's disappointment she also seemed determined to remind him as often as possible over the next few months that regaining her career was the only thing of importance in her life.

Maybe it was. Maybe he should do himself a favor and accept that. Whatever desire she'd felt for him had been an aberration, gratitude for her housewarming gift disguised as desire.

She intended to run again, and she'd made it perfectly clear that no doctor, no therapist and certainly no paraplegic coach wearing his heart on his sleeve was going to interfere with her plans. Yes, indeed. She had her life all mapped out, and the name Mac McCandless wasn't anywhere on the map that he could see.

He watched her now, giving an interview to a Pensacola television reporter outside the city's sports complex. He knew what she was saying without actually hearing the words—knew because the words were rehearsed, along with the assured smile that always accompanied them.

Yes, I'm back in training.

No, I'm as strong as ever and completely recovered from the accident.

The Olympics in Sydney? Of course I'm going to compete. She even believed what she was telling the guy. She used the same convincing lines on Mac at every opportunity.

True, she was doing well, better than he had anticipated. The leg and hip had healed, and she'd graduated from walking to light running. Her limp had even disappeared. But her weakened lung would never allow her to do more than run for pleasure.

He shook his head and pushed off through the crowd of race spectators and wheelers before Keely could see him and wave him over. No way was he going to be put on the spot.

After her accident he'd managed to dodge questions about her chances of a comeback by feigning a lack of firsthand knowledge about her condition. He couldn't do that now. The reporters knew she'd been back at Courtland with him through the summer. They knew he was in charge of her training. Sooner or later someone could turn a camera on him and ask, "Will Keely Wilson run professionally again?" He'd have to lie or tell the truth. And he wasn't sure which was worse.

Two of his students were about to race on the adjacent track, so he quickly made his way over to them. The Courtland team had arrived in Pensacola late that morning after a six-hour drive that was supposed to be four—the oldest van in their three-vehicle caravan had blown a tire. Keely had surprised him by driving down to Florida on her own to watch the events.

"Hey, your guys look great," a buddy called out to him as he passed the wheelers from the Hartford rehab hospital.

"Thanks, Steve."

"You racing in Detroit next month?"

"Not this time." He pushed aside the regret that accompanied his response. Maybe next year, when his life was a little less hectic, he'd concentrate a bit more on his own racing.

On the track the race was about to begin, so he quickly gave last-minute instructions to his students while Dean reloaded the camera. After that, Mac got the team together near the fence. "You guys had a great morning. This heat's a killer, so watch yourselves during the lunch break. Let's meet back at this spot at about one-forty."

They wheeled off in different directions, some to meet girlfriends, others to find a shady spot and eat snacks provided by the race officials. Mac was contemplating finding a shady spot himself, hoping to catch up on the sleep he'd missed because of their middle-of-the-night departure from Georgia. As he headed toward the concession area for something to drink, a slim man approached. He asked Mac if he was the Courtland coach. Mac said he was.

The man started to say something, stopped and then sneezed. He sneezed several more times before he could talk again.

"Sorry," he said, wiping his nose with a handkerchief he'd pulled from his pocket. "Allergies. Drive me insane all year. This ocean air will probably kill me."

Mac felt sorry for the guy. He sounded as if someone had stuffed socks in his sinus cavity.

The man stuck out his hand. "Beatty Redmond of Coxwell Industries down in Miami. I've been hearing wonderful things about your team. Watching them today, I'd say the praise was well deserved. Very impressive."

"Thanks."

"I was wondering if you might have a few minutes to talk to me. Our company president is interested in sponsoring a team and sent me here with specific instructions to, to… Oh, excuse me a moment."

He started another sneezing spell.

"To what?" Mac prodded.

"To…" (sneeze) "find…" (sneeze) "the best team" (sneeze). Redmond blew his nose so loudly that people around them turned to look and laugh. "I think your team might be it. Do you have a few minutes?"

"Mr. Redmond," Mac said, hardly able to keep the excitement from his voice, "you can have as much of my time as you need."

"You're kidding. Thirty thousand dollars?" Keely pushed aside the bottle of mineral water she'd taken from his motel room's minibar and leaned across the table toward him, as if she hadn't heard correctly. "And he's giving you more this fall?"

"Fifty for the next fiscal year. He's also going to provide uniforms."

"That's wonderful!"

"The company has a licensing agreement for some new kind of breathable material that not only wicks moisture but uses your own body to regulate temperature. Insul-something or other. Redmond thinks within two years everyone will be wearing it, even nonathletes."

Dean slapped Mac on the shoulder in congratulations and flopped down on the bed. "Does this mean we can finally buy a team van and burn that wreck you got from the baseball team?"

Mac grinned, hardly able to suppress his glee at what they might finally be able to do. Buy equipment. Manage travel expenses. The offer wasn't eight hours old and he'd already started to calculate the possibilities.

"*Maybe* we can buy a van. But let's not make any plans or tell the team until we actually have the money. I still have to clear the sponsorship with the university."

"Do you foresee any problem with that?" Keely asked him.

"No, it should be pretty much a formality."

"I think we ought to celebrate tonight," Dean said. "Food? Beer? Dancing? The over-twenty-one crowd will hit the Aquarium. Want to join them?"

"You want to go look at fish?" Keely asked.

"No, I want to go *eat* fish. This place has the best seafood you ever ate, a huge dance floor, and it's gimp-friendly." He looked at Mac. "You in?"

Mac nodded. "You know it. But I'm buying."

"No argument from me," Dean told him. "Keely, you in?"

She hesitated, and Mac wondered how she was going to get out of Dean's invitation. Keely got up at five every morning to work out and rarely stayed up past ten. He was pretty sure she didn't date, although she had plenty of opportunities;

he knew she did very little that wasn't directly related to her training. Chances were, she hadn't been to a nightclub in years, if ever.

"I don't eat anything fried or drink beer," she reminded them. "The dancing is pretty iffy, too."

"Dean's grandmother has more fun than you do," Mac said, giving Dean a wink.

"Yeah, Mac," Dean said, "let's dump her and find some younger women. This one's too old."

Keely's hands flew to her hips in mock indignation. "I am *not* too old."

"You just act old, then," Mac said. Getting her out for a good time might show her that running and relationships could coexist. "You need a night out, Keely. Do you even know *how* to dance?"

"Of course I do! I just haven't done it in a long time."

"How long?"

"Uh, years."

"Unreal!" Dean said. He pulled her to her feet and toward the door. "Mac's right. Go change clothes. You're in serious need of a good time and we're the guys to provide it."

THE AQUARIUM had once been what its name indicated, a seaside tourist attraction with fish, dolphins and a whale show. The outdoor facilities were no longer open, but one tank remained with an underwater viewing window. The current owners had converted an enormous rectangular room in the main building to a combination restaurant and nightclub.

The place was popular not only with the wheelers in town for the race but with the military from the nearby naval air station. Sailors in uniform, and women apparently hoping to catch one, crammed the place. Men and women in and out of wheelchairs moved across the center dance floor, creating a sea of flesh and metal that seemed to undulate in rhythm to the rock and country songs the band played.

Nets, shells and boating memorabilia hung from the ceiling and three of the walls. The fourth wall was the focal point of the room, the lighted tank stocked with strange and colorful creatures that swam right up to the glass and looked at you as you looked at them.

The place fascinated Keely, and yet it had its drawbacks. The music was too loud. The air carried the fishy scent of the ocean, which was fine if you were standing on the beach or eating fish, but not so fine if you were trying to eat salad. Even worse, she felt a disturbing alien emotion each time someone pulled Mac away from the table to dance.

The women—and there had been an endless parade of them—seemed most interested in the slow songs, when they could sit sideways in Mac's lap and nestle against his chest. The woman nestling against him now had her arms around his neck and was telling him something funny that had him braying like a jackass.

"I didn't realize people in wheelchairs could dance," Keely told Dean, mentally berating herself for caring that Mac's right hand had shifted from the wheel on that side to the woman's jean-clad thigh.

"Not a whole lot crips can't do when it comes right down to it," Dean said.

"So I see." Obviously Mac could move the chair with one hand while groping women with the other. Well, it wasn't exactly groping, but it bothered her to watch, anyway.

Was he trying to torture her in exchange for that night on the patio? Or was she simply getting very good at *self* torture?

Someone touched her shoulder, and she turned to find Steve Sasser, one of the Hartford wheelers Mac had introduced her to. "Would you like to dance?"

"Oh, no, thank you. I haven't danced in so long I don't remember how."

He patted his lap. "All you have to do is sit. I'll do all the work."

She contemplated saying no again, but then relented. He was nice. A good-looking man. She couldn't think of a single reason she shouldn't dance with him.

After Steve came Jimmy, Ben, Wade, Erik and two dozen more men, both disabled and able-bodied. "This is getting ridiculous," she told Dean. "I'm exhausted just walking back and forth from the dance floor."

"Yeah, but having fun for a change, right?"

Yes, she admitted, she was having fun, though feeling a little guilty about it. Growing up, her dad had often hammered into her the consequences of breaking training.

"Act like ordinary people and you'll be ordinary," he was fond of saying.

He'd been right, of course. During high school, while her friends worked on their summer tans, Keely worked on endurance and strength. She'd skipped the parties, the dates, the hours on the telephone talking about boys. Instead, she'd concentrated on making the Olympic team. She'd won her first silver medal at seventeen.

Adhering to her father's rules all those years had paid off. The lessons she'd learned had followed her into adulthood, and she was loath to deviate from them too often. When you were bad, you paid for it with poor performances and you lost the respect of the people counting on you. It wasn't worth it.

Not that she was a complete social misfit. The very nature of her business dictated that she attend dinners and put in appearances at various functions. She dated occasionally. She'd even had a physical relationship that lasted a whole six months. It had turned out badly, of course, and the failure had been entirely her fault, but that was the way things worked. With so much time and passion expended on her career, she had none left over for a man.

"My turn to dance with you," Dean said, standing. He held out his hand. Keely allowed him to lead her through the crowd.

"I don't know if I'm ready for this," she shouted as the slow song segued into a faster one.

"Just be careful and don't throw that hip out. Mac would kill me."

Maybe it was the music. Maybe it was Dean's youthful exuberance rubbing off on her. Whatever it was, Keely allowed herself to flow with it, letting her natural rhythm guide her body and release her from her inhibitions. Dancing, she rediscovered, was like running, controlled by an inner mind that moved you without true conscious thought.

The next song was slow. Dean insisted they dance to it, too, but his attention—like her own—was more on Mac and his current partner. The girl was young and petite, with dark hair that fell past her waist. "She's very pretty," Keely commented.

"Beautiful."

Dean's gaze kept going back to the couple.

"Do you know her?" Keely asked. "She looks familiar."

"Ginny Sasser. Steve Sasser's daughter. I met her here last year and I've bumped into her a few times since then at races. You probably saw her at the track this morning."

Ah, that was it. Keely didn't remember the face, but that long hair was hard to forget. "Is she single?"

"Yeah. And smart. She's in her second year of law school."

Keely grinned at him. "You sure seem to know a lot about her."

"I've had a bad case of the hots for her ever since I met her last year."

"If you're attracted to her, why haven't you done anything about it? I haven't seen you dance with her once."

"You should talk."

"Meaning?"

"You know exactly what I mean. You and Mac. You've spent all night trying to stay away from each other, yet you can't keep your eyes off him and I'd bet money he could name every man you've danced with."

Was he watching her? She hated being thrilled at the thought of it.

She wasn't going to allow herself to be drawn into a conversation about Mac, so she ignored Dean's comment and told him again to go ask Ginny to dance.

"I haven't worked up my courage yet," he said.

"Do it now, Dean. You can't simply stand back and worship her from a distance."

"She might turn me down and then I'd be crushed." He grinned. "The rejection might scar me for life."

"Oh, sure, like anything would ever scar you for life. Go on—do it," Keely said again.

"She might be tired of dancing."

"Then ask her if she wants to go look at the fish with you."

"Well...maybe. I'll think about it."

As they looked at Ginny, she smiled at them. Or more precisely, at Dean.

"See?" Keely said. "She's sending you signals. She wants you to come over."

"Think so?"

"I'm positive. She obviously likes you, too."

Keely took the lead and danced them closer to Mac and Ginny.

Dean danced her back the other way. "What are you doing?"

"Helping you out." She danced them forward.

"I don't need help." He danced them back.

"Quit being difficult and let's get over there."

She nearly had to jerk him this time, but he followed her lead. They ended up dancing right next to Mac as the song ended and Ginny got up from his lap. Perfect timing.

"Hi," Keely said.

"Hi," Mac replied.

Keely turned her attention to the girl. "I'm Keely and this is Dean. We're friends of Mac's."

"I'm sorry," Mac said, and took up the introductions. "I think you already know Dean. Ginny Sasser, meet Keely Wilson. Ginny is Steve's oldest daughter."

"Oh? Steve's daughter." Keely pretended ignorance. "I'm glad to meet you. Are you here with your dad?"

"Uh-huh, just my dad." She cut her gaze to Dean. "I mean, I'm not here with a date or anything."

Dean seized his opportunity. "If you're not otherwise engaged, would you care to walk over and look at the fish?"

Ginny quickly nodded assent. "I'd love to see the fish with

you." She turned to Mac. "Thanks for dancing with me, Coach McCandless."

"Thank you, Ginny."

"Nice to meet you, Keely."

"You, too, Ginny."

Dean took Ginny's hand. "See you guys later." He winked at Keely over his shoulder and mouthed, "Don't wait up," as he led Ginny off to the aquarium wall.

"'If you're not otherwise engaged'?" Mac mimicked Dean. "What was that all about? Who talks like that?"

Keely chuckled. "I believe young love does something to the syntax."

Mac's forehead wrinkled. "You're kidding. You mean those two…"

"Uh-huh. The heat between them nearly singed my eyebrows. I had to force him to come over here, he was so nervous about talking to her."

"Man, I must be getting old if can't recognize sexual attraction anymore."

Probably because he was too busy radiating sexual attraction himself.

The soft slow intro of the next song filled the air, and men and women around them began to move into each other's arms. Putting Dean together with Ginny left Keely alone with Mac and both of them partnerless.

Mac gazed up at her expectantly. "Looks like my dance partner deserted me."

"Looks like it."

"And it was partly your fault because you forced Dean to talk to her."

"I…I guess it was." She knew what was coming next, but was uncertain how to handle it.

"You'll have to take her place, you know."

She didn't move an eyelash. Inside, though, her vital organs were turning to jelly.

Dancing with him…the intimacy of it…buttocks to groin. One breast pressing against his chest. With the other men she hadn't given it a thought, but this was Mac. Mac, who made her feel liquid. Mac, who with a simple smile could make her breath catch in her lungs and her heart flutter like a thousand hummingbirds in flight.

She wasn't sure she could dance with him. Yet she couldn't walk away without being cruel. Deep down she suspected the tiny part of her that longed for intimacy with Mac had even purposely put her in this terrible situation.

Physical fear of him still stood as a wall between them, a lower wall than when she'd first learned of his injury, but a wall nonetheless. Over the past months, he'd helped her learn to touch him without cringing, but dancing with him was a big jump from putting ointment on his scraped hands or rubbing sunscreen across his shoulders. His hands and shoulders weren't paralyzed. His legs were.

She worried how his legs would feel under her. How did they look?

She'd never seen him when he wasn't wearing long pants. Even on the hottest days this summer, he'd worn sweats or a long-legged body suit. For work he preferred khakis or jeans, although the rest of the staff dressed in shorts. Tonight his legs were covered again, in a dark-gray pair of cotton twills.

He held out a hand at her hesitation. "Remember how much fun we had dancing the night of your graduation?"

"I remember. You had some pretty fancy moves, as I recall."

"I still do," he said, grinning. When she didn't move, he sobered. "Come on, Sport Model. This is Mac. Your best buddy. You don't have any reason to be afraid of this. I promise."

Sport Model. He'd given her the nickname in college, teasing that she was built for speed like a fancy racing car.

As if disconnected from her body, she saw her hand inch forward and into his, without having made the decision to move it.

"That's it," he coaxed, gently urging her down toward his lap. "Trust me and everything will be fine. You know I'd never ask you to do anything that would hurt you."

Her pulse pounded in her ears. The first contact with his

lap sent a sizzle of fear through her body, but the fear quickly turned to a delicious curl of pleasure that stretched like a contented cat in the pit of her stomach and below.

His legs felt fine. The curves of her backside settled in against them without any problem, and her lower legs found a comfortable place to nestle between his.

Her arms and hands were a different story. She didn't know where to put them. Her right arm was the one closest to his body, and she moved it this way and that, trying to find an appropriate place for it, until he took the decision from her and hooked it on his shoulder.

He pulled her forward a bit and placed her other hand against his chest. She knew his soft cotton shirt hid muscle and delicious masculine angles, and her fingers ached to touch the naked flesh in reality, as they had done so often lately in her dreams.

She had danced with Steve Sasser the very same way only thirty minutes ago and the position had felt merely functional, a way to keep her off the wheels of the chair and balanced in his lap. With Mac, it was more of an embrace.

"This okay?" he asked. "If it's not, all you have to do is say so."

"It's fine." Sexual arousal had taken root at the heart of her and was making her feel a little bold.

As they began to move to the lazy rhythm of the song, she remained aware of the people around them, but her focus reduced itself to one man, to the musky smell of his cologne and the warmth of his breath against her cheek.

His face was just a whisper away and she studied it, the contours of his jaw, the crinkly lines at his eyes, the ever-so-slight dip in the center of his chin. They were flesh-and-blood magnets drawing her with an invisible charge.

And that mouth. A torture device for women if she'd ever seen one. Perfect teeth. That tiny, heart-shaped bow at the top of his upper lip.

She was thankful she wasn't alone with him. Had they been alone, she might have pushed foolishness to recklessness and touched her lips to his, just to see if they really felt as good as she imagined.

"This isn't so bad, is it?" he asked, giving her a reassuring smile. She liked the way his eyes seemed to smile right along with his mouth.

"No, it isn't so bad." She didn't think it was wise to tell him that, in fact, it felt very very good.

Their gazes held for a moment, for too long a moment. In the dark depths of his eyes she saw her wildest dreams and her worst nightmares. He desired her. He wanted to make love to her.

Quickly she looked away, afraid her own eyes might reveal the truth: she wanted the same thing. And it wasn't that other Mac she wanted, the Mac from ten years ago who had run so gracefully and been so physically perfect. It was *this* Mac. The older Mac. The Mac who couldn't run and wasn't perfect. The Mac who'd been to hell and survived it.

She wanted the Mac in the wheelchair.

WHEN HE TOOK HER back to the motel that night, awkwardness made her tongue-tied. She stood at her door, shuffling from foot to foot, not knowing what to say or how to act, hoping she could say good-night without throwing herself on top of him.

He was attractive, charming, witty and oozed sexuality from every pore of his skin, a dangerous combination of traits in any man, but downright deadly in this one.

Her brain cells screamed for her to get away, and as quickly as possible. Every time he touched her arm tonight, or smiled at her, or whispered something amusing in her ear, it put another chink in the wall she had erected against him. The wall was beginning to crumble.

Now she needed time to repair the damage. Time alone. Sleep, if possible. Maybe even a few notes jotted in her journal to soothe her. She had to force her concentration away from him and back to her goal. She couldn't allow herself to become distracted.

She thanked him for a good time and scurried into the room

as fast as she could without being rude. As on countless other nights, she found she was afraid to sleep or even turn off the lights, so she got out her journal and read back through past entries.

May 7: Mac says I'm making great progress, but he treats me as if I might break. He's always around. He's always looking out for me. It's annoying at times. Other times I find I like it way too much. Have to work on that.

June 28: Mac let me increase my exercises slightly today. He's such a sweetheart. I need to thank him somehow. Dinner out as my treat? A gift? The leather shop at the mall has a briefcase in the window that's perfect. It's the same incredible brown as his eyes.

August 17: Today Mac...

Mac this. Mac that. It read more like a teenager's diary than the journal of a grown woman. She was supposed to be recording her training progress, not talking about Mac Mc-Candless.

In disgust she tossed the journal back into her bag. This was ludicrous! She couldn't give in to this...this...admiration.

Admiration? Who was she trying to fool? Call it by its real name—lust. Wet, aching, nipple-hardening, I-want-to-rub-myself-all-over-you kind of lust.

As Dean might phrase it, she had a bad case of the hots for Mac. And she had to find a way to control herself—before she ruined everything.

CHAPTER TEN

September

"PLEASE, MAC, let me ride you. I'll try not to squeal this time."

"Aw, Linda, not today. I've got tons of work to do."

He had appointments all morning, a board-of-trustees meeting that afternoon and a stack of telephone messages on this desk left over from yesterday.

"Yes, today. Please, please, let me. Just an itty-bitty ride?"

The secretary gave him a pleading look, dissolving Mac's better judgment. He'd always had trouble resisting a woman when she wanted something. All she had to do was poke out a lip or act hurt, and he melted quicker than butter on a hot ear of corn.

"Pleeeeeeeeease," she whined again.

"Since when am I an amusement ride?"

"Since you got these fun wheels. Oh, come on. It won't take five minutes."

He sighed, knowing he was defeated. Okay, he'd take her for a ride. It wasn't seven yet and few people were at work. No one important would see them. As long as the other women he worked with didn't find out, it was okay. If they did, they'd want a ride, too, and he didn't have time to entertain them this morning.

"Climb on," he told her. "But we've got to be quick. And you have to promise—no squealing. You know I hate squealing."

"I promise."

She plopped down in his lap. He shifted her sideways so

her hips wouldn't touch the wheels. Pushing off was difficult, but in seconds he had overcome the slow start and the added weight of his passenger. Quickly they picked up momentum. By the time they hit the ramp at the end of the hall, they were flying.

"Eeeeeeeeeeee," she squealed despite her promise, just like they'd both known she would.

They barreled up the ramp and onto the concourse, scattering people in their wake, picking up speed again as they left the carpet and hit the concrete floor. As they whizzed through a group of students, someone yelled, "Go for it, Coach." Another opened a door.

Mac raced through the upper level to the outside without slowing. The college had placed ramps across one end of both sets of steps and he hit the first one with a loud *whomp*. The chair nearly jumped the second one, becoming airborne and slamming onto the pavement with a jolt that bounced Linda several inches off his lap. The planters loomed ahead.

"Hold on," he warned, but there was no real danger. He had maneuvered this course so many times he could do it in his sleep. The trick was maintaining the right speed so he didn't have to brake, cutting to the right of the first tree to avoid the uneven pavement and making sure he didn't hit anyone.

"Coming through!"

The student athletes on their way into Coach Layton's early-morning conditioning class scrambled onto the planters and out of the way, cheering Mac on as he expertly snaked through the trees and toward the street. As always, he waited until the last possible second to brake. And as always, Linda screamed loudly as they slid to a stop inches from the curb.

This time he looked up to find he had also stopped inches from Keely.

"Keely! Hey."

She opened and closed her mouth several times. Finally she whispered, "Excuse me, I have to go," and slipped around them.

"Oops," Linda said with a chortle. "Mac, do yourself a

favor and let your friend know I'm an old married woman who dearly loves her husband.''

"Huh?"

She rolled her eyes, then knocked on his head as if it were made of wood. "Think about it, you big dunce and maybe you can figure out why she's upset." She hopped up. "Thanks for the ride. See ya."

"See ya, Linda."

Mac pivoted the chair so he could better watch Keely's progress up the long walk. She charged ahead at full steam, almost at a run, forcing people to jump out of her way. Clearly something *had* upset her.

When the answer hit him, he wanted to knock himself on his own head for his stupidity.

"SLOW IT DOWN a bit," Dean said from behind, sounding like he was beginning to tire. "We still have over 1200 steps to go."

Instead of slowing down, Keely began climbing faster. The sound of her soles hitting the concrete steps was like a drumbeat, urging her to run faster, to make it up and down the steep rows of the coliseum without stopping to rest.

"If you can't keep up, Averhardt, don't blame it on me," she said, ignoring the growing pain in her side.

"Don't start this again, Keely. You know you're pushing too hard. For some reason you've been antsy ever since we started today."

Running the lower circle of the 1,956 steps of the coliseum with Dean was a twice-weekly ritual Keely enjoyed, but his constant admonishments to slow down and not overdo were getting on her nerves. Today of all days she needed to push herself. She needed to feel strong and alive, to feel she had overcome her injuries.

September twenty-seventh. A year ago today, she'd been hit by that car and nearly died. This day marked a whole year away from competition. Other elite women runners were celebrating victories and breaking her records left and right. She, meanwhile, was stuck here in classes that bored her to tears and being nagged by Mac and Dean every time she lifted a leg to exercise.

Seeing Mac this morning with that woman on his lap hadn't helped her feelings, either.

She needed to work a little harder, run more miles, exercise another couple of hours a day. By spring maybe she could race again.

"I'm not slowing down," she told Dean, taking two steps at a time. She called over her shoulder, "And I'm doing all twenty-four rows without stopping."

"You're *not* doing all twenty-four. That's crazy."

"Oh, yes I am."

The pain deepened, making Keely struggle to bring in more oxygen. Faced with the unexpected barrier, she did what she always did; she denied the pain and pushed herself harder.

"Please slow down," Dean urged again. "You've been doing so great these past few months. You don't want to do anything to wreck your progress."

"Ooh, you're such a nag."

"Fine. Don't listen. You're on your own, then. I can't handle this pace."

Dean pulled back, letting her go ahead without him.

She reached the place where the steps met the topmost aisle, raced over to the next row and began the descent. Down she ran to the floor, then up again to the top, moving as fast as she could. Down. Up. Down. Up.

The pain in her side worsened, but pain was good. Pain meant she was alive.

Focus, she told herself. *Work harder.*

An image of Mac riding that woman on his lap flashed in her head to intrude on her concentration.

Focus!

She pressed ahead. Down. Up. Down. Up.

A couple of steps into her descent on the next row, someone hit her in the ribs with a brick—at least, that was what it felt like. An intense fire consumed her side and made her cry out, propelling her forward. One second she was on her feet and the next she was sprawled facedown, bumping down the steps on her belly and feeling every hard edge.

"Keely! Are you all right?" Dean's voice seemed miles away.

Finally she thumped to a stop. She rolled onto her back and lay there with her eyes closed, trying to catch her breath.

Not again, she prayed. *Please, not again.*

Dean was next to her now, giving his best imitation of a man having a panic attack. "Did the hip go out? Did you break anything? Is it your lung?"

She struggled to turn around and sit up. She put her head between her knees, frantically drawing in oxygen through her mouth. One of the athletes doing steps on an adjacent row called out to ask if she was okay and did they need help.

"Tell her—" she paused to take a couple of deep breaths "—I'm fine."

"Are you sure? I can have one of the trainers here in two minutes."

She shook her head.

Ten minutes passed before the fire in her side died out and she could breathe and talk normally.

"You cut yourself," Dean said, wiping blood off her arm and below her eye with his shirt. "And I think you're going to have a shiner."

The throbbing in her cheek told her he was right. She must have hit the edge of one of the steps with her face when she fell.

"What happened?" Dean asked.

"I fell over my own feet." She glanced sideways to see if Dean believed the lie. He didn't.

"You were gasping for breath and your face was purple," he pointed out. "For a second there I thought your lung was about to collapse again. You scared me to death."

"You're making a big deal out of this when all I did was trip and fall down a few steps."

"Keely, I don't buy that excuse. You cried out and grabbed your side before you fell."

"Dean, please."

The last thing she needed was him running to Mac with some wild story. Admittedly the lung was still bothering her, but even the respiratory therapist she'd worked with after the surgery said that was to be expected for a while. She'd had a lobe removed; she'd lost tissue. She hadn't yet built back to full capacity. The lung would be okay. She only needed a few more months to recover.

"You know Mac's going to ask me what happened," Dean said. "I'm not going to lie to him."

"I'm not asking you to. I *told* you what happened. I tripped. That's all there was to it."

Regardless of whether or not he believed her, Dean had the good sense not to bring it up again. He walked her downstairs to the locker rooms and left her with a reminder to take care of her eye as soon as possible.

She doctored her cuts and stretched out on a bench with an ice pack on her face. Soreness in her arms and legs set in immediately, a combination of falling and not cooling down properly. As soon as she was able to drag herself upstairs, she went to Mac's office, hoping to talk to him before Dean and do a little damage control.

Mac wasn't in. The monthly board-of-trustees meeting, Miriam said. He'd be gone most of the day and would even miss wheeler practice.

"I can leave him a note," Miriam offered, not looking up. "He probably won't see it until morning."

"No, don't bother. I'll catch him later."

For Keely "later" meant that night. Dinner at seven. Three or four nights a week they had dinner at his house or hers while she studied and he graded papers. Sunday afternoons, if he wasn't gone with the football team, he grilled fish or chicken on her patio. A couple of times they'd taken day excursions out of town: the zoo, the art museum, the Egyptian exhibit up in Nashville.

Somehow they had settled into the routine of an old married couple, and it was, for the most part, comfortable, like slipping your foot into a soft old shoe. The fit was good.

Lately, though, it had become less comfortable for her and

she suspected for him, too. The attraction between them hung in the air all the time; it colored every decision, every action. She found herself carefully choosing her words. She avoided sitting too close to him, not sure she could keep her hands to herself. The effort that went into being friends, being *only* friends, was wearing her out.

"What happened to your face?" Miriam asked, just now looking up.

"I took a little tumble down the steps."

"You're going to have a black eye."

"Do me a favor and don't mention it to Coach McCandless, okay? I'd rather tell him about it myself."

"Sure, hon, but be prepared. He's going to have a fit when he sees it."

CHAPTER ELEVEN

KEELY WENT to wheeler practice that afternoon, but she skipped lab, opting to go home early and take a hot bath to ease her aching muscles.

After that, she made her weekly call to her mother, since she'd missed doing it the previous Sunday. Holding the receiver between her ear and shoulder, she stood at the bathroom mirror and dabbed makeup on her face. The skin of her cheek and around her eye was an artist's palette of purple in varying shades. The makeup didn't hide the bruises.

At six she drove from her house to Mac's and used the spare key he'd given her, letting herself in through the front door. While the squash and broccoli cooked, she fixed her homemade chocolate pudding and stuck it in the refrigerator to firm, a consolation for Mac who wasn't crazy about vegetables and enjoyed a calorie-laden treat. The pudding wasn't really chocolate and didn't have a gram of fat or sugar in it, but he didn't know that.

She tore lettuce for salad as she skimmed a chapter of the advanced chemistry text she'd picked up at the campus bookstore a couple of days earlier. Finally something interesting!

She made a mental note to talk to her adviser about auditing a class. Her nutrition class was okay, had already given her an idea for an electrolyte drink she was itching to put together, but the rest of the classes...boring. She deserved an A for simply staying awake in Principles of Recreational Management. If she could get access to one of the chemistry labs to have a little fun, she might actually survive this quarter.

At six-thirty she heard Mac's van pull into the garage.

Upbeat. Calm. That was the way she had to play this. She

was pretty sure Dean hadn't yet had a chance to tell Mac about her fall, and that would work in her favor. Quickly she rehearsed what she was going to say.

He pushed through the door, calling out a tired greeting. "When's supper?" he added. "I'm starved."

"Ten minutes," she said, not turning around. She continued to stand at the counter, tearing up the lettuce, although she'd already broken the leaves into minuscule pieces.

"Can I help?"

"No, it's nearly finished. Just relax. How was your meeting?"

"Long and uneventful." She heard him toss his keys on the table and put down his briefcase. The fragrance of roses filled the air. "How was your day?"

No, he definitely hadn't talked to Dean yet.

"Well," she said, clearing her throat, "there *is* something I need to—"

Before she could get the rest of the sentence out, the telephone rang. Her shoulders slumped. Now she'd have to work up her courage all over again.

He pulled out his cell phone. "Hello. Hey. Yeah, I just walked in the door. What's up?"

He paused to listen to something the caller said. When he spoke again the hard inflection in his voice put Keely's senses on full alert. "No, Dean, I haven't talked to her. Maybe you better tell me what happened before she fell."

Her body stiffened.

Listening over the next few minutes to the one-sided conversation was like waiting in front of a firing squad while the executioners loaded their guns. Dean, no doubt, was recounting every gory detail of this morning's mishap. Mac said little in response, but that in itself was an ominous sign.

"...No, Dean, you did the right thing. No, I'm sure she won't hold it against you." He hung up the phone and Keely braced herself. "I believe you have something to tell me."

"I fell down a couple of steps. Surely I'm not the first person to do that."

"Keely, turn around."

He swore loudly when he saw her face. He made her sit at the table so he could study the damage. A bouquet of red roses lay on his nearby briefcase, and she inhaled their heady fragrance as he assessed her injuries.

His hands trembled as he lightly pressed his fingers against her cheek. "I don't think you chipped the bone, but have Doc Ramsey take a look at it in the morning to see if it needs an X ray. You'll probably have a tiny scar from that cut, but you'll hardly see it."

"One more won't make any difference."

He examined a cut on her forearm and a second one on her hand and dismissed them as minor. "That all of them?"

"Yes."

"Any hip or knee pain?"

"No, just muscle soreness. I soaked in the bathtub and it helped, but my legs are still really sore."

"I can take care of that."

He moved his chair at an angle. Before she could protest, he picked up both her legs and placed them across his lap. He still had on the suit he'd worn to his board meeting, and he looked like a million dollars.

"I'll mess up your suit."

"Forget my suit."

He began to run his hands over her calves, feeling the muscles through her thin leggings, stroking to lengthen and relax them.

Oh, my! All protest died on her lips.

"Tell me what happened before you fell," he said, working his way up her right calf.

"Dean already told you what happened."

"I want *you* to tell me."

"I was going too fast. Dean warned me to slow down, but I was feeling edgy this morning and wanted to see how far I could get. You know me. Miss Impatience. But it's no big deal, because I'm fine."

Lord, he had great hands. She could die right now and be content. Forget checking the broccoli. Forget supper completely. She just wanted to sit here in this chair and let him put his hands all over her.

"Did you have trouble breathing before you fell?"

"Hmm?" Concentrating on his words was hard when he was doing such erotic things to her. "I guess I was a little winded. That's natural, though, isn't it?"

"Did you have pain?"

"No, just trouble catching my breath. You aren't going to cut back on my training schedule, are you?"

He didn't indicate one way or the other, telling her he'd wait until Doc Ramsey had a chance to check her over before he made a decision.

"Are you angry with me?"

"Furious."

He didn't seem furious. He seemed concerned but calm. He hadn't even given her a lecture for disobeying his orders.

He nodded at the bouquet of roses and baby's breath. "I stopped and got those for you on the way home. They aren't much, but I thought they might help cheer you up."

"They're gorgeous. Thank you. But...you didn't know about my fall until a few minutes ago."

"No, but when I looked at the calendar this morning and realized what day it was, it occurred to me that you might be feeling a little down. Today's the anniversary of your accident, isn't it?" She nodded. "Depressed?"

"A little. I've lost the whole last year of my life. Falling down those steps today didn't help." *Or seeing that woman's arms around your neck.*

His hands slid upward to her thigh, making her breath catch in her lungs.

"Four thousand years ago the ancient Chinese used massage to treat not only physical symptoms but emotional ones," he told her. "They believed that touch was necessary for the well-being of the soul and that a good massage could do wonders for you when you had a bad day."

That made sense to her. At this very moment she felt better than she had all day, possibly in her entire life. Heat infused her. Little ripples of pleasure radiated through her body.

"Close your eyes. Relax."

If she got any more relaxed, she might fall from the chair, but she closed her eyes, anyway, and let him work on her aching spots. One of his hands was kneading her upper thigh, his fingers only inches away from sending her to heaven, while the other had slipped behind her knee to gently massage. She had to bite her lip to keep from moaning out loud.

As he worked, he told her about the importance of massage to the Greeks, how warriors in Egyptian, Persian and Japanese cultures received massages both before and after battles and bathed in public pools scented with fragrant oils to relax.

The tension of strained muscles gave way to tension of another kind that made her body quiver. Her blood raced through her veins. Desire pooled between her legs.

"You're boiling over," he said.

Her eyes flew open. "What?"

"You're boiling over." He pointed to the stove. "The food."

The water in the pot sizzled as it hit the burner. The vegetables. Oh! He was talking about the vegetables!

His face was a mask of pure innocence, but she thought she saw a twinkle of amusement in his eyes.

Blushing, she jumped up and quickly removed the pot from the burner. "I, um, supper should be ready in a few minutes," she told him, struggling to regain her equilibrium. She had a sneaking suspicion he knew how aroused he had gotten her. Even worse, she suspected he'd done it on purpose.

AFTER SUPPER, Mac changed into jeans and a T-shirt, then joined Keely in the living room. She was curled up on the couch with her shoes off, using the remote to click through the TV channels.

"No homework tonight?" he asked.

"Finished." She stifled a yawn. "I only had one chapter to read."

"Maybe you should turn in early. You've had a rough day."

"Are you kicking me out?"

"No, of course not."

"Then, can I stay here with you for a while? If I go home, I'll only sit around that empty house and get depressed again."

"Stay as long as you want. How about we find a movie to watch?"

"Okay, but I get to pick. Your taste in movies is as bad as your taste in music. If I never have to watch *Rio Lobo* again, it'll be too soon."

He chuckled. They had a friendly, ongoing squabble over what radio station to listen to when they rode in the van. He liked country. She liked the weird New Age stuff the campus station played. Their respective tastes in movies were incompatible, as well. They always disagreed on what to watch. But they'd learned to compromise.

"You choose tonight," he told her. "Scoot over, and I'll sit with you."

He transferred to the couch, pushing his chair to the side, out of the way. Keely scanned the channels and stopped on one that showed a fake-looking squid attacking a submarine.

She smiled at his expression of disbelief. "Just kidding," she said, changing to another channel. "Here we go. *The Quiet Man*. John Wayne for you. Ireland for me. And it looks like it just started."

"Good choice."

They settled in to watch, but it wasn't long before Keely's chin dropped and she nodded off to sleep. She swayed, fell against him, then jerked awake. "Sorry." The second time she fell, she didn't move.

"Keely."

No answer.

Careful not to wake her, he lifted his arm and let her slide the rest of the way down. She snuggled in with a sigh, her face in the crook of his neck and her arm loosely around his middle.

Mac closed his eyes to capture the moment, knowing it might be the only intimate one he'd ever have with her. Years from now, he wanted to be able to instantly recall every detail:

the way she felt in his arms, the soft sound of her breathing, even the clean fragrance of her hair. She must have dusted herself with powder or sprayed on perfume because she smelled like flowers. He inhaled deeply and pressed the alluring scent into his memory.

The movie ended and another one began. When a loud commercial came on, he looked for the remote to turn down the volume, but it was on Keely's other side, out of his reach. She mumbled something and stirred. Then she lifted her head and looked at him with eyes that didn't want to stay open. It took her a moment to realize where she was. *And* that she was plastered to his side.

She didn't draw away in horror, as he expected. Instead, she dropped her gaze to his mouth. An invitation, he told himself, so he lowered his mouth to hers.

Nice. Her lips were sweeter than he'd imagined. Even nicer was the fact that she began to kiss him back. Her hand slid up to his neck. A little gurgle of pleasure escaped her throat.

Heat poured into him. His equilibrium shifted. If blood could boil, it was boiling in him now.

Touching her, being touched by her, caused the dam inside Mac to break. The feelings he'd kept carefully hidden rushed out, filling him with an urgent need to hold her close to his heart. He gave in to that need because he had no choice.

By the end of the kiss, they were both gasping for breath. She stared at him in wide-eyed confusion. Her face carried a bright red flush and her lips the dampness of passion.

"We shouldn't have done that," she said, still clinging to him.

"Why not? Felt damn good to me."

"You're my coach."

"I'm also a man, Keely."

"Believe me, I'm aware of that."

She moved from his arms. She stood and found her shoes. Her backpack was on the floor, and she stuffed her books inside it.

"You're not leaving?"

"It's late. I'm tired." She picked up her keys. "Bye."

"Wait!" He took a fortifying breath. "Stay here tonight."

"In your bed?"

"Yes. With me. In my bed."

Her brief hesitation gave him hope. But then she shook her head. "I can't."

"You can't? Or you don't want to?"

"I don't want to."

Fair enough. At least she was honest. But it didn't take away the sting of her rejection.

"Okay. But if you're determined to leave, I'll follow you home."

"I'd rather you didn't. I'll see you tomorrow."

By the time he got into his chair, she was already out the door and in her car. He watched in frustration as she cranked it and drove off.

There was a pattern here. He got close. It spooked her. She retreated.

But what could he do about it?

Be patient, he supposed. Let her come to him when she was ready. *If* she was ever ready. One thing was certain, he wouldn't be foolish enough to ask her a second time to share his bed. The next move was hers.

CHAPTER TWELVE

THE FRONT LAWN of the Sizemore house looked like a toy department after an explosion—bikes, bats, balls, tanks, toy soldiers, brightly colored plastic cars you could sit in and peddle, enough action figures to fill a railroad car, some with missing legs or arms, a few with missing heads.

Keely picked her way through the graveyard of overturned bicycles and rang the doorbell. A herd of trumpeting elephants answered it.

"Ma-ma, company!" Savannah yelled as she ran past without a backward glance. Six or so little girls, all chattering at the same time, and several older boys followed her.

"We're goin' to Jack's," Bay yelled, bringing up the rear of the pack. He and the boys jerked up bicycles and prepared to ride off.

Vicki appeared at the door with J.P. on her hip. "You be back by noon, Savannah," she called after her daughter. "And Bay Alan, don't you make a pest of yourself with Mrs. Wyatt." She smiled at Keely, a genuine smile that told her she was glad to see her. "What a nice surprise. What brings you out so early on a Saturday morning?"

"I need to talk to you if you can spare a minute."

"Sure, come on in. Don't you just love this autumn weather?" She led the way to the kitchen. Black fabric covered the table. A crisp white apron and cap lay on a nearby chair.

"I love the cooler temperatures but I'm not ready for it to drop below freezing," Keely said. "Who's the pilgrim costume for? Savannah?"

"Yeah. I'm trying to get a jump on her costume for the

Thanksgiving play, since this is my busiest time of year.''
Putting J.P. on the floor with a cookie, she joined Keely at
the table. ''I'm glad to have someone to visit with this morning. Alan's tailgating with Mac and some other guys before
the football game.''

''I know, and that's why I hope you don't mind me dropping in. I need to ask you something and I don't want either
one of them to know I'm here.''

''Mm, sounds wonderfully sinister. I like it already. What
secret are we keeping from them?''

''No secret really.'' Nervousness made her fumble with the
cuffs of her sweater. ''I feel awkward talking to you about
this.''

''We've gotten to be friends these past months, haven't
we?''

''I wouldn't be here if I didn't think so.''

''I promise whatever we talk about will stay between us.
Now, what is it you want to ask me?''

She took a deep breath and let it out. ''I have some questions concerning Mac.''

''Uh-huh.'' Vicki didn't look surprised.

''He and I have become...much closer lately. I guess
you've noticed.''

''Hard to miss. You spend so much time together Alan has
started referring to you as the Siamese twins.''

''I've tried not to be attracted to him, but I am. I've tried
not to act on the attraction, but I do, anyway. It's like I'm no
longer in control of my brain or my body. I find myself brushing imaginary pieces of lint off his shirt so I can touch his
chest, or asking him to look at something in a textbook so I
can put my head next to his just to smell him. To smell him!
Isn't that the most awful thing you've ever heard?''

''Absolutely horrible.'' Vicki looked as if she was trying
not to laugh.

''And suddenly I'm jealous of every woman he's nice to.
A few weeks ago I bumped into him while he had one of the
secretaries on his lap. You know how they're always bugging
him to give them a ride. I literally saw green. Here was this

woman sitting on him, with her arms around his neck, and I wanted to scratch her eyes out.''

"Did you?"

"No, of course not! I walked away. But I came *this* close to telling her to get her bony behind off him if she knew what was good for her because she was sitting in *my* seat!"

Vicki broke up then, laughing loudly.

"This isn't funny!"

"Oh, sweetie, I'm sorry, but listen to yourself. You're a normal woman with normal desires and he's a very attractive man. What you're feeling is natural. Why are you fighting it?"

Keely wasn't sure she knew. For months she'd been telling herself that a relationship with Mac wasn't possible because he could distract her from her training. But she couldn't be any more distracted than she was already. Her mind wandered. Her timing was off. Whenever he watched her workout, she couldn't concentrate on what she was doing and ended up dropping weights or stumbling.

Yesterday, while he was bent over her ankle taping it, she got so turned on by how sexy the back of his neck was that she leaned forward to get a better look at it and fell off the table, nearly knocking them both to the floor. She'd decided right then and there that she had to do something. She had only two choices—either get away from Mac or get closer to him.

"You're not still afraid of his physical condition, are you?" Vicki asked. "That's not what this is about?"

"No, not afraid of his condition exactly. I'm afraid more of doing something stupid, hurting him, humiliating him, expecting something from him that he's physically unable to do."

"You're afraid of your *ignorance*."

"Yes. That's it. Also...I've only had sex with one man before, so my expertise is sorely lacking. I'm not sure I even know how to go about this."

Keely let out a breath, relieved to finally put a name to her fears and to talk to someone who would understand.

"Vicki, you told me once that if I had any questions, all I had to do was ask. Well, I'm asking. Mac's wary of me, so if anything's going to happen between us, I'll have to be the one to initiate it. Only...I don't know how."

"You need the Vicki Sizemore crash course in seduction."

"Exactly. But how on earth do I seduce a man in a wheelchair?"

Vicki's eyes sparkled with mischief. "His birthday's in a few days. Let's put together a surprise he'll never forget."

THE SOUND OF KEELY singing and the soft fragrance of perfume met Mac when he opened the door. He stopped in the kitchen for a moment and savored both, realizing how much he'd missed having a female around since his sisters had grown up and moved away.

He sighed at his own foolishness. Miss stockings hanging over the shower rod? Miss makeup cluttering his bathroom vanity?

Yes, he had to admit he did. Women added disharmony to a man's life, but there was something comforting about that disharmony. He couldn't explain it, but the chaos created by women was somehow necessary for a man's survival, and he had lived too many of the last few years alone and without it.

Keely walked out of the bedroom and around the corner, jumping in fright when she saw him. "You aren't supposed to be here yet!" She took a nervous glance behind her. "I wasn't expecting you for another fifteen minutes."

"I finished early." In truth he'd left a mountain of paperwork on his desk. Knowing she'd be here waiting for him to celebrate his birthday had shot holes in his concentration.

He put his keys on the table, along with the box filled with birthday presents given to him by the staff, then made a more leisurely examination of Keely's outfit. The blue strapless dress sparkled and showed a generous amount of both breast and leg, two of his favorite parts of her anatomy.

"You look nice."

She smoothed her hand across an imaginary wrinkle. The

dress didn't have enough material to wrinkle, but Mac couldn't say he minded.

"I thought we'd dress up for dinner tonight since it's your birthday. You don't mind, do you?"

Not if it meant getting to stare at her in that dress, he didn't. "No, I don't mind." His gaze roamed over her again with appreciation, then stopped at her feet. "But I think we'd better find you some shoes."

She laughed and wiggled her bare toes. "I brought some heels. I just don't want to put them on until I absolutely have to." She walked over and kissed him lightly on the forehead. "Happy birthday."

"Thanks."

"Do you feel older?"

"Older and *old*," he admitted.

"You're not old. I was just thinking a little while ago that you're even more handsome now than when I first met you ten years ago." She brushed her fingertips through the hair at his temples. "This little bit of gray is incredibly attractive. And these little lines by your eyes—" she slowly slid her finger along one "—somehow make you even sexier."

"Wrinkles are sexy?"

"On you they are." His heart bubbled into his throat as she caressed his jaw, then slid her hand across his chest in a gentle intimate motion that set his skin on fire. "You certainly don't have the body of an old man. Of course, I haven't seen all of it yet."

Yet? "Keely..." He reached out to touch her, but she grinned and scooted back. What was she up to?

"Your brother called earlier," she said, making sure she stayed just inches past his reach. "Did he catch you at work?"

Mac nodded. "I talked to him."

"You also have a package from California. I assume it's from one of your sisters. And Vicki brought over a cake and some gifts from the kids."

"I'll open everything when we get back. Where did you make reservations?"

"Mm...I can't tell you. That's part of tonight's surprise."

"Am I allowed to eat real food, or are you going to make me have bean sprouts and all that other stuff you eat?"

She smiled. "Tonight you get steak. Now hurry up and have your shower. I want this to be a very special night for you and I'm anxious to start."

He pushed into the bedroom, found underwear and socks, then got his best suit out of the closet. He threw everything on the bed. Shrugging out of his shirt, he tossed it in the hamper, then took off his belt, shoes and socks. He rubbed his hand across his stubbled jaw. Maybe he'd shave first.

The bathroom door was closed. He slid it open, pushed forward and stopped in surprise. What...? Glowing candles filled the room. "Keely!" he called, going inside.

She walked up behind him. "I'm here."

He turned his chair so he could see her. "What's this?"

"Your appetizer." She leaned toward the vanity and pressed the button on a small CD player that hadn't been there that morning. Soft music spilled out. "I thought it might be fun for us both if I gave you a bath."

He swallowed hard. His body tensed. Was she serious?

"You'd enjoy that, wouldn't you?" she asked. "The two of us naked in the tub?"

Numbly, he nodded.

"I thought you might."

She reached back and unzipped her dress, purposely moving it down an inch at a time while she swayed to the rhythm of the low seductive music. His gaze was glued to the riveting sight as bare breasts, a bare midriff and then a bare stomach danced into view. Finally the dress pooled around her feet, revealing her perfect—and perfectly naked—body.

Her breasts were breathtakingly beautiful, as if they had been carved to exact proportions, and were tipped with nipples that were rosy and erect. Her hips flared gently from a tiny waist before melding into those impossibly long legs. The hair between her legs was blond, like that on her head.

She had the sleek body of an athlete. Her muscles added delicate curves that were exquisitely feminine and lovely.

Mac sat there staring, stunned, wanting to touch her but

afraid of making a move that would alter their relationship forever. Once they crossed the boundary from friends to lovers, there was no going back for either of them.

She stepped out of the dress. "I've been reluctant to have a relationship with you because I thought we might both get hurt by it. But something very strong is going on between us, and I think that trying to suppress it is hurting us more. I don't know if what I'm doing is right or wrong. I don't have much experience with romance or sex, and I'm probably making a fool of myself. But if I am, I don't care. I'm tired of fighting my attraction to you. I want to be with you more than I've wanted anything in a very long time. If you want to be with me."

She rubbed a hand across her breasts, down to her feminine mound, then back up to her breasts, while Mac watched, mesmerized. The shadows created by the candles danced on her skin. Her own shadow danced in tandem on the wall behind her.

The slow sensual motion of her hand was meant to seduce him. He didn't need any prompting, but did she realize what she was letting herself in for?

"You understand I can't... Physically, I can't..."

"I know, and it doesn't matter. You don't have to hold me or touch me or even say a word to me if you don't want to. Ever since I saw the seat that goes across your tub, I've been having the naughtiest thoughts about you sitting there while I slowly wash you. You have an incredible body and I want to touch every part of it."

"Some parts aren't the least bit incredible. They don't work like they're supposed to."

She reached for his T-shirt and he lifted his arms automatically so she could pull it off. "That honestly doesn't matter to me. If you can't do anything more than take a bath with me, it'll be enough."

Oh, he could do a little more than that. And he intended to show her.

She helped him out of the rest of his clothes. For a moment, when she peeled off his underwear, he felt self-conscious. He wondered if she would ignore the lower half of him as women tended to do, perhaps even be unwilling to look at him. She'd once been so afraid of his body.

"You're beautifully made," she said, and he suddenly felt that way for the first time in a long while.

He transferred to the seat across the tub. She stood behind him washing his hair, an act he discovered could be wildly sexual, although his head was all she touched. He closed his eyes and let her work her magic, feeling all traces of tension ease out of him as she scratched his scalp lightly with her nails. She was making love to him with just her touch and her words, and it was as arousing an experience as he'd ever had.

"I know you're very sensitive in places," she said in a throaty voice. "When I get through with your head, I'm going to find every one of those places and see just how sensitive they are. I might touch them with my fingers or my lips...or run my tongue over them."

He groaned and begged, "Touch them now."

"Be patient. We have all night."

"Do we?"

"Yes. If you don't feel like going out, I can cook. Steaks and vegetables are marinating in the refrigerator. We can lie around here being sinful, feeding each other...and doing whatever else comes to mind."

"I don't have to dress up?"

"You don't have to dress at all. In fact, I'd greatly appreciate it if you didn't so I can enjoy looking at you."

"Lady, I didn't know you could be so wicked."

"Me, neither, actually. I like it."

Finally, when he didn't think he could stand it any longer, she rinsed his hair with the hand shower and soaped his shoulders and back, tormenting him with the gentleness of her strokes. She teased his sides and his neck slowly and deliberately; she ran her tongue along the back of his ears and nipped them playfully with her teeth.

He sat without moving and let her have her way until she soaped her breasts and began to rub them across his back.

"Do you like that?" she asked with a low purr in his ear. The last of his control deserted him.

"You're killing me."

She chuckled with glee. "That's the idea. You've been killing me for weeks, Mac McCandless, and now it's payback time."

"Come around to the front where I can touch you, too."

"Not yet. I'm in charge here. Just enjoy."

"Obey your coach and get over here."

"You're not my coach tonight. You're my lover. And I want to give you pleasure."

Her *lover*. He liked the sound of that. "Please, come around before I lose my sanity. I can't stand much more of this."

"All right, but I'm not through playing and, remember, I'm still in charge."

She rinsed them both, stepped over the seat and moved in front of him. This was fantasy come to life. Her lips were dewy. Her skin was flushed from passion. But it was the wantonness in her eyes as she looked down at him that did him in.

"I'd give my soul," he said, "to be able to move inside you."

She skimmed her fingertips across the muscles of his chest. "Vicki assured me that people with spinal injuries who can't have traditional sex can at least have a satisfying experience if they stop worrying about what they *can't* do and concentrate on what they *can*. She says they have to be inventive."

"You told her you were planning this?"

"I had to. I needed advice. When you and Alan were at the Auburn game, I went over to the house."

"Were you worried about having to touch me?"

"Yes," she admitted. She kissed his forehead. "I won't lie to you. Anticipating what something might be like and actually doing it—well, they're two different things. Even though I wanted this, I was still a little afraid of it."

"And now?"

"And now, I can't imagine how I went so long without

touching you. And I want to know what it feels like for you to touch me back.''

He didn't need a second invitation. Her breasts were at just the right level to take into his mouth, and he did so with the right and then the left, licking and sucking the hardened nipples while his hands touched her hips, her back, her buttocks—all the places that had been forbidden to him before.

He pulled her down to straddle his lap. Following his instructions, she lifted her legs over the seat and wrapped them around his hips.

He touched her gently at first, wanting to drive her to the edge without going over it too quickly. He held her gaze and watched the emotions play across her face, watched desire turn her eyes to molten blue, as he slid the pad of his thumb back and forth between the folds and across the sensitive nub hidden there.

"Is this a prerequisite for your class in Rehab 102?" she asked thickly.

"Are you interested in my class?"

"Can I be teacher's pet?"

"You already are."

He quickened the motion of his thumb and slipped his fingers in and out of her, using her own moisture as lubrication. She gasped in pleasure, threw back her head and closed her eyes, tightening her legs around him.

Tomorrow he would have bruises where her fingers clutched his shoulders, but it was worth it to see that wild look on her face.

Her body began to slide back and forth toward release, moving against his hand, forcing him to increase the pressure. He slipped his other arm around her waist and aided her in her rocking.

Faster. Harder. She was soaring now and he was soaring with her, fueled by the incredible sexual energy she was creating. Her deep moans infused his blood with fire.

She cried his name, and the explosion in her body washed through him like a giant wave, carrying him along. Keely was on the crest of the wave and he was somewhere in the churning water below, but it was still a pleasurable trip—and unexpected. He had heard paras and quads talk about feeling "something" during sex that was like a climax, but he had never experienced it firsthand.

He almost cried from sheer joy.

Keely had collapsed on his shoulder, unaware of the wonderful gift she had just given him. He stroked her back, realizing suddenly what had made the difference between tonight and the times before.

This time, he loved the woman in his arms.

She moaned as if in pain. "No fair," she said. "I was supposed to make love to *you*."

Mac hugged her close. "You did, sweetheart. You did."

KEELY STRETCHED against Mac's side and let out a long sigh of contentment. Lying in bed with him was sheer bliss. She could do this every night for the rest of her life and never get tired of it.

Their lovemaking had exceeded all her expectations. Intimate and special, it had been the most wonderful experience she'd ever had. Finding out he'd also gotten pleasure from it had made her weep.

"Want more?" he asked now.

"Mmm, yes, more," she said suggestively, putting aside her plate of half-eaten birthday cake.

He chuckled. "I meant *food*. My, my, but you've turned into a lusty young thing."

"You make me lusty." She ran her hand over his middle. He really was beautiful, despite his injuries. His legs were a little thin from atrophy, but other than that he was taut, well shaped. The dark hair across his chest was just thick enough to be sexy without obscuring his lovely muscular form.

The tattoo on his hip had been a surprise, very out of character for Mac. Once he'd explained Alan's role, though, it made perfect sense.

The circular scars on his stomach and lower back had also given her a moment's pause when she'd undressed him, but only because they were so small, so inconsequential-looking, and she had prepared herself for something horrible. How puzzling that a bullet could cause such little damage on the outside yet be so devastating.

He picked up another piece of birthday cake from his plate and took a huge bite. The man's diet was a disaster, full of fat and cholesterol. His kitchen cabinets were a junk-food addict's paradise. The only time he ate vegetables or fruit was when she prepared them.

"I don't see how you can eat the way you do and still look so good."

His mouth was stuffed with chocolate and cream filling. "Itz-er-zize," he managed to get out.

"Exercise?"

"Uh-huh. Itz-er-zize."

"You need to eat something other than cake and Doritos." They never had gotten around to cooking dinner, so Mac had made a raid on the kitchen for snacks. "Why didn't you bring back some of the raw carrots and cauliflower I cut up? They're full of vitamins."

"Ugh! Vim-ma-mins."

He was hopeless. "Keep eating like that and you'll be too fat to fit into your new gear."

He swallowed the rest of the cake and licked icing off his thumb. "You shouldn't have bought all that stuff for me, Keely. You spent too much money."

"You'll need it now that you'll be racing more. You're forty, and you can't use your students as an excuse any longer. You can race seriously." He didn't say anything. "Right?" she pressed.

"Maybe."

She sighed at his indecision. "I don't understand your attitude. You're so good. With some discipline in your life and diet, and some intensive training, you could be one of the best wheelchair racers in the country. In the world."

"I'm not sure I want to make that kind of commitment. I don't have the time unless I take it from something else I love. My students need me. My wheelers need me."

And Keely Wilson needed him, too. The time he spent

coaching her he could use for his own training. But she was too selfish to give him up. Without him, she didn't believe she'd race again.

"Maybe we could train together," she suggested. "That would help with your time problem, wouldn't it? You're always saying we make a great team."

"That might shortchange you, and I'm not going to risk that."

"No, it wouldn't. Ooh, you're so self-sacrificing it makes me furious. You're so busy taking care of other people that you don't take care of yourself. For a change, do something because it helps *you*."

"You sound like Alan."

"Well, Alan's right." She lifted her head so she could see him better. "You told me once that you couldn't pursue your own dream of being an athlete because of family commitments. Maybe God is giving you a second chance."

"You mean He crippled me just so I could race wheelchairs?" he said with a smile, but she didn't think it was very funny.

"No, of course not. But you're always telling me people have to accept their physical *disabilities* and rise above them. Isn't that the same thing as accepting your physical *abilities* and using them? Seems pretty hypocritical to me that you urge to your students to go out and try their best, regardless of their physical condition, but you won't do it yourself."

His smile faded.

"Will you at least think about it?" she asked when he didn't say anything.

"Yes, but not tonight. The only thing I want to think about tonight is you and me." He set his plate on the bedside table and pulled her up to lie on top of him. She put her hands on his chest and leaned her chin there.

"Did you *really* feel something when we made love?" she asked. "You're not just saying that to make me happy?"

"I really did feel something, but I want you to understand it probably won't happen every time. It might never happen again, and if it doesn't, I don't want you disappointed or thinking I didn't enjoy it.''

"I understand. But the more we make love, the more opportunities you'll have to feel something, right?"

Her logic made him chuckle. "I guess that's one way of looking at it."

Wiggling her eyebrows, she asked, "Ready to try again?"

He rolled, taking her with him, pinning her to the mattress beneath him. "Lusty *and* demanding. What am I going to do with you?"

She slid her arms around his neck and pulled him down for a long hard kiss. He tasted of chocolate. "Mmm, does that give you any ideas?"

"A few. Sit up here in front of me and I'll show you one."

She followed his directions. "Are you about to do what I think you're about to do?"

He put her legs over his shoulders and buried his dark head between them. The feel of his mouth on the most intimate part of her brought an embarrassingly loud moan to her lips. Her breath nearly stopped.

Rehab 102. Her first class.

"Can I get a degree in this?" she wondered out loud, and his body shook with amusement.

THEY CLUNG TO EACH OTHER in the dark, Keely sleeping soundly, Mac only half-awake. He needed to get up and prepare properly for the night, but she felt too good. Her head was on his shoulder, and her body was half on top of his, seeking his warmth in the cold room. He pulled the covers over her back and kissed her on top of her head.

He'd waited so long to hold her like this. He would wait one more minute before getting up. Just one more. Maybe two.

He drifted into sleep, feeling confident about himself and their relationship. Things were going to be okay. She cared about him and he cared about her. The problems he'd imagined hadn't materialized.

He slept soundly, waking only when the first rays of dawn

streamed through the window. He glanced at the clock, relieved to see it was before five and he hadn't overslept. Still, there was something wrong. He wasn't sure yet what it was.

Keely stirred just as the horrible truth struck him. Humiliation washed over him and sent heat to his face and chest.

She awoke and made a sound of disgust. "What in the world? What is this?"

She crawled to her knees, turned on the lamp and pulled back the covers. The sheet, the blanket, even the shirt she had on were soaked.

"Oh, please!" he prayed out loud. Not now. Not with this woman. But it was already too late for prayers, too late to do anything but wait for the awful reality to destroy the dream. The stupid cripple had done the one thing he feared above everything else. The stupid cripple had wet the bed.

CHAPTER THIRTEEN

HE COULD RECALL every humiliating experience in his life. In fifth grade he'd touched Lucy Henderson's breast—an accident, of course, because actually trying to touch a breast hadn't occurred to him until a couple of years later.

Lucy hadn't had much of a breast to touch, even by fifth-grade standards, but she had screamed, anyway, and called him a pervert in the middle of art class, accusing him of trying to "feel her up." The humiliation had stayed with him a long time past the punishment—a three-day suspension from school and an I'm-disappointed-in-you lecture from his dad.

He'd thought nothing could ever embarrass him like that again, but he'd been wrong. This was worse.

At the rehabilitation hospital, he'd been hoisted in and out of the pool for therapy with a harness-and-pulley mechanism that treated him like a packing crate and made him feel just about as human. He'd been bathed and dressed as if he were a child, until he'd learned to do it himself. He'd suffered the horror of having a nurse stick a sixteen-inch tube into his bladder several times a day just so he could take a leak.

Those months after the shooting had been the worst of his life, and probably nothing could surpass the pain he felt when he thought about them. But this came close. This came damn close.

"Hosing the bed" while with a partner was one of his greatest fears. In rehab he and the other single men with spinal-cord injuries had talked and worried about it a lot. And now he'd gone and done it, ruining any chance he had of making Keely forget his physical problems and think of him as normal.

But who had he been trying to kid? He wasn't normal, hadn't been for a long time. Why was he trying to pretend he was?

That's right, McCandless. Start feeling sorry for yourself. Start wallowing in self-pity again and make everything that much worse.

This wasn't the first time he'd waited too long to use a catheter and had wet himself, but it *was* the first time he had wet someone else in the process. He hated that the "someone else" was Keely, the one woman he'd hoped would never see him as less than a man.

"I'm sorry," he said stiffly. He swore to himself, knowing that no matter how often he apologized, it would never erase what had happened. Might as well just accept that things between them would never be the same.

"Mac, there's no reason for you to be upset," she said, her luminous blue eyes reflecting compassion rather than the disgust he'd expected. She tried to smooth back his hair, but he turned his head, not wanting to be touched right now. How could she bear him when he couldn't bear himself?

"I don't want to talk about it," he said.

"All right. We'll just forget it."

Fat chance of that.

They had both showered and changed into dry clothes, Keely borrowing one of his shirts so she wouldn't have to put on her dress, and Mac slipping into a pair of sweatpants. He was struggling to change the sheets and the waterproof pad on the mattress, but he was so angry with himself he couldn't get them right. He jerked a corner down only to have the opposite corner pop up.

She walked to the other side of the bed. "Let me help you."

"I can do it myself," he snapped. "I'm crippled, but I'm not helpless."

She let go of the sheet and straightened, throwing up her hands. Now he saw disgust in her eyes, but it wasn't because he had wet the bed; it was because of the way he was handling it. "Did I say you were helpless?" she asked.

He was being an ass and it wasn't like him, but he couldn't seem to help himself. Why didn't she just go home? He didn't want her here. He wanted to sulk in private, go a little crazy for once, maybe even throw something, but he couldn't do that with her looking at him, trying to touch him every two seconds. He didn't want her witnessing just how far into self-pity he was about to sink.

Several minutes later, after an almost comical battle with the fitted sheet, he got the bed made. He pushed into the kitchen and on to the laundry room, where he threw the sheets into the washing machine. Back in the kitchen, he filled the coffeemaker. A jolt of something was what he needed, and since even he couldn't stomach a beer this early in the morning, he figured caffeine and the sugar high from some powdered doughnuts would have to do.

She followed him and leaned against the counter silently watching, the wet hair and too-big shirt making her more desirable than any woman had a right to be before six in the morning. This time he knew for sure that she wore nothing under the shirt, because he'd seen her put it on.

And it was hell knowing.

Memories of the night before flooded back to torture him— that erotic striptease she had done to coax him into the bath, her exquisite body aroused, her legs wrapped around his waist as she screamed her release. He had been with a lot of women, before and after his injury, and enjoyed every experience, but none had given him as much pleasure as this woman had last night. None had gone beyond the physical aspect of sex to touch the man underneath.

He loved her. Heaven help him, he'd tried not to fall for her again, but he'd tumbled like a stone the second she'd come back to town. The relationship had no chance of working, though. This morning's fiasco was proof of that.

"Go home," he said sharply. "Getting involved with me was a mistake. I'd rather go back to being just your coach."

She shoved herself away from the counter and stood in front of him. "A mistake?"

"A big one."

"I understand you're embarrassed, but why do you want to throw away our whole relationship because of one unpleasant incident? That doesn't make a bit of sense."

"I'm not talking only about what happened this morning. All kinds of things make this impossible, things you don't even know about. I don't want to go through this every day as you find out the bad side of being with a paraplegic." He turned the chair around and pushed forcefully toward the bedroom, intending to get dressed. "We'll both be better off if you'll go home and forget last night."

"So it was a big lie when you acted like you cared about me?"

He stopped abruptly and turned the chair enough so he could see her. "I didn't lie."

"You must have, or you wouldn't be trying to hurt me like this."

Her statement was like a fist to the gut. "I don't want to hurt you and I do care about you." *I love you,* he wanted to say, but it would only make things harder. "You deserve more out of a relationship than a paraplegic can give you."

Her forehead crinkled in thought. She chewed the inside of her cheek. "Well, let's see. I know you can give me a satisfying sexual relationship, so you must mean you can't give me something else I need. What? Friendship?"

"You know what I'm talking about."

"Understanding? Compassion?"

"That's not what I'm talking about and you know it."

"How about…time together? A shoulder to cry on? A confidant? Can you give me those things or does that take someone who can walk?" He didn't answer because she was exaggerating, saying something ridiculous to make a point. "I need someone to tell me when I'm being bratty. Can you do that or is it too much for a paraplegic to handle?"

"Yes, I can. You're being bratty right now."

That made her smile a little.

"I'm talking about my physical problems and how they can affect a relationship. They can kill romance in about thirty seconds flat. I don't want you repulsed by me again."

"Ah, now I understand where this sudden desire to flee is coming from."

She sat in his lap against his objection, but this time he let her smooth his hair from his brow. The touch of her fingers raised goose bumps on his flesh.

"Mac, I have limited experience with romance, so I don't know what the standard is, but last night was the most romantic night of my life. And I don't mean because of the sex, although that was fantastic. Just lying in your arms and having you stroke my back as I fell asleep made me feel safe. Do you know, last night was the first time in over a year that I've slept through the entire night?"

"A year? Why?"

"Since my accident I've had this irrational fear of the dark and dying in my sleep. I've only been able to sleep a few hours at night. That's why I take so many naps and get cranky in the afternoon. I think maybe it's because the accident made me realize how fragile I really am and how little control we truly have over what happens to us."

"You should have told me. I could have helped you find someone to talk to."

"You're right. I should have told you and not let it continue so long. And I guess I have to talk to someone about it eventually. But I'm telling you now to show you how important last night was to me. I felt so cared for and so contented being with you that I dropped off to sleep without the slightest hesitation."

"And then I ruined everything this morning."

"No, you didn't. I'm sorry about what happened because it's upset you so much, but it didn't bother me. It doesn't bother me now. I don't care if you wet the bed every night as long as you let me sleep with you once in a while. More than once in a while." She put her arms around his neck and kissed him lightly on the lips, but he remained unyielding. "Getting to this point took us so long, Mac. Please don't mess things up over something so stupid."

"Keely..."

"You're not getting rid of me, so you might as well quit arguing."

"Baby, it's no good. You and me together—it won't work. I fooled myself last night into believing it could, but now I see that was just wishful thinking."

She blew out a breath in impatience. "Please, don't do this. Please don't throw away what we've found together just because you're embarrassed."

"That's not it at all."

"Oh, no? Well, answer this—what if it had been me?"

"But it wasn't you."

"Well, what if it had been? What if I was the one who'd wet on you? Would you want me to be embarrassed about it? Would you allow me to be so embarrassed that I ended our relationship?"

"No, but that's not the situation here. And you didn't wet on me, so you have no way of knowing how I feel."

She looked at him oddly.

"What?" he asked, wondering what she was thinking.

"You're absolutely right. Maybe you'd feel better if we evened things out."

"Evened them out?" She didn't say anything, only sat there contemplating something. Then he realized what. "Oh, hell, you're not thinking...?" She nodded. "You wouldn't!"

But she would. And she did.

Before he could push her off his lap the crazy sweet wonderful woman wet on him.

THE GREEN PEPPERS were out of season and outrageously expensive, but full of vitamin C. Keely picked over them, found some she liked and put them in the cart. She checked them off the grocery list.

"You're insane," Mac said at her elbow.

"I know. A dollar a pepper is highway robbery, but I've got a taste for them."

"I was talking about that crazy stunt you pulled this morning."

"Oh. You're never going to let me live that down, are you?"

"I can't get it off my mind." He grabbed her hand and gave it a little squeeze. "Thank you. No one's ever done anything like that for me before."

"The situation was drastic and called for drastic measures."

"You shocked me into submission."

"I couldn't think of anything else to do. Pleading with you wasn't working." She playfully tweaked his chin. "You're awfully hardheaded at times."

Mac had been so overwhelmed by what she'd done he had given up trying to send her home. With a great deal of coaxing she'd been able to convince him that he was overreacting to his little mishap in bed and she could handle any problems his condition caused in their relationship.

He'd tried to scare her off, telling her in graphic detail about the problems paraplegics deal with every day. She'd taken a deep breath and told him the truth—those things frightened the wits out of her and she wasn't sure she'd handle them with any degree of grace. But she *would* handle them.

"My legs are thin and ugly," he'd said.

"I wouldn't care if you didn't have legs," she'd countered.

That had done it. He'd given in, knowing further argument was useless, although he'd made her promise to be open with him about her fears.

They had also agreed to be discreet. Technically there was no conflict of interest. Mac wasn't her supervisor, her teacher or responsible for her grades. Their coaching arrangement was private and had nothing to do with the university. But the gossips would have a grand time if they found out she was involved with him.

And she was very much involved with him. Physically. Emotionally. Whether it was only a killer case of lust or went deeper, she wasn't sure. Trying to label it would probably be useless, maybe even dangerous. She had little experience with romantic love, particularly how it felt when it happened to you, so this might be something else entirely.

She only knew she liked being with Mac more than she had ever liked being with anyone. She trusted him, liked him, desired him. Definitely desired him.

When they'd settled things this morning, they'd made love, and again when he'd come by to pick her up after work for their weekly grocery-shopping trip. She couldn't seem to keep her hands to herself now that she was allowed to touch him. And every time she touched him, even looked at him, she wanted him.

Like right this minute in the middle of the produce section.

"I laughed all day," he said, unaware of the devastating effect he was having on her and the naughty things she was imagining. "Miriam thought I'd lost my mind. I almost busted a gut when she told me that whatever was wrong with me, I needed a daily dose of it."

"Maybe you do."

"Oh, no! You're not getting a second chance."

"Behave and I won't need one. Act up again and next time I'll wet on your *head* instead of in your *lap*."

He laughed but warned, "And I'll get you with my grabbers." He clicked together the two metal hands of the tonglike device he used for getting cans and boxes down from the shelves. He pointed it at her crotch.

Keely slapped it away. "Stop it before someone sees you."

She looked both ways in the aisle, relieved that none of the other shoppers had observed his latest bout of mischief. He was full of it tonight, using his grabbers to pinch her on the behind every time she turned her back to him and bent over.

They had decided there was probably no harm in continuing to shop together, since people would just assume she was helping him. She *was* helping him, although he managed just fine by himself if he was careful about how he packed his laptop basket.

In truth, they simply liked shopping together. They ate together most nights, anyway, either at her house or his, so it seemed senseless to make separate shopping trips.

Usually her biggest problem was keeping him from putting junk food in the basket when she wasn't watching. This teasing tonight was considerably more difficult to deal with because while it was embarrassing, it was also fun. She liked his playful side; she liked to see him happy and smiling.

"Behave. Let's find the stuff on this list so we can get out of here. I still need to read over my notes for class tomorrow. Coach Stewart is letting me teach by myself for the first time."

"Solo? Are you nervous?"

"Terrified. Actually, I could really use help preparing. Want the job?"

"What does it pay?"

"Oh, hugs. Kisses."

"Scratch my back and you've got a deal."

"Done."

"I don't know why you're nervous. You're a good teacher and coach. The couple of times I sat in on the nutrition class you're helping with this quarter I was really impressed. Even I learned something."

"Too bad you don't practice what I teach."

"Yeah, but as you've pointed out to me at least a million times, I'm a hopeless case." She smiled. He had that right. "You're a good teacher and coach, Keely. One of these days you're going to realize it."

Maybe. She still wasn't comfortable in front of a class, and the thought of teaching by herself scared her to death. She liked it okay, but she'd much rather spend her time in the weight room or playing around in the chemistry lab. Her teaching assistant's job and her courses were all right temporarily, but as soon as she was able to run again, she'd put them aside.

And it wouldn't be long now. She'd already decided what she wanted her first race to be—the Los Verdes Marathon in April, which gave her five months to train. Five months to prove to Mac that she was ready. She glanced at him, wondering how he was going to react when she told him.

"Have you given any more thought to what we talked about last night?" she asked. They moved down the aisle and Keely picked through the poor offering of lettuce.

"What specifically was I supposed to think about?"

"Wheelchair racing. We could even go together. You know, pick some races that have a wheeler division so we can both compete. How does that sound? Wouldn't that be fun?"

"Mmm," he said noncommittally.

"Maybe this spring we could try it."

"Yeah, right, like either one of us would be ready for that." He plucked the list from her hand and started reading as if the conversation bored him. "What else have you got down here?"

She hid her disappointment. Maybe this just wasn't the appropriate time to bring up racing. "Potatoes," she said.

"I'll get them."

He pushed over to get potatoes, or so she thought. He came back with a bag of chips and a container of onion dip in his lap basket. He transferred them to the cart.

"That is *not* potatoes," she said. "Can't you get something else?"

He grinned. "You're right. I forgot the beer." He took off around the corner.

"Hopeless," she muttered. "Utterly hopeless."

One aisle over, she strained to reach for a box of no-fat crackers on one of the upper shelves when a masculine arm reached around from behind and got them for her. She squealed and whirled, coming up hard against the man's chest. He grabbed her elbow to steady her.

"Whoa! Didn't mean to scare you," Doug Crocker said, his own eyes wide with shock. "Sorry."

"Coach…I…" She stepped back, feeling uncomfortable at his closeness, then laughed at his expression, realizing she'd scared him as much as he'd scared her. "I didn't know it was you."

He chuckled. "That's okay. You looked like you were having some trouble, so I thought I'd give you a hand." He passed her the crackers.

"Thank you. They always seem to put the things I want on the top shelves." She glanced quickly past him, wondering where Mac was and whether he knew Crocker was in the store.

"I'm glad I ran into you, Keely. I've been wanting to tell you what a good job you're doing with the freshman runners. Laura Stewart says you've been a great help with the fall conditioning program."

"Oh? Well, that was kind of her. I don't know how much help I've been, but I've enjoyed it."

"You have a real knack for coaching."

"I appreciate your saying that."

She smiled politely, wondering what he wanted. He was being too friendly. Crocker didn't give compliments, and he hadn't said more than ten words to her in the months she'd been at Courtland.

"You and McCandless seem to be spending a lot of time together lately. I guess that's part of the arrangement he has worked out with you. Or is it personal?"

Ah, now she understood. He was fishing for information about Mac. Well, he wasn't going to get it.

"Coach McCandless is a very generous man. I've been lucky he's willing to help with my training."

"I bet that's not too much of a hardship for him, although I guess it might be for you."

"I'm sorry, I don't know what you mean. Why would working with Coach McCandless be a hardship?"

"Him being a cripple, I meant."

Her blood pressure soared. "Coach McCandless may be in a wheelchair, but he's less *crippled* than anyone I've ever met. He's a fine coach and a fine man. If you spent more time talking *to* him than *about* him, you might realize that."

He smiled, but it wasn't sincere. "Ah, now I've offended you, and here I was getting ready to ask you to have dinner with me. I thought you might like to know what it feels like to spend time with a real man for a change, instead of half a one."

Before she could tell him what she thought of his invitation, Mac pushed up from behind him. He had obviously heard every word. His complexion was ruddy; his eyes were hard and cold as ice.

"The lady prefers cripples to asses, Doug. And for the record, Keely's with me tonight, tomorrow night, every night. Got it?"

Crocker looked between them, his hard gaze mirroring Mac's. "So it's like that, is it?"

"Yeah, it's like that."

Keely groaned inwardly. So much for being discreet. Now the whole world would know they were sleeping together.

She saw that Crocker had clenched his hands, but now he opened and closed them rapidly, as if he wanted to jam one into Mac's face.

"Go ahead," Mac said, sensing the same thing Keely had. "You've been itching to do it for a long time. Take your best shot."

Crocker didn't move. Finally, giving Mac a cold smile, he dipped his head. Without apologizing to either one of them for his rudeness, he turned and stalked away.

"Sonova..." Mac muttered.

"He's definitely that."

"I meant me."

"You? Are you crazy?"

"Yeah, me, because I lost my temper with him and I hate giving him the satisfaction of knowing he has the power to do that. But when I heard him hitting on you, I couldn't help myself. I saw red."

"I don't know why you don't get rid of him and end your misery. He's given you more than enough cause. He's disrespectful to you in front of the staff, and he says awful things about you behind your back. He even tries to undermine your orders. No one would blame you for firing him."

"Yeah, I know, but he used to be a good coach and he could be again, if he'd just put his feelings for me aside. Besides, I owe him."

"Owe him how?" He looked away, as if he'd said too much, but she made him face her again. "Owe him how?"

"Never mind. I was just running off at the mouth."

"Oh, no. You're the one who brought it up, and now I want to know what you're talking about. How could you possibly think you owe Doug Crocker *anything* after all the things he's done?"

"Because...sometimes..." He frowned. "Sometimes I think he may just be right and that one of the reasons I got the A.D.'s job, instead of him, was so I could be the university's token cripple."

CHAPTER FOURTEEN

THE BACK DOOR opened that evening and Keely raced by like a whirlwind, the force of her entrance and the cold wind that followed her scattering the tests Mac was supposed to be grading for his Sport Management class. He quickly slapped a hand down on them before they flew off her kitchen table.

Glancing at Keely to make sure she wouldn't see the racing magazine he'd been reading, he put it in his briefcase. He wasn't sure why he'd bought it, or circled the upcoming races with wheeler divisions. Even if he decided to enter one, he'd have a hard time getting ready physically.

Crazy. Ridiculous. He didn't know why he'd allowed Keely to put the idea in his head. He was forty, after all, too old to be thinking about racing professionally.

"Did you have a good workout?" he asked, suddenly noticing Keely's silence.

"No."

"Problems?"

"No."

"Want me to fix you something to drink?"

"I don't care."

He heaved a heavy sigh, wondering how long she was going to stay upset over the stupid comment he'd made in the grocery store. Her mood was even worse than it had been before she'd left to ride her bicycle.

"I can't believe you're still worked up about this," he told her, putting the papers in order.

"And I can't believe you would even *think* you didn't deserve the job as athletic director."

She was wrestling with her jacket and grumbled under her

breath when she got the fabric caught in the zipper. Unable to get the zipper up or down, she pulled the jacket over her head, then stepped out of her tights.

Mac watched with fascination as she retracted her arms into the sleeves of her T-shirt like a turtle, did some kind of contortionist maneuver with her bra and pulled it out one of the armholes. She tossed the flimsy piece of cotton on top of the tights on the floor. Getting a bottle of water out of the refrigerator, she sank with a groan into the chair next to him, wearing nothing but her T-shirt and panties.

"I couldn't keep my mind on my workout because of what you told me," she said, pushing sweat-soaked hair out of her eyes. "I got upset every time I thought about it, and I'm especially upset with you for throwing something like that at me and then refusing to talk about it. How can you expect me to just forget it?"

"Because it was a stupid thing to say, and it's not worth discussing. I wish you'd just drop the subject before we end up fighting."

"You wouldn't have said it if you didn't believe it."

"You're going to nag me about this all night, aren't you?"

"Yes, I am. You know how irritating I can be when I set my mind to it, so you might as well just give in and talk to me."

He chuckled despite his frustration. Even her railing could be endearing.

"Listen," he began. "Sometimes I let the prejudices of people get to me. I feel a little insecure because of being in this chair and I think dumb things. I'm entitled to be human and have an occasional lapse in good judgment, aren't I?"

She started to argue, then her hard look faded. "Of course you are. You're so easygoing and you never complain, and I guess I forget what a rough time you've had dealing with your injury. Oh, I'm such an idiot for bugging you about this! Especially considering how I acted when I found out about your paralysis. I'm the last person in the world with the right to give you a lecture."

"It's okay. Forget it." The misery on her face made him

add, "And I don't honestly believe I got the job because I have a disability, so you can quit worrying."

"You don't? Really? You promise?"

"I promise."

"But Crocker planted a seed of doubt and made you worry just a little, didn't he?"

Mac answered carefully, not wanting to upset her again, but not wanting to lie to her, either.

"I guess that's true, but I also know I'm good at what I do. If my disability did play a role in the search committee's decision, even unconsciously, I've proved I'm as capable as any able-bodied person. They got the best person for the job. I wouldn't have taken it if I didn't believe that."

"Mac, I'm absolutely positive you were the best person and you should be, too. You're a great coach and a great athletic director. You're good with the athletes. You never show favoritism for one sport over another. You set a wonderful example for the staff."

"And next week I apply for sainthood."

"I'm serious."

"I know you are, and I like that you think I'm such a paragon of virtue even if I'm not."

"You *are* a paragon of virtue. You're kind and compassionate. Handsome. Sexy. Incredibly sexy. I had a terrible time keeping my hands off you when we were in the store. I almost attacked you in produce and again in frozen foods."

He reveled in her description of him, even if it wasn't accurate. "We aren't in the store now," he said with a lazy grin.

She grinned back. "No, we're aren't, but I'm hot and sweaty and I probably stink, so I doubt you want me too close until I've cleaned up."

He leaned toward her and sniffed. "Yeah, Wilson, you stink. Go take a shower."

"Come in there with me and I'll make it up to you for getting mad." Her voice had turned low and throaty.

"If I'm playing with you, when am I supposed to get these test papers graded?"

"I'll help you after supper, and you can help me study for
my teaching assignment tomorrow. Come on. Thirty minutes
in the tub isn't going to put either one of us behind and it'll
relax us." Her eyes darkened with the suggestion of passion.
"You've had a hard day. Let me scrub your back and take
care of you."

He let his gaze slide to her breasts, remembering how she'd
rubbed them against his back last night and driven him to the
brink of madness. With a mental groan he forced himself to
look up. If he wasn't careful, he was going to develop an
obsession with those breasts. He already had one with her legs
and that curvy little backside.

"I like it when you want to take care of me," he said, "but
you're forgetting one very important obstacle to this plan of
yours. I can't get in and out of your bathtub."

"Mmm, yes, you can."

"And why is that?"

Her teeth toyed with her bottom lip, as they often did when
she didn't want to tell him something.

"What have you done?"

"Bought a transfer seat for the bathtub so you can take a
shower here whenever you want."

"Agh!" He threw down his pen. "You promised you
wouldn't make any more changes to the house."

"The seat's portable and inexpensive. It lifts right off and
you can even take it with you when you go out of town with
the teams."

"You shouldn't have spent any more money on me."

"I didn't spend much, and when I cooked up my little
seduction scheme, I got to thinking that if it worked, you'd
occasionally want to spend the night here and take a shower.
And if it failed and you *didn't* want me, I'd just give you the
seat as a gift."

"You really believed there was a chance I wouldn't want
you?"

She looked at him with sincere confusion. "Well, yes. I'm
certainly no prize, and you could have any woman you want.

They throw themselves at you all the time, baking you brownies and sweet-talking you into riding them on your lap.''

''That's only because I'm in this chair. A disability brings out the mothering instincts in a woman.''

''No, it's you, not your disability. You're a magnet for anything female between the ages of eight and eighty. I've seen the way those young coeds drool over you. And I'm seriously considering strangling that redhead in the Sports Information office if I see her stick those big boobs of hers in your face one more time on the pretense of fixing your collar.''

Amused, he tried not to laugh.

''Please don't be mad at me for buying the transfer seat,'' she pleaded. ''I want you to feel as comfortable here as you do at your house, and it was such a tiny expense.'' She lifted a leg and put it in his lap, rubbing back and forth across his midriff with her toes. ''Besides, it's as much for me as it is for you. It gives me more opportunities to get you out of your clothes.''

Mad? How could he be mad when she looked at him with those enormous eyes and told him she wanted him naked?

Caressing her leg from ankle to thigh, he followed the soft curve of her calf and ran his finger along the scars that marred the otherwise perfect flesh. The bones were healed and the rod attached to them should be removed, but he knew she wouldn't agree to surgery right now. He wouldn't even bring it up.

''I'm not mad, Keely, but I wish you'd check with me before you do things like this. Is the seat all you bought?'' She nodded. ''Do you promise?''

''Yes. Well, except for the bathtub faucet gadget and some extra grab bars.'' She grimaced at his look of exasperation. ''And a few other very minor things. But that's it.''

Her thoughtfulness overwhelmed him. She had a wide streak of generosity in her, too, although she tried to conceal it. He'd seen it over and over again in her treatment of the students, particularly the wheelers. They had come to rely on her not only for instruction, but for a sympathetic ear about their romances and personal problems.

"I'm suddenly reminded of what I like most about you," he said. "You always keep me slightly off balance. Just when I think I've figured you out or I'm sure I know what you're going to do, you surprise me."

She smiled. Her dimples peeped out to lure him. "Come play in the bathtub and I'll give you more reasons to be crazy about me."

Without a word he took her arm and pulled her into his lap. In two seconds he had her shirt over her head and her body angled to the side. He rubbed his big hand across her small perfect breasts, teasing the peaks, making them harden.

"Is this a yes?" she asked, laughing.

He slipped his hand lower.

"Mmm. Definitely." Her laughing turned to a catlike purr. "John Patrick McCandless, I *do* love the way you say yes."

THE QUICK BATH melted into a leisurely one, taking far longer than the thirty minutes they had planned. The transfer seat fit fine on the tub in the bathroom off the hall, but Mac suggested they see if he could get in the larger tub in her private bathroom, instead. The tub was like a five-foot-square shallow swimming pool, and its tiled side proved high enough and wide enough for him to slip down onto it and into the water without help.

Once in, he didn't want to get out, especially with Keely naked and fussing over him. Only one tiny thing spoiled the fantasy-come-to-life.

"This stinkin' stuff wasn't part of the deal," he grumbled as she worked lavender-scented soap into a frothy lather and rubbed it across his back. When she was through with his back, she poured shampoo in her hand and massaged it into his hair. He got a whiff of herbs and groaned. "Ah, Keely."

"Now, Mac, don't be a baby. Did I whine when I had to use your shampoo and soap this morning?"

"No, but my shampoo doesn't make me smell like I've been dragged through a flower garden."

"No, but your shampoo makes me smell like I've been drenched in men's cologne. This is so much nicer. Quit squirming or I'm going to get it in your eyes. Hold your head back."

He obeyed and let her rinse his hair. "Remind me to wake up early enough in the morning to go home and wash off this smell before I go to work. I'll get laughed out of the locker room if anyone gets a whiff of me."

"I thought you liked my smell."

"On *you* I love it."

"Complaints, complaints."

She slipped to the front and sat between his legs, facing him so she could soap the rest of him. He took her legs and hooked them over his, then grabbed her bottom and pulled her onto his lap.

"You've got a great rear end, Wilson. I get turned on just thinking about the way it undulates when you run."

"Undulates? My rear end does *not* undulate. And you're supposed to be watching my running form, not my behind."

"Baby, I'm no fool," he said, making her giggle.

Several minutes passed and she still kept washing, lingering on his shoulders, giving extra attention to his chest. The playful movement of her fingers across his flesh had him fighting for control.

He eased his hand up and tweaked one nipple, but she slapped it away. "Uh-uh-uh," she scolded, playing coy. "Not your turn yet. When I get tired of touching you, you can touch me." Running both hands slowly over the muscles of his arms, she added huskily, "But the way you're built, that might never happen."

With an impatient growl, he pulled her forward until their bodies touched intimately. She laughed, but it turned to a moan when his mouth covered hers and he kissed her deeply. She put her arms around his neck and kissed him back, coyness replaced by eagerness.

With his hands locking her in place, he rubbed her against his slight arousal, although he had no sensation there and the pleasure of it was all in his mind. For her, thank God, the pleasure was real. She moaned again, a sound that was half-way a sigh, and ground herself against him, letting him know she wanted more.

Pain mingled with his desire. The act of penetration was only a memory to him now, but it was powerful enough to make him ache for what he could never have again. He loved her with his heart. He wanted also to love her with his body.

Perhaps she sensed his pain; perhaps he'd unknowingly hesitated, for she whispered exactly what he needed to hear—*"I never knew being with someone could be this perfect."*

The flame within him flared to a roaring fire.

Sweet heaven, it *was* perfect, better than anything he'd experienced prior to his paralysis. He had no reason to grieve for what he'd lost. *This* was what lovemaking was meant to be, not just a sensory experience, but a melding of the physical being with the emotional. Body touched body, but spirit also touched spirit. Two fused to become one.

"Fly for us both," he told her, moving her faster and harder against him. When her climax ripped through her like an explosion, she cried his name, and he was certain he had never heard sweeter music.

MAC TRAVELED to Augusta with the football team for a Thanksgiving Day bowl game, and wasn't expected home until late Sunday night. Keely backed out of going to Atlanta to spend the holiday weekend with her mother. She thought she'd enjoy staying in Courtland and having some time to herself. But by Friday night she was irritable and bored. Lonely, she realized. Without Mac around, nothing seemed to interest her.

Saturday she ran with Dean and was further off her time than the previous week, which concerned her. Then she had lunch with him and two of the other female teaching assistants, which ended in disaster when a fan made a nuisance of himself and she finally had to ask the manager to make him leave the café.

"I felt bad about it," she told Vicki that night, when she

went over to the Sizemores' for coffee and dessert. "But he just wouldn't take no for an answer."

Vicki hung Keely's jacket in the hall closet, and they walked to the den, where Alan played Chutes and Ladders with Savannah and J.P. on the floor. Bay was stretched out in front of the TV.

"You handled it the right way," Vicki said. "If it had been me, I'd have probably decked the guy."

"Decked who?" Alan asked.

"Some jerk who wanted Keely to sign her autograph on his body."

That tickled Alan, who wanted to hear the details and couldn't stop laughing when she got to the part where the guy lifted his shirt, hefted his beer gut onto the table and handed her a pen.

Keely found herself laughing along with him, no longer feeling down. "I'm glad you two talked me into coming over here tonight. I needed to be around friends after the day I've had."

"We wish you'd come over more," Vicki said. "You don't have to wait until you're with Mac."

Mac. Keely continued to smile, but her insides constricted at the mention of his name. She wondered what he was doing. Her watch said eight-fifteen, and the game had been over for about four hours. This morning when he called, he'd said he would probably go out with friends tonight. The team had won, according to the radio. They'd want to celebrate.

"Daddy, J.P.'s eatin' the game again," Savannah complained.

Alan quickly pulled the toddler forward and took away the cardboard cutout Savannah had been using to move around the board. As a result the usually good-natured J.P. began to cry. When Alan tickled him, he immediately stopped, but the child was obviously sleepy and getting fussy.

"Time for this one to wind down and go to bed," Alan said.

Vicki walked over and picked him up. "I'll take him. He needs a bath first. Come on, Keely. You can help."

"Uh, okay, but I warn you the only thing I've ever bathed is a dog."

Alan snickered. "Kids aren't that different. Clean their ears, neck and tail good, and don't let them shake water all over the floor."

"I can handle that."

"Good," Vicki said, leading the way to the bathroom. "You can put him to bed, too. Know any lullabies?"

"Not a one."

"Improvise."

MAC CAUGHT a commercial flight home Saturday night, rather than waiting to ride back on one of the team buses Sunday, but the flight nearly did him in. He hated to fly commercially, hated having to be carried into the plane like spoiled royalty, hated especially having to check his wheelchair and worry that it might get broken.

The airline hadn't broken it, but when he landed in Columbus, Georgia, he discovered they'd temporarily misplaced it. Agony was a mild word for what he experienced until the baggage handler brought it out. To add to his irritation, he had to pay for an expensive shuttle trip from Columbus to Courtland because he'd left his van parked at the athletic department.

Now, finally home, he felt a bone-deep weariness. And anticipation. He took out the sack of presents for the kids and tossed his suitcase in the house. Keely's car was parked in Alan's driveway, so he headed across the street, wondering how he was going to explain his arrival a day early.

But Alan didn't seem surprised when Mac appeared at the door. He seemed downright amused. "Well, well, well. Look who's back. What's wrong, Mac? Did you miss me and have to rush home?"

"Yeah, I couldn't stand being away from you another minute. Broke my heart."

Savannah had to hug him, and Bay, currently going through a fascination with airplanes, wanted to hear about his flight.

Mac took an aviator's cap out of his sack and handed it to him.

"Oh, wow! Thanks, Uncle Mac."

"Me. Me," Savannah begged, jumping up and down. He buckled a Mickey Mouse watch on her wrist and showed her the button that made Mickey announce the time.

"Don't drive your mom and dad crazy pressing that," he warned her. "Only every once in a while, okay?"

"'Kay," she promised, immediately pressing it. She pressed it twice more before she sat down.

Vicki walked in and kissed him on the cheek. "Hey, I thought you weren't coming home until tomorrow. What gives?"

"I had things to do. You know." He glanced down the hall. Where was Keely? He felt as if he hadn't seen her for a month. If he had to wait one more minute, he was going to explode. "J.P. still up? I brought him a little something."

"Keely's putting him to sleep. Tell us about your trip."

Mac groaned inwardly. "We won. Nothing special."

"Are you hungry? I have an apple pie in the oven, or I can fix you a turkey sandwich."

"Later, Vic," Alan told her. "Can't you tell the man has other business?"

"Huh?"

"Sweet thing."

"Oh!" She chuckled. "Sorry. Go on back. I know she'll be as eager to see you as you are to see her."

He pushed down the hall to where the two younger children shared a room, hearing soft singing. The door was partly open and he could see Keely lying on the bed next to J.P., lightly patting his back as he fought sleep, singing him a very slow version of "A Hard Day's Night." Mac smiled. Only Keely would use a Beatles song as a lullaby.

As he watched her, watched the pleasure on her face at the simple act of putting a child to bed, happiness turned to regret. With him, she could have no children to sing to at night. With him she would have to be content to love someone else's children. The thought of it filled him with a pain that was almost physical.

Of all the things he had lost because of the shooting, losing his ability to father children bothered him the most. Fatherhood might theoretically be possible, but the odds against conception were high. He didn't know anyone among his paraplegic and quadriplegic friends who had tried artificial insemination and been successful.

He slowly opened the door. Seeing him brought surprise to Keely's face and then a look of joy that was a tonic to his weary body. She checked J.P. and finding his eyes closed, eased from the bed. Two seconds later she was in Mac's lap, kissing him wildly, making the difficulties he'd endured to get home seem unimportant.

"Let's get out of here." He was nearly breathless from wanting to be alone with her.

"I'll race you to the door."

"WELL?" ALAN ASKED from across the room, urging Vicki to hurry up and have a look out the window. He'd bet her twenty dollars Mac and Keely wouldn't make it across the street to Mac's house before they kissed.

"Shut up and let me... Oh, my goodness!" Vicki walked over to her purse, got some money and handed it to him. Included with the twenty was an extra ten.

Alan grinned. She must have seen a lot more than a kiss. "Well, way to go, Mac!"

CHAPTER FIFTEEN

DECEMBER ROARED IN, bringing colder-than-normal temperatures to Georgia. Mac and Keely spent most nights at his house on a quilt in front of the fireplace, the open fire a luxury that safety prevented him from having while alone.

The quilt had belonged to his mother and was a crazy jumble of patterns, textures and colors. The scraps came mostly from clothes she'd sewn him and his siblings growing up. Some were special, like the piece leftover from Megan's baptismal gown. Others were more ordinary but still held a memory of some sort. A patch in one corner represented Mac's favorite pair of shorts at the age of five, the ones with the little cowboys on them. The "S" from Brand's Superman pajamas was there, as was a patch from Christine's favorite sundress, with the big daisies.

Keely called it his "memory quilt" and insisted he drag it out every night to cover the hardwood floor. Comfort wasn't the reason. She'd become fascinated by the quilt, by the stories behind each scrap of fabric, and begged to hear a new story whenever he was willing to indulge her.

With her curled against his side, her hand under his shirt stroking his chest, Mac didn't mind indulging her often.

"And what's this one?" she asked one night, pointing to a triangle with tiny flowers in the design.

Mac chuckled, remembering a happy time and place. "You'll love this story. That was Jilly's party dress when she was about thirteen. I think she was in the eighth grade, or maybe the ninth. She and her best friend, Lisa, weren't old enough to date, but the party was at a neighbor's house, so my mom and Lisa's mom got together and agreed it would be okay if these two boys in their class escorted them. Jilly talked nonstop about the party for weeks and couldn't wait for that night to get there. Only, things went a little haywire, thanks to Brand.''

"What did he do?"

"About ten minutes before the kids came by to walk Jilly to the party, Brand handcuffed her to a kitchen chair."

"Oh, no," Keely said with a snort of laughter.

"Brand had gotten a magic kit for his seventh birthday and was the only one who knew how to open the handcuffs. But he wouldn't, and no matter how much we coaxed, he just stood there with his arms crossed, shaking his head, saying a magician never reveals his secrets. Dad was so furious he threatened him with every kind of punishment he could think of, but it still didn't do any good. Dad was yelling, Mom was pleading, and Jilly was bawling her head off. In the middle of this chaos Lisa arrives with these two boys in tow who couldn't wait to run down the block and tell all the other kids what was going on. So five minutes later we had a kitchen full of laughing kids."

"Did Brand finally turn her loose?"

"No, my dad had to cut off the handcuffs with a hacksaw. Brand couldn't watch TV or sit down for a month."

"I'll bet he never pulled a stunt like that again."

"You don't know Brand. He was a terror back then, especially when it came to his sisters. To tell you the truth, he still plays pranks on them every chance he gets."

When she stopped chuckling, Keely let out a wistful sigh against his shoulder. "You're so lucky. I always wanted sisters to pull pranks on. When I was little, one Christmas I somehow got it in my head that Santa was responsible for bringing sisters. Christmas morning I woke up expecting to find at least one under the tree and was shattered when I didn't. My mother had to sit me down and explain where babies really come from. And, of course, I was disgusted by that."

"Did your parents ever consider having other children?"

"I don't really know. In the few years after I was born, I

think they might have tried, but my mother never got pregnant again to my knowledge. I'm not sure if something was wrong or they simply stopped trying. They fought so much I doubt there were too many opportunities to conceive a child.''

"Sometimes even the nicest people aren't nice together.''

"I guess so, but my dad was such a great guy I can't imagine anyone having trouble getting along with him. He took me to the track almost every weekend when I was growing up so I could practice, and I never heard him complain about all the hours of free time he gave up for me. He was never very good at sports himself, but he saw something in me and he encouraged it. He supported me a hundred percent.''

"Your father would be proud of you if he could see you today. All the titles you hold. All the medals you've won.''

"All but the gold. That one has always eluded me for some reason. In 1996 I thought I finally had it in the bag because I'd trained hard and the Olympics were in my hometown. But that morning it rained and turned cool. I hadn't expected that and it threw me. I got a slow start and was never able to gain any momentum.''

"But you still got a silver.''

"Yes, but the gold is what's important. I wanted it. I still want it.'' She sat up and turned cross-legged to face him. "When I was little, my dad made me a medal out of a piece of wood. He painted it gold and threaded it with red, white and blue ribbon. He put it around my neck and said, 'One day, kitten, you'll win the marathon and this will be a real Olympic gold medal.' I still have a piece of the ribbon and I wear it for good luck when I race. It's all faded and falling apart, but I keep it because it represents my dream. *Our* dream. Mine and my dad's.''

An uneasiness grew in Mac's chest. Until now, he hadn't realized how closely her running was tied to her feelings for her father.

"I *have* to win that gold. I have to. I've dreamed all my life of taking that victory lap around the Olympic stadium and holding the American flag high while thousands of people cheer. I want that for myself and I want it for my dad. You remember how supportive he was of me when I was running for Courtland. Every weekend we had a meet, if it was within driving distance, he'd be there to watch.''

''I remember.''

''I could always count on him to be in the stands rooting for me, encouraging me to do my best.''

''But he wasn't alone.'' She cocked her head in confusion. ''Your mom was always with him,'' Mac reminded her. ''I don't remember a time your dad came that your mom wasn't right there, cheering you along.''

Keely looked away, but before she did, he saw a flash of pain in her eyes. ''I suppose she was,'' she said softly. ''I really don't remember.''

KEELY'S UP-AND-DOWN relationship with her mother moved toward a crisis the following week, and Mac found himself in the middle of it. Liz called to say she was driving over Friday night and bringing her male friend, Everett Lathom. The unexpected visit sent Keely into a panic.

''You have to come and help me entertain them,'' she said. She sat on the corner of his desk sticking pencils in his electric sharpener, grinding them one after another into useless nubs. ''Good grief! I call her every week without fail, and I've already promised I'd spend a few days with her between Christmas and New Year's. What more does she want from me? I can't *believe* she's going to pop in like this without an invitation.''

''Maybe she got tired of waiting for an invitation. Or maybe she's afraid you'll back out at the last minute like you did at Thanksgiving.''

She gave him a hard look. ''Whose side are you on?''

''Are there sides?''

''Yes, of course there are.'' Then she realized how ridiculous that sounded. ''I don't really mean it.''

''I know you don't. Look, I think you should do this alone. You haven't seen your mother in months. And it also couldn't hurt you to get to know this Everett fellow better, since she seems serious about him.''

"I won't survive without you there."

Survive. A strange word to use for getting through a visit with your mother.

In the end he agreed to come, not because he believed Keely really needed him, but because he figured Liz Wilson might.

When he got to Keely's house shortly before seven Friday night, she was at the stove stirring the red beans she was planning to serve over rice. Judging by her expression, he would have sworn she was going to a funeral, rather than having dinner with her mother and her mother's friend.

"You know it's pretty stupid for you not to be comfortable around your own mother," he told her.

"You don't understand. My mother and I can't spend five minutes together without fighting. And I can't imagine why she insisted on bringing that man with her."

"What's so wrong with this guy that you can't stand to be in the same room with him?"

Two hours later Mac knew exactly what was wrong with the guy—nothing. Except that he wasn't Keely's father. And in Keely's book, that was an unforgivable sin.

Everett Lathom was friendly, interesting and clearly crazy about Liz. Mac also had to give the guy credit for effort. He was bending over backward to be nice to Keely, to draw her into the conversation, but she was as sullen as Mac had ever seen her.

Liz and Everett were pretending they didn't notice, but the air was so thick with tension, it would take a chainsaw to cut it. Mac was pretty sure he'd count this among the longest nights of his life.

"This is such a lovely meal," Liz said, and Mac wondered how she could do it with a straight face.

"And such a beautiful house," Everett added.

Keely mumbled an almost unintelligible thank-you, then pointed out—for the third time—the photograph of her father hanging on the wall to the left of the fireplace.

"Mac gave it to me," she said.

Her mother's smile was laced with indulgence. "Yes, dear,

you told us, and it's a wonderful gift. Such a good likeness of you.''

"And Daddy."

"Yes, and Daddy."

Liz and Everett exchanged glances. Mac could almost hear Liz's silent plea for Everett to continue being patient with Keely—and not to be offended by her latest reference to her father.

They had decided to eat in the living room at a small table set up near the fireplace for the occasion. Liz reached over and patted Mac on the arm, acting as if nothing was wrong. "John, I'm so glad Keely invited you to join us. I was thrilled when she told me tonight you two are seeing each other."

Mac smiled, but Keely made a noise of impatience. "He likes to be called *Mac,* Mother. Nobody calls him John."

"Actually, quite a few people still call me John," he said. Keely gave him a hurt look for not supporting her, but he ignored it. "They're mostly people I grew up with. I didn't become Mac until my dad died. He'd been called that all his life."

"Where did you grow up?" Liz asked.

"Benevolence, a little town about fifty miles from here."

"I have a cousin who married a man from Benevolence and lived there for several years," Everett said. He turned to Liz. "Honey—" Keely jerked at the endearment "—you remember Reba and Charles Abernathy, don't you? We ran into them at the symphony last year when they were in Atlanta visiting."

Liz put her hand over his, a loving gesture that didn't escape Mac's attention, or Keely's. "Yes, I remember the Abernathys. Nice people."

"Charles Abernathy," Mac repeated. He called up a memory from more than twenty years ago. "I played high-school football with a Charles Abernathy. He was a big guy with thick black hair. He was a senior when I was a freshman and went on to play for Georgia."

"That's him," Everett said, chuckling, "although he lost that thick hair a long time ago."

A lengthy discussion ensued among the three of them about the Abernathy family, then about their own families. Mac told them about his siblings and pulled pictures from his wallet to show off their children. Everett responded with pictures of his two grown daughters and their children.

Mac was impressed by Everett and Liz. They didn't seem that much older than him, probably in their early fifties, and they had an easiness about them he liked. The open affection they showed each other reminded him of how things had been between his own parents.

"Mac, Liz tells me you and Keely are working with some wheelchair racers at the college. How's that coming?" Everett asked.

"Really good. Keely's been a great help. She's turning into a first-class coach." He glanced at her, hoping for a comment, but he didn't get one. "I was really proud of how well she did last quarter, and she's doing even better this quarter. I know it hasn't been easy for her—going back to school, being a teaching assistant and training at the same time, but she's really put everything into it."

Still no response. Keely sat stoically, picking at some stewed apples.

"Are you still enjoying school, sweetheart?" her mother prodded.

"It's all right."

"Just all right? What's your favorite class?"

She shrugged. "I don't have one."

"She does great in my Rehab 102 class," Mac said, hoping to make her giggle or at least shock her out of her stupor, but all she did was pinch him under the table.

"Oh?" Liz remarked, looking at Keely. "What do you do in that class?"

"It involves a lot of oral presentations," she answered without a change in expression.

This time Mac pinched Keely under the table.

"And what about your other classes?" Liz asked her. "What kinds of things are you learning?"

"I don't know. Nothing really exciting."

"I would think you'd be more enthusiastic about school, considering how well you're doing. And if John—Mac—thinks you'd make an excellent coach, perhaps you should consider that."

"School and coaching are just temporary diversions, Mother, until I can run again. I'm only doing them because Mac made them a stipulation of my training. I don't *enjoy* them, for heaven's sake."

Temporary? She didn't enjoy them? Mac couldn't conceal his surprise or hurt at her revelation. Just what else, he wondered suddenly, did she consider a temporary diversion? Him?

He muttered a low expletive that let Keely know she'd pushed him too far tonight with her childish behavior and spiteful tongue. "Should I strangle you now or wait until the company leaves?" he whispered through gritted teeth.

Keely ignored him, but he was certain he saw a smile touch the corner of her mother's mouth.

Everett cleared his throat and made a desperate attempt to salvage a situation that was rapidly going downhill. "Well, er, I'd like to see one of these wheelchair races sometime. I didn't know there was such a thing. Do you use special chairs?"

Mac took a deep breath and regained his composure. "I have photos with me from some of the practices and races," he told Everett stiffly, choosing to postpone the confrontation with Keely until they were alone. He pulled the photo pack out of the sling under his seat. "I brought them along because I thought you and Liz might like to see what Keely is helping me do."

When they'd finished eating, Keely cleared the dishes and Mac arranged the photographs on the table, where Liz and Everett could both look.

Liz picked up one of the photos and looked at it more closely. "Why, that's Ross Hewitt. I didn't know he'd been down from Chicago."

Liz pointed out a dark-haired man talking to one of the wheelers at the race in Pensacola. "No," Mac said, "that man's name is Redmond. He represents a company that partially funds our program. He's really been a lifesaver. I've been able to replace our old chairs and create a decent expense fund for the athletes, something we've never had before.''

"I'd swear..." She leaned over to Keely and showed her the photograph. "Doesn't that look just like Ross?"

Keely glanced at it and released a dismissive snort. "No. It favors him a little, but Ross has a much bigger build. And the hair is different.''

"Oh, Keely! How can you say that? This is Ross Hewitt. I'd stake my life on it.''

"Who's Ross Hewitt?" Everett asked.

Keely stood so abruptly she almost overturned the chair. "A little cheese and fruit would be nice, since I don't have dessert,'' she said, plastering a smile on her face. "Let's put the photographs away so they don't get messed up.''

She reached for them, but Mac grabbed her hand and entwined his fingers with hers. "In a minute,'' he told her, suspicious of her behavior. "We're not finished.'' She tried to pull away, but he wrapped his other arm around her hip and held her close.

"Ross is Keely's agent and business manager,'' Liz said, clearly oblivious to the drama being played out across the table. "He manages her investments. A nice man, but he has terrible allergies and this awful voice because of them. He coughs and sneezes constantly.''

The uneasiness that had haunted Mac the moment Liz began this conversation now hit him full force. No, he'd told himself, it couldn't have been Hewitt he talked with at the track that day in Pensacola. Redmond must coincidentally resemble him.

But the voice...the allergies...

Liz was going on about Ross Hewitt, how helpful he'd been to Keely right after her accident, but Mac only half listened. He looked up at Keely, praying he would see innocence on her face, but all he saw was a guilty stain creeping up her throat, and eyes that confirmed what she'd obviously hoped he would never find out. Through Ross Hewitt—the fictitious "Beatty Redmond"—*Keely* was covertly sponsoring Mac's wheelers.

CHAPTER SIXTEEN

KEELY SLAMMED the lid on the pot she was drying, bent down and tossed it with more force than necessary into the cabinet. The other pots crammed inside tumbled to the floor in a chorus of clanging metal.

It was bad enough that she'd suffered through two hours of watching old what's-his-name paw her mother, and right beneath the photograph of her father, too. It was bad enough that Mac—the one person she'd thought she could count on to support her, no matter what—was furious at her for having Ross pose as the fictional Beatty Redmond, but her mother had shattered what nerves Keely had left by announcing over the fruit and cheese that she was planning a spring wedding. She was actually going to marry that old geezer!

"You acted like a spoiled three-year-old!" Mac yelled from behind her, continuing the verbal attack he had started the second they were alone. "I can't believe you pitched that fit. I've never been so ashamed of anyone in my life!"

She plopped down on the floor and started picking up the pots, stacking them in the cabinet so they'd stay this time. Her hands shook with anger, and the tears that had threatened for days began to come now, even though she tried to hold them back.

The news hadn't been unexpected, just more devastating than she had imagined. All week, since her mother's call, she had worried that an engagement announcement might be the reason for the visit. All night she'd been waiting for the bomb to fall. And it finally had, widening the emotional fissure between her and her mother.

"I didn't pitch a fit," she told Mac in defense of herself,

although she knew he was right. She'd pitched a humdinger of one. But it just hurt so much to see her mother and old what's-his-name happy.

"Like hell you didn't pitch a fit! You were abusive and deliberately rude to both of them. You made your mother cry when you said you wouldn't be at the wedding, and for that alone you ought to be ashamed of yourself. You'll be lucky if she ever speaks to you again after what you've done."

The lines in his face and the narrowed eyes showed just how angry he was. So did his voice.

"How can you be so selfish? Don't you think your mother has a right to happiness and to marry the man she loves without you acting like she's committing a crime?"

"I didn't tell them not to get married. I only said I thought they hadn't known each other long enough. I'm not going to pretend I like it when I don't. But they're adults. They can do whatever they want."

"And thank God for that. At least they're smart enough not to let your childish behavior keep them from going ahead with their plans."

She slammed the cabinet shut and stood, planting her fists on her hips. "You know, I'm getting really tired of you calling me names and treating me like you do. You tell me I'm selfish, yet you get furious when I try to do something unselfish for your wheelers. You accuse me of being childish, but you treat me like a child, always having to approve every step in my training, not allowing me to run when you know I'm ready. I'm sick to death of you smothering me. You swore you wouldn't let our sleeping together affect my training, but that's exactly what you're doing."

"Now wait a minute! Don't twist this around to make it sound like I'm to blame here, and don't pretend this has anything to do with us sleeping together. You and Ross Hewitt were wrong setting up that bogus sponsorship and lying to me about it. If you didn't think you were doing something wrong, you wouldn't have had him pass himself off as someone else."

"I've already explained all this. The sponsorship isn't bogus and neither is Coxwell Industries."

"You just happen to own the company."

"Yes, I own it. Ross had been bugging me for a long time to license the InsulCare formula and produce it, so I used the money from my buyout of the Aztec contract. I had a company and you needed a sponsor for the wheelers. What was so wrong with me trying to help?"

"Nothing, except you went behind my back, you lied and manipulated me, and I don't like that one bit. That tells me you don't really care about my feelings."

"That's not true! The only reason I went behind your back is because you wouldn't have taken the money from me otherwise. You're so irritatingly noble at times."

The veins in his face looked like they were ready to pop. "You don't know what I would have done, because you took the choice away from me!"

She bit back her scalding reply. Okay, he had a point about the money, but she'd honestly been trying to help. She had assumed his pride wouldn't allow him to accept if she offered it outright, so she'd come up with a way to give it to him. She'd told a few white lies. But they certainly weren't worth getting this upset about.

He took her silence as an admission of guilt.

"Sometimes, Keely, I think you purposely try to be hard to get along with, and when problems don't materialize the way you expect, you invent them. Just like this thing with school. You love school, but you sat here tonight and made us all think you hate it. You love coaching, but you won't admit to yourself or anyone else that it's something you'd like to try professionally."

"Why on earth would I consider coaching when I'll be running again soon?"

"You know why. You're afraid of the truth."

"I don't have the slightest idea what you mean."

She turned to the dishwasher and busied herself, filling it with tonight's dishes. All the activity was an excuse to avoid looking at him. She didn't like the way he could see inside her and recognize what was going on when she didn't always understand her own feelings.

"Keely, don't lie to me and don't lie to yourself anymore. You worked hard and you gave this comeback your best shot, but it wasn't enough. The reality is, even if you want something badly, that doesn't mean you're going to get it."

"You don't know what you're talking about."

"I don't? Can you look at me in this chair and tell me I don't understand what it feels like to want something so badly you'd do anything to get it?"

She didn't answer him, didn't know *how* to answer him.

"Well, can you?"

"You're comparing my situation to yours and they're not the same at all," she said. "We're totally different. Just because you stopped believing in dreams and miracles doesn't mean I have to."

He pushed up close and took her arm, forcing her to turn around. Then he held her tightly by both forearms. "Listen to me. It's exactly the same thing. We've both been permanently injured and we both have to accept that nothing we ever do is going to change that."

"I am *not* permanently injured."

"You can barely breathe when you run."

"That's not true! I could run a race tomorrow if I had to. I've already gotten my entry form for the Los Verdes Marathon in April."

He let go of her abruptly. His jaw worked back and forth in anger. "That just proves what I said a little while ago. You're not honest with me. You go behind my back and do things you know you shouldn't."

"Would you have supported me if I'd told you I was thinking about entering a race?"

"No, because physically you can't run it."

"That's not true!" she said again. "You're not in my body. You don't know what I can and can't do. From the way you hold me back, sometimes I think you don't *want* me to run again."

"Do you really believe that?" He gave her an incredulous look.

"No," she said honestly, body sagging. He had done everything he could to help her. She was just angry about tonight's events, and taking it out on him was easy because he was here. "I know you'd never do anything to hold me back. But I'm starting to get the feeling you never believed I could do this, not even in the beginning when you agreed to help me."

He didn't respond.

"Well?" she prompted. "Did you?"

A sickening knot formed in her throat because she was afraid she already knew the answer. Tears streamed down her face.

"Keely, you're upset. I'm upset. Right now isn't a good time to talk about this. When we're both calmer, we can—"

"It's true, isn't it? I thought at least *you* believed in me, and that's what kept me going all these months. Whenever I got discouraged or afraid I couldn't do it, I'd remind myself that you would never have agreed to help me if you didn't think I had a chance of racing again. So I'd work harder and I'd push a little bit more. But you've been lying all this time, haven't you?"

"Wait a minute. I've never lied to you."

"Then, what *is* the truth? Did you believe for an instant that I *could* race again? And if you've ever cared for me, don't lie to me now."

The anger seemed to leave him in one great expulsion of breath, to be replaced by an overwhelming sadness. "No, I never believed you'd race again," he said with obvious regret. "You're counting on a miracle that's never going to happen."

KEELY CRIED HERSELF into a sick headache and fell into bed. Mac was afraid to leave her alone. He cleaned up the kitchen and put the leftover food away.

Later, when he was sure she had no more tears left to spill, he went to her in the darkness and pressed himself against her back, wrapping his arm around her. She hadn't even bothered to take off her clothes. She lay awake but unresponsive on top of the covers.

He kissed her neck, longing to make love to her, but knowing she needed something different from him right now.

"I wasn't trying to hurt you," he said softly. "I wanted you to have your chance, even if it didn't work out, and I knew from my own experience that it was going to take you time to accept things."

"You should have been honest with me." Her voice was flat, emotionless. "You yelled at me tonight about not being honest, and all these months you've been deceiving me. How honest is that?"

He clenched and unclenched his jaw. "You're right. I should have told you the truth in the very beginning and not agreed to coach you. I did it to stall for time."

"To waste my time, you mean."

"How was it a waste of your time if it helped you heal? The past months have been great for you. You've gone back to school and now you have the chance to try coaching as a new career."

"I don't need a new career. I already have one—running. I *will* run again. I *will* be the best in the world. I *will* win a gold medal in Sydney. And no one, not you or anyone, is going to tell me not to try. I'd rather go after my dream and fail than be like you—afraid of even trying."

He forced down the anger rising in him again, ignored the sting of her words. He smoothed her hair. "Baby, you can't run."

"Yes, I can!"

With a sigh Mac rolled onto his back, put his arm under his head and stared at the shadows on the ceiling cast by the pale light in the hall. Continuing this conversation was useless. She wasn't going to listen to him, didn't want to listen to him. Nothing he said would convince her.

He could think of only one way to make her see the truth, but it would probably kill them both.

CHAPTER SEVENTEEN

December

THE MORNING WAS COLD and clear, the ground still covered with a thin layer of frost the sun had yet to burn away. On the side of a four-lane road, Keely paced and stretched to keep her muscles warm and tried to rid herself of the uncommon nervousness that clawed in her belly.

Stay focused, she warned herself silently. *Be patient. Conserve your energy.*

She took several deep breaths and visualized the test marathon course ahead of her; it would follow the bypass for nearly a third of the twenty-six miles, taking her along the newest, and for the most part, uninhabited section of the road. The surface was smooth and the road had a bike lane she could use. The only hill was at mile six, when she would be warm but not tired.

At mile eight, before the first traffic light, she would exit right onto a meandering dirt road for less than a mile, then take a left that would put her on a relatively flat two-lane country road for eleven miles. Miles twenty-one to twenty-six, the hardest part of any marathon, would be another country road with a slight downhill grade.

The course was incredibly easy, with every part of it working to her advantage. She was certain Mac had intentionally drawn it that way, just as she was certain he had given her every other advantage within his control.

Exams were over, so she didn't have to worry about school. The three-week Christmas break had begun two days ago with a mass exodus of students, which meant the streets in and around Courtland were virtually deserted. She wouldn't have to worry about the bypass being crowded with other runners, or running in heavy traffic, which made her uneasy since her accident.

As the only participant in this "race," she wouldn't be jostled at the start or fighting for position at the finish. It would be just her against the clock.

Even the weather was cooperating, she thought, as she jogged to Dean's truck and took off her jacket and the old sweats she'd put on over her running tights. The cool air would reduce her chances of dehydration from sweating. Since their arrival a light tailwind had come up to push her along the course.

"Drink," Dean said. He handed her a cup of a carbohydrate-replacement solution, and she stopped jogging to sip it. "I know you said you don't usually eat during a race, but Mac made me get bananas, dried fruit and energy bars just in case." He offered her a banana. "Want to eat something before you start?"

Grimacing, she waved it away. "I've carbo-loaded for days. I don't think my stomach can handle anything solid right now. My butterflies might not appreciate it, either."

"Nervous?"

"A little. Mostly excited." She drained her cup and placed it in the trash sack on the floorboard. "I've spent months working toward this day."

"I wish I felt as good about it as you do. You haven't run a full marathon in practice, and that worries me."

"Mac gave me more than four hours to finish," she reminded him. "And I always run better in a race than in practice. I can handle it in that time with no sweat."

"Maybe, but it might not be as easy as you think. You know what happens when you try to push yourself."

"I'll be fine. I haven't had problems in months."

Reaching into her bag, she brought out a baseball cap and her father's ribbon. She rubbed the ribbon for strength before pinning it to her shirt. Everything depended on her performance over the next few hours.

According to Mac's deal, she only had to finish today's trial within an hour of her *worst* recorded time at this distance. She could make it. And when she did, Mac would have to concede that she was able to return to racing.

His sweetheart of a deal, though, had come with a big stipulation: "If you don't make it, Keely, you have to retire. No more comeback attempts. No more putting off the inevitable. You have to accept that your career is over and give me your word that you'll go on to something else."

She had agreed. She had no reason not to. Her training had gone well over the past months, except for a few setbacks she blamed on tension caused by the situation with her mother. Recently she'd done extensive hill work, deep-pool running, and speed work on the track, returning her muscles and cardiovascular system to top form.

She jogged back and forth for a few yards, then did easy stretches, testing her muscles. They felt good.

"If you need to drink between the designated stops," Dean reminded her, "wave and I'll pull around."

"Will do."

"I'll be right behind you if you need anything."

"Just don't follow me if I suddenly plunge into the woods to drop my tights."

"Got it," he said with a chuckle. He closed the door of the truck. "You greased up and ready to go?"

She nodded but looked to her right, hoping to see Mac's van approaching. The gloomy sight of an empty road met her. A horrible thought worked its way from her head down her spine. Maybe he wasn't here yet because he wasn't coming.

Admittedly, things had been strained between them for the past two weeks. Dean had relayed his messages and helped her with her prerace training program. The couple of times she'd tried speaking to Mac directly he'd been maddeningly businesslike, as if she was just another of his students.

Two nights ago on the telephone, they'd had a terrible argument because of Mac's insistence that one of the team doctors be here today in case she had problems. She hadn't talked to or seen Mac since.

He wanted her to quit and she wouldn't. She wanted him to believe in her ability and he couldn't. Their difference of opinion over her career had driven a wedge between them that had wrecked both their professional and personal relationship.

But regardless of their problems, she'd expected him to be here for her start. *Wanted* him to be here.

Taking her gaze from the road, she looked at Dean for reassurance, but he was wearing an uncomfortable expression.

"He isn't coming, is he?" she asked.

"He had things to do—checking the course, picking up Doc Ramsey. They're ahead of us somewhere."

Disappointment brought a lump to her throat. "Did he give you a message for me?"

Dean shifted in place, like a little boy asked by his mother to confess a sin. He knew she and Mac had argued about her unwillingness to retire.

"No, I'm sorry, he didn't."

Keely looked away, trying not to feel upset but failing. Mac wasn't coming. He wasn't even going to bother to wish her luck.

"I can get him on the radio."

She realized Dean was still talking to her. "What?"

"Do you need me to get Mac on the headset?"

"No, it's okay. I don't need him," her mouth said, but her heart said she needed him very much, not only today, but every day. And more than she'd realized until this moment.

"MAC, WE'RE ROLLING. Starting time nine-zero-seven and thirteen seconds."

Dean's voice startled Mac, although he'd been waiting for the signal. He made a note on his clipboard and tossed it onto the dash. The sound made Doc Ramsey, who'd been half-asleep in the passenger seat of the van, sit up and rub his eyes. Mac raised the microphone arm on the headset so he could respond.

"Okay, don't crowd her, but stay close enough to tell when

she starts having problems. If she even stumbles, I want to know about it.''

"Will do. Where are you and Doc?"

"Parked at the fire station. We'll move and stay just ahead of you. We can be there in a couple of minutes when you need us.''

"Copy." There was a moment of silence on the line. "Hey, Mac…''

"Yeah?''

"This thing between you and Keely is none of my business, but I think you should know she seemed hurt you didn't come see her off.''

Mac's heart gave a lurch. He'd debated for two days whether to see her this morning and had spent a sleepless night worrying about it. Ultimately he'd decided it was better to stay away. Better for Keely not to get angry right before she had to run. Better for him because his insides couldn't survive another fight with her.

And the truth was, the thought of talking to her this morning, when he knew she was about to get the biggest disappointment of her life, was more than the coward in him could take.

"Mac, did you hear me?''

Mac glanced at Doc, thankful the older man didn't have a headset on and couldn't hear the conversation. "Yeah, I heard you. Sorry to put you in the middle of things.''

"No problem. I just hope, well, you know, y'all can work things out after this is over.''

Me, too, Mac thought. *Me too.*

EVERYTHING WENT SMOOTHLY until ninety minutes into the run when Keely began to feel an increasing pressure along the ribs on her bad side. Taking shallower breaths helped, but that robbed her of oxygen and slowed her pace, something she couldn't afford in this middle leg when she needed to record her fastest miles.

A slow start. A fast middle. A moderate end. That was the pacing plan Mac had devised to keep up her energy and bring her in at four hours. With the tailwind, she'd expected to gain some time, but she hadn't. Instead, she was steadily losing time. And she had to make it up.

Ignore the pain. But it was difficult to ignore. It was so smothering.

She tried to concentrate on keeping her form smooth and efficient, to gain time through economy of motion and block out the burning that now consumed her whole side.

Breathe normally, her mind screamed at her. She tried, but every time she inhaled deeply, it felt as if someone was jamming a spear in her ribs.

Suddenly Dean drove around and pulled over, indicating a water stop. Keely almost cried with relief. Mac had ordered her to stop and drink, rather than drinking on the run, and the few seconds of rest at each stop had helped keep her moving. The few she'd get at this stop would mean the difference between staying on her feet and going down.

Dean thrust a cup in her hand when she got to the truck. "You look bad and you're still slowing down. Are you okay?"

She nodded and drank the liquid as fast as she dared. Too slow and she'd lose precious seconds. Too fast and she'd be fighting stomach cramps.

"Answer me orally," Dean ordered. "You know procedure."

According to Mac's rules, she had to orally respond to questions at each water stop. If she didn't, Dean wasn't supposed to let her continue. So far, she'd been able to. This time, she tried but no sound came out.

"That's it," Dean said, reaching in the cab to get the headset. "I'm pulling you in and calling Mac."

Ignoring him, she tossed the cup and headed out, Dean's curses following her.

"MAC!"

"Yeah?"

"I got no oral response at this stop and she's fighting for air. I tried to pull her in, but she got away from me."

"We're on the way."

Stubborn infuriating woman! She was already so far behind time she had little chance of finishing, but that wouldn't stop her from injuring herself trying.

Mac drove like a wild man to intercept Keely. He passed her and Dean, then made a quick U-turn and pulled up next to her so Doc could talk to her out the window of the van. Dean hadn't exaggerated. She was laboring for breath and pushing herself forward on willpower alone. Only by a miracle was she was still going.

She tried to wave them away. Where she got the strength to lift her hand, he didn't know.

Mac watched for oncoming traffic while Doc visually assessed her condition. Doc asked her to touch her pulse monitor and give him a reading. She followed his instructions, and the reading was in line with what Doc expected, easing Mac's concern, but only slightly.

"As long as her vitals and fluid intake stay okay and she can communicate, I think it's safe for her to continue," Doc said. "Let's start checking her at each stop."

"Your call, Doc," Mac told him, not trusting himself to decide. "Her safety is the issue here. Nothing else matters."

"Her oxygen intake is the only thing really concerning me right now," he told Mac, then turned back to Keely and asked, "How's your respiration? Are you feeling any pain in your chest? Any pressure when you inhale?"

She shook her head.

"Just tired and hot?"

She nodded.

"C'mon, talk to me so I'll know you're breathing okay and can go on."

No response.

Mac leaned forward on the steering wheel and yelled, "This is insane! Give it up before you hurt yourself."

Still no response.

"Talk to me," Mac warned her, "or I swear I'll bring you in and physically restrain you."

She turned her head and looked at him, and he could see

the determination in her eyes, along with the pain she was fighting. She opened her mouth to speak, but the three words she forced out were the very ones he didn't want to hear. "I...won't...quit."

KEELY TOOK A FEW BREATHS of oxygen from the portable unit Doc passed through the window. That eased her pain, revived her temporarily, so they did it several more times over the next few miles and let her continue to run.

But Mac frequently expressed his unhappiness with the situation and wouldn't let her out of his sight. He was in front of her now in the van, leading the way. Keely focused on his emergency flashers and just kept putting one foot in front of the other, trying not to think about how far behind she'd fallen.

At each water stop she sat in the side door of the van and let them fill her with liquids. Doc checked her vital signs and made sure her temperature didn't get too high. Dean gave her oxygen and rubbed her leg muscles to keep them from cramping while she wasn't moving.

Mac, frustrated by his inability to get down on the floor to help, barked orders at everyone from the driver's seat.

Repeatedly they urged her to quit, but Keely kept going. She kept going when her energy deserted her and the oxygen no longer did any good. She kept going when the pain in her lungs became so intense she felt she was inhaling fire with every breath.

Even when her watch told her she had only four minutes to finish—and seven miles to complete—she kept going.

"SHE'S DOWN! She's down!"

Dean's words ripped through Mac's brain at the same moment he looked in the rearview mirror and saw Keely collapse.

Doc was out the door before Mac could pull off the road and stop.

Doc and Dean hauled her in the side door of the van and

put her on the floor. Cursing his useless legs, Mac threw himself from the driver's seat to the floor, dragging himself to her side.

As he reached her, the timer beeped on her watch—the death knell of her career.

"Maaaaac..."

"I'm here, baby."

He held her in his arms and tried to comfort her as the first sob racked her body. She didn't have enough liquid left to produce tears, and her wails were punctuated by great gasps for air. Her face, etched with the pain of what she had endured, also carried the anguish of failure.

"I...couldn't..." She clung to him and tried to cry. "I... couldn't...do it."

"It's okay," he said, pulling off her baseball cap to cradle her head. "Everything's going to be okay."

"I tried...so hard."

"I know you did, baby. You did everything you could." He put the oxygen mask Doc handed him over her nose and mouth. "Now just breathe for me and don't worry about anything. I promise everything's going to be all right."

Her temperature had risen to 103, high enough for concern, so they plied her with more liquids, changing to watered-down fruit juice when the sugar in the replacement drink made her throw up. Doc kept a continuous check on her blood pressure.

Her arms were scraped and bloody from elbow to wrist because of her fall, but they weren't a priority at the moment. Helping her shocked system was. With Dean on one side and Doc on the other, they walked her back and forth along the road to keep blood moving to her muscles and stave off post-race collapse syndrome.

After several agonizingly long minutes, they brought her close enough to the van for Mac to talk to them. He had pulled himself into his wheelchair and used the lift to get down onto the road. "Is she dizzy?" he asked Doc when they approached. "Headache?"

"She's okay," Doc said. "Breathing easier and keeping down undiluted juice. She's stabilizing."

Mac had set up a recovery unit at the athletic department, where she'd spend the next few hours replenishing her body fluids and getting her blood sugar back to normal. His only thought now was to get her there as soon as they had her regulated.

But when he suggested it, Keely balked.

"No...I have...to finish," she said as they helped her sit in the open door of the van. Her skin was bright red and her muscles quivered, making her hands shake so badly she could hardly hold the cup Dean had given her. Although her breathing had improved, she still had to breathe through her mouth to get enough oxygen, which made talking difficult.

Her pronouncement that she had to finish the race had the three men looking at one another with concern. Mac knew they were all thinking the same thing—she must be out of her head.

"Sweetheart..." Mac folded his hand around hers and brought the cup to her lips. He helped her drink. "You're dehydrated and confused. The trial is over. There's nothing to finish."

"Not over. Have...to finish." She stopped to catch her breath, then continued in her halting speech, determined, it seemed, to make them understand, to prove she wasn't out of her mind. "Not confused. Have to...keep going. Have to cross...the finish line."

"No! Absolutely not! There's no way in hell I'm letting you go on!"

"Please...listen...please."

"You don't have to finish. We all know you ran the best race you could."

Dean and Doc expressed their agreement.

"Matters to me," Keely said. "Please...this is my...last race. Know I can't go out a winner. But...don't want to go out a quitter."

"No, no way. You aren't physically able to run."

"No, but, Mac...I can still walk."

She crossed the finish line eight hours after she began, walking, instead of running. It was a small victory compared to what she had expected of herself today, but in the eyes of the three men who watched her take her last faltering steps, she might as well have won the gold medal in the Olympics.

"That woman is ninety percent guts," Doc said, sounding a little choked up.

"And the rest is heart," Dean added.

Mac swallowed a lump in his throat the size of a baseball. He'd never felt more love for anyone, never been prouder of anyone, in his life.

They drove her to the recovery unit at the athletic complex. She lay on a table with her feet elevated to ease the flow of blood to her heart and prevent edema in her legs. Doc swabbed antiseptic on her scraped arms and helped her change into dry clothes.

Physically she seemed okay, no worse off for having walked those last seven miles, although with every step Mac had agonized over his decision to let her do it.

"Please, Mac," she'd pleaded with him, "let me go out with some dignity."

He hadn't been able to refuse her.

Her emotional health was what worried Mac now. She couldn't stop crying—quiet private tears, not the sobbing he expected—which tore at his heart every time he tried to talk to her. "Try and sleep a little while," he told her. "That might make you feel better."

She looked at him with big sad eyes that said nothing would ever make her feel better. "What do I do now, Mac? How do I go on without the one thing that made me who I am?"

"You just will." He wished he knew the right words to say, but instead, he felt useless. "You'll dig down and grab hold of some of that incredible strength you have, and you'll find a new direction in your life."

"I can't imagine any other life."

"Can't you? I can. When I met you, you were a gangly seventeen-year-old kid with the best set of legs I'd ever seen on a runner and no idea how to use them. I came away that day sure of two things—You were going to be a champion and you were going to steal my heart. I wasn't wrong about either prediction.''

He stroked her hair. He hadn't intended to say any of this now, but the words tumbled out.

''The feelings I have for you started as physical attraction and admiration for your talent, but they've had a lot of time to grow into something stronger. I love you. You're hurting right now and it's going to take a while to put the hurt behind you. But don't think for an instant that your life is over, because it isn't. If you'll have me, I intend to spend the next sixty years making you glad to wake up every morning.''

''What are you saying?''

''I'm asking you to be my wife and grow old with me.''

''Marriage?''

''Yes. Marry me. I know I can make you happy.''

For a long time she didn't respond, and he began to regret the suddenness of his declaration. She had too much to deal with now. When she was feeling better, when he had champagne and a ring, he'd ask the proper way.

''You don't have to say anything right now or even think about it,'' he told her. ''Close your eyes and rest. We'll talk when you're feeling better.''

With intravenous fluids, she improved steadily over the next hours. At nine-thirty that night Doc checked her a final time and decided she was well enough to go home.

''I think I should stay with you tonight,'' Mac told her in front of the men, propriety having crumbled the minute he'd taken her into his arms in the van. ''You shouldn't be alone.''

She nodded but said nothing.

At her house, Mac fixed dinner while she took a shower. When he went to tell her it was ready, he found her asleep on the bed, her face stained with tears and her father's ribbon clutched in one hand. He covered her with a blanket but left the lamp on the bedside table burning. He looked in on her several times during the night, until he himself fell into an exhausted sleep on the couch sometime around dawn.

He didn't wake until after noon. He pushed to the bedroom and peered inside, but she wasn't there. "Keely?" When he didn't get an answer, he checked both bathrooms.

In her private bathroom he found the ribbon in the trash; that sent an uneasiness skittering along his nerve endings. He took out the ribbon and laid it beside the sink, then went through the bedroom into the hall.

"Keely, where are you?" Only an eerie stillness greeted him.

Slipping on his sweatpants and jacket, he pushed out to the driveway. Her car was no longer next to the van. He stared at the empty spot, trying to think where she might have gone. He'd expected her to sleep most of the day.

"Hello, Coach McCandless," a voice said.

The elderly woman, whose little dog often ran with Keely in the mornings, waved to him from the neighboring yard. Her son was on a ladder stringing Christmas lights around the eaves of the house while she directed him.

Mac nodded to the man, then told her, "Your decorations are going to be the hit of the neighborhood, Mrs. Martin."

She smiled. "I hope so. I do love this time of year."

"Mrs. Martin…did you happen to see Keely earlier?"

"Yes, I did. She was leaving as I was coming home from church."

"Did she mention where she was going?"

"Well, no. I didn't actually talk to her, just noticed her as she walked to her car."

"Okay, thanks. I guess she drove to the store for something."

He started to push back through the gate, but her call stopped him. "Oh, Coach McCandless, I don't believe she's coming back for a while."

His heart pounded wildly. Turning, he asked, "Why would you think that, Mrs. Martin?"

"Because she took a suitcase."

THE DOORBELL RANG as Liz Wilson was coming down the stairs. "I'll get it, Louise," she called out to the housekeeper.

Everett had promised to take her to the park to see the lighting of the Christmas tree, and afterward they were going shopping for gifts.

Her smile of expectation changed to surprise when she opened the door and found, not Everett, but a pale, gaunt Keely standing there with a suitcase in her hand and desperation on her face.

"Keely?"

"Please don't turn me away, Mother. I don't have anywhere else to go."

CHAPTER EIGHTEEN

KEELY WIPED HER BREATH from the windowpane with the hem of her nightgown. After sleeping more than twenty-four hours, she still felt terrible. Sore. Depressed. The antics of the squirrel outside would have lightened her mood on any other day, but now she knew nothing would ever make her feel better. She'd lost everything.

The squirrel again scampered down the tree until it had nearly reached the ground, then stopped and scouted the backyard with quick jerks of its head. The object of its attack—the bird feeder—sat atop a four-foot post in the center of the garden, an easy climb for the hungry squirrel, except for the metal guard that ballooned like a skirt from the base of the feeder.

Unable to climb under or over the guard, the squirrel had resorted to a series of well-planned attacks that Keely had been watching for several minutes. He'd tried jumping on top of the feeder from the oak tree, only to smack the ground because the limb didn't reach quite far enough. He'd tried jumping at it from the patio table, only to hit the rim of the guard and bounce off.

This time he was trying a sprint-and-leap attack. So far it hadn't landed him where he wanted to be, but he'd shaken loose so many sunflower seeds with each attempt, he no doubt thought he was making progress.

He raised his head and looked around, apparently satisfied that neither the cat nor the yard man was around. He ran again and launched himself, sending the feeding sparrows to the air in a panic and hitting the squirrel guard with a loud thud.

Keely shook her head as he slid, spread-eagled, down the guard.

Stupid squirrel. He didn't have enough sense to know when the odds were stacked too high against him. *Just like you,* her inner voice nagged. Too stupid to know when her career was over. Too stupid to know when to quit.

Her throat clogged and her eyes watered. *Why me?* Because a driver had been in too much of a hurry, her dreams had been taken away. The man had ruined her life. In return, he'd only lost his driver's license for a year. The unfairness of it still rankled.

She thought of Mac, who had lost so much more than dreams, and wondered if he hated the man who had shot him. No, unlike her, Mac didn't have the capacity for hate. He'd made the best of his situation, had even managed to use his disability to be a better coach. In every way that was important, he was a stronger person than he'd been before.

I can't waste my life grieving over lost dreams any more than I can waste my life grieving over being in this chair, he had once told her.

If only she could be like that. She didn't want to spend her life grieving over something that was beyond her power to keep, but how did she let go of what had always been so much a part of her? Without her career, she was only a husk. There was nothing inside of any substance or importance.

The squirrel was getting into position for another attack on the feeder, but Keely had grown tired of his antics. She banged on the glass and yelled, "Get out of here!" sending him scurrying up the tree and out of sight.

"Who on earth are you talking to?" her mother asked from the doorway. She walked into the bedroom accompanied by a whisper of silk.

"No one. Just scaring away some crazy squirrel trying to get the bird seed."

"Oh, that pesky thing. He's been at it for weeks."

"Aren't squirrels supposed to hibernate or something in the winter?"

"I have no idea. If they do, someone obviously forgot to tell him."

Liz put a tray on the nightstand and took a seat on the bed, her back ramrod straight, her hands folded just so in her lap, like the proper lady Grandmother Bradshaw had raised her to be. Regal was how Keely had always thought of her mother. Elegant. Beautiful. Unbending.

Had she ever looked like normal people? Even now, at nine in the morning, her hair was swept up in some fancy twist and her face was perfect, right down to the soft coral of her lipstick. The emerald-green dress looked like something out of the pages of a fashion magazine.

"Come eat," she said. "Louise made you a nice big plate of fruit. The strawberries and peaches aren't fresh, but the oranges are. Or there's bacon and toast if you'd rather have that."

"I don't eat bacon," Keely said automatically, then realized the ridiculousness of it and sighed. She wasn't in training, would never be in training again, and could eat anything—bacon, chocolate, pizza loaded with cheese. All the unhealthy things everyone else ate that she'd given up.

"At least eat the fruit and toast," her mother prodded. "You haven't eaten anything since you got here yesterday, and you know that's not good for you. You need to rebuild your strength."

"For what?"

"Sweetheart, I know things are very difficult for you right now, but if you don't eat and you get sick, it won't make your problems any easier to deal with, now will it?"

"I'm really not hungry."

"I know, but humor me, please?"

Stifling her natural urge to continue arguing, Keely walked to the bed and sat with a repressed groan of pain, tucking her sore legs underneath her.

Her mother had taken her in when she could rightfully have slammed the door in her face. If eating a couple of strawberries would make her happy, then she'd eat a couple of strawberries.

She was determined to be nice, no matter what. And that meant no arguing. No smart remarks when her mother criticized her or tried to tell her what to do. And definitely no mentioning old what's-his-name.

She'd apologized for her recent rude behavior, an apology her mother had stiffly accepted, but Keely wasn't going to press her luck by bringing up the subject again. If her mother wanted to spend her life with Everett Lathom, it was her life. Keely wasn't going to say another word against him.

"Come downstairs for a while," her mother suggested. "You could read or watch television."

"No, I don't feel like it. I haven't even been able to work up the energy to get in the shower yet."

"Do you feel well enough to talk to Mac? He was frantic yesterday when I called to tell him you were here, and he's called several times since wanting to speak to you. He's terribly worried."

Keely threw her half-eaten strawberry on the plate, no longer able to even pretend hunger. She hadn't meant to worry him. When she'd opened her eyes yesterday morning, her first thought had been, *Time to get up and run.* Then she'd remembered she didn't have running to look forward to.

Overwhelmed by the reality of that, and by Mac's out-of-the-blue proposal of marriage, she'd gone a little insane. She'd thrown clothes in a suitcase and left, with no idea where she was going or what she would do, only that she had do *something.* She'd surprised her mother and herself when she'd arrived on Liz's doorstep.

"Is Mac all right?" Keely asked softly.

"He's upset you left so abruptly and without telling him where you were going, but he'll be okay, I think, once he's talked to you."

"I was thoughtless. I should have written him a note so he wouldn't worry."

"You've been through a terrible ordeal, and you're not thinking straight right now. Mac understands that."

"Has he called this morning?"

"Four times. He wanted to drive up here, but I convinced him not to do anything until he's talked with you."

Keely closed her eyes briefly and said a prayer of thanks. No way could she deal with him in person. Talking to him on the phone would be hard enough. He'd ask when she was coming back—and she didn't know. He'd ask what she was going to do with the rest of her miserable life—and she didn't know that, either.

"I feel so…" She felt the sting of tears and lowered her gaze, chastising herself again for being such a mess.

"So what, sweetheart? Tell me what you feel."

"You wouldn't understand."

"Oh, I think I might." She smoothed Keely's hair from her face, a motherly gesture Keely normally disliked but endured. Today it felt almost…nice. "You feel empty, like someone pulled the plug and all the important parts of you simply drained out. Your determination, your strength, your optimism, all the things that have always kept you going when life got tough suddenly don't seem to be there anymore, and it scares you."

That was exactly how she felt, but how had her mother known? "What do I do about it?" she asked.

"You cry. You rail over the injustice of what's happened and wallow in self-pity for a few days because you've earned the right. Then, when your head's clearer and you realize you're *not* really empty, you'll be able to take the next step."

"What?"

"Deciding what makes you happy. And going after it with all your heart."

THE BOLT SLIPPED from Mac's hand and hit the concrete floor, bouncing under the workbench where he and Alan were trying to repair Alan's racer. Mac threw down the wrench, and in an uncharacteristic display of temper, vented his frustration over his separation from Keely by throwing the heavy roll of tape across the garage…then the spoke wrench…then the pry bar.

"Missed this one." Alan handed him the rubber mallet

without so much as blinking. Mac threw it, too, hitting the waist-high rack where Alan had stored his lawn tools and garden hoses for the winter, making the hoses uncurl and writhe across the floor like snakes. A split second later, the rack itself crashed down. Tools flew everywhere.

Vicki appeared in the doorway before the echo of the clatter died down. "What is going on out here? I'd swear we're in the middle of a war zone." She surveyed the damage with a surprised, "Oh!"

"The rack fell," Alan said casually. "Go on back to the house and we'll take care of it. Too cold out here for you."

She looked at Alan with narrow-eyed suspicion, then at Mac, then back at Alan.

Mac waited for her to scold them both for the mess. But as if communicating with Alan by telepathy, she grasped that this wasn't the time to be scolding. With a quick compassionate glance at Mac but not a word, she walked back into the house.

"How many years does it take before you can read each other's minds like that?" Mac asked.

"More than I want to count." Alan took two beers from the cooler and handed them to Mac for opening, his dexterity limited to less difficult tasks. Alan could write, eat and do almost every other chore with the help of adaptive devices, but the simple ability to get his finger in a pull tab and manipulate it eluded him.

Mac opened the beers and handed one back, then took a swallow of his own and apologized for his lack of restraint. His anger had fizzled, but the dull throb of frustration remained. "I've been like dynamite ready to explode ever since Keely took off. I guess it's a miracle I haven't blown before now, the way I feel."

"You look bad, too."

Mac rubbed his jaw, darkened by a four-day growth of beard. "J.P. asked if I'd been eating dirt."

Alan chuckled. "That's because his face resembles that after he's been eating dirt. He recognized the look."

"You ought to feed the kid real food, Alan."

"Why, when it's so much cheaper for him to forage in the neighborhood and dig up his meals?"

Mac laughed despite his bad mood. This was what he'd needed for days, a heavy dose of Alan Sizemore and a chance to let off some steam.

They pushed to the wall and began picking up the fallen tools, deciding to wait until some other time to rehang the rack. "So tell me," Alan said, "did you get bad news from Keely or have you gotten all worked up like this just for fun?"

"*You* tell me if it's justified," Mac said, passing over the hedge trimmers. "I've only talked to her directly once, and that was for about one minute. All the other times I've called, she's either been asleep or doesn't feel like coming to the phone. I've had more of a relationship with her mother the past four days than I have with Keely."

"You going up there?"

"I want to, but she made me promise not to, says she needs some time alone to think and she can't think with me there. I don't even know what that means. How would I stop her from thinking?"

Alan offered no explanation.

"Then, and this really worries me, when I asked her when she thought she might be coming home, she started to cry. She wouldn't give me a straight answer about the plans we made to spend the holidays together, begged me not to press her, and right after that, she suddenly decided she had to get off the phone. She said talking to me only makes her feel worse."

"Ah, man, I'm sorry."

"See what I'm up against? I feel like I'm banging my head against a brick wall."

He forced down the hot lump of pain beginning to rise in his throat. He'd really been looking forward to spending Christmas with Keely, had already told Christine and Megan not to expect him to fly to California this year because he had other plans.

Keely had been looking forward to it, too, or so he'd

thought. "We'll buy a tree and decorate your house and have a Christmas with all the trimmings," she'd suggested a few weeks ago.

Amazing how your life could go from terrific to desolate in a matter of hours.

"Has she given you any idea what she'll do now that she can't run?" Alan asked.

"No, and I'm afraid to push her about it, because she's so messed up right now. I don't want to urge her to finish school and coach if that's not what she really wants to do."

"But I thought you wanted her to coach. Wasn't that the whole idea of getting her back in school?"

"I *do* want her to coach, because I think she's got a natural talent for working with people, but as long as she's happy, it doesn't matter to me what she does. The decision is hers to make and I'll support her in whatever she decides."

"What if she decides on something that takes her out of Courtland? What will you do then?"

That was a question Mac had thought about constantly the last few days. He wanted to be part of her life, and if she wanted that, too, he would go wherever he had to go to be with her, even if it meant giving up his job.

"I'll deal with that problem when or if it happens. Right now I can't even get her to talk to me or return my phone calls. We don't seem to have a future." He took a ragged breath and ran a hand roughly through his hair. "I asked her to marry me the other day, Alan, and she just stared at me in horror like I'd lost my mind."

"Hell."

"Then she ran away in the middle of the night. I have to believe she loves me, but I can't understand why she wouldn't want to be with me when she's feeling so bad. Does it make sense to you?"

"She's a woman. Women aren't designed to make sense. I've been married to Vicki for seventeen years, and she still sometimes does the opposite of what I think she'll do. Women are built to confuse men. It's in their genes or something."

"I don't understand Keely at all. Our physical relationship

is good. Her running isn't a barrier anymore to our being together. But the minute I proposed, she took off like a scalded cat. I don't get it. Have I fooled myself into believing she cares for me?''

"Nah, man, don't start thinking like that. She has a lot on her plate right now. Sounds to me like she just needs time to sort things out.''

"I know, but I hate the idea of her up there in Atlanta, suffering. I should be there. Or she should be here where she belongs.''

"I wouldn't worry. She's got her mom to help her if she needs it, and there still must be some feeling between the two of them, or Keely wouldn't have gone to her in the first place.''

True. Maybe mother and daughter could find a way to resolve the years of pain that separated them.

"She's tough," Alan said. "If anybody can get through this, it's Keely.''

Mac nodded, remembering how courageous she'd been during her running trial, the way she'd held on even when she was in so much pain and knew she couldn't make it. She'd given it everything she had, gone after her dream despite the incredible odds against her.

He almost felt shamed by her courage. She had so much of it. And he had so little.

"Alan, do you still get angry about what happened to you? Your accident, I mean.''

His friend registered surprise at the question. Mulling it over a few seconds, he shrugged and said, "I guess so. Not as much as I used to, but yeah, I still get angry. I guess it comes with the wheels. You know, a package deal—wheelchair, anger, depression, insecurity.''

"Insecurity? You? You're the most secure person I know. Nothing gets to you.''

"Don't bet on it." He narrowed his gaze. "Why did you ask me that?''

"No particular reason." Taking a long swallow to finish his beer, he crumpled the can and sent it sailing toward the trash. "I hate to bug out on you, but if you don't need that racer right away, I think I'm going to head on home. I haven't slept much the last few days and I'm dead."

"I'm in no hurry."

"Then I'll see you later." Mac hesitated and added, "Thanks for letting me bend your ear tonight. Being able to talk helped."

"Sure. Anytime." As Mac rolled to the door, Alan called, "Cheer up, buddy. This thing with Keely will work out. And hey, shave in the morning, will ya? You're ugly enough without that all over your face."

Mac pushed across the street, smiling. The telephone was ringing as he got in and he snatched it up. "Keely?" But it was only a salesman wanting him to switch long-distance telephone services.

He took a quick shower and went to bed, but the moment his head hit the pillow, he started feeling depressed again. He missed Keely's warmth, the way she held him and sighed contentedly in her sleep, the way she often awoke in the morning, her eyes heavy-lidded with desire. He loved to put that soft purr in her throat.

Although the sheets had been washed since she'd slept beside him and it had been weeks since she'd even been in his house, he imagined he could smell her sweet scent in the room.

He picked up the phone and called her, but Liz said she'd already gone to bed. "I'm sorry, Mac. She dropped off to sleep a couple of hours ago."

He muttered a curse under his breath, feeling both disappointment and anger. He had an overwhelming need to talk to her tonight, to reassure himself that everything between them was okay.

Okay? Who was he kidding? Nothing was okay. Nothing was even close to okay. She'd made that clear when she'd run away. She made it clear every time she refused to talk to him or return his calls. The last thing she wanted to do was spend her life with him.

"Let me wake her," Liz said.

He rubbed his tired eyes. "No, don't bother."

"Then let me give her a message first thing in the morning. What would you like to tell her?"

Tell her I'm going insane without her and I want her to come home. Tell her I love her.

"Just…that I won't call again. Obviously she doesn't want to talk to me. If she decides she does, she knows where I am."

"I'm so sorry, Mac."

"Yeah, Liz, I'm sorry, too."

After he'd hung up, he tried to sleep but couldn't. Was it possible for a man to be addicted to a woman? Because that was what this felt like. An addiction. And the pain of withdrawal was excruciating.

HIS WEEK WENT from bad to worse the next afternoon when Coach Stewart visited his office.

"Are you telling me Doug Crocker gave this kid Falcon tickets and spending money?" he asked her, bile rising in his throat.

Laura Stewart turned her palms upward in a gesture of uncertainty. "I don't know if it's true, but that's what I heard. This supposedly happened weeks ago, so maybe it's only a rumor. But I thought you should know before it got outside the department."

He felt sweat pop out on his brow as he mentally weighed the consequences if these allegations were true.

Giving gifts to athletes you were trying to recruit was a violation of National Collegiate Athletic Association rules. The track program could face sanctions, probation, fines, a loss of scholarships. Mac would have ample reason to fire Crocker, but he himself might face a reprimand or be fired or demoted by the administration, even though he had no knowledge of Crocker's actions.

"Lack of Institutional Control," the NCAA called it, and he'd seen more than one good athletic director lose his job because of the improper actions of someone beneath him. If the association decided a violation was severe, it could result in the dreaded "Death Penalty," the termination of a program.

But he was getting ahead of himself here. As much as he disliked Crocker, he wouldn't judge him on gossip. He needed more information.

"Someone might be trying to cause trouble for Doug," Laura said, reflecting Mac's thoughts. "You know he's not the most popular person around here because of the way he acts and the things he says about…" She hesitated and flushed red.

"For the things he says about me behind my back?"

"Yes."

"I'm aware of what he says, Laura."

"I don't think a single person in the department would regret seeing him gone, but I hope he didn't do it. If he did, we're all going to suffer for it."

"I'll launch an internal investigation right away. I don't want to make any hasty judgments and ruin a man's career over some locker-room gossip. In the meantime, let's keep a lid on this. The staff doesn't need to be spreading it around."

"I'll do whatever I can to help you."

After getting all the information Laura had, he dismissed her and got on the intercom to Miriam. "Angel, I need you." She was in his office in an instant. "Where's Coach Crocker?"

"Left early. He'll be back Monday morning."

Monday. That was good. That gave Mac the weekend to check out the story and know what he was dealing with.

"What's on my schedule Monday?"

"You have a nine o'clock appointment with Mr. Hartselle from Hartselle Racers to discuss sponsoring the wheelers, but the rest of the day is open."

"I want Doug here waiting when I get out of that meeting. No excuses from him. Whatever else he has, tell him to cancel it."

Rusty Adair, responsible for the university's compliance with NCAA rules, also needed to be in on this, whatever it turned out to be. Mac told her to locate him immediately.

"I'll take care of it."

"Also, look up the number for a kid we're trying to recruit by the name of Willie Jackson, and see if you can get him on the phone for me. He lives with his grandmother in Carrolton. Ida Mae Jackson, I think her name is. The info should be in his file."

"Anything else?"

"Find me a couple of aspirins before my head falls off." He rubbed his throbbing temples and imagined his track program being destroyed because of the stupidity of Doug Crocker. Or maybe it was his *own* stupidity for not facing the demons that had haunted him since the shooting. "Hey, Miriam, better bring the aspirin bottle and leave it here."

CHAPTER NINETEEN

SOMETHING WOKE HER. Keely wasn't sure if it was the rain pounding on the window or something else. The erotic dream still clung to her like a mist, leaving her groggily aroused and her body damp with sweat. For a moment she lay suspended between the dream and reality, not understanding they were separate. She could feel his lips on her breasts and the excruciating pleasure of his hand between her legs, could smell the musky odor of sex on the sheets.

"Mac," she whispered to her phantom lover, but lightning suddenly illuminated the darkness and the empty bed beside her, thrusting her unwillingly toward reality. Mac wasn't here. She was alone.

Happiness gave way to emptiness.

Abruptly she sat up. She turned on the light next to the bed to make the frightening shadows in the room disappear. The clock showed eleven-forty. Mac would be asleep by now, his mouth a little open, a muscled forearm across his eyes. He snored slightly sometimes when he slept on his back, but she found odd comfort in the sound. She missed it now. Missed him.

Perhaps that was what had caused her to wake—the absence of that lulling snore and Mac's arm around her. With him she felt safe from the terror that skulked in the darkness, the one that wore the mask of death.

No, not death. The evil thing that disturbed her nights wasn't death, as she had once believed. Loneliness was its name. At night she was more vulnerable, and the loneliness closed in on her.

She picked up the telephone to call Mac, then quickly put

it down. Picked it up again, only to put it back. With a cry of frustration she fell back on the bed.

This longing inside her was too much to bear. She'd never needed anyone like this, never *allowed* herself to need someone so badly. Even though she knew she had no choice but to give him up, she didn't want to.

She had deceived herself into believing she could make a life with Mac, but she was too much like her mother to succeed. Controlling. Self-centered. And Mac, dear sweet Mac, was an open generous person like her father had been. Marriage between them would be a grave mistake, just like marriage between her mother and father had been a mistake. Their differences would eventually tear them apart.

She had no skills, no talent. The invention of her InsuCare fabric, the only good thing she'd done outside of running, had been a fluke. She hadn't set out to create a medical product and save lives. Oh, no, she wasn't that noble. Her goal had been something as frivolous as exercise clothes.

She was worthless now that she couldn't run. What could she possibly offer Mac that some other woman couldn't? Nothing. Absolutely nothing.

Knowing sleep would elude her, she slipped on a robe and quietly descended the stairs on her way to the kitchen for something to drink. It was quiet except for the occasional rumble of thunder and the ticking of the grandfather clock at the end of the hall. The housekeeper had retired hours earlier to her rooms at the back of the house. And Keely's mother had never been one to stay up late.

But someone was up. The doorway to the den expelled a pale flickering light. Keely walked toward it but stopped short at the sound of a feminine giggle and a man's voice.

"Mmm, that feels so good," the man said. "A little lower and to the... Hey, watch it. You promised no tickling."

"I lied. I love to watch you squirm."

"Oh, yeah? Well, let's see *you* squirm, Miss Prissy Pants."

The sound of a scuffle and more giggling echoed down the dark hall. Keely eased forward until she could see their reflections in the mirror just inside the den. Everett Lathom had her mother pinned to the couch and was tickling her unmercifully. Her hair, always up and tidy, was down and spilled over the cushion, and she had discarded her silk for a pair of jeans and a simple white shirt. Her feet were bare.

Jeans? Bare feet? Keely had never seen her dressed so casually. And the two of them were fooling around like a couple of giddy teenagers in love.

"No more, no more, please," her mother begged.

"Do you give?"

"I give." Instead of turning her loose, he kissed her long and hard. She put her arms around his neck. "Yes, I definitely give. Have I told you today how much I love you?"

"About fifty times, but tell me again."

He laughed as she placed countless kisses across his face and told him she loved him with every one. "Promise me you'll tell me that every day of our married lives."

"That's an easy promise to keep, Everett. I only wish we were getting married tomorrow so I could start."

"We can, you know. All you have to do is say the word. I already have the marriage license and we've taken our blood tests."

"Very tempting, but I want to do this marriage right, with our children and our friends there to bless it. I've never had a real wedding. Spence and I eloped because we were young and foolish, and because my parents didn't approve of me marrying an insurance salesman. I want a real wedding with you. A long dress, flowers, someone singing 'Oh Promise Me.' A storybook wedding. I've dreamed of it."

"Then you'll get it, my love. Whatever makes you happy. I intend to spend the rest of my life pleasing you."

Keely stepped back where she could no longer see, feeling like a voyeur. The moment had been unmistakably tender. To see her mother as a woman with hopes and desires, to hear her dream of a special wedding with the man she loved—it made Keely feel strange, disoriented.

"Are you sure Keely's asleep?" Lathom asked. "She hates me enough without catching me making out with her mother.'' More kissing noises and murmurs of pleasure reached Keely's ears.

''She was when I peeked in on her a little while ago. And she doesn't hate you.''

''She gives a pretty good imitation.''

Her mother sighed loudly. ''I know. At times I want to throttle her for the things she says and does, but she can't help herself. She sees our marriage as a betrayal of her father. If she accepted you, that would simply make the betrayal worse in her mind.''

''You're making excuses for her again. She's a grown woman and she should be acting like one.''

''I'm not making excuses. I know she behaves badly sometimes. But underneath that defensive exterior is a sweet generous woman with a great capacity for love. She's had a difficult life, Everett. All the fighting that went on in this house when she was growing up would have scarred any child. She's never had the emotional security your children had. She has a hard time expressing affection to me because of that.''

Keely, touched by her mother's defense of her, felt a warmth spread through her body.

''Darling,'' Liz continued, ''I'm positive that if the two of you got to know each other better, you'd be friends. You really have so much in common. Maybe if you'd spend some time with her while she's here, you—''

''No. We've already been through this. Every attempt I've made to get along with her she's thrown back in my face. For your sake I'll tolerate her, but I won't go out of my way to see her or be nice to her. She's made it clear she doesn't want anything to do with me.''

With another huge sigh and acceptance of defeat, her mother said, ''All right. I can't say I blame you.''

''How's this week been with the two of you cooped up together? Every night when I get here, I expect to find one of you murdered.''

Every night? So that was why Keely hadn't seen him. He was waiting until she went to bed and then sneaking into the house.

"The week's been surprisingly nice," her mother told him. "She's trying so hard not to get in the way or do anything to upset me."

"Because she doesn't want to derail the gravy train and have you kick her out."

"Now, that's not true. For the first time I believe she truly wants us to get along and put the past behind us."

"You're kidding yourself, Liz. She treats you with contempt. If one of my daughters had talked to me the way yours talked to you the night we told her we were getting married, I'd have put her over my knee and spanked the living daylights out of her, regardless of how old she is."

"She apologized."

"Only because it was to her *advantage* to apologize so she could stay here," he said shortly. "I'll bet you money it wasn't because she was really sorry about hurting your feelings. Has she even once wished you happiness? Has she even once said, 'Mother, I might not agree with your marriage, but I love you and I'll support your decision'? Whether or not she likes me, she should support your getting married again. But she's too busy thinking of herself to see how her attitude is ruining our plans."

In the deafening silence that followed his speech, Keely raised a hand to her throat, feeling a tightness there. His words held a disturbing ring of truth. She'd never said those things to her mother, never even *thought* to say those things.

Guilty as charged.

"You don't think she loves me and wants me to be happy?" A hitch in her mother's voice signaled that tears were imminent. "Just because she doesn't say it doesn't mean—"

"Oh, honey, no, please don't cry. I didn't mean she doesn't love you. Of course she does. I guess it's like you said. She doesn't know how to tell you what she feels."

"I love her so much. She means everything in the world to me."

"I know she does. Please don't get upset."

"I want the three of us to be a family."

"We can. I promise I'll try again with her. Please don't cry."

Lathom tried to quiet the flood without success. Keely's own tears coursed down her face, and she covered her mouth with her hand so the couple wouldn't hear her. She hadn't realized the hurt she'd caused her mother, not only over her impending marriage, but over so many things. As Lathom said, she'd been concerned only with her own feelings.

She backed away and fled to her room, burying her face in the pillow to muffle her tears.

How had things grown so out of whack? As a small child, she and her mother had been close. Nothing had been as comforting after a nightmare or a fall from the swing as putting her head in her mother's lap and feeling that soft hand on her back, to hear her mother say that everything was going to be all right. Her mother's attention had made her feel safe, cherished.

But as she'd grown older, she'd become increasingly less comfortable with Liz's mothering, seen it more as an attempt to orchestrate her life than an expression of love. She'd grown closer to her father. He had never tried to tether her independence, but told her to take risks and follow her heart. He'd encouraged her to resist her mother's control.

And she had. As *he* had resisted it.

She braced herself against the sudden storm of unpleasant memories—of lying awake in this very bed listening to her parents fight in the next room. The worst part had been waiting for the inevitable slamming of the bedroom door and the pounding of her father's footsteps as he angrily marched down the stairs and left the house. Each time she'd been afraid he wouldn't come back.

She'd tried to be good so that wouldn't happen. She'd openly adored her father, tried to be like him. But perhaps she'd taken her struggle for independence from her mother a little too far, needlessly alienating herself from someone who had once been very important to her.

The thought suddenly occurred to Keely that by coming here she might be seeking something she had once treasured, perhaps even needed in her life again—a close relationship with her mother. Only, to have that meant forgiving her mother for the anger and pain her sometimes overbearing ways had caused during the past twenty-five years. *Could* she forgive her? She wanted to so badly. Was it possible to wipe away all the hurt and all the bad memories?

Keely closed her eyes and tried to sort out her feelings, but dawn found her still awake and no closer to the answers she was seeking.

LIZ WALKED INTO THE KITCHEN the next morning to find Keely already dressed and eating one of Louise's orange muffins at the table. For the first time this week she hadn't had to physically pull her daughter out of bed and force her to get dressed.

"Are you all right?"

"Mmm-hmm."

"What are you doing up so early?"

Keely shrugged and slouched in the chair. "I just woke up early and couldn't go back to sleep."

She sounded normal enough, although she'd obviously been crying again. Her eyes were red, as was the tip of her nose. Liz longed to hug her but feared rejection. An occasional touch was all Keely ever allowed. Even then she sometimes stiffened.

"I'm on my way to Sunday School and church," Liz told her. "Would you like to come with me?"

"No, thanks."

"Please don't mope around all day. You've been here over a week and you haven't left the house. Take a walk or sit outside in the garden."

"Well, actually…" She straightened and picked with nervous fingers at her muffin. Two bright spots of color appeared on her cheeks. "I thought I might get the Christmas stuff down from the attic. I could put up the tree and we could decorate it together when you get home. That is, if you want some help."

The offer made Liz stop in the middle of putting on her

coat. Decorate the tree? Had she said *together?* That had always been Keely and Spence's job. After Spence moved out, Liz had done it alone because Keely either wasn't here for Christmas or avoided doing anything with her.

She slid the other arm into her coat and reached for her purse. "That would be wonderful," she told Keely, careful not to act too excited. If she made a fuss, she had no doubt her daughter would withdraw the offer. "I'll see you in a little while."

"Okay, I'll get everything ready while you're gone."

ACCESS TO THE ATTIC was through a set of narrow stairs in the closet of the master bedroom. An unusual place for stairs, Keely had always thought, but as a child she'd loved the idea of having a "secret" room with a hidden entrance. She'd often come here. Creaking noises and shadowed corners hadn't frightened her then, and only added to the room's appeal.

She opened the door at the top of the stairs. When she stepped into the unheated space, a blast of frigid air hit her and almost sent her scurrying back downstairs for a jacket.

She pulled the string to turn on the overhead bulb, revealing a junk lover's paradise of castaway furniture, toys, old hiking gear and boxes upon boxes of what turned out to be clothes sprinkled liberally with mothballs.

Sorting through the clutter wasn't hard, but resisting the treasures among it proved impossible. Each piece of clothing she pulled out and examined brought back a memory: the boots she'd used hiking with Daddy in the mountains in north Georgia, the gown she'd worn to the only high-school dance she'd ever attended, an Easter bonnet from when she was six. She lingered over each article and each memory.

The wardrobe contained some of her father's old suit jackets, and she slipped one on against the chill. The fabric smelled faintly of cedar from the wardrobe and of the cigars her father had enjoyed. Pleasant smells. Pleasant memories.

The rhinestone tiara she'd worn for Halloween when she'd dressed as Cinderella's fairy godmother was lying on top of some costumes in a nearby box. She put it on, then picked up the accompanying magic wand and waved it in the air, in her mind's eye seeing a pumpkin turn into a coach. Foolishness, but it was nice to remember that not all of her childhood had been bad.

A stack of boxes next to the wardrobe had "Keely" written on the cardboard, and a peek inside the top carton revealed Barbie dolls, doll clothes, and the horse figurines she'd developed a passion for collecting one year.

Shaking off the dust from the cardboard flaps, she carried the box to the center of the room and sat down to go through it.

A wistful smile curved her lips when she took out one of the horses. She'd once so loved to play with these. But then she'd starting running and hadn't had time for play. Her father had said that if she wanted to be the best runner in the world, she needed to practice all the time and give up her silly horses. Because she wanted to be the best, because she wanted to please him, she had put the horses, her dolls, all her toys away.

No distractions, kitten. You have to put your whole heart into your running.

She was still on the floor, surrounded by the pieces of her childhood, when her mother climbed the stairs some time later.

"You're back early," Keely said, noticing she'd changed out of her dress and into a pair of slacks and matching sweater.

"The worship service was brief today." Liz rubbed her arms and shivered. "It's freezing up here! I see you got the tree put together in the den. Did you find the decorations?"

"Not yet. I found these and forgot about the decorations." She picked up one of the horses and showed it to her. "Remember when I went through that horse craze?"

Her mother took the horse and turned it over in her hands. "How could I forget? For a whole summer you lived in cowboy boots and jeans, and you wore that awful straw hat everywhere."

"And I begged for a real horse, thinking we could keep it in the backyard."

They both chuckled.

Her mother looked at the oversize jacket Keely was wearing. "Nice outfit, but I don't think the tiara is really you. A little too gaudy."

"I forgot I was wearing it," Keely said with a laugh, touching her head.

To her astonishment her mother sat down next to her, apparently unconcerned about the dirty floor, and together they looked through the figurines. Keely found one of polished wood and only about two inches tall, an intricately carved horse with a female rider. She held it up for her mother to see.

"This was always my favorite. I liked to pretend that was me on the back of the horse."

"It's beautiful."

"Maybe it's not too late for me to be a cowgirl."

Her mother smiled. "I'm glad to see your sense of humor returning. Being able to laugh at yourself will help you get past the hurt."

"I don't have much choice but to laugh at myself. Crying about it hasn't changed anything."

"You know, it might not be a bad idea for you to talk to Ross and tell him what's happened. He needs to know you're not going to be running so he can advise you on what to do."

"I already have an idea what he'll advise me to do. I've had some offers."

"Oh?"

"They came in after I got hurt, before I knew I'd have to retire. I didn't take them seriously at the time, but I'm sure Ross will want me to consider them now—if they're still available."

"What kind of offers?"

"A couple of endorsements for television commercials and print ads. One's for a soft-drink company. The other is modeling underwear. And a job with ABC Sports."

"Underwear?" Her mother's surprise turned to amusement.

"Somebody wants *you* to model underwear? Do they realize you have an aversion to underwear?"

Keely's lips twitched. "I guess it is pretty ironic."

"What's the sports job?"

"Doing commentary and interviewing competitors for track events and for the Olympics in Sydney. The offer's good. Nice pay. I'd be traveling all over the world between now and then, visiting the athletes in their hometowns and putting together reports on their training. Most people would kill for the opportunity."

"Are you considering it?" Her mother's look said she hoped not.

"I probably should, but it's just not right for me. I'd planned to compete in the next Olympics, not sit in a commentator's booth and talk about who's competing. I'm not a broadcaster or an underwear model or a soft-drink hawker. I'm an athlete." With a humorless smile she added, "At least in my heart I still am."

"Have you given any thought to what you'll do?"

"A little bit but I haven't made any decisions yet."

"Why not get more involved in your company?"

"I've considered that, but I don't have any business experience. I balance my checkbook, and that's it. Ross handles everything else." She began putting the horses and dolls back in the box with her mother's help.

"It's never too late to learn, Keely."

"I suppose that's true."

"And what about Mac? The man's in love with you, and unless I've completely misread the situation, you're in love with him. You have to include him in any plans you make."

"Do I?"

"Yes, of course you do."

Keely just shrugged, not commenting.

"Sweetheart, it *is* possible for a man and woman to have a healthy lasting relationship. Just because your father and I couldn't make our marriage work doesn't mean that all marriages fail or that marriage brings unhappiness. You do understand that, don't you?"

"Yes."

"Do you? Then why are you here when the man who adores you is hundreds of miles away?"

Keely shook her head. "Maybe because I haven't figured out yet how our being together could work. We're such opposites."

Her mother squeezed her arm. "You'll figure it out. Stop looking at it with your head and see it with your heart."

"Okay, I'll try." Keely closed the box, had a thought and opened it again. She took out the miniature carved horse. "Can I keep this one? Gran gave it to me, and except for the jewelry she left me when she died, I don't have anything that reminds me of her."

"Of course you can keep it. It's yours. Keep all of them if you want and the dolls, too, if you have a use for them."

Keely put the horse in her pocket. Her hand touched paper, and she pulled it out and unfolded it.

"Maybe the children of that friend of yours would like them," her mother was saying. "What's her name? Nicki something?"

"Vicki Sizemore."

"Didn't you tell me she had two or three children? We could pack these up and send them to her."

Her mother's voice seemed to come from far away. The blood had drained from Keely's head, making it impossible to think clearly or even respond. Her attention wasn't on the dolls but on the handwritten note she'd found in her father's jacket. She read it a second time, because her mind refused to accept what it said.

Spencer, darling, I can't wait another minute to see you. Eight tonight. I've reserved our usual room. The wine will be room temperature but I'll be very, very hot. I love you.

Your wicked Angela.

Stunned, Keely could only sit there and stare at the paper, trying to reconcile the apparent adulterer with the sweet lov-

ing man who was her father. Her heart said he could never
have been so deceitful, yet reason told her she held the damn-
ing evidence in her hand.

"Sweetheart, what's wrong? You're white as a sheet."

Keely's body began to shake uncontrollably. No, it was all
a mistake. Her father wasn't capable of this.

"Keely?" Panic threaded her mother's voice. "What have
you found?"

Keely looked up to find herself staring into a face as white
as her own. "Nothing. Nothing...really." Her mother reached
for the paper, but Keely crumpled it. "Only trash," she said,
but her shaking, the warble of her voice, revealed the lie.

"Keely, give it to me."

"No, Mother. Don't read it."

"Give it to me." She pried the letter from Keely's fist.

"Please, don't read it."

But she did. And when she did, her eyes closed briefly and
her body seemed to sag with the weight of the discovery. The
letter slipped from her hand onto the floor. "Oh, no," she
whispered so softly Keely had to strain to hear her. "I thought
I'd burned all the letters years ago."

"You knew about his relationship with this woman?"

Then it had to be true. Her father had had an affair! In an
instant, years of respect, love and pride for him turned to
disillusionment.

No! *This* was what had broken apart their marriage. *He* had
destroyed their family. Not her mother!

With painful clarity she remembered the many times she'd
taken her father's side against her mother, times when he'd
come in late from "working" and her mother had been furious. She remembered the many times she and her father had
excluded her mother intentionally by choosing activities she
didn't like—the ball games, the hiking trips—and left her to
sit home alone. And Keely had let her mother know she preferred to be in her father's company.

How that must have hurt her.

A sob tore from her throat. The room began to spin and

her breakfast started to come up. "I think I'm going to be sick."

Her mother was kneeling next to her in a second, pushing her head down. "Put your head as low as you can and take deep breaths."

"I didn't understand!" Keely cried, the tears pouring from her eyes. "I've been so hateful to you about the divorce because I thought it was your fault, but all the time it was him who wrecked everything. I'm so sorry. I'm so very sorry."

"Hush, now. Don't talk. Just close your eyes and take deep breaths."

Several minutes passed before Keely felt well enough to sit up. Unable to stand the touch of her father's jacket, she pulled it off and threw it on the floor. "I hate him!"

"No, you don't hate him. He was a human being who made mistakes. And regardless of how he felt about me or our marriage, he loved you."

"Was he in love with *her?*" The question took all of Keely's courage to ask.

"You don't want to know about this," her mother said, brushing the hair back from Keely's face. "Knowing will only hurt you. And it happened such a long time ago. The best thing is to accept that it happened and then put it behind you."

"I couldn't hurt any more than I'm hurting right now."

"Yes, you can, and I've tried so hard to protect you from it. You'd be better off not knowing the details."

"No, don't protect me anymore. I need to know what happened. All this time I believed the problems between you and Daddy were your fault. I've blamed you for everything. For the fights. The divorce."

Her mother's tears began to fall now, leaving streaks on her cheeks and dark mascara smudges under her eyes. "I know you have, and it ripped me apart."

"Please, tell me the truth. Did he love this woman?"

An ominous silence stretched between them and Keely held her breath. At last her mother spoke. "No, he didn't love her. I don't think he ever really loved any of them."

CHAPTER TWENTY

"IT'S WAY TOO QUIET in there," Alan said, straining to hear the muffled voices through the closed door of Mac's office. For the past forty-five minutes the level of the conversation had gone up and down. At the moment it was low, but Alan wasn't sure if that was a good sign or a bad one. He pushed to Miriam's desk. "Buzz him and pretend he has a call or something. Maybe you can hear what they're talking about."

She gave him one of her not-on-your-life looks.

"What'll it hurt? Buzz him and say I dropped by to take him to lunch. See if you can tell what kind of mood he's in, at least." Miriam didn't seem to be softening, so he leaned toward her and added with his most engaging grin, "Come on, beautiful, you know you're just as curious as I am about what's happening in there."

"Mac gave me strict instructions that he wasn't to be disturbed on the intercom or in person for any reason—so shoo." She waved him back. "And don't think you can bat those long eyelashes and get your way with me, Dr. Sizemore. I'm wise to your tricks."

"Oh, doll, you wound me. If only I *could* get my way with you, I'd be the happiest man on earth."

She scolded him for being an outrageous flirt but couldn't quite hide her amusement. "I don't know how your wife puts up with your antics."

"I'm so cute she can't help herself." That made her chuckle so he pressed his advantage. "Okay, buzzing him is a bad idea, but can't you tell me what's going on and who the third person is? I recognize Crocker's voice but not the other guy's. Is Mac firing Crocker? What did he do?"

"What Mac wants you to know, I'm sure Mac will tell you."

"Aw, Miriam, you're killing me."

"Don't 'aw, Miriam' me. I honestly don't know what Coach Crocker did, and even if I did know, I couldn't say a word. Mac would have my hide."

"He didn't tell you anything?"

"Not a hint, but I've never seen him in such a black mood as he's been in during the past week."

"That's not all work-related."

"I guessed that, since I haven't seen a certain young lady around here lately, but I don't pry into Mac's personal life. There's enough gossip about the two of them in this department without me adding to it."

"Crocker-initiated gossip?"

"Uh-huh."

"Figures."

Alan scratched his jaw. What *was* going on? Mac had taken a mysterious business trip out of town on Saturday, canceling their plans to work out together. When Alan had asked him about the trip and if something other than Keely had him so on edge, he'd said it was a problem with one of his coaches and he'd tell him about it later.

Alan didn't have to wonder who the coach was, but he was curious about what that coach had done. And he was itching to know what Mac planned to do about him.

The volume of the voices on the other side of the door escalated again, this time to an alarming level. Crocker's angry voice rang out.

"You can't fire me! I've given seventeen years of my life to this place!"

Mac's calm response was too low to hear, but Crocker told Mac loudly what he thought of him, his speech sprinkled with expletives and accusations of unfair treatment. The verbal attack brought the third man into the dispute; he warned Crocker repeatedly to "back off and sit down."

Alan and Miriam looked at each other in concern. "This is

getting way out of hand,'' Alan told her. He pushed toward the door.

Miriam jumped up and blocked his way with her considerable bulk. ''Don't even *think* about going in there, buster.''

''But Mac might need my help.''

''He's capable of taking care of himself.''

''Yeah, but—''

''No buts. You're not going in there.''

From Mac's office they heard the sound of a scuffle. A split second later someone yelped in pain.

Miriam's confidence wavered and she whirled and reached for the knob. Before she could open the door, Crocker opened it from the other side and barreled out. Miriam, knocked backward by his hasty exit, landed in Alan's lap with the force of a cannonball being fired. She pressed the breath right out of him, along with his voice.

Mac pushed through the door right behind Crocker, followed by the third man from the office, Rusty Adair, Mac's rules-compliance officer. Both jolted to a stop at the sight of Miriam sprawled in Alan's lap.

''Miriam? Alan? What the…?'' Mac asked.

Before Alan could answer, Miriam gasped in horror. ''Mac, you're bleeding!'' She leaped to her feet and rushed over, trying to find the source of the blood.

Alan saw big splotches of it down the front of Mac's white shirt, blood and red marks on his neck, but no wounds. ''Buddy, you okay?''

''Yeah, I'm okay.'' Mac gently clasped Miriam's hands to stop their probing. ''Angel, I'm okay. The blood's not mine— it's Doug's.'' He turned to Adair. ''Rusty, see if you can find him and get him to the emergency room. I think I broke his nose.''

THE TRACK at Keely's former high school was nearly deserted. Only three runners were dedicated enough to be out in the freezing weather. They puffed as they made their laps, their breath turning to steam in the frigid air.

Keely sat on the steps and watched them for a long time,

remembering how this place had once been an important part of her life, as it probably was now for these young people. Here was where she'd come so many Saturdays with her father to train. Here was where she'd gained attention as a high-school runner.

She could almost hear her father as he coaxed her to work harder. *You can be the best in the whole world. Fight for it. C'mon. That's it. Faster. Keep going. Get tough. Show me you want it.*

She had wanted it more than anything, or so she'd believed back then. Now she wondered if maybe what she'd wanted most wasn't to be the best but to please her father. When she'd run well, it had made him happy, and when he was happy, it had eased the tension at home and given her a brief taste of what it felt like to be part of a loving family.

These many years after his death, maybe she was still trying to please him, or at least equating happiness with living up to his expectations.

After her failed running trial, she had looked at the good-luck ribbon her father had given her, and her first thought had been, *I've failed him. Now I'll never be happy.* She'd thrown the ribbon in the trash because it no longer represented her hope but her failure.

The loving father she'd adored and been so desperate to please hadn't been worth her adoration. Spencer Wilson. Cheater. Adulterer. She had spent most of her life believing he was a saint and blaming the unhappiness in her family on her mother.

The only time your mother's happy is when she's telling people what to do and how to act.

His words had been so easy to believe, growing up. Her mother had often seemed exactly as he described her, domineering and critical. She'd nagged about everything, found fault with every decision Keely had made from the clothes she'd bought to the few friends she'd chosen. She still nagged.

Was it like her father said, out of a need to control? Or was it merely a mother's way of showing concern?

Keely couldn't trust her memories to tell her the truth, because they were tainted by her father's deception.

Disturbed, she let out a long rattling breath. How could she put everything in perspective? She had too much pain to sift through, too many decision to make about her life.

A burst of wind danced across the track, reaching out to touch everything with its icy fingers. The force of it whirled bits of trash and sent the slender pines between the track and the baseball field swaying in an out-of-kilter rhythm. She shivered and slid her feet closer, tugging her jacket over her knees. She slipped her hands into the slash pockets. The night would be cold, perhaps the coldest of the season.

A bittersweet smile curved her lips as she thought of Mac and cold nights in front of the fire on his mother's quilt. They would talk and laugh and warm each other with hot sex. Oh, how she missed those times, missed the I-belong-here feeling she got when she was with him.

Those months she'd spent in Courtland had been good for her spirit, as well as her body, even though she hadn't saved her running career. For the first time in years she'd felt needed. By Mac. By the wheelers. By the students. The adrenaline high she'd experienced when a student suddenly understood a difficult problem was every bit as powerful as the high from winning a race.

But was a career in coaching and teaching really what she wanted?

No. With a heaviness of heart she had to admit it wasn't. She liked working with the students, but she couldn't see herself doing it every day for the rest of her life.

Out on the track, one of the young men slowed to a jog to cool down, then did a few easy stretches. He walked to the edge where he'd left his gear bag and changed into tennis shoes, also swapping his woolen hat for a baseball cap. Covertly, he looked at her from beneath the bill.

Keely pulled up the collar on her jacket to bury as much of her face as she could, but he was openly staring now. He walked toward her. ''Hey, aren't you Keely Wilson, the run—?''

"No, I'm not. I'm not her." She retreated up the steps and fled to the house, tired of being defined only by what she used to do. Mac was right. She could start over and do something else. She was bright. She had good ideas. She could learn to do anything she set her mind to. She was more than just a set of legs.

"Miss Keely's coming up the front walk," the housekeeper called from upstairs.

The fear that had risen in Liz with the passing hours melted to relief. "Thank you, Louise." She rushed from the den to the front door and ushered her daughter inside where it was warm. "I wish you'd told us you were going out. I got scared when I realized you weren't in the house."

"You were on the telephone and Louise was busy vacuuming." Keely coughed and cleared her throat. Her face looked frozen and she had nothing on her head or hands.

"Where on earth are your hat and gloves?"

"I forgot them." She slipped out of her lightweight jacket.

"Honestly, what were you thinking, going out with nothing on your head and only that flimsy thing when it's thirty-five degrees? Your system's already had a shock. Do you want to make yourself sick?"

"Mother, I'm not five anymore. Please don't nag me."

Liz's heart filled with regret. "You're right. I'm sorry." She took the jacket from Keely's arms and searched the foyer closet for a hanger. "I guess when I see you do something I think will hurt you, it's hard for me not to speak out. My concern for you didn't go away when you grew up."

When she didn't get a response, Liz glanced over her shoulder. Keely was staring at her as if she'd spoken in an unintelligible foreign tongue.

"You nag because you love me, don't you?" Keely asked.

The strange question surprised Liz. "Yes, of course. Because I love you very much."

Keely's face softened and one corner of her mouth eased upward into a soft smile. "Just checking."

Liz hung the jacket on the rod and closed the door. "How about a nice cup of hot tea to knock off the chill?"

She led the way to the den where a fire burned in the grate and a fresh pot of tea sat steeping on a silver tray on one of the end tables. The bare Christmas tree stood to one side of the fireplace, a visual reminder of things left unfinished.

When they were comfortably seated on the couch, Liz poured tea into a china cup and squeezed lemon into it. "Here, the lemon will soothe your throat."

Keely took the cup and saucer in her cold-reddened hands and inhaled the vapors. "Hot tea and lemon. How many times do you suppose you made my sore throats feel better with hot tea and lemon when I was little?"

"Oh, a few, as I recall." She shifted and tucked one leg under her so she could face Keely and not have to turn her head. Keely did the same. "You were never a sickly child, but you were prone to getting a tickle in cold weather."

"You always worried that the tickle would turn into something more serious, so you'd rub that menthol stuff on my throat and chest, then pin a washcloth to the inside of my nightgown so it wouldn't get greasy. I almost enjoyed getting sick because it felt so good when you fussed over me." Keely frowned suddenly. Her throat worked as if trying to handle something too large to swallow. "I'd forgotten that until this moment. I haven't thought about it in years."

"Sometimes the mind hides away memories, even good ones, until we're ready to face how they make us feel."

Keely nodded slowly. "Maybe that's true. This morning I've been flooded with memories of growing up in this house, of spending time with Daddy." She looked down into her cup. "And not being willing to spend time with you."

Her hand trembled, making the cup clatter on the saucer, so she set both on the coffee table. She hugged her arms tightly to keep them still, but they shook, anyway, as did her whole body. "I think my mind's trying to tell me it's time to face those memories, the good ones and the bad ones."

Liz prayed that was true. In the forty-eight hours since Keely had learned of her father's affairs, she'd done little but lie on the bed and gaze at the ceiling, tuning out everything around her. Liz, meanwhile, had spent those same hours torturing herself with questions. Would the revelation finally bring her daughter back to her? Or break the remaining threads holding their relationship together?

Guilt accompanied the questions, guilt for thinking about her own needs when her only child was dealing with two devastating events that had occurred in the past ten days.

"I'm sorry you found out about your father, especially now when you've already had so much other disappointment."

"I never thought anything could hurt me as much as not being able to run again, but finding that letter…"

"Oh, honey, I know. That's why I kept the truth from you when you were living at home. I thought it would be so much easier for you if you believed your father and I didn't get along because of our different personalities and backgrounds. That was the heart of the problem, yes, but not what finally ended the marriage."

"Why did you continue to keep the truth from me after I left to go to school? Or after you and Daddy separated? Even after he died and I so stupidly accused you of causing his heart attack, you never fought back. We've argued about the divorce a million times in the past eight years, and not one of those times did you tell me the real reason for it. Why?"

"Answer me truthfully. If I'd told you I filed for divorce because your father was unfaithful, would you have believed me?"

Keely's eyes provided the answer long before she spoke. "No, I would never have believed that, not in a million years."

"Of course not. You worshiped him. You would have resented me even more than you already did if I dared make an accusation like that. I couldn't risk alienating you further."

"I'm sorry." Keely's bottom lip trembled. "I never even gave you the chance to tell me the truth."

"No, don't apologize. I don't blame you for anything that's happened. I know I'm often too rigid and you resent it. I suspect your father also set out to deliberately turn you against me. Am I right?''

Keely stood and walked to the fireplace to stare silently into the flames. Liz followed. She wanted to put her arms around her daughter, but years of rebuke had made her fearful. She stood a comfortable distance away, pretending to straighten a photograph on the mantel, and waited for Keely to decide if she truly was ready to face her memories.

''At the time,'' Keely finally said, her voice small and filled with hurt, ''I didn't understand that's what Daddy was doing, but I've been thinking about it, and yes, he did his best to make things worse between us. He said things, did things, to make sure I didn't trust your love. Finding ways to exclude you got to be a game between us.''

Liz had thought so, but whenever she confronted Spence, he'd denied it. He'd said she was too critical of Keely and only had herself to blame if her daughter didn't like being around her. For a while Liz was too occupied with trying to keep her marriage together to even see that Keely had started to withdraw from her. When she did finally notice something was wrong, it was already too late to repair the damage.

''I suspected it. When you were small we were so close. You used to throw those sweet little arms around me and hug me as tightly as you could and say, 'I love you, Lis-bet,' trying to imitate your grandmother.''

''I didn't have any front teeth and I couldn't pronounce Elizabeth.''

''Then, suddenly, I became 'Mother' and you didn't even want me touching me. I know the fighting between me and your father didn't help, and that your running was something you and he shared that we couldn't. But I always sensed there was more to your sudden aversion to me.''

''He warned me that I'd gotten too close to you and that you would use that to hurt me. He said...no matter what I did or how hard I tried to please you, it would never be enough, that you were cold and could never love me as much as he did.''

''Dear God!''

"So I stopped trying to win your approval. Only his."

The tears that had pooled in Keely's eyes when they started this conversation began to fall quietly now. Liz, too, felt the sting of tears; the depth of Spence's deceit was like a knife to the heart.

"Why, Mother? Why did he do it?"

"I'm not sure I know. His desire to hurt me. Fear of losing you in a custody battle if we divorced. He seemed to have a constant need for validation, to see proof that people loved him, yet even when he had proof, he wouldn't believe it. He wasn't treated well as a child. His mother showed him little affection, and his father left them when he was very small. I can only guess that had something to do with his affairs and his lies."

Keely swiped at her tears. "I thought I hated him, but all I feel is this dull empty ache where my feelings for him used to be. I don't feel hate or love, just...nothing."

"Perhaps one day you can feel love again. Or at least forgiveness. Despite his faults, he was your father and he loved you very much."

Keely turned her head. "Do *you* forgive him?"

Liz wanted to answer honestly but wasn't sure how. The affairs, the years of lies, had devastated not only her marriage but her self-esteem. She'd been a carefree trusting girl when she married Spence, but he'd quickly changed her into a hard suspicious woman. Only with Everett's love had that carefree girl come to life again.

And yet, for most of the years of her marriage to Spence, she had to admit she loved him desperately. She'd clung stubbornly to the ideal of commitment and to her vows, despite every horrible thing he said and every woman he'd thrown in her face. Even now, even when she no longer loved him, she wanted to believe that something good had come from their marriage, something other than this child who stood next to her.

Could she forgive him? She had to. For Keely's chance at a happy future and for her own.

"Yes, I forgive him," she said. "I forgive him because

that's the only way I can free myself of him. I want to go forward without regret, to wake up every morning without having the pain of the past influence my every thought, my every decision.''

''I wish I could find the same peace of mind, and not only over this thing with Daddy but the accident and the other problems in my life.''

''You can. Take one step forward. Then another. And another.''

''Kind of like running a race.''

''Yes, I suppose it is.''

''Do you think that approach would work for mending a relationship? I've badly hurt someone I love.''

Mac, Liz thought. *She's talking about Mac.*

''I don't see why not. You can damage love, but it isn't easily destroyed. Take the first step and let Mac know you love him. See what happens.''

Keely's face, always an open reflection of the emotion that lay underneath, was a dark canvas of sadness, regret and pain; but also held the paler colors of resolution and hope.

To Liz's surprise, she took a step closer. Her heart stilled as her daughter reached out her arms, asking to be held for the first time in more than fifteen years.

''I meant you,'' Keely said softly, her chin quivering. ''I love you, Liz-bet.''

CHAPTER TWENTY-ONE

CHRISTMAS EVE had turned the athletic complex into a cata-comb of eerily empty rooms. Reporters wanting a comment kept the telephones ringing all afternoon, but the calls finally died off at about eight. The two souls, besides Mac, who'd been foolish enough to come in today had long ago gone home to be with their families. Mac had no one waiting at home, so he lingered, the silence here somehow easier to bear than the silence of his little house.

He could go to Alan's or catch a flight out to spend the holiday with his sisters or brother, but the idea of kissing someone else's wife under the mistletoe and playing with someone else's children after Christmas dinner didn't appeal to him this year. He preferred, instead, the mindless act of updating files, of rearranging the books in his office according to subject.

His written report on the now-infamous nose-breaking in-cident was typed and ready to deliver to the university pres-ident after Christmas, a follow-up to his oral report, already given. Neither he nor the university had yet released an offi-cial statement on Doug Crocker's dismissal, but the story had shot through the staff, then the college community, like wild-fire. The news had hit the Associated Press sports wire that afternoon.

A cold. A stupid cold had saved the track program from sanctions. Mac shook his head, still unable to believe it. The kid, Willie Jackson, hadn't used the tickets Crocker had im-properly given him. He'd caught a cold and his grandmother had made him stay home from the game.

Willie also claimed Crocker hadn't given him any money.

Mac was certain that was a lie, although he couldn't prove it. But neither could anyone else.

Because the kid hadn't used the tickets and because no evidence of a gift of money existed, technically Crocker hadn't violated NCAA rules. The track program was safe from sanctions.

But Crocker *had* killed his career at Courtland. The university supported Mac, both in his investigation of the alleged violation and in his subsequent firing of Crocker for unethical recruiting practices. If the broken nose became an issue, Rusty Adair could testify that Mac had only defended himself against an unprovoked physical attack. The bruises on Mac's throat, where Crocker had tried to choke him, were evidence enough.

Still…the situation should never have gotten to the point of physical violence. Mac had screwed up. Maybe not in the eyes of his superiors or staff, but in his own eyes.

He'd done the right thing in firing Doug. He was comfortable with his decision. If he was going to be honest, he'd even admit he'd *enjoyed* popping him in the nose. But Mac knew he'd definitely done the wrong thing in letting his disability interfere with doing his job. By failing to deal with Doug Crocker's improper behavior months ago, he'd created an explosive situation. He'd turned Doug into the living, breathing personification of the fears Mac still had about being in a wheelchair.

Pretty stupid, McCandless.

Down the hall a drink machine burped as if in agreement.

Never again would he let self-doubt keep him from doing what was right. Never again would he allow this wheelchair to keep him from going after what he wanted in his professional—or personal—life.

He was giving Keely twenty-four hours to get her feelings straightened out. Let her spend Christmas with her mom, but then he was going to Atlanta to bring her home. Never mind his promise to stay away. If she loved him, she had to tell him so. If she didn't love him, she had to tell him that, too. And to his face.

With no filing left to be done and the books arranged in a long colorful row, he decided it was foolish to hang around any longer. He locked up the office and headed home.

The streets of downtown were deserted, the stores dark. The garlands of green that looped in intervals along the utility wires swayed in the cold wind as he passed underneath them.

At the Sizemores' house, the multicolored lights on a tree in the window blinked on and off in cheery welcome, and a lighted Santa in the yard waved hello. But at Mac's house...

He stopped the van in the street and stared.

His front window also had a tree.

"Vicki," he grumbled. He wished she hadn't bothered. Sometimes women had a hard time understanding that men need their own unviolated space.

He punched the remote to open the garage door, then parked. The soft light of the Christmas tree spilled into the kitchen to guide him to the living room. Beneath the tree he recognized the packages he'd wrapped for Alan, Vicki and the kids, but the others had been put there by a different hand.

Shrugging out of his jacket, he tossed it toward a nearby chair. He picked up a red-foil package with an elaborate bow and read the name tag. "To Mac, from Keely."

Keely?

"I was beginning to think you were never coming home."

Startled by the voice, he dropped the package, sending it sliding across the hardwood floor. He whirled the chair around. His heart beat in double time as he saw what he couldn't see before. Keely lay on her side on his mother's quilt before the fireplace watching him, her head resting in one hand.

She sat up and tucked her jean-clad legs under her. "I was afraid you might run the other way if you saw my car, so Alan let me park it in his garage," she said, as if that explained everything. It didn't. Not by a long shot. "I heard about your fight with Crocker. Are you okay?"

She'd momentarily stunned him, but he found his voice quickly now. "Is that why you came back?"

"No, Alan only just told me about it."

"Then what are you doing here?"

"Getting cozy. I hear it's going to be a cold night." She patted the quilt. "Come down here with me? We can start a fire. I'd love to hear one of your family stories." When he didn't move, uncertainty clouded her face. She retracted her hand. "I was hoping you'd be at least a little glad to see me."

"Glad? I'm angry as hell at you! You ran out on me without a word, and the worry from that alone took a good ten years off my life. Then you gave the knife a couple of extra twists by acting like I wasn't important enough to talk to when I called your mother's. Do you have any idea how that made me feel?"

"Foolish. Abused. Unloved."

"You've got that straight!"

She blew out a troubled breath. "Okay, that's fair. I hurt you deeply and you have every right to be angry. But do you think you might put your anger aside for a few minutes and give me the chance to talk to you, to apologize?"

He didn't answer immediately.

"Mac, please don't be hardheaded. That's *my* job."

Begrudgingly he agreed. "Okay, I'm listening."

"I'm sorry I hurt you. I wish I could say I was only running away from the pain of losing what I thought was the most important thing in my life. But the truth is…I was running away from you, too. You're the first man to tell me he loved me and truly mean it. And then on top of everything else I was dealing with at the moment, you said you wanted to marry me. Pretty serious stuff to throw at me right then."

"My timing was lousy," he said stiffly.

"Yes, it was. But I'm not telling you this to make you feel bad for what you said, only to try and explain why I ran away. Failing my running test and having you propose was way too much for me to handle at one time. You know the old saying—Out of sight, out of mind. I thought getting away would make my problems disappear."

"Denying your problems doesn't solve them. I've learned that lesson the hard way."

"No, you're right. But leaving did turn out to be good for

me in one way. Mother and I cleared up the misunderstandings that have been keeping us apart. We talked and got everything out in the open, and I feel really good about our
relationship now. It still needs work, but the hard part is behind us. She and Everett even agreed to let me be part of the
wedding.''

"You're okay now with them getting married?"

She nodded. "Daddy made her miserable for years. Everett
is a nice man who's very much in love with her. He'll be
good to her. With him she can finally be happy."

"So old what's-his-name isn't such a bad guy, after all?"

"No, old what's-his-name is pretty okay. I invited him to
the house to help decorate the Christmas tree, and I actually
enjoyed talking with him. Having a stepfather will take some
getting used to, but it might be nice."

"And you'll be getting the sisters you always wanted."

"Sisters?"

"Remember the pictures he showed us of his two daughters
when he was here? They'll be your stepsisters."

"Oh, I hadn't thought of that," she said, her eyes shining.
"Sisters. I got sisters for Christmas, just like I asked."

"I'm glad for you, Keely. Sounds like the time spent at
your mother's was pretty special."

A sudden shadow of pain crossed her face. "Yes, mostly.
Something not so special happened, too, something I won't
go into right now. But the result of it was like finding the
missing piece in a big puzzle. Once I had that piece, I was
able to step back and see the complete picture of my life. For
the first time I could put running, and why it meant so much
to me, into perspective. Finding that piece also helped me
come to terms with some hard truths about myself."

"Like what?"

"Like understanding that I'm very much like my mother.
For years I've tried to convince myself it isn't true. But it *is*,
and I'm not ashamed to admit it. I'm even proud of it, because
I've discovered she's a very strong woman."

"You inherited her strength."

"I hope so. I also inherited some of her faults, like the

need to always feel in control. That, too, has bothered me for a long time. But I've come to accept that being like my mother doesn't automatically mean I'm going to make the same mistakes she did."

Keely moved forward and knelt in front of him, but thankfully not so close that he could reach out and touch her. The temptation to draw her into his arms and try to soothe the tired lines around her eyes with his lips was overwhelming. Only distance saved him from the humiliation of letting her know how easily he could forgive her.

"Mac, when I realized I could never compete professionally again, it devastated me. Running has always been a major part of who I am. It doesn't have to be the only part, though. You've forced me to understand that. You've made me peel back all the outside layers to find a person inside me that I had no idea was even there. And you know what? I can learn to like that person. She's not as worthless as she thought she was."

"I've been telling her that for months."

"I know," she conceded. "But…the next thing I'm going to say will disappoint you, I'm afraid. She also doesn't want to be a coach. I know you hoped that by getting me back in school, I'd come to love coaching as much as you do, but I'm sorry, I don't. Getting my master's degree in Health and Human Performance is a waste of my time."

Hope shattered. She was dropping out of school and leaving town permanently. Leaving him. He tried to keep his voice level when he asked, "What will you do?"

"I've decided Coxwell Industries needs a working president rather than one who only playacts. I enjoy being in the chemistry lab a great deal, and I have hundreds of ideas for products I'd like to develop, so I've told Ross I'm going into full commercial production with the InsulCare fabric. I'm going to run my own business."

For her sake he tamped down the sorrow of losing her. He would deal with it when he was alone.

"Keely Wilson, corporate bigwig. Sounds pretty good."

He tried to smile, but couldn't. The thought of her living

hundreds of miles away in Miami was as awful a thing as he could imagine.

"That description isn't at all what I had in mind," she said. "I want to be Keely *McCandless,* corporate bigwig."

He wasn't sure he heard her correctly. "Run that by me again?"

"What I'm clumsily trying to tell you is that I've realized no career alone can make me happy. Running my own business appeals to me very much. I'm even looking forward to finishing school once I change my major to chemistry. But if I woke up tomorrow and discovered by some miracle I could race and compete professionally again, even that couldn't make me happy. Only you can do that."

Something warm and beautiful filled her eyes. She seemed to glow in the twinkling lights from the tree.

"Mac, the instant you walked across that track eleven years ago and introduced yourself, my life changed. I've spent years caring for you in one way or another. You've been my mentor, my teacher and my coach. Eventually, you became my friend and my lover. But I panicked when you said you loved me. My parents failed miserably at their relationship, and I convinced myself the same thing would happen to us. I didn't believe I had enough substance to truly make you happy."

He opened his mouth to tell her that wasn't true, but she held up her hand and stopped him.

"No, let me finish. You need to hear this and I need to say it. I've never been thoughtful enough of other people. Lord knows, you deserve to spend your life with someone who's a lot smarter and a lot less emotional than I am. Ever since you proposed, I've racked my brain trying to come up with even one thing I have to offer you that no other woman can. Now, finally, I've done it. I know what makes me perfect for you and why we have to get married."

"And that is?"

"No other woman on this earth could possibly love you as much as I do."

He closed his eyes for a moment and thanked God. "I

thought you came here to tell me you were leaving me for good.''

"Leaving you? No, my love, I'm not leaving you. You're the best thing in my life, and I want the chance to prove I can be the best thing in yours. I intend to spend the next sixty years making you glad to wake up every morning beside me. If you'll have me.'' She held out her arms to him. ''Will you grow old with me?''

He wasn't sure how he got from the wheelchair to the floor so fast, but suddenly he was holding her, and she was laughing and crying at the same time.

"Is this a yes?'' she asked. He kissed her hard, then more slowly with passion, again and again, until the familiar catlike purr of desire started in her throat and her body hummed with desire. ''Mmm. John Patrick McCandless, I do love the way you say yes.''

CHAPTER TWENTY-TWO

October 2000
Sydney, Australia

THE MARATHON was the longest of Keely's life, two hours
and thirty minutes of torture that had her insides churning and
her heart beating so fast it threatened to explode from her
chest.

She tried taking deep breaths. She tried shallow ones, but
neither made her feel better. Every passing minute brought a
new agony and reinforced doubt. Had attempting this race
been a terrible mistake?

Just when she thought she might pass out from the stress,
the race leaders entered the Olympic stadium. Torture turned
to sheer terror. Mac and a member of the Canadian team were
in front of their division, side by side, racing their wheelchairs
for the finish line. Even on the huge video screens overhead
it was impossible to tell who was leading.

One man would take home the gold medal; the other would
take home the silver.

"Please," Keely prayed out loud, but the cheering of the
crowd behind her obliterated her words.

More than 125 nations were represented here in Sydney,
but international boundaries dissolved the moment the announcer said Mac's name. He was a hero. His and Keely's
story, leaked by his staff to *The Atlanta Journal* and broadcast
by the wire services, had endeared him to people all over the
world. They knew he was trying to win a gold medal for her.
Now, 110,000 fans let him know by their screams and waving
arms that they supported him.

Amid the chaos, Keely continued to stand in the trainers' area and pray. Mac had worked so hard to make the U.S. team. He'd raced on weekends and trained every night after work for more than two years. This moment meant everything to him, to both of them.

The marathon wasn't his usual event. He was so much stronger in the four hundred and eight hundred meters. But he'd insisted that with her help he had a chance.

"I have to try the marathon," he'd told her. "For my dreams and for yours."

Now he was only seconds away from either capturing their dreams or losing them forever, and the crowd, the millions of people around the world watching live on television, knew what was at stake.

Thirty yards to go.

Fifteen yards to go.

"You can do it," she whispered, as if he could hear her. Before the race, she'd pinned her father's faded ribbon to Mac's jersey for luck. But it would take more than luck now. Everything was up to Mac. He had to *want* to win, not for her, but for himself.

He seemed to surge. He crossed the finish line half a wheel in front of the Canadian, and the victory sent the spectators and the U.S. team into a frenzy.

People began hugging and kissing Keely. Television reporters tried to snag her for a comment, but she fought her way through the gate and onto the track where Mac was about to take his victory lap.

He scanned the track apron for her. She raced forward and dropped to her knees. His arms were already open to receive her.

A teammate handed him an American flag and he tried to pass it to Keely. "Run alongside me, Coach," he said to her over the noise. "You earned this gold as much as I did."

Keely's heart swelled with emotion. She had wanted for a lifetime to do this, to hear the cheers of the crowd and experience the thrill of a gold-medal win. He was offering her the chance.

She kissed him. "I love you more than anything," she said.

And then she stepped back into the crowd and let him take the victory lap without her.

[partial text at top of page, faded]

perience that will only perfecting it. He was nearby her
[illegible line]

She continued, "I had just been thinking, now that
[illegible line]
in the trainer would be *[illegible]*

EPILOGUE

Three years later...

"PLEASE, PLEASE, let me ride you. I'll try not to squeal this
time."

Mac groaned. "Aw, Linda, not tonight. We still have a ton
of inventory to take."

"Please? One little ride? You rode Roberta and Miriam last
night, but I didn't get a turn."

He was about to give in to the secretary's pleading when
he looked down the hall.

"Sorry, Linda, but you know my wife gets mad if I let
anyone have her seat." He smiled at Keely and pushed forward to meet her. "Hey, Sport Model."

"Hey, handsome." She bent down and brushed his lips
with hers.

"You're off early," he said.

"I finished the prototype for the portable trainer ahead of
schedule. Do you think I can ask the wheelers to field-test it
next weekend when Dean takes them to Augusta? I could use
some feedback."

"Sure. He'd love to test it."

A runner could warm up or cool down off the track, but
an athlete in a wheelchair needed track space. When the
wheelers traveled, they often didn't have that space. Keely
had come up with an idea for lightweight portable trainer they
could take with them.

Her ability to see a problem and find a solution continued
to astound Mac. Her company produced a range of equipment
used by able-bodied and disabled athletes and held several

patents for medical equipment. The commercial application of her InsulCare fabric alone had made a tidy profit.

With a plant in Miami and now a second one in Courtland, she had expanded Coxwell and increased profits ten percent. But what mattered most to both of them was that she loved what she was doing.

"I brought a picnic supper and put it in your office," she said. "I was hoping you could take thirty minutes to eat with me. We've hardly talked all week."

"I know, and something's got to give. I feel like I never see you anymore, and I don't spend enough time with my students, either. That bothers me."

"Dean's doing a good job with them, isn't he?"

After his graduation, Dean had joined the staff as an assistant coach. Mac had put him in charge of the wheelers.

"Dean's doing a great job. The problem isn't him, baby, it's me. I miss you. And I miss not having the time to coach. What if I told you I've been thinking about retiring from racing? What would you say?"

She cocked her head. "Seriously?"

"I wouldn't trade these past three years for anything, but I've accomplished what I set out to do. Now I want to coach again. I want to be with my students. That's where I belong."

"I can't say I'm surprised."

"Do you have any problems with it?"

"No, not if that's what you want."

"Are you sure you won't be disappointed? I know you enjoy the races as much as I do."

"I'd miss it, but to be honest, I've been thinking I might start staying home on the weekends, anyway, if you could manage without me. There's a quilting class I want to take Saturday mornings, and I've also got a big project coming up that's not the kind of thing I want to be carrying around to races every weekend."

"What kind of project?"

"Oh, something very special. Actually, you initiated it, so I'm going to need your help. You can coach me."

Coach her? Doing what?

He patted his lap. "Hop on. I'll ride you to the office. We can have our picnic and talk about this coaching thing. I've got news about Ginny Sasser and Dean you'll want to hear, too."

"Can you ride both of us?" she asked.

"Both?"

He glanced past her to see if he had overlooked J.P. or one of the other Sizemore kids. The hall was empty.

Then he had another thought, a crazy one, and his insides turned to mush. He looked at Keely's stomach. She'd been putting her hand there a lot lately, the way she did when she felt queasy.

He was afraid to hope. They had only recently started trying again for a child.

The first year he'd been so sure he could impregnate Keely. Every couple of months she'd undergone intrauterine insemination with sperm they'd taken from him through electro ejaculation. They'd pooled and specially processed the sperm to increase its effectiveness, but still Keely hadn't gotten pregnant.

Time after time the news was the same: no baby. Mac finally accepted there never would be.

Keely, though, had refused to give up on the idea and she'd talked him into trying again. He'd indulged her, but he hadn't allowed himself to hope for success.

He looked up to find her beaming down at him.

She patted her stomach. "Instead of Sport Model, you're going to have to start calling me Family Sedan. You may even have to put a bumper sticker on my behind that says 'Wide Load.'"

"A baby?" he asked, his voice cracking.

She nodded. "I've suspected since last week. But I didn't want to get your hopes up and then find out it wasn't true. The fertility clinic confirmed it a little while ago."

"But it's only been a couple of months. How...?"

"Haven't you heard? I'm terribly impatient. And I never quit until I get what I want."

An image flashed into his head. A little girl. Big blue eyes. Dimples. Strong-willed like her mother.

He smiled, and then his smile turned into a chuckle. His chuckle turned into laughter. He pulled Keely onto his lap, needing to touch her, to hold her.

"A baby," he said with wonder.

"I'm going to need a birthing coach. Want the job?"

"What does it pay?"

"Oh, let's see. Hugs. Kisses. Your back scratched whenever you want." Her expression softened. "Love for a lifetime."

"Sounds like a great deal. I'll take it."

She kissed him and caressed his cheek. "My beautiful perfect husband, you've given me a miracle, after all."

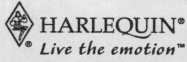

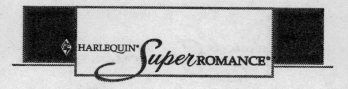

HARLEQUIN SuperROMANCE®

Receive 75¢ off your next Harlequin Superromance® book purchase.

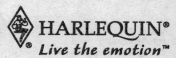

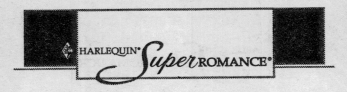

HARLEQUIN *Super*ROMANCE®

Receive 75¢ off your next Harlequin Superromance® book purchase.

75¢ OFF!

Your next Harlequin Superromance® book purchase.

52604339

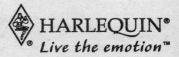

HARLEQUIN®
Live the emotion™

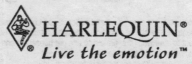

FTD.COM

SHOP ONLINE OR DIAL 1-800-SEND-FTD

$10.00 OFF
COUPON

Expiration Date: April 30, 2003

To redeem your coupon:

**Log on to www.ftd.com/harlequin
and give promo code 2196 at checkout.**

Or

**Call 1-800-SEND-FTD
and give promo code 2194.**

Terms and conditions:

NCP2196